TERR

Blade swung into act... ...moment he saw Jared's hand sweep toward the holster. He lunged to his left, his huge arm encircling Jenny and Gabe, bearing them to the ground, shielding them from the anticipated shot. Expecting to feel a searing pain as the slug tore through him, he twisted as he went down, training the Commando on the scavengers. He could see Jared sighting the Smith and Wesson, apparently intent on making an accurate shot, but the revolver wasn't aiming at Blade, Jenny or Gabe.

The scavenger was pointing the gun at something behind them.

A snarling form hurdled over the Warrior and his family, springing at the scavengers. The Smith and Wesson boomed, but the shot missed. Before Jared could fire again, a feral feline landed on all fours, uttered a piercing, raspy scream of rage, and launched itself at one of the scavengers....

DEVIL STRIKE

The Devil cut loose with an assault rifle. Bullets plowed into the outer wall on the right side of the doorway. Instead of retreating into the shadows, Blade automatically did the unexpected; he stepped into the center of the street, trained the M60 on the dune buggy, and let them have it. The big machine gun bucked in his arms as he poured a veritable hailstorm of lead into the grill, hood and driver. A short swing to the left stitched the pattern of slugs into the other Devil, and the man screamed as his chest was transformed into a series of miniature crimson geysers.

The driver slumped over the steering wheel and the dune buggy veered into a house on the right, smashing through the wall and coming to an abrupt rest as a portion of the roof collapsed upon it.

Blade whirled, and saw the first dune buggy returning for another attack....

The *Blade Double* Series:

TERROR STRIKE/
DEVIL STRIKE

DAVID ROBBINS

LEISURE BOOKS   NEW YORK CITY

Dedicated to
Judy, Joshua and Shane.
To Sylvester Stallone, who demonstrated the
value of persistence.
To Scott and Fran Charles, for dedication
above and beyond the call of duty.
And to Jerry and Linda Jeffries, who give the
word friendship its true meaning.

A LEISURE BOOK®

March 1993

Published by

Dorchester Publishing Co., Inc.
276 Fifth Avenue
New York, NY 10001

TERROR STRIKE Copyright © MCMXC by David L. Robbins
DEVIL STRIKE Copyright © MCMXC by David L. Robbins

Printed in the United States of America.

TERROR STRIKE

PROLOGUE

"**W**here the hell are we?"

"Beats me."

"You're a lot of help."

"Hey, you're the jerk who lost the map."

The two grungy men halted and glared at each other. Both stood about six feet in height, and both were lean and sinewy. One had blond hair, the other black, and both had brown eyes. The blond wore a ragged green shirt and faded, torn jeans, while his companion was attired in a dirty brown short-sleeved shirt and patched blue corduroy pants that had seen their prime a century earlier. The men's footware consisted of crudely made deerskin shoes.

"Who are you calling a jerk?" the blond demanded angrily, his hands tightening on the Remington Model Seven rifle he held.

"There's no one else within miles of here, Merrill," the man in the corduroy pants said. Cradled in his arms was a Beeman/Krico Model Six Hundred, and strapped to his left hip a Caspian Arms .45-caliber pistol.

"It wasn't my fault the damn map slipped out of my back pocket," Merrill said, and frowned.

"You were carrying it."

"Get off my case, Emerson," Merill snapped. He turned and headed due south, moving down the slope of the low hill they were on.

"Boy, are you in a lousy mood," Emerson said, following.

"No thanks to you, turkey," Merrill shot back over his left shoulder.

"I didn't lose the map," Emerson said.

"No, but this stupid plan was your idea, not mine."

"My plan was sound."

Merrill snorted derisively, his eyes scanning the waist-high vegetation in front of him and the forest less than 50 yards distant. "Sure it was."

"So my information was unreliable," Emerson said. "Shoot me."

"Don't tempt me," Merrill replied.

"I believed the gambler in Shantytown when he told us about Canada," Emerson said wistfully.

"You believed his story about Canada being unaffected by World War Three? About Canada hardly being touched by the radiation, the chemicals, and all that other crap?"

"Well, I—" Emerson began.

"You actually believed his tale about cities teeming with people, about cities where they still have cars that run, and food can be bought at stores, and there's electricity and running water and everyone has a roof over their heads?" Merrill asked resentfully.

Emerson sighed. "It could've been true."

"Yeah. Right. Just like the stories we've heard about California, the Civilized Zone, and Miami could also be true," Merrill said sarcastically, and stopped. He faced Emerson. "When will you learn? You know as well as I do that those stories are all a load of bull. There's no truth to any of them. People wish it was true, because everyone yearns for the good old days when living was easy, when all a person had to do to get light was flick a switch, or if they were hungry they went to a store and bought all the food they needed." He paused. "But things aren't that way any more. The war threw everything out of whack. If we want to eat, we have to kill game or trade for provisions at Shantytown or one of the other rat-infested towns. If we want light, we have to build a fire or use a lantern."

"There are generators in use," Emerson said lamely.

"Yeah. A few here and there. So what? A few generators don't change the fact that you're always chasing pipe dreams. You think we're going to find paradise, a city exactly like those in existence before the war. It won't happen."

"You never know."

"I know you're crazy, and I know I'm tired of going with you on these wild-goose chases."

"Answer me this, then, Mister-Know-It-All. If you're so smart, if you're positive that cities like those before the war don't exist, then how come you go with me all the time? How come you offered to go with me to Miami, even though we changed our minds when we found out we'd have to go through the Russian sector? And how come you came with me on this trip to Canada?"

Merrill shook his head and resumed his trek. "Because I'm your friend, your dipstick."

They hiked in silence for several minutes.

"I'm sorry I got on you about the map," Emerson said.

"You should be."

"Look, I'm trying to apologize and you're treating me like dirt."

"No, I'm treating you like a chump. There's a difference."

"I'm a chump?"

"We both are," Merrill stated bitterly. "We've always been chumps. From the day we were born in run-down shacks near what's left of Duluth, we've been busting our butts to get ahead. And what has all our effort got us? Nothing. Zip. The clothes on our backs and our guns. That's it."

"We're still friends after all these years."

"Yeah. When we were kids, living within a half mile of one another, I never figured I'd be seeing your ugly mug every day twenty years later."

"Don't you want to be friends any longer?"

Merrill gazed at the western horizon. "What I want is to find us a place to bed down for the night. We have about two hours of daylight left."

"There's plenty of time," Emerson said.

"There you go again."

"What am I doing?"

"Being your usual, disgusting, optimistic self."

In short order they came to the forest and discovered a game trail winding in the direction they were heading.

"Let's take it," Emerson proposed.

An eerie hush enveloped the pair as they wound among the trees. No insects sounds could be heard, and the birds, if there were any, were strangely silent. Even the breeze was silent.

"This is spooky," Emerson said softly.

"Maybe there's a bear or a bobcat in the vicinity," Merrill suggested.

"Maybe there's a mutation."

The dreaded word made Merrill stroke the trigger on his rifle nervously. He despised the vile genetic abominations so prevalent since the nuclear holocaust, and the mere thought of a two-headed wolf or an enormous snake lurking in the undergrowth gave him goose bumps. He couldn't begin to imagine what life had been like prior to the war, before the radiation and the chemicals had polluted the environment and deranged the wildlife. Once, in International Falls, he'd spoken to a man who claimed the "warping of the ecological chain" meant all future generations would have to contend with a world overrun by mutants, which was a disheartening scenario if ever there was one.

"This game trail might lead us to water," Emerson commented.

Merrill nodded. Game trails usually did, sooner or later, lead to water. The animals used the trails like ancient men and women had once used their roads and highways.

"We must be in northern Minnesota," Emerson mentioned.

"That'd be my guess," Merrill concurred. Their swing into Canadian territory, which they had entered near Fort Frances, had taken them northward, around the Lake of the Woods, then to the west, encompassing hundreds of miles and three months. And all for nothing. Their search for an inhabited Canadian metropolis had been fruitless. Oh, they'd found a few towns inhabited by trappers and hunters, but not the utopian city they were seeking. If Emerson had had his way, they would still be looking. The dummy had wanted them to try and push on to Winnipeg, but Merrill had put his foot down and refused to continue.

"I don't want to sleep in these woods," Emerson stated nervously.

"Then you'd better hope we get out of these trees before nightfall," Merrill said.

In a quarter of a mile they did. The forest abruptly ended at the edge of a field. Beyond the field, in an oval configuration aligned from north to south, was a small lake, its deep blue surface tranquil, the sunlight shimmering on the water.

"Fish for supper!" Emerson declared.

"We'll camp right next to the lake," Merrill said, then glanced to the right. "What the hell!"

"What?" Emerson responded, looking around.

Not thirty feet away, situated close to the trees, was an old log cabin, its roof and glass windows still intact.

"Will you look at that!" Merrill exclaimed happily.

"Do you suppose someone lives there?"

"There's only one way to find out."

They approached the structure warily, circling to the front on the south side, their rifles trained on the closed door.

"I doubt anyone has lived there in years, maybe since the war," Merrill speculated.

"If it's empty we can spend the night inside," Emerson said.

"Open the door," Merrill directed.

"You open it."

"What's the matter? Chicken?"

"No."

"We're not in the woods any more," Merrill stated.

"Meaning what?" Emerson asked.

"Meaning you're having a bad attack of nerves, and the best way for you to get over the willies is to go open the damn door," Merrill said. "I'll cover you."

"Okay. Okay. Don't rush me." Emerson edged closer and closer to the cabin, his eyes flicking over the two windows, one to the right and the other to the left of the door. He held the Beeman at waist level.

"Hurry it up. We don't have all day," Merrill snapped.

Emerson ignored him and moved to the door. He grasped the knob with his right hand, twisted, and shoved, then crouched, braced for the worst. The door swung inward to reveal a room that hadn't been occupied in decades. Dust covered everything. A sofa was positioned along the west wall. Shelves crammed with books lined the east wall. A blue shag rug covered the floor. In the center of the room stood a rocking chair, a straight chair, and a coffee table between the two.

"Anything?" Merrill inquired.

Emerson stepped inside. In the northwest corner was a kitchenette complete with a wood-burning stove and a rack containing an assortment of dishes. Across from the kitchen area was an open door.

"Anything?" Merrill repeated.

Without answering, Emerson walked to the open door and peered into a narrow bedroom in which there were three items of furniture: a bed, a dresser, and a nightstand.

Merrill came into the front room. "I asked you a question."

"I heard you."

"Then why didn't you respond?"

"Because I'm tired of you riding herd over me today," Emerson said, stepping to the sofa and sitting down. "No one died and made you boss. We're partners, remember?"

"Hey, I wasn't trying to upset you," Merrill said.

"Too bad. You did a good job."

Merrill glanced down at their footprints on the dusty carpet. "What did I tell you? Nobody has been here in ages."

"It's been one hundred and six years since the war. Do you think this cabin has been abandoned that long?"

"Who can say?" Merrill replied, and moved to the kitchenette. "Do you still want to spend the night?"

"The night, hell. Let's take a week off and relax."

"Fine by me. But if we're going to have fish for supper, one of us had better get to fishing while the other does the cleaning. I don't intend to breathe dust the whole week."

Emerson rose. "Okay. I'll do the fishing."

"Let's pick for it."

"All right," Emerson said. He reached into his right front pocket and extracted a bullet, then placed the Beeman on the sofa. Hiding his hands behind his back, he palmed the cartridge in his left hand. "Ready?"

"I was born ready."

Emerson extended his arms, fists clenched. "Pick the one."

"Now which hand has it?" Merrill asked rhetorically, and scratched the stubble on his chin.

"You'll never guess."

"The left one."

Dejected, Emerson opened his left hand, disclosing the bullet. "Damn. How'd you know?"

"Simple. You took it out of your pocket with your right hand, and I just figured you'd naturally transfer it to your left," Merrill said, and smirked triumphantly. He strolled to the front door. "I'll be back in an hour with more fish than we'll need. Try to have the place dusted out by then."

"Don't rub it in."

Merrill snickered.

"Hey, wait," Emerson declared.

"We're not going to pick two out of three," Merrill stated.

"Not that. Look," Emerson said, and pointed at the southwest corner.

Merrill pivoted and spied the closet. "Now what do you suppose is in there?"

"Let's see."

They converged on the closet and Merrill opened the door.

"Wow! Will you look at that!" Emerson exclaimed.

The previous owner had filled the closet with camping, hunting, and fishing gear, including two fishing poles leaning against the left wall.

"There aren't any guns, but these will do nicely," Merrill said, and withdrew the poles. He propped the shorter of the pair against the door and hefted a black and white model fitted with a black reel. "Now I won't have to use the roll of wire in my pocket."

"I get the other pole."

"It's yours. But you don't get to use it until the cabin is cleaned. A deal is a deal."

"Crap," Emerson said.

Merrill smiled and exited. He slung the Remington over his right shoulder and made for the lake, experimenting with the rod and reel as he went. He'd never seen a fishing pole in such superb condition! And now it was his! He toyed with the idea of taking the pole to Shantytown and trading the rod for a week of women and wine, but he discarded the brainstorm after concluding there were more important things in life than a week in the sack with a wench. Like fishing.

Once again he noticed the quiet in the air, and he paused to gaze at the forest to his rear. Nothing moved. Not even a leaf or a pine needle.

Damn! He was getting as bad as Emerson!

Eager to try out the new rod, Merrill hastened to the lake shore, a narrow strip of dirt ringing the water. He wondered if the line would hold up as he unfastened the hook from the top. His first step was to dig some worms. He looked at the cabin, approximately 20 yards from the water, and saw Emerson moving about inside.

Something splashed in the lake.

Merrill turned and saw the ripples where something had broken the surface and then submerged, and prompted by his hunger he walked along the shore, seeking a suitable spot to dig. In 15 yards he found a moist, soft track of soil and began scooping out the dirt with his hands. At a depth of two inches the familiar form of a nice, juicy worm squiggled into view. He plucked the bait from the soil and proceeded to slowly insert the hook.

Another splash left concentric wavelets on the lake.

The worm wriggled violently, resisting the impaling.

Merrill applied more pressure with his right thumb and fore-finger and finished preparing the bait. He hefted the pole, admiring its balance, and inspected the reel. In comparison to the wire and any thin tree limb he ordinarily employed, the fishing pole was exotic and alien. He knew nothing about operating the reel. There must be, he reasoned, a method of unwinding the line smoothly. He saw a red button with three distinct settings, and he switched from one setting to another, testing the rod.

Yet another splash sounded, this time much nearer.

The prospect of hauling in a tasty bass or trout caused Merrill's stomach to growl. Unsure of how to cast the pole and afraid of tangling the line, he unwound 20 feet, backing away from the sinker as he did. Then he swung the pole in an arc overhead, the line whipping through the air, and brought his arm down when the pole pointed directly over the lake. To his amazement, the line not only sailed out over the water, it kept going, the reel spinning and buzzing like an angry bee, until the sinker plopped into the lake almost 40 feet from where he stood.

Terrific!

Merrill chuckled and settled down to await the first nibble. Within minutes a fish took the bait, and after a brief, exciting contest, Merrill reeled in a feisty lake trout 18 inches in length. Encouraged by his success, he spent the next 40 minutes fishing, hauling in seven healthy specimens for the supper table. He used a short piece of wire, tied to a stout section of tree branch he found next to the lake, to rig a string for his catch. The sun was sinking below the western horizon when he ambled to the cabin, holding the fish in his left hand.

The cabin door was open.

"Emerson! I hope you're hungry," Merrill declared as he entered the cabin. "Look at what we have."

Engaged in checking the fire he'd kindled in the wood-burning stove, Emerson looked up and beamed. "Wow! Did they jump into your arms?"

"No. My superior fishing skill caught them."

"I don't suppose the new rod helped?" Emerson asked, rising.

"It's incredible," Merrill admitted, surveying the furniture and the floor. "Hey, you got rid of all the dust."

"I found a broom in a closet in the bedroom."

"Then let's get to feeding our faces," Merrill proposed.

They set about preparing the fish. The delicious aroma of their simmering supper filled the cabin. Merrill closed the cabin door.

Emerson arranged plates and glasses on the kitchen counter. "Look at what else I found," he mentioned, and reached into a cabinet on the north wall to produce salt and pepper shakers.

"Is that real salt?" Merrill queried.

"You bet."

Merrill could hardly wait to tear into their meal. Salt was a luxury in postwar America, and a bag or bottle of the condiment could be worth its weight in gold to an astute trader. His mouth salivated in anticipation.

"Did I show you this?" Emerson mentioned, and leaned down to tug on the knob on a cupboard located to the left of the sink. The three shelves inside the cupboard were stacked high with canned goods.

"We must've died and gone to heaven," Merrill said.

"I say we stay here for a month, at least."

"It's only the end of May. Why don't we stay until the end of summer? We don't have anything else to do."

Emerson nodded and closed the cupboard. "Why not? We have all the comforts. I found lanterns, kerosene, matches, all kinds of goodies. We'd be stupid if we just stayed here a week."

So with the prospect of a idyllic summer spent fishing and loafing before them, they savored their meal of piping hot fish. The twilight faded into darkness.

"I'll get a lantern," Emerson offered, and walked into the bedroom.

Merrill relaxed in the rocking chair, gazing out the right-hand window at the lake. He heard a match being struck and light flared in the bedroom.

"Here we go," Emerson announced, returning with the lit lantern in his left hand. "There's another closet in there crammed with stuff."

"I think we should keep our mouths shut about this place," Merrill commented contentedly. "This cabin will be our little secret."

Emerson deposited the lantern on the kitchen counter, and the pale yellow glow illuminated the entire interior. "I agree."

"Maybe we could move in here permanently," Merrill recommended.

"It's too far out."

"How do we know that? There might be a town nearby where we can replenish our supplies now and then."

"If there was a town, someone would've discovered the cabin," Emerson said.

"You never know."

Emerson walked to the front door. "I need to take a leak. Be back in a jiffy."

"You'd better take your rifle," Merrill advised, pointing at the Beeman and the Remington. Both of their guns were leaning against the wall to the left of the entrance.

"I have my pistol," Emerson responded, and patted the Caspian on his left hip. He opened the door and stepped outside.

Feeling full and happy, Merrill lazily watched his friend pass the right-hand window. He swiveled his head to the right, expecting to see Emerson pass the side window on the west, but his companion didn't appear. Surmising that Emerson had stopped somewhere between the windows, probably at the corner, to take the leak, Merrill closed his eyes. His mind drifted, and he thought of the many childhood experiences he'd shared with Emerson.

Emerson?

Merill's eyes snapped open and he stared at the front door in confusion. He knew he'd dozed off, but for how long? A minute? An hour? He couldn't have been asleep very long because the front door was still ajar. "Emerson?"

A cool breeze blew into the room.

"Emerson?" Merrill called.

There was no reply.

Perplexed, Merrill rose and moved to the entrance. He poked his head outside, craning his neck to gaze at the bright stars dotting the firmament. "Emerson?"

Still no answer.

What the hell was going on? Merrill asked himself. He retrieved his Remington, ensured a round was in the chamber, and ventured outdoors. "Emerson? Where are you?"

The breeze rustled the trees in the forest behind the cabin.

Merrill walked to the southwest corner and scanned the terrain, his anxiety mounting. His chum would hardly have gone for a nighttime stroll. But if Emerson had been attacked, he would have managed to shout or fire a shot. So where could—

A tremendous commotion sounded from the direction of the lake, loud splashing punctuated by inarticulate, gasping cries. As quickly as the noise began, it abruptly ceased.

"Emerson?" Merrill yelled, and jogged toward the water. The night was moonless, and the surface gave the illusion of being a vast black pit. He listened for more splashing. Twelve feet from the lake he halted. "Emerson? Are you there?"

In the distance a wolf howled.

His body tensed. Merrill advanced to the edge of the water and surveyed the lake. A tingle ran down his spine. "Emerson! Answer me!"

A faint splash came from the water directly in front of him. Merrill leaned forward, licking his lips, peering into the night. Try as he might, he couldn't detect anything unusual. He resolved to return to the cabin and wait for daylight, and he was about to pivot and leave when a great, hulking form reared up out of the water and lunged. He felt bands of steel constrict around his arms, and he opened his mouth to scream as the creature surged backwards, bearing him into the lake. Water flooded down his throat, and he kicked and heaved in a vain attempt to break free. Panic seized him. And then something clamped on his neck, and he went oddly numb from his head to his toes. His lungs seemed to explode, and his mind shrieked a mental wail of despair.

Eternity claimed him.

CHAPTER ONE

The three women were standing near the base of the towering oak tree, conversing. Two of the three were blondes; the third had flowing black tresses.

"How'd you talk him into it?" asked the taller of the blondes. She was endowed with a slender figure, and her features were distinguished by a high forehead, prominent cheekbones, and thin lips. Her green eyes were matched by the color of her shirt, and brown pants and moccasins completed her attire. Around her slim waist was strapped a Smith and Wesson .357 Combat Magnum.

"Yeah, what did you do?" added the woman with the black hair. Her attractive countenance showed her Indian heritage. A buckskin dress, which she had designed and sewn together herself, accented her shapely build. Like the blonde, she wore moccasins.

"I didn't do anything special," responded the shorter blonde. She grinned, exposing her even white teeth, her rounded chin jutting downward. Her apparel consisted of a yellow blouse, blue pants, and brown leather shoes.

"Come on, Jenny. You can tell us," urged the tall blonde. "Cynthia and I are your best friends."

"That's right," Cynthia echoed, running her left hand through her dark hair.

"I know I can trust both of you," Jenny said, glancing from one to the other. She focused on the tall blonde. "Really, Sherry, I'm telling the truth."

"We know your husband better than that," Sherry responded.

Cynthia nodded. "And you know *our* husbands. So tell us how you did it so we can use the same tactic on them."

"Did you beg him?" Sherry inquired.

Jenny laughed lightly. "Of course not!"

"I'd never beg Geronimo for a thing," Cynthia stated. "He told me once that he married me because he considers me to be a strong-willed woman. If I begged him for something, he'd accuse me of being an imposter."

"I didn't beg Blade to go on a vacation," Jenny said.

"Then what *did* you do?" Sherry demanded. "Promise him extra whoopie?"

"Be serious," Jenny responded.

"I am. It works for me with Hickok," Sherry disclosed.

Jenny and Cynthia glanced at each other.

"You're kidding," Cynthia said.

"Nope," Sherry answered.

"You really promise Hickok more sex if he'll do what you want?" Jenny queried in disbelief.

"Well, I don't exactly promise him more sex," Sherry said. "I *give* him more sex."

"I don't follow you," Jenny remarked.

"Let's face facts. Most men are sex-starved maniacs," Sherry declared. "They can't get enough. And have you ever noticed how they always get romantic at the weirdest times?"

"Have I!" Cynthia interjected. "The other day I was doing the dishes and Geronimo came up behind me and started nibbling on my ear."

Sherry snickered. "Just like a man. What did you do?"

"I made him dry the dishes," Cynthia revealed.

All three enjoyed a hearty laugh.

"Anyway," Sherry went on when their mirth subsided, "if I want to wrap my hardheaded hunk around my little finger, all I have to do is give him more sex. We're accustomed to doing it on certain nights of the week when our work schedules don't conflict. With both of us being Warriors, one or the other has night duty every few days. And it's next to impossible to find time for lip locks when you have two kids running around the cabin."

"Lip locks?" Cynthia repeated quizzically.

"What do you call it?" Sherry rejoined.

"Making love," Cynthia said.

"In front of your son?" Sherry asked.

"No. We don't discuss sex in front of Cochise," Cynthia said. "He's only four, you know."

"Well, Ringo is almost five and Chastity is almost seven," Sherry stated. "They pick up on everything we say, so we use the term lip locks to discuss our plans for the evening in front of them without them being the wiser."

"Don't they get curious about what the expression means?" Jenny inquired. "Don't they ask you about it?"

"Sure. Now and then."

"And what do you say?" Jenny questioned.

"If they ask me, I tell them that I'll explain when they're older."

"And if they ask Hickok?" Cynthia queried.

"He always tells them it's a secret technique for summoning the stork."

"What stork?" Jenny wanted to know.

"The dummy keeps telling them that babies are delivered by storks," Sherry elaborated. "I'm going to have a heck of a time setting them straight when they're older."

"We're getting off the track," Jenny said. "You didn't finish your story about using sex to persuade Hickok to do what you want."

"It's simple. If I want something, and if I know he might

give me grief, I become romantic when he leasts expects it, when we have a spare moment. Afterwards, he's always a regular pussycat, and I can usually talk him into anything I want.''

Jenny shook her head. "You're the last person I would have expected to use sex to get her way."

"Hey, I'm a Warrior, remember? I've been trained to employ psychological-warfare strategies," Sherry replied.

"But against your own husband?"

"Hickok is a man, and in the battle between the sexes a woman has to use every weapon she has," Sherry said.

Jenny frowned. "I don't think of sex as a weapon."

"Don't you ever use sex to influence Blade?" Sherry asked.

"Never," Jenny said.

Sherry glanced at Cynthia. "What about you?"

"The Sioux regard sex as a special, spiritual expression of love between the wife and husband. If I used sex as a weapon, I would betray the heritage of my people."

"Thanks heaps. The two of you are making me feel like a hussy."

Cynthia looked at Jenny. "So how did you persuade Blade to take this trip?"

"I used the same method women everywhere have used for ages. I nagged him to death."

"I don't like to nag," Sherry said. "It's too demeaning. I'd rather use sex to get what I want."

"Are you still planning to leave tomorrow?" Cynthia asked Jenny.

"Yep. Tomorrow morning. Which gives me about twenty-four hours to get all packed."

"Are you taking Gabe?" Sherry inquired.

"Yes."

"Hickok and I will baby-sit him if you want. He's the same age as Ringo and they're the best of buddies," Sherry said.

"Thanks, but no. Blade and I discussed whether to take Gabe along, and we decided we'd hurt his feelings if we left him behind," Jenny explained.

"You're missing a chance to have a second honeymoon," Sherry commented.

"Gabe is an integral part of our family. I know that many parents before the Big Blast viewed their children as hindrances to their careers, or as nuisances they couldn't wait to raise and boot out of the house. But the Elders have taught us better than that. We know children are a blessing bestowed on us by the Spirit so we can understand the Spirit's parental relationship to us by experiencing being parents ourselves," Jenny said.

Sherry sighed. "Sometimes I really wish I'd been born here at the Home instead of in Canada."

"You're part of the Family now," Jenny noted.

"Yeah. And I've been through the Warrior training courses. But I'll never know what it was like to be raised in the kind of environment where everyone sincerely tries to live the Golden Rule. Don't get me wrong. In the small town of Sundown where I was born, life was hard but relatively peaceful. We had to struggle just to keep food on the table. The people were generally nice, except for the usual scumbags. And, of course, we had the mutations to deal with," Sherry detailed.

"I know what you mean," Cynthia mentioned. "Since I was raised in the Dakota Territory, my background was similar to yours."

"You're both full-fledged Family members now," Jenny stressed. "It doesn't matter to the rest of us whether you were born at the Home or not. We love you just the way you are."

"Yeah. I know. It's funny. I never expected to wind up living in a Utopia," Sherry said. She gazed about her at the 30-acre compound constructed by a wealthy survivalist named Kurt Carpenter shortly before World War Three in northwestern Minnesota, near the former Lake Bronson State Park. Carpenter's foresight had ensured that his descendants, and those of the 30 people he had gathered together at the compound, would be able to hold their own in a world deranged by the ultimate insanity—devastating nuclear self-destruction. It was the idealistic Carpenter who had dubbed his retreat the Home and designated his loyal followers as his Family.

The man had built well, Sherry admitted to herself. To the west she could see the 20-foot-high brick wall that completely enclosed the compound on all four sides. At the inner base of the wall flowed the moat Carpenter had installed as another line of defense. A large stream entered the Home at the north-west corner, through an aqueduct, and was diverted to the south and the east along the bottom of the wall. At the southeast corner the two branches joined again and passed out of the Home through a second aqueduct. An enormous drawbridge situated in the middle of the west wall served as the entrance.

Carpenter's practical side was further demonstrated by his dividing the Home into sections. Almost the entire eastern half of the compound was preserved in its natural state or utilized for agricultural purposes. In the western portion were located six immense concrete bunkers, each devoted to a specialized use. And in the center of the Home, arranged in a line from north to south, were the cabins for the married couples. Sherry glanced over her left shoulder at Jenny and Blade's cabin, not 15 yards off, and thought of her own home, the next cabin to the south. Beyond hers was Cynthia's.

"So where is Blade taking you?" Cynthia asked Jenny.

"I don't know. He's keeping it as a big surprise. Apparently he got the idea from Plato."

"Did I hear someone mention my name?" asked a kindly voice to their rear.

They turned to find the Family's current Leader approaching at a leisurely stroll. His blue eyes seemed to twinkle with amusement as he regarded them. Long gray hair and a gray beard made him look older than his 50-odd years. A brown wool shirt and faded jeans clothed his lean frame. "How are you this morning, ladies?"

"We're fine," Jenny responded.

"Are you excited over your impending trip?" Plato asked.

"You know it."

"Where is Blade taking her?" Sherry inquired.

Plato chuckled as he reached them. "I'm not at liberty to divulge their destination. Blade requested that he be allowed to spring the surprise."

"Can't you give me a clue?" Jenny questioned eagerly.

Their wizened Leader reflected for a moment, then grinned. "Fair enough. You're aware, of course, that our Founder kept a journal of his activities and beliefs?"

"Certainly," Jenny said. "Carpenter's journal is kept in E Block, the library."

"Well, I was studying the journal several months ago when I came across an obscure reference to a two-week trip the Founder took. Intrigued, I checked through all of his material we have on file, and in a drawer containing copies of Carpenter's correspondence I found additional information."

"About what?" Jenny asked.

"Sorry. That's the only clue I can give you," Plato responded.

"You're a lot of help," Sherry muttered.

"I wouldn't want to spoil Blade's plans," Plato stated.

"Can you at least tell me if we'll be traveling very far so I know whether to pack a lot of extra clothes?" Jenny inquired.

"You're fishing, my dear," Plato said, and unexpectedly laughed.

Cynthia cleared her throat. "Will other couples be permitted to take trips to this mystery spot?"

"Perhaps," Plato answered.

"We should be allowed to go," Sherry declared. "Hickok and I could use a break, and so could Cynthia and Geronimo. For that matter, you'll probably need to keep a waiting list of those who want to go."

"Whether other couples are permitted to go will depend on what Blade and Jenny find when they arrive at their destination," Plato elaborated.

"You don't know what's there?" Jenny probed, taken aback by the revelation.

"If Carpenter's records are accurate, and if the ravages of

time haven't taken a severe toll, then I know," Plato said.

"You're not exactly brimming over with confidence," Sherry remarked.

Plato shrugged. "The best I can do is hope."

"It doesn't much matter," Jenny stated. "I'm so happy about going, I wouldn't care if Blade was taking us to a tar pit."

"How will you get there?" Cynthia brought up.

"We're taking the SEAL."

"Then you shouldn't have to worry about scavengers or mutations. The SEAL will make mincemeat out of any scuzzies who try to give you grief," Sherry mentioned.

"Scuzzies?" Plato repeated distastefully.

"Yeah. You know. Dirtballs. Lowlifes. Bloodsuckers."

"Are you referring to those misguided unfortunates who have succumbed to their own abysmal ignorance and who live by the admittedly brutal credo of might makes right?" Plato inquired.

"They're the ones. The scuzzies," Sherry said.

"Your husband has the rather quaint habit of alluding to them as cow chips," Plato noted.

"That's my hunk. He's as smart as a whip."

Plato idly glanced over Sherry's right shoulder and the corners of his mouth curled upward. "Are you making light of Hickok's powers of perception?"

"Didn't you hear me?" Sherry responding, raising her voice slightly. "I'm proud of my man. Hickok is as smart as they come. Of course, I'd never tell the lug to his face."

From behind them came a delighted cackle. "Too late, gorgeous. I heard that!"

CHAPTER TWO

A trio of newcomers, all men, joined the quartet.

"Oh, no!" Sherry declared, placing her hands on her cheeks, addressing the man on the right, a sinewy six-footer wearing buckskins and moccasins. Blond hair crowned his handsome features, and a blond mustache framed his mouth. In a holster on either hip rested a pearl-handled Colt Python revolver. "What are you doing here? I thought you were at the armory."

"Is that any way to greet your better half?" the gunman replied.

"As usual, Hickok, you've got it backwards," said the man on the left. The shortest of the three men, he possessed a stocky, powerful build. His clothing consisted of a shirt and pants fabricated from material that had once been part of a green canvas tent. Tucked under his belt next to his buckle was a genuine tomahawk, and under his right arm, snug in a shoulder holster, was an Arminius .357 Magnum. His features, like those of Cynthia, showed Indian ancestry.

"Who asked you?" the gunman retorted.

"Geronimo is right," stated the man in the middle, a giant

endowed with a herculean physique. Seven feet in height, his body rippled with layers of prodigious muscles scarcely contained by the black leather vest, green fatigue pants, and combat boots he wore. His hair was dark, his eyes were a striking gray. On each side of his waist, in a brown leather sheath, hung a big Bowie knife.

"And who asked you, Blade?" the gunman countered.

"Are you claiming to be the better half of our marriage?" Sherry demanded.

Hickok hooked his thumbs in his gunbelt and smirked. "I reckon I'd be plumb foolish to make such a claim, but I have it on good authority that I'm as smart as they come."

"See?" Sherry said, glancing at the others. "This is precisely the reason I didn't want him to hear me complimenting his brains. He'll walk around with a swelled head for a month!"

"Probably longer," Geronimo quipped.

"Not me," Hickok disagreed. "I'm the modest type."

"Right," Geronimo said sarcastically. "And so was George Armstrong Custer."

"Don't go pickin' on Custer," Hickok stated. "He would've won that scrape at the Little Big Horn if the weather had cooperated. That's why the Indians whipped Custer's tail."

"What are you babbling about? Custer, against orders, attacked an Indian encampment without bothering to verify the number of braves who would oppose him. He lost because he was stupid, not because of the weather," Geronimo said.

"Oh, yeah? I've read a few books on Custer, pard."

"So have I," Geronimo responded.

"Then you must have read about the haze," Hickok said.

"The what?"

"Custer rode to the crest of the hills overlooking the Little Big Horn and tried to spot the Indian camp through his field glasses, but there was too much haze," Hickok related. "Do you remember readin' about that?"

"Yeah, but—" Geronimo began.

"I rest my case," Hickok declared.

Plato smiled at Blade. "I can't imagine how you'll manage for a couple of weeks without your two compeers."

"I'll get by," Blade said, and grinned.

"Com-who?" Hickok asked, looking at Geronimo. "Were we just insulted?"

"The ladies have been pumping me for information concerning your trip," Plato mentioned.

"Oh?" Blade responded, his eyebrows arching as he gazed at his wife.

"We simply asked a few questions," Jenny said. "You can't blame us for being curious."

"Did you learn anything?" Blade queried.

"No," Jenny replied.

"I guess you'll just have to be patient and wait until we get there," Blade said.

"Why do women hate to be surprised?" Hickok wondered aloud.

"We do not," Sherry said.

"Bet me. Whenever I try to surprise you, you drive me nuts until you find out what the surprise is."

"No, I don't," Sherry insisted.

"Okay. Just remember you said that on your birthday."

"What are you planning to give me?" Sherry asked.

The gunman snickered. "I'm on a roll today."

Blade draped his right arm around Jenny's shoulders. "If you'll excuse us, we have preparations to make."

"Is that a hint?" Hickok inquired.

Sherry grabbed the gunfighter's right wrist. "Let's go. We have the cabin to ourselves until the kids get home from their schooling."

"What do you have in mind?" Hickok asked, and then an impish grin creased his face. "Oh." His blue eyes gleamed lecherously.

They walked off, heading to the south.

"Speaking of kids, where's Cochise?" Geronimo asked his wife.

"Spending the morning at Samson's," Cynthia disclosed.

"Cochise wanted to play with Benjamin, and Samson and Naomi offered to watch both boys until noon."

"Then we have *our* cabin to ourselves?" Geronimo asked.

"Yes. Why?"

Geronimo nodded at Blade, Jenny, and Plato. "We'll catch you later." He took hold of Cynthia's left arm. "Let's go."

"What's your rush?" Cynthia queried, then did a double take. "You mean right now?"

"I don't see any dishes in your hands."

Cynthia chuckled, gave a little wave, and they departed.

"Perhaps I should advise the midwives and Healers to be prepared for a busy spell nine months from now," Plato joked.

"Count us out," Jenny said. "We have too much packing to do."

"We could delay the start of our vacation for a day," Blade suggested to Jenny.

"Not on your life, buster. I've been after you for months to take time off from your job with the Freedom Force and your post as the head Warrior. You gave me your word that we can leave tomorrow morning, and I'm holding you to it."

"One more day wouldn't make a difference."

"It would to me," Jenny asserted.

Blade gazed tenderly at her for a moment, then sighed. "Okay. You're right. The vacation comes first. So why don't you begin packing and I'll check on the SEAL?"

"It's a deal," Jenny responded. She spun on her heels and hastened toward their cabin, humming softly.

Plato stepped up to Blade. "I haven't seen your wife this happy in years."

"Neither have I."

"You, however, don't seem to share her joy," Plato observed.

"I need to check on the SEAL," Blade reiterated, and started walking to the west.

"Mind if I accompany you?" Plato inquired, keeping pace with the giant.

"Suit yourself."

"What's bothering you?"

"Nothing," Blade said testily.

"I may not be an Empath, but I know when you are upset," Plato said. "If I'm prying, if I'm overstepping the bounds of our friendship, I'll desist. But I know you're troubled about something."

Blade glanced at the man who had been his mentor since the death of his father years before, his lips compressing. "I'm sorry, Plato. I shouldn't take out my frustrations on you."

"What frustrations, if I may ask?"

"The same ones I've been trying to deal with for almost a year and a half," Blade said. "The frustration of holding down two demanding jobs at the same time, when now I'm not wholly convinced one of the jobs is necessary. The frustration of having to constantly shuttle back and forth between Los Angeles and the Home, never spending more than a couple of weeks at either location. And the supreme frustration of struggling to deal with a wife who definitely doesn't want me on the Force, who wishes I would confine my activities to the Home and my post as the top Warrior."

"Perhaps if we examined each of your frustrations, we might resolve them," Plato recommended.

"Fat chance."

"Let's take a look at the first one," Plato said. "You say that you're not convinced one of your posts is necessary. May I assume you are referring to the Freedom Force?"

Blade nodded.

"But when the Force was first conceived, you believed the unit would be a critical component in enabling the Federation to deal with sundry threats," Plato reminded the Warrior.

"Yeah, I did, didn't I?" Blade replied, reflecting on that day in Los Angeles when the governor of the Free State of California had proposed forming a special strike squad, a team that would be prepared to fly out on a moment's notice to handle trouble spots as they arose. Was it *really* only 18 months ago?

Blade could recall the summit meeting as if it had taken place the day before. The leaders of the Freedom Federation, the league of seven organized factions dedicated to fostering the flickering embers of civilization in a country where barbarism reigned, had assembled in Anaheim, California, for a momentous meeting. The governor of California, one of the few states to retain its administrative integrity after the war, had been there. So had Plato. Also in attendance was the President of the Civilized Zone, the area in the Midwest including the former states of Wyoming, Colorado, Nebraska, Kansas, New Mexico, and Oklahoma, and part of Arizona and the northern portion of Texas. The U.S. government had evacuated hundreds of thousands of its citizens into this area during the war. Later, after the U.S. government collapsed and a dictator arose, the area was designated as the Civilized Zone.

Four other leaders were also at the meeting. The Flathead Indians, who now controlled Montana, sent the woman who presided over their tribal councils. The Cavalry, a group of superb horsemen who ruled the Dakota Territory, were represented by their top man. And the leaders of two other factions from Minnesota, the Clan and the Moles, were on hand to cast their votes on the creation of the Freedom Force.

Initially, Blade had favored the idea behind the force. An elite tactical unit, he reasoned, might help to neutralize the machinations of the Russians, who had wrested control of a section of the eastern United States during the war. And in addition to the Soviets, there were countless other menaces: scavengers, raiders, mutations, petty tyrants, despotic city-states, and more. In fact, there were too many menaces. Between his responsibilities as a Warrior and his duties on the Force, Blade seemed to spend all of his time away from his loved ones, confonting one danger after another. And most of the dangers, he had to admit, were encountered in his capacity as a Warrior.

Emotionally, though, his position with the Force had taken a harsher toll. In ten months of action he'd lost five of his team. Five! He blamed himself for each and every one. They'd died being true to their commitment to defend the Federation, but they had perished while under his command. Even as the thought entered Blade's mind, he heard Plato speak.

"Are you certain the Force isn't necessary, or are you endeavoring to justify your decision to disband the unit for a year?"

"My decision to disband the Force for a year stemmed from the problem my extended absences were causing at home. Jenny and Gabe were extremely upset. I needed the time to be with them, to stablize my family."

"And there was no other reason you disbanded the Force?"

"Like what?" Blade asked.

"Like perhaps the deaths of those five Force members affected you more than you have been willing to reveal. Perhaps the real motive was your desire to avoid losing any more personnel," Plato conjectured.

Blade looked at the Family Leader, impressed by Plato's insight. He shrugged. "Maybe it was a combination of the two."

"You were operating under a considerable strain," Plato suggested.

"That's the understatement of the decade."

"What will you do five months from now when the Federation leadership expects you to render a decision on whether or not you'll continue as the head of the Force?"

"I don't know."

"What does Jenny want you to tell them?"

"To go fly a kite."

They fell silent as they approached the vicinity of the six huge concrete blocks. The Founder had arranged the buildings in a triangular pattern, and each structure was known by a letter of the alphabet. At the southern tip was A Block, the Family armory, stocked with a variety of weapons. The Family Gunsmiths were responsible for ensuring the weapons were kept in perfect functional condition for the Warriors. One hundred yards northwest of the armory was B Block, the sleeping quarters for single Family members. The men were housed on the upper floor, the women on the lower. In a north-westerly line, again one hundred yards distant, stood C Block, the infirmary. Due east the same distance was D Block, which served as the Family's carpentry shop and all-purpose construction facility. One hundred yards farther to the east was E Block, the massive library Kurt Carpenter had personally stocked with almost five hundred thousand books. Family children were taught to read early, and nearly everyone at the Home read avidly. Finally, one hundred hards southwest of the library was F Block, the building utilized for storing their farming equipment and supplies, for preserving and preparing food, and for whatever other purposes the Tillers deemed appropriate.

Blade and Pluto angled toward the wide expanse between the blocks, the Family's primary area for socializing, where worship services were conducted, where the Elders held their open-air meetings, where the Musicians held their concerts, and where many of the older children congregated to play. Adults gathered there too, if they weren't working, to pass the time in pleasant conversation.

"So tell me again about this spot the Founder described as beautiful and restful," Blade prompted. He spied the vanlike SEAL parked in the middle of the open tract.

"I found a reference to the spot some years back, but the earlier reference was in error because it claimed the site was east of the Home. Actually, it's approximately ten miles to the northeast. The Founder described it as 'a small, beautiful lake undisturbed by the destructive hand of humankind,' a place where he could go to commune with the Spirit and sort out his thoughts," Plato detailed.

"And you're positive we won't need to take along sleeping bags and tents?" Blade queried.

"You shouldn't require them. The Founder had a cabin built near the north shore of this lake, a retreat he used frequently while the Home was under construction and before the war began. Logically, the cabin should still be there. In light of its remote location, I doubt the looting bands of scavengers have found the site. They tend to roam close to the cities and towns.''

''We've been attacked by a few here,'' Blade noted.

''True. Then maybe you should take the tents and sleeping bags, just in case.''

''I hope you're right about the lake and the cabin. Venturing into the Outlands is always a risky proposition, but the trip will be worth it if Jenny, Gabe, and I can forget all our cares and woes and have fun,'' Blade said.

Plato smiled. ''Don't worry. You'll undoubtedly have the time of your lives.''

CHAPTER THREE

"I saw something!" Jenny exclaimed, leaning forward in her seat to stare out the windshield.

"I saw it too," Blade said, and quickly applied the brakes. Twenty-five yards ahead and slightly to the left, at the edge of a stand of trees and dense underbrush, something had appeared for an instant. He'd glimpsed a brownish creature moving near a towering pine.

"What do you think it is?" Jenny asked.

"I don't know," Blade said.

"Maybe it's a mutation," Jenny noted.

From the seat behind them a childish voice piped up. "Can a mutant get in here, Dad?"

"No, Gabe," Blade answered. "The SEAL is virtually impervious."

"Im—what?" Gabe said.

"Impervious means the SEAL's body can't be penetrated by a bullet, cut by a knife, or smashed by a hammer," Blade explained.

"Wow! I wish my body was impervious," Gabe stated.

Carpenter's foresight served them in good stead. The Founder had spent millions of dollars to have the Solar Energized Amphibious or Land Recreational vehicle developed. Carpenter had realized his descendants would need a versatile, durable vehicle capable of negotiating the rugged postwar terrain, so he'd offered to foot the bill to have a prototyle built. The automotive executives he'd approached had welcomed the opportunity to construct the ultimate all-terrain vehicle. They had viewed Carpenter as a strange eccentric who possessed enough money to indulge his fascination with ostentatious toys. Little did they suspect his true motive.

The automakers had performed their job well. The transport's green body was composed of a shatterproof and heat-resistant plastic fabricated according to Carpenter's rigorous specifications. As a security precaution, the shell was tinted to enable those within to see out while preventing anyone outside from observing the occupants. A set of puncture-resistant tires, each one two feet wide and four feet high, supported the vehicle.

Knowing that the war would drastically reduce the availability of fossil fuels, Carpenter had insisted that his "toy" be solar powered. Sunlight was collected by a pair of solar panels attached to the roof, and the energy was converted and stored in a bank of six revolutionary new batteries in a lead-lined casing underneath the SEAL. The experts had informed Carpenter that, if the solar panels weren't broken and the battery casing wasn't damaged, the transport would run forever.

"There! I saw it again!" Jenny said.

"What will you do if it's a mutant, Dad?" Gabe inquired.

"Blow the sucker to smithereens," Blade responded.

And well he could. After the automakers were done with their work, Carpenter had taken the SEAL to the Home and called in specialists, mercenaries who converted the seemingly innocuous transport into a four-wheeled arsenal. Four toggle switches on the dashboard controlled four armaments. The first toggle activated two 50-caliber machine guns mounted in recessed compartments directly under each front headlight. When the toggle was flicked, a small metal plate would slide upward and the guns would automatically fire. The second toggle launched the miniature surface-to-air missile mounted in the roof above the driver's seat, in front of the solar panels. Once the toggle was pressed, a panel in the roof moved aside and the heat-seeking missile shot into the sky toward its target. The third toggle was for the flamethrower hidden behind the front fender. At the proper moment, the driver worked the toggle and the fender lowered, the nozzle of the flamethrower would extend six inches, and anyone or anything in front of the SEAL would be fried to a crisp. For their last bit of handiwork, the mercenaries had included a concealed rocket launcher behind the grill.

"It's coming toward us!" Jenny declared.

Blade's brawny hands clasped the steering wheel tightly. Ever since one of the genetic deviates had killed his father he'd dreaded the sight of mutations. He glanced at the toggle switches, then at the trees, and abruptly laughed.

A mule deer, a four-point buck, stepped into the open and regarded the SEAL with curiosity. After several seconds it wheeled and bounded into the undergrowth.

"It was just a deer!" Gabe said, giggling.

Jenny frowned and leaned back in her seat. "I was that worried over a measly buck?"

"You'll have to relax more if you want to enjoy our vacation," Blade remarked.

"Weren't you concerned?" Jenny asked.

"Yeah," Blade admitted. "We both have to unwind, or we'll be seeing mutations and who knows what else behind every boulder and tree."

"I wasn't scared," Gabe declared.

"You weren't?" Jenny responded.

"Nope. Daddy will beat the crud out of any mutant that tries to hurt us," Gabe said.

Jenny gazed at Blade and grinned. "Yes. I bet he will."

"One day when I'm big like Daddy I'll have knives of my

own, and then I'll beat the crud out of those suckers,'' Gabe vowed.

''Where did you ever hear about beating the crud out of things?'' Jenny inquired.

''From Ringo.''

''Figures,'' Jenny said.

Blade chuckled and accelerated, glancing at both of his loved ones. The spacious interior of the SEAL afforded more than ample room. In the front there were two bucket seats with a console between them. Behind the bucket seats was a single seat running the width of the transport. The rear section was reserved for storing provisions. Under the storage area, in a recessed compartment, were tools and two spare tires. Jenny sat in the passenger-side bucket seat, while Gabe was sitting in the wide seat.

''How many miles have we traveled?'' Jenny asked.

Blade consulted the odometer. ''Seven miles.''

''How far do we have to go?''

''That's my secret.''

''You still won't tell me?''

''Nope.''

''Turkey.''

Blade smiled. ''Hickok was right,'' he said, and surveyed the landscape in front of the transport. He was making a beeline to the northeast as Plato had advocated, driving overland, avoiding the denser tracts of vegetation. With its nearly indestructible body and enormous tires, the SEAL easily lived up to Kurt Carpenter's high expectations, traversing the rugged terrain effortlessly. Although the ride was bumpy, there were few obstacles the SEAL couldn't handle.

Patches of forest alternated with fields and low, rolling hills. Once they came to a steep ravine, and Blade skirted the eroded gorge rather than contend with the precipitous incline. Wildlife was abundant. Birds roosted in the trees or flew overhead. Rabbits darted from the path of the SEAL. Squirrels chittered at them. They saw other deer, and Jenny spotted a black bear on a nearby hill.

"Isn't it odd we haven't seen any mutants at all?" Jenny mentioned after they had covered eight and a half miles.

"There you go again," Blade said.

"I'm not being a worrywart," Jenny stated defensively. "But we know there are mutations out here."

"Yeah, Dad," Gabe interjected. "How come we haven't seen any?"

"To answer that, I'd have to explain about the three kinds of mutations," Blade replied.

"Go ahead. We have time to kill," Jenny prompted. "Gabe has to get the facts straight."

"What's the scoop, Dad?" Gabe added.

Blade bypassed a boulder half the size of the SEAL, and settled in his seat. "There are three kinds of mutations we know about, son. The first are those caused by the massive amounts of radiation unleashed during World War Three. Do you know what radiation is?"

"The yucky stuff that came from the missiles and the bombs?"

"Close enough. The radiation is responsible for animals born with two heads or six legs."

"Like the time those mutant wolves attacked the Tillers?"

"Exactly," Blade confirmed. "The second type of mutation is produced by the regenerating chemical clouds."

"The what?" Gabe queried.

"Do you know those green clouds that appear out of nowhere, floating low over the ground and swallowing people up?"

"Yep."

"They're the regenerating chemical clouds. They were used as a chemical-warfare weapon during the Big Blast, and they got out of control. They dissolve people, bones and all, but the clouds don't always dissolve animals because the agents in the clouds are specifically designed to leech onto the human metabolism."

"Huh?" Gabe said.

"The clouds don't swallow up all the animals. Many animals

are transformed into what we call mutates. They lose all their hair, their bodies become covered with pus-filled sores, and they try to eat every living thing they find," Blade detailed.

"They're gross," Gabe declared.

"The third kind of mutations are those genetically engineered by the scientists. Both before the war and afterward, there were scientists who created hybrids in test tubes, creatures that are half human and half something else. You name it, the scientists probably made it. Bear-men. Cat-men. Dog-men."

"Turtle-men?"

Blade smiled. "I don't know about turtle-men. I'll have to check on those."

"How about butterfly-men?"

"I don't think so."

"Or dinosaur-men?"

"We're getting off the track," Blade said. "We're supposed to be discussing why we haven't seen any mutants yet."

"Oh. Right."

"I doubt we'll see any of the genetically engineered mutations because they aren't that numerous," Blade said.

"Say, Dad?"

"Yes?"

"Are Lynx, Ferret, and Gremlin gene-ticklely engineered?" Gabe inquired.

"That's genetically engineered. And yes, they are," Blade said, thinking of the trio of mutants who were created by an insane scientist known as the Doktor to serve in his assassin corps, and who later defected to the Home and were now trusted Warriors.

"Will we see any mutates?" Gabe questioned.

"We could, so keep your eyes peeled at all times."

"And the other kind?"

"We might run into some of them. They're out there, but they're not lurking behind every tree, as I said before. The odds of bumping into one are about the same as those for bumping into a bobcat or a cougar."

"Uh-oh," Gabe said.

"What?" Blade responded, looking over his right shoulder.

"There," Gabe said, and pointed to the left.

Blade twisted in his seat, his eyes widening in surprise at the sight of a cougar 75 yards from the SEAL. The graceful feline, over six feet in length, was hurrying into a thicket, and it disappeared without a backward glance.

"I've seen pictures of cougars in books at the library," Gabe said. "That was a cougar, wasn't it?"

"Yes," Blade acknowledged.

"Then I bet we see a lot of mutants," Gabe stated.

"It was a fluke," Blade declared. "It doesn't mean we'll run into a lot of mutations."

"But you said we would if we saw a cougar."

"I said the odds were the same."

"Then we'll see mutants," Gabe insisted.

"Not necessarily," Blade remarked, hoping to allay any fears his son might have.

"Well, I hope we do," Gabe said.

"Why?" Jenny asked.

"Because I want to see Daddy blow the suckers to smithereens," Gabe answered.

Jenny laughed. "You're a chip off the old block."

"The what?"

"Never mind," Jenny told him.

Blade drove across a wide field, reflecting on the presence of the cougar. The big cats had been rare in Minnesota prior to the war, but afterwards, with the number of humans severely reduced and much of the cougars' range reverting to raw wilderness, they'd make a comeback.

"There's something I've been wondering about," Jenny commented.

"What?" Blade asked.

"A few years ago the countryside around the Home was crawling with those chemically spawned horrors, the mutates. But now there are hardly any. What happened?"

"We discovered the reason in the notes the Doktor kept. In an effort to destroy the Family, his assassin corps regularly released the green chemical clouds in the vicinity of the Home. Naturally, after the Doktor and his assassin corps were dealt with, the number of mutates dwindled.''

"What about the clouds already unleashed?''

"We know the clouds are regenerating, but we don't know if the regeneration is sustained indefinitely. We suspect they have a limited life span,'' Blade replied, and his gaze drifted to the north. Immediately he tramped on the brake pedal.

"What's wrong?'' Jenny asked, facing forward.

Rising above the trees, approximately a half-mile ahead, there reared a vertical column of smoke.

"A campfire, you think?'' Jenny inquired nervously.

Blade nodded and drove in the direction of the smoke. "We must check it out.''

"Why not go around? It's none of our business.''

"I have to make it our business,'' Blade said.

"But why?''

"Because that campfire is about a mile from our destination,'' Blade divulged. "Whoever made the fire must still be there, and we need to learn if they're friendly or not.''

"We're that close to our vacation spot?'' Jenny queried in surprise.

"Yep.''

"What will we do it they're raiders? Return to the Home?''

"If they're raiders, they'll regret being this close to the Home. We have our hearts set on this vacation, and I'm not going to allow anyone or anything to stand in our way.''

"Go get 'em, Dad,'' Gabe stated.

The SEAL entered a stretch of woods, and Blade reduced speed to five miles an hour, skillfully weaving the transport among the trunks. His window was down, and he leaned to the left, listening for alien sounds, for voices, laughter, or any noises indicating the presence of another party. "Get the Commando,'' he directed.

Jenny climbed from her seat, over the console, and knelt next to Gabe so she could reach into the storage section.

The woods thinned and Blade pressed on the accelerator,

pushing the speedometer to 20. He focused on the spiraling plume of smoke, gauging the distance. He didn't want to blunder into the camp of whoever made the fire. The SEAL's air-cooled and self-lubricating engine produced a muted whine, instead of the raspy gowl so prevalent in prewar vehicles, and he doubted the SEAL could be heard more than 30 yards away. With luck, he might be able to catch the fire-makers off guard.

Jenny returned to her seat, laden with weapons. In her hands she held one of Blade's favorite autoloaders, a Commando Arms Carbine. Converted to full automatic capability by the Family Gunsmiths and fitted with a 90-shot magazine of .45-caliber ammunition, the Commando, which Blade found reminiscent of the ancient Thompson submachine guns, was a devastating piece of firepower. Over Jenny's left shoulder was slung a Beretta BM 62 auto-rifle, and in a holster on her right hip a Ruger Super Blackhawk .44 Magnum, a powerful handgun she had to hold with both hands to fire accurately, a gun she had practiced with many times.

"Hey, don't I get a gun?" Gabe asked, leaning on the console.

"No, you don't," Jenny said.

"Why not? Daddy has taught me how to shoot."

"I know. But there might be danger up ahead."

"That's why I want the gun," Gabe noted with childish simplicity.

"Not now," Blade interjected. "Sit back in your seat and keep quiet."

"But I want to help. I want to blow some of the suckers to smithereens," Gabe offered.

"First of all, we don't know if we'll be blowing anyone to smithereens," Jenny said. "Second, you're too young to be shooting people."

"How old do you have to be, Mom?"

"Be quiet, Gabe," Blade ordered. "I won't say it again."

Gabe made a hissing noise and sat back in his seat.

"Thank you," Jenny said.

Gabe crossed his arms on his chest and pouted.

Blade drove forward, watching the smoke. He slowed when he estimated he was within 100 yards of the campfire, and the SEAL crawled another 50 yards before he applied the brakes. "You stay here with Gabe," he told his wife. "I'm going to go have a look."

"Nothing doing. Where you go, I go."

"And leave Gabe here by himself?"

Jenny gazed to the north. "Why risk exposing yourself? Why don't we drive right up to the campfire in the SEAL? There hasn't been a bullet made that can penetrate the SEAL's synthetic shell. You said so yourself."

"Bullets, no. But a hand grenade or a bazooka could damage the transport extensively. If they're raiders, there's no predicting the type of weaponry they might have."

"I don't like you leaving us."

"It can't be helped," Blade said.

Jenny frowned. "I'll give you two minutes. Then I'm coming to get you."

"You'll stay put."

"You're my husband. Don't be ridiculous."

"All right," Blade said. "But give me fifteen minutes."

"Here," Jenny stated, extending the Commando. She glanced at the steering wheel. "Too bad you've never given me driving lessons."

"I will the first chance I get," Blade promised, taking the carbine and opening his door. "I won't be long." He dropped to the ground and took a moment to double-check the magazine.

Jenny and Gabe materialized at the window.

"Be careful, Daddy."

"I will, son."

"Fifteen minutes," Jenny said.

"Close the windows and lock the doors," Blade instructed her. "If anyone or anything tries to get in, lean on the horn."

"I'll blow 'em to smithereens!" Gabe declared.

"Enough, already, with the smithereens," Jenny said. Her

eyes locked on her husband, silently expressing the depth of her affection. "Take care."

"You know it," Blade replied, and jogged toward the smoke.

CHAPTER FOUR

Blade advanced warily, moving bent over at the waist, scrutinizing the undergrowth carefully. There were fewer and fewer trees the farther he went. When he reached a point approximately 20 yards from the smoke, he heard a peal of laughter. Someone was having a good time. He cocked his head and detected the murmur of conversation.

There was definitely more than one person.

He stalked through the waist-high weeds, the Commando at the ready, pausing between each step to listen. Twenty more yards were covered, and then he saw the flickering flames of the campfire. Dropping to his elbows and knees, he continued to narrow the range. The voices became louder, and after a bit he could distinguish individual words. In another 15 yards he could hear them clearly, and he flattened and crawled to within eight yards of the speakers.

"—waste of our damn time!"

"We'll find the place yet."

"Like hell we will!"

By cautiously parting the weeds with the Commando barrel,

Blade could see the fire and the eight people seated around it. Five were men, three were women. All wore filthy clothes. Their hair was unkempt, and all bore smudge marks on their faces. Their clothing consisted of a mix of tattered jeans, torn shirts, and old leather garments.

"We'll find it!" declared a man with a bushy brown beard and brown eyes. "We know it's in this area somewhere."

"But where?" snapped a weasel of a man whose oily black hair was plastered to his head. "It's like looking for a needle in a haystack!" He wore jeans, a tan shirt, and a black leather jacket.

"Lighten up, Roy," said a young redheaded woman. Her tight-fitting clothes, a blue blouse and jeans, seemed to have been molded to her shapely contours. "One minute we're shooting the breeze, and all the vibes are mellow, and the next you're griping and whining and spoiling the whole mood."

"I don't whine, you bimbo," Roy retorted angrily.

"Don't call Tammy a bimbo," the man with the beard warned. "I don't like to have my wife insulted."

"No offense meant, Jared," Roy said, but his contemptuous tone belied his statement.

"I know we're in the right area," Jared said. "And just think of what it will be like if we find this place! We'll never go hungry again. We'll never have to scrounge for food."

What place were they talking about? Blade wondered. He could see they were well-armed. Each person carried a rifle slung over a shoulder and a handgun in a hip holster.

"They have weapons there, an entire armory we can use," Jarad went on. "I heard tell they even have a library with thousands of books—"

"Who the hell cares about books?" Roy sneered.

A library! An armory! Blade's eyes narrowed.

"Those of us who can read care about books," Jared said. "Trust us, Roy. All we have to do is find the Home and we're set for life."

They were raiders planning to attack the Home! Anger washed over Blade, a sense of outrage at the thought of the harm the band could inflict on the Family, and heedless of his personal safety, he stood and strode toward the camp, the Commando level at his waist.

A brunette was the first to notice the enraged giant coming through the weeds. "Look out!" she cried, and leaped to her feet, her left hand going for her revolver.

"Don't even think of it!" Blade barked, stepping into the clear, swinging the Commando from side to side, waiting for one of them to grab a gun. He hoped they would give him an excuse to finish them right there.

Eight faces gaped in astonishment at the Warrior.

"Who the hell are you?" Roy demanded.

"Someone who was in the right spot at the right time," Blade said cryptically.

"We don't know you, mister," Jared stated, "and we don't want any trouble."

"You've got it, in spades," Blade declared.

"What did we ever do to you?" Tammy asked.

"It's what you were planning to do to those I'm sworn to protect that matters," Blade responded.

"What are you talking about?" Jared queried nervously.

"Don't play innocent with me. I overheard you discussing the Home. I know you plan to try and raid our compound."

"Your compound?" Jared said, and glanced at his companions in bewilderment.

Blade took a pace nearer and trained the Commando on the man named Jared, and as he did a hard object jammed him in the small of the back and a flinty voice spoke from right behind him.

"Let go of the hardware or you're dead!"

"Okay!" Blade deliberately blurted out, allowing his shoulders to droop dejectedly, and he made a motion as if he were tossing the carbine to the grass. Instead, he pivoted, spinning in a tight arc even as he sidestepped to the left, and he brought the Commando around and up.

A hefty man in a leather jacket, brown shirt, and jeans was just beginning to react when the stock of the Commando jammed into his arms, deflecting his Marlin 336 CS aside. An instant later the Commando's barrel struck him in the temple and he staggered backward and slumped to his knees. The Marlin slipped from his fingers.

The rest of the men and women were rising.

Blade rotated, covering the band, standing sideways so he could keep an eye on the one he'd slugged. "Put your hands up!" he commanded.

"You don't understand!" Jared declared, and took a step toward the Warrior.

Blade pointed the Commando at the bearded man, his finger tightening on the trigger.

"We don't want to hurt you!" Jared said, extending his arms with the palms out. "Really!"

"Sure," Blade replied sarcastically, his finger easing off the trigger.

"You misunderstood," Jared asserted. "We don't plan to attack the Home. We've heard wonderful things about the Home, and we came all this way to see if we could *live* there."

Amazement replaced Blade's anger, and he looked at each of them, stunned to behold evident sincerity on every countenance. "You what?"

"We've traveled hundreds of miles in the hope of being allowed to live at the Home," Jared said.

"Explain yourself," Blade directed, still suspicious of a trick.

Jared gestured at the others. "We were in Grand Rapids when we first heard about the Home. Grand Rapids, Minnesota, that is. Have you ever been there?"

"No," Blade admitted while continually scanning the band for a hint of treachery.

"It's a small town east of the Chippewa National Forest. About seven hundred people live there, making their living by fishing and hunting and trading. We were at a bar when we heard an old trapper talking to some men concerning the time he was captured by the inhabitants of an underground city in the north-central part of the state. He was out exploring,

trying to find prime game areas for trapping, when he wa
caught by these people called the Moles. Do you know wh
they are?''

Blade nodded. Indeed he did. He had had many dealing
with the Moles in their capacity as an ally of the Family i
the Federation.

"These Moles told the trapper to stay away from that region
They apparently aren't too fond of strangers and don't permi
anyone near their underground city.''

Blade pursed his lips. Everything Jared had said so far ran;
true. The Moles' underground city had initially been a serie
of hasty fallout shelters dug by a man named Carter and som
others shortly before the outbreak of the war. Certain that th
war was imminent and doubting they had the time to construc
a suitable retreat, Carter and company had driven far from
civilization and hiked into the Red Lake Wildlife Managemen
Area. Once there they'd simply started digging. They survive
the war, and their descendants had expanded on the origina
shelters, adding on a network of tunnels and chambers. O
the ground, over the heart of their complex, they had buil
a massive mountain of clay as added protection and insulation
Eventually their city had become known as the Mound.

"They released the trapper and sent him packing," Jare
was saying. "While he was there they told him about thei
allies in something called the Freedom Federation. One of th
allies they mentioned was the Family.''

Blade relaxed slightly. He was beginning to believe Jared
and he was gratified to learn the Moles were not indulgin;
in their old practice of slaying or enslaving every stranger the
encountered. Or were they? "Wait a minute," he interrupted
"How long ago was the trapper caught?"

"Not quite two years ago," Jared said. "Why?"

"No reason. Continue.''

"Excuse me," Tammy spoke up.

"What is it?" Blade asked.

"Can I take care of Harold?" she inquired, and pointed a
the hefty man still on his knees, blood trickling from a gash i

his temple, his eyes open but unfocused. "He was on guard duty, and he must not have seen you sneak in."

"Go ahead," Blade said. "But keep your hands where I can see them."

The woman walked to the guard and knelt beside him. She started inspecting the wound. "Harold? Are you all right?"

"Is it night?" Harold asked, swaying unsteadily.

"No?"

"Then why am I seeing stars?"

Tammy went to reach into the right back pocket on her jeans.

"Not so fast!" Blade warned. "Use two fingers."

Tammy froze, staring at the Commando, and slowly removed a red bandanna from the pocket. "This is all I wanted," she explained, and used the bandanna to dab at the blood.

"Go on with your story," Blade told Jared.

"Well, the information we learned about the Family fascinated us. The trapper talked about the Home, about the library and the huge armory and a tall wall that keeps out all the wild animals and the mutants. But what interested us the most was the news that married couples live at the Home in peace and security. Their children are educated and raised in relative safety."

Blade's mouth curved downward. He didn't like the idea of the Moles relating so much information about the Family, particularly not the fact that the armory existed. Weapons were valued at a premium in the Outlands, and any large band of raiders might be tempted to try and destroy the Family simply for the sake of acquiring an immense arsenal. "You seem to attach a lot of importance to the security and safety the Home and the Family have to offer," he commented.

"All of us were born in the Outlands. We've spent our entire lives living by our wits, barely surviving at times. No one is safe in the Outlands, mister. You must know that."

"I do," Blade said. The Outlands was the designation for any and all territory outside recognized jurisdictions, and included a major portion of the country. With the collapse of civilization, most of the U.S. had reverted to a barbaric level and survival of the fittest was the law of the land. Life in the Outlands, as the staying went, was cheap. People could be shot without provocation, or have their throats slit in the middle of the night. Killings, robbery, rape, and worse were commonplace. Blade had ventured into the Outlands a number of times, and on each occasion he had barely escaped with his life.

"Then you know why we want to find the Home, why we want to live there," Jared stated, and nodded at Tammy. "She and I want to have kids. We want to see them grow up healthy and strong. Most of all, we want to see them grow up, period. The Outlands is no place to try and raise a family."

"You have a point," Blade conceded.

"What's your name?" Jared asked.

"Blade."

"I'm Jared." He pointed at Tammy. "That's my wife, Tammy. Harold is the one you clobbered." He indicated the weasely man. "That's Roy. He joined us in Bemidji."

"Howdy," Roy said.

Blade said nothing, his gray eyes regarding the man coldly. He instinctively distrusted the weasel.

Jared pointed at each of the others. "That's Lloyd, with the torn T-shirt, and the brunette is his wife, Betty. The guy with the Winchester is Jim, and the woman next to him is Alice, his squeeze. The guy wearing the jeans with the holes in the knees is Tom."

Each person offered a friendly greeting.

"Hello," the Warrior said when the introductions were completed.

"And you're really from the Home?" Jared queried.

"I don't make it a habit to lie."

"Will you take us there?" Tammy asked hopefully.

"Not so fast," Blade replied. "Did all of you live in Grand Rapids?"

"None of us did. We were just passing through," Jared said.

"You wandered around a lot?"

"All over."

"And how did you feed yourselves?"

Jared blinked a few times and looked at his wife before answering. "Oh, we did odd jobs for food. Or we scrounged if we had to."

Blade scrutinized the group. "In other words, you're scavengers."

"You could call us that," Jared conceded reluctantly. "But we're not like most scavengers."

"Oh?"

"No. We don't go around killing people for the fun of it. We don't steal and loot. We try to live our lives honestly."

Blade studied Jared's features, measuring the man's integrity. "I've never heard of honest scavengers before."

"You must believe me! We're not murderers. The only times we've killed were when we were attacked, in self-defense. Why do you think we can't stand living in the Outlands any longer? Because we're sick and tired of all the senseless killing. We're sick and tired of always having to be on the alert for danger. And some of us want to have children. Could you imagine raising a kid under such conditions?" Jared inquired passionately.

The Warrior glanced at Tammy and Harold. She was assisting him to his feet. "No, I wouldn't like to rear a family in the Outlands."

"Then tell us. Do you think we have a chance to be admitted to the Home?"

"I don't know," Blade replied, facing Jared. "The decision isn't mine to make. Whether you're permitted to live there is for the Elders to decide."

"Who are the Elders?"

"Our Elders decide policy issues, and their decisions are implemented by our Leader."

"Will they let us live there?" Jared asked.

"I really don't know. Our compound can only handle so many people, and we already have about a hundred living there."

Jared frowned and his shoulders slumped. "We didn't know."

"You still might be granted permission," Blade said encouragingly. "And even if the Elders deny your petition, you might be allowed to live at Halma with the Clan."

"The who?"

"Another of our allies. The Clan were refugees from the Twin Cities, and the Family helped relocate them in Halma, a small town west of the Home," Blade explained.

"Do you—" Jared began, then stopped, staring past the Warrior, his eyes widening.

Blade turned.

Coming through the weeds were Jenny and Gabe. She had the Beretta pressed to her right shoulder. Gabe walked behind her, his head craned to the right so he could see the scavengers.

"These are my wife and son," Blade introduced them. "Jenny and Gabe."

"This is just great!" Jenny stated as she moved to Blade's left side. "Here I was, fearing for your life, and I find you socializing." She lowered the rifle.

"Who are these people, Dad?" Gabe wanted to know.

"Don't worry," the Warrior said. "They won't hurt us." He looked at the band.

Jared's right hand streaked to his revolver, a Smith and Wesson Model 65, and the handgun swept up and out, the barrel aimed at Blade and his loved ones.

CHAPTER FIVE

Blade swung into action the moment he saw Jared's hand sweep toward the holster. He lunged to his left, his huge arm encircling Jenny and Gabe, bearing them to the ground with his body in front of theirs, shielding them from the anticipated shot. Expecting to feel a searing pain as the slug tore through him, he twisted as he went down, training the Commando on the scavengers. He could see Jared sighting the Smith and Wesson, apparently intent on making an accurate shot, but the revolver wasn't aiming at Blade, Jenny, or Gabe.

The scavenger was pointing the gun at something behind them.

A snarling form hurdled over the Warrior and his family, springing at the scavengers. The Smith and Wesson boomed, but the shot missed. Before Jared could fire again, a feral feline landed on all fours, uttered a piercing, raspy scream of rage, and launched itself at the man named Harold.

For the space of a second, as the creature had alighted and girded its leg muscles to execute the leap at Harold, Blade glimpsed the thing clearly. Goose bumps broke out on his skin.

He recognized their attacker immediately. The characteristics were unmistakable; there was the hairless body covered with blistering sores oozing sickly yellowish pus, the otherwise dry, cracked, peeling skin, the two mounds of green mucus in place of ears, and the overpowering stench associated with animals caught in the green chemical clouds and transformed into ravenous horrors.

The thing was a mutated bobcat!

Harold screamed as the 60-pound fury pounced on his chest, its front claws slashing at his face and neck, its rear claws digging deep into his flesh. He staggered backwards, flailing at the mutate to no avail.

Jared tried to get a bead on the mutate, but couldn't shoot for fear of hitting Harold.

Blade shoved himself erect and closed in, gripping the barrel of the Commando and swinging the machine gun as if it were a club. The stock smashed into the mutate and dislodged the beast, sending it tumbling to the ground, where the creature promptly regained its footing and growled at the Warrior.

"Look out, Dad!" Gabe yelled.

The mutate vaulted at Blade's midriff, its claws extended to rake his stomach.

Blade whipped the Commando in a vicious swipe, catching the feline on the head and knocking it to the grass a second time. As it rolled and rose to its feet, Blade reversed his grip on the Commando, and was about to cut loose when he realized Tammy stood a few yards behind the bobcat, in his line of fire. Instead, he released the Carbine and drew his Bowies, meeting the mutate's next rush head-on.

With its mouth wide open, exposing its tapered fangs, the bobcat took two bounds and leaped.

The Warrior twisted his torso, evading those razor claws, and buried his left Bowie in the mutate's neck, sinking the blade to the hilt and impaling the bobcat in midair. The mutate went limp, but Blade still brought the right Bowie around and down, driving the point of the knife into the creature's skull.

Blood spurted from the mutate's nostrils and a putrid bile

spewed from its mouth. Unexpectedly, the bobcat came to life again, convulsing violently, its legs kicking wildly, and then it sagged, suspended by the knives, lifeless.

Blade placed the body on the ground, pressed his right boot onto the mutate's spine, and wrenched the Bowies out. Both knives dripped blood and pus. He heard a cough and looked to his right.

Harold lay flat on his back, his face severely lacerated, his throat literally torn to ribbons. His hands were clasped to his neck, and crimson spilled over his fingers and sprayed in all directions. He gasped and groaned, his mouth opening and closing, sheer terror reflected in his eyes.

"Are you okay?" Jenny asked Blade, standing and lending a hand to Gabe so he could rise. "I don't see any scratches. Did the mutate nick you?"

"No," Blade said, squatting. He wiped the Bowies clean on the grass and slid them into their sheaths. "I'm fine."

The band of scavengers gathered around Harold. Jared leaned over their companion. "Do you want us to try and get word to your mother and brother?"

Harold didn't respond. His lips quivered, his eyelids fluttered, and he expelled a protracted breath.

"That poor man," Jenny commented sadly. "Is there anything we can do?"

Blade shook his head. In addition to the deep cuts and slashes, splotches of pus were visible intermixed with the blood on Harold's neck, and mutate pus was as toxic as the deadliest of known poisons. Once the pus entered the human bloodstream, the affected individual seldom lasted more than a few days.

There were tears in Tammy's eyes when she bent down and kissed the doomed man lightly on the forehead. "We're so sorry, Harold. You're one of our best friends. I wish there was something we could do for you."

Harold suddenly arched his back, his arms dropped to his sides, and he stiffened and expired.

"Harold!" Tammy cried.

"It's no use," Jared said, feeling Harold's left wrist for a pulse. "He's gone."

Blade stared at the scavengers, noting their expressions of legitimate sorrow. All except for one. The weasel, Roy, was staring at Jenny.

Jared glanced up at the Warrior. "I'm sorry if I startled you. I saw the thing coming at you and there wasn't time to give any warning." He paused. "I thought I could nail the damn mutation before it got to us."

"You tried," Blade said.

"Not hard enough."

The scavenger wearing the torn T-shirt cleared his throat. "We should bury Harold. He's been with us for years, and I'm not about to let the buzzards or any other animals get to him."

"We'll bury him," Jared assured him.

Jenny leaned closer to her husband. "Who are these people, anyway?" she whispered.

Blade made the introductions, leaving the weasel for last. "And this one is Roy," he concluded gruffly.

"Hello," Jenny said.

"Hello, yourself, beautiful," Roy responded, smirking. "So you're the big lug's wife, huh? I can't imagine what you see in him. If you—"

Before Roy could continue, Blade was on him. He grabbed the scavenger by the front of the tan shirt and lifted, his enormous shoulder and arm muscles bulging, hoisting Roy overhead. A flaming scarlet tinged the Warrior's cheeks.

Transfixed by the abrupt assault, the other scavengers gaped.

"Let me go!" Roy demanded angrily, pounding his fists on the giant's forearms.

"Gladly," Blade responded, and hurled the weasel at the ground.

Roy hit hard on his left side and rolled several yards. He rose unsteadily to his knees, striving to unsling his rifle, but the tip of a combat boot rammed into his abdomen, doubling him over in agony.

Blade drew back his right foot to kick the scavenger again.

"Blade! Please! Don't!" Jenny interceded.

The Warrior stopped, his foot ready to lash out, and looked at her.

"He's not worth it," Jenny said.

"I should break every bone in his body," Blade stated harshly.

"Why stoop to his level? No harm has been done."

Blade hesitated, his fists clenching and unclenching. He saw Gabe watching in rapt fascination, and he thought of the example he was setting for his son. He wanted to beat the weasel to a pulp, but what effect would the sight have on Gabe?

"You bastard!" Roy fumed, shoving to his knees again. "I'll get you for this!"

Blade reached down and clamped his right hand on the scavenger's throat. He pulled Roy to a standing posture and glared into the man's defiant eyes. "Don't push me."

Roy tried to pry the Warrior's fingers fron his neck, but the steely vise only constricted tighter.

"This is the first and only warning you'll receive," Blade stated flatly. "I won't tolerate anyone treating my wife with disrespect. And no one—absolutely *no one*—comes on to my wife more than once. If you make the same mistake again, you'll answer to me. Do you understand?"

The scavenger merely glowered.

"You're a stubborn little turd, aren't you?" Blade remarked, and shook Roy until the weasel's teeth chattered. "What's it going to be? Are you going to behave yourself?"

"Yeah," Roy hissed, and sneered contemptuously.

"Why don't I believe you?"

"I won't try and put the make on your wife!" Roy snapped. "What else do you want me to say?"

"Not a word," Blade replied, and released his grip.

The scavenger toppled to the grass. He sat up and rubbed his sore neck.

Jared stepped over to the Warrior. "I'm sorry about this. He's been this way ever since we met him."

"Why'd you let him hook up with you?" Blade asked, his flinty gaze on the weasel.

Jared shrugged. "We can always use another gun. To his credit, he always did his share of the work."

"I can tell you here and now that he won't be permitted to live at the Home, and I doubt the Clan will accept him either. The rest of you can still apply to the Elders, but he might as well return to whatever hole he crawled out of," Blade said.

"You won't hold his actions against us?"

"You're not to blame for his behavior."

Jared breathed a sigh of relief. "Thanks. Will you take us to the Home as soon as we're done burying Harold?"

"No."

"No?" Jared repeated, perplexed. "Why not?"

"We're on a special trip, a vacation, the first I've taken away from all my duties in years. I'm not about to let anything interfere with it. I'm sorry."

Tammy joined them. "Are you sure you're not holding Roy's conduct against the rest of us?"

"I give you my word I'll take you to the Home after our vacation is over," Blade promised.

"How long will that be?" Tammy queried.

"About two weeks."

"Two weeks!" Jared exclaimed. "But we've come so far."

"Which is why another two weeks won't make much of a difference," Tammy said, taking his hand and squeezing reassuringly.

Jared glanced at her, then at the giant. "I guess we don't have any choice."

"Blade, we could take the time out to return to the Home," Jenny proposed.

"And what if a new threat has arisen? What if the Elders want to send me on another run, or the leaders of the Freedom Federation require my services again?"

"We've only been gone half a day," Jenny said.

Blade stared at her. "Do you want to take the risk of spoiling our trip?"

Her forehead creased as she pondered the question. "No," she finally admitted. "I don't."

"Then we continue to our destination," Blade said, and faced the head of the band. "Can you survive out here for two weeks?"

Jared nodded. "No problem. We'll hunt game for our food, and we know how to make sturdy shelters. We'll be okay."

"Then I'll swing by on our return trip and pick you up. We can cram most of you into our transport and the rest can sit on the roof. What do you say?"

"We'll be counting the minutes," Jared said, and smiled.

The Warrior offered his right hand. "Until then."

Smiling broadly at the prospect of achieving their goal, Jared shook vigorously.

Blade nodded at the others, but purposely ignored the weasel, and departed with Jenny and Gabe, making for the SEAL.

"Take care!" Jared called after them. "Don't let anything happen to you!"

"We'll be back," Blade pledged, and waved.

With hopeful expectation on their faces, the scavengers watched until the trio were no longer visible.

"I can't believe it!" Lloyd declared. "Our dreams have come true!"

Jared pivoted and gazed at Roy. "No thanks to you. I want you to leave. Now."

His lips compressing in resentment, Roy stood. "And what if I don't want to go?" he demanded. He saw Lloyd, Tom, and Jim close in on him and suddenly found himself surrounded.

"You don't have any choice," Jared said. "We've tolerated your attitude for as long as we can. Lloyd, Jim, and I have all seen you looking at our wives. But you were never blatant about it, so we let your conduct pass. This Blade has made us realize we've been fools. I can safely say I speak for the rest when I tell you to take a hike. And don't ever come back."

Roy glared at each of the men. "Just like that?"

"Just like that," Jared said.

"After all we've been through?"

"Don't play on our sympathy. We don't have any for a man who lusts after every woman he meets. Just leave, Roy, before we're tempted to hurry you along."

Roy glanced at the women, and the loathing he perceived on their countenances added to his simmering fury. "Fine! Be that way! I'll leave. And all you can go to hell."

"If I were you, I wouldn't head south," Jared advised. "That's the way Blade went, and I doubt you want to bump into him again." He stepped aside and motioned with his right arm. "Don't try to sneak back and cause us any trouble. We'll kill you if you do."

"Bastards!" Roy fumed, and walked away from them to the east. "I hope the mutants get the bunch of you!" He stormed into a stand of trees, his blood boiling, tempted to take a few shots at his former comrades. But he knew Jared was a man of his word, and he didn't like the odds. For 50 yards he tramped through the brush until his rage began to abate. He remembered the mutate, and quickly unslung his Ruger Model 77R.

There was no sense in being careless.

He absently gazed at the sky, thinking of the giant, and hatred welled within him. This was all the giant's fault! He told himself. He'd only hooked up with the lousy band because he planned to eventually get into Tammy's pants, with or without her consent, and now the damn giant had ruined his scheme. Months of biding his time and waiting for Tammy and him to be left alone, and it was all for nothing!

Damn!

Damn!

Damn!

Several minutes elapsed, and he stalked onward until he heard an odd whine. He was almost to the edge of a field, and he crouched, gazing to the southeast in the direction of the noise. Seconds later a large green van came into view, driving slowly to the northeast. The driver's window was down, and Roy blinked in surprise when he recognized the man behind the wheel.

The rotten giant!

He watched intently as the vehicle cruised across the field and vanished over a low hill. Then he rose and walked to where the van's immense tires had flattened the vegetation and left rutted impressions in the soil. Where were they headed? he wondered. The giant had mentioned taking a vacation. But to where? Probably not very far, if the bastard intended to return within two weeks and pick up Jared and the others.

Roy glanced at the low hill, wishing he could avenge himself on the man he hated most in the world. An idea occurred to him, and a crooked grin twisted his visage. The van wasn't moving very fast, and the vehicle was leaving a trail any idiot could follow. Shadowing them would be easy. And if he stayed on their tracks, sooner or later they would stop to enjoy their vacation. They'd undoubtedly be engrossed in their fun and off their guard. The very last person they would expect to see would be him.

He snickered.

Yes, sir! This must be his lucky day! He could take his revenge on the son of a bitch, and then have his way with the prick's foxy momma. The thought of kissing her lovely body made him salivate, and Roy cackled as he changed direction and hastened to the northeast.

CHAPTER SIX

"Is this your surprise spot?"

"Yep."

"Oh, Blade! It's lovely!" Jenny declared happily.

"What do you think, Gabe?" Blade asked, shifting in his seat and looking at his son.

"Can we fish in the lake?"

"You bet."

"Will we live in a tent like we do when we camp out in the Home?" Gabe inquired.

"No. We'll be staying in a cabin."

"What cabin, Dad?"

Blade turned and nodded at the log structure on the north side of the lake. He had braked the SEAL next to the western shore, 500 yards from Kurt Carpenter's retreat. "That cabin."

"Does anyone live there?" Gabe questioned.

"Nope."

"Then why is the door open?"

Blade's eyes narrowed and he leaned over the steering wheel. To his consternation, the cabin door was hanging wide open.

"Maybe someone does live there," Jenny said.

"Maybe," Blade concurred, wondering if someone had found the cabin and moved in. What should he do if the place was occupied? The Founder had built the cabin, but no one from the Family had been there since the Big Blast. Could he rightfully claim it?

"How did you learn about this spot?" Jenny asked.

"Plato told me about it. The Founder used the cabin as a retreat," Blade explained, and pressed his right foot down on the accelerator. The Commando rested on the console between the bucket seats, and he placed his right hand on the weapon as a precaution.

"Maybe the cabin has been ramsacked," Jenny speculated.

"I hope not," Blade said. He drove along the western shore until the SEAL reached the field bordering the north end. Twenty yards off, at the edge of the forest, stood the cabin. He braked and shifted the transport into Park. "Stay here."

"I'll cover you," Jenny offered, leaning out her window, the Beretta in her hands.

"Watch out, Dad," Gabe said.

Blade nodded and climbed from the SEAL. He eased his door shut quietly, then advanced on the cabin. The structure appeared to be intact and sound, despite the passage of over a century. He stepped to within five yards of the doorway and halted. "Hello. Is anyone there?"

No one responded.

He trained the Commando on the door and cautiously moved closer, glancing at the windows on either side. The cabin seemed to be deserted, but there might be someone hiding inside. He edged to the right of the doorway and peered into the interior. His nostrils detected a distinct fishy odor, and his brow knit when he spied a pan resting on a stove in the northwest corner of the room. "Is anyone here?" he repeated. "I mean you no harm."

Again there wasn't any reply.

Strange.

Blade walked into the cabin, his eyes roving over the blue shag rug, the sofa, the bookshelf against the east wall, and the rocking chair, straight chair, and coffee table in the middle of the room. There was hardly any dust on the furniture or the rug, indicating someone had cleaned the place recently.

But who?

He moved to the kitchen area and noticed two dirty plates and silverware lying on a counter near the stove. A few pieces of dry fish remained in the pan on the stove. He reached out with his left hand and touched the pieces. They were cool, and separated into soft bits when he squeezed them, leading him to conclude that the meal had been cooked two or three days ago.

Where was the person who'd done the cooking?

"Hello," Blade declared, and angled to an open door on his right. He discovered a furnished bedroom, and he stared at the tidy bedspread in perplexity. The bed obviously hadn't been slept in, which only compounded the mystery. He went to each of the closets and cabinets, inspecting the contents, and was pleased to find the cabin fully stocked.

How weird.

From the evidence, he surmised someone had used the stove to prepare a single meal and then departed without pilfering any of the valuable items in the cabin. Such behavior was extraordinary. He turned from the closet in the southwest corner of the living room, bewildered that even the fishing tackle had been left alone, and his eyes strayed to the section of wall behind the open front door. There, leaning on the jamb, was a rifle.

Thoroughly confounded, Blade examined the weapon. He recognized the model as a Beeman/Krico Six Hundred. The Family Armory contained the same kind of weapon, and he'd fired it on a few occasions. He checked the three-shot detachable magazine and the barrel, and found the gun loaded and clean.

The enigma deepened.

No one in their right mind would go off and leave a perfectly good weapon, not in a day and age when a reliable rifle could mean the difference between life and death. Blade replaced the Beeman behind the door and stepped outside. He studied the grass and weeds in the vicinity of the entrance, hoping to find tracks. He located a few partial prints, but nothing unusual, nothing to explain the deserted cabin.

"Is it safe?" Jenny shouted.

Blade looked at the SEAL and nodded. He returned to his family, scrutinizing the small lake, impressed by the serenity of the scene. Two weeks at the retreat would give him the rest he sorely needed, but the puzzling state of the cabin bothered him. Was it really safe? None of the evidence conclusively proved foul play was involved, but the only reason he could conceive of for someone going off and leaving their rifle behind and the cabin door ajar was if the person had been slain. But if the occupant or occupants had been killed, why didn't the killer or killers plunder the cabin? Perhaps he was making the proverbial mountain out of a mole hill. There might be a perfectly innocent explanation. After all, as a Warrior he was inclined to evaluate every situation in terms of the potential for danger, and perhaps he attached too much significance to the gun, the open door, and the fish in the pan.

"What did you find in there?" Jenny inquired as Blade reached the driver's side.

"No one is home," Blade said. He took his seat in the SEAL and related the discoveries he'd made.

"It's sounds to me like someone left in a big hurry," Jenny conjectured when he concluded.

"But why?" Blade asked.

"Can we stay there until the people come back?" Gabe inquired.

Blade stared at the cabin, pondering their options. "I don't see why not. We've come this far, so we might as well enjoy ourselves."

"I agree," Jenny said. "If the occupants return, we'll explain the situation to them. I'm sure they'll understand."

"Then let's settle in," Blade proposed. He drove the SEAL to within a yard of the entrance and parked, aligning the transport so the driver's door was near the cabin doorway in case a quick exit became necessary. After switching off the ignition, he dropped to the ground, the Commando in his left hand.

Jenny and Gabe slid to the grass on the passenger side, and Jenny led their son inside to check out the interior.

The Warrior turned, surveying the surroundings, bothered by a vague sensation of unease, an inexplicable feeling that they were being watched. But there wasn't a soul in sight. He shrugged and went into the cabin.

"Oh, honey! This is wonderful!" Jenny exclaimed, delighted at the homey atmosphere. "I wish we had known about this retreat years ago."

"I'll begin unloading the things we need from the SEAL," Blade offered.

"From the looks of this place, we won't need much," Jenny said.

"Do you want me to bring in our spare clothes?"

"No. Just Gabe's pajamas. I can get whatever other clothes we need out of the SEAL anytime. But we'll need the brown bag containing our toilet articles. And don't forget the plastic jugs of water. Until we test the water here, we don't want to take any chances."

"Is that all?"

"Did you bring one of the flashlights?"

"Yes," Blade confirmed, knowing she was talking about one of the half-dozen flashlights the Family had received in trade with the Civilized Zone.

"We'll need the flashlight if we go outside at night," Jenny mentioned.

"Okay. Anything else?"

"Yeah. The food bag."

"But I told you about the canned goods in the cupboard."

"The way you two gorillas eat, I'll need all the food I can get," Jenny joked.

"All right. Now is *that* it?"

"It's all I can think of at the moment."

"Lucky me," Blade quipped. He slung the Commando over his left shoulder and returned to the SEAL.

The next several hours were spent at various tasks. Blade unloaded the SEAL and was conscripted to assist Jenny in washing every dish, glass, pot and pan, and piece of silverware in the cabin. Jenny replaced the sheets on the bed with a clean set she found in the bedroom closet. Because she wasn't quite satisfied with the cleanliness of the cabin, Jenny enlisted Gabe to give the place a dusting.

"We're only staying here for a couple of weeks, not a lifetime," Blade commented at one point.

"I refuse to sleep on a bed if I don't know who slept in it before me," Jenny said. "And I'm not about to use dishes and silverware any old scavenger might have used."

"I still think you're going overboard."

"Baloney. I keep our cabin at the Home this clean."

Blade glanced at his son, who was busy dusting the books. "I never realized you go to this much trouble."

"Of course not. You're a man."

"Meaning."

"Meaning men don't have the foggiest idea of how hard women have to work to keep a house neat and tidy. You think all we have to do is swish a dust cloth around and make a few passes with a broom and the place is spotless. But it doesn't work that way, especially if there are children in the family. A wife's work is never done."

"I try to help out," Blade said.

"You do," Jenny acknowledged, "when you're not off fighting dragons."

"I thought we agreed we weren't going to discuss my work once we got here?"

"Sorry," Jenny said.

"Hey, Dad?" Gabe interjected.

"What?"

"This is our vacation, isn't it?"

"Yeah," Blade replied.

"And didn't Mommy and you say our vacation is for having fun?"

"Yes," Blade responded.

"Then how come I'm not having fun yet?"

"Ask your mother."

Forty-five minutes later Jenny shooed them out of the cabin so she could prepare their supper in peace. She decided to open several of the cans in the cupboard to determine if the contents were edible, and began searching a drawer for a can opener.

Blade and Gabe strolled toward the lake. To the west the sun dipped closer and closer to the horizon.

"This place is neat," Gabe declared.

"You think so?"

"Sure do. Can we go fishing tomorrow?"

"First thing in the morning, unless your mom wants us to paint the cabin instead."

Gabe looked at his father in dismay. "Was that a joke?"

"Yep."

"Whew! You scared me," Gabe said.

Blade chuckled, stooped down to pick up a rock, and tossed it far out over the lake. He saw water spray upward as the rock splashed down.

"Dad, can I ask you something?" Gabe inquired.

"Anything."

"Why didn't you beat the crud out of the bad man today?"

"I wanted to."

"Why didn't you?"

Blade put his left hand on his son's shoulder. "Do you understand why I treated the man so roughly?"

"A little."

"I acted the way I did because the man wasn't treating your mom with the respect she deserves. He knew she's married to me, and yet he looked at her and talked to her as if she wasn't. I could tell he wanted her for himself."

"The bad man wanted to steal Mom?"

"In a way."

"When I get big, I'll beat the crud out of him for you," Gabe vowed.

"I doubt we'll ever run into him again," Blade said. "But remember what happened. One day you might find yourself in a similar situation. The relationship between a husband and a wife is very special, and you should do everything in your power to ensure others treat your wife with the courtesy she deserves. My dad told me there are certain rules a man should stick to if he wants to have a happy marriage."

"He did? Like what?"

"A man should never take his wife for granted. He should always treat his wife as his partner, not as a piece of property. Never keep a secret from your wife. And above all, never let anyone criticize her or abuse her," Blade recited from memory.

"Does Mom have rules too?" Gabe queried.

"I don't know. We'll ask her later. If she doesn't, she should," Blade said.

"Like what?"

"Let me see," Blade said, and scratched his chin. "A woman should never nag her husband. She should always be ready to sympathize with him when he stubs his toe. And she should always be in the mood when he is." He laughed and grinned.

"Was that another joke?"

"I wish it was."

They came to the edge of the water and halted.

"What kind of mood?" Gabe asked.

"Never mind. I'll explain when you're thirty," Blade said, and rested his hands on his Bowies.

"But I still don't get it. Why didn't you beat the crud out of the bad man?"

"Because I couldn't set myself up as his judge, jury, and executioner."

"Huh?"

"I made his punishment fit the crime. When someone oversteps their bounds and insults us or hurts us, we can't go overboard. We must always be fair in all our dealings with others, even when they're cow chips, as Uncle Hickok would say.''

''I bet Uncle Hickok would've shot the bad man.''

''Maybe. But Hickok would have given the man a chance to go for a gun. Uncle Hickok has his own set of rules he lives by.''

Gabe gazed absently at the water near their feet, his young mind trying to comprehend the imponderable riddle of adult existence. ''Does everyone have a set of rules they live by?''

''Nowadays most do. Before the war the situation was different.''

''Why?''

''Before World War Three, most people lived by the rules set by the society they lived in. For instance, in America the people were regulated by hundreds of thousands of laws. The laws were the rules the people had to live by. If they broke the laws, they were punished by the legal authorities, by the government. The government used laws to control the people.''

''The government controlled the people?''

''From the cradle until they passed on to the higher mansions.''

''I don't think I would've liked living back then.''

''Me neither. Nowadays everyone pretty much sets their own rules. But in California and the Civilized Zone the governments have a lot of laws, like America did, because California and the Civilized Zone have a lot of politicians. Politicians love to make laws.''

''What's a politician?''

''They claim to be public servants, to serve the will of the people, but a lot of them serve themselves. They're always trying to get richer or become more powerful. In the worst cases, politicians are second-rate power-mongers. Always remember, Gabe, that laws are the chains power-mongers use to enslave people.''

''Are all laws bad?''

"No. Just as all politicians aren't bad. There are a few sincere ones who want to do good."

"Why don't we have any at the Home?"

"Because the Founder warned the Family not to allow a professional political class to be developed. Being a power-monger is one of the few grounds for expulsion, for being kicked out of the Family," Blade said. "Our Founder never liked the fact that politicians in his time expected to be treated as if they were special. They always had special titles, and they allowed themselves special privileges. In the end, right before the war, the politicians had set themselves up as a special class above the ordinary citizens. Kurt Carpenter never wanted that to happen at the Home."

"I'm glad I live at the Home," Gabe remarked.

"That makes two of us."

They strolled to the east, covering a dozen yards, gazing over the lake.

"I bet there are big fish in here," Gabe declared.

"We'll find out tomorrow."

"Are there fish big enough to eat me?' Gabe asked.

"I doubt it."

"But what—" Gabe began, when a shout from the cabin cut him short.

"Gabe! Blade! Time for supper!" Jenny yelled.

"Good. My stomach is growling," Blade commented. He turned on his heel and strode toward their vacation hideaway. "Come on, son."

"Dad!" Gabe suddenly cried.

Blade spun. "What is it?"

"There!" Gabe declared, pointing at the lake, at a point 20 feet away. "Did you see it?"

"What?" Blade responded, scanning the surface and finding nothing unusual. He could see the bottom out to 15 yards or so.

"The biggest fish in the universe! It was bigger than me. Almost as big as you."

Blade smiled. "You're starting early."

''What?''

''Most fisherman don't start telling tall tales until they're a little older,'' Blade said.

''But I saw something,'' Gabe insisted. ''It was big and dark and swimming under the water.''

The Warrior scrutinized the lake. ''Whatever it was, it's gone now. Let's go eat.''

They walked off, with Gabe constantly glancing over his right shoulder.

''Do you believe me?'' he asked.

''Of course. Now we know there are big fish in the lake. We'll catch one tomorrow morning and Mommy will cook it for lunch.''

''If the thing doesn't eat us first.''

CHAPTER SEVEN

Their evening supper consisted of venison sandwiches Jenny had packed for the trip, along with a can of green beans and, for dessert, a can of peaches, both of which she took from the cupboard. After their meal, Blade carried an empty lantern he found on the kitchen counter into the bedroom, where several cans of kerosene were stored in the closet. He filled the lantern, lit the wick, and walked to the living room to deposit the lantern on the coffee table.

"I'll do the dishes," Jenny volunteered.

Blade sat in the rocking chair and gazed out the left-hand window at the lake. Twilight had descended, enveloping the landscape in shadows. He saw several ducks alight on the water and paddle about. Behind him arose the clatter of dishes as Jenny cleaned their supper plates. "I like it here," he announced.

"So do I," Gabe stated. He moved around the rocking chair and stepped to the left window, blocking Blade's view.

Jenny started humming.

Feeling content and peaceful, Blade closed his eyes and

rocked slowly back and forth.

"Where'd he come from?" Gabe unexpectedly asked.

The Warrior's eyes snapped open. "Who?"

"That man."

"What man?" Blade demanded, rising.

"The man standing in the water."

Blade was to the open door in two long strides. He stood next to the left jamb and stared at the lake, but there wasn't anyone in sight. "Where? I don't see a man."

"He was there," Gabe asserted. "Standing near the shore."

Blade's eyes narrowed. He discerned a series of concentric ripples approximately ten feet from the north shore. "What happened to him?"

"He went under the water."

Jenny came over and joined them. "What's going on? Is there really somebody there?"

"I saw him," Gabe said.

The Warrior waited expectantly, his eyes ranging from one end of the lake to the other. Nothing moved. Even the ducks had disappeared.

"Perhaps you saw a shadow. The light can play tricks on you at this time of the day," Jenny postulated.

"I saw a man," Gabe maintained, his tone signifying his hurt at not being believed.

"Wait here," Blade directed them. He advanced to the edge of the water, unslinging the Commando as he crossed the field. The ripples had subsided and the surface was placid. He tried to peer into the depths, but the growing darkness had transformed the underwater domain into a murky realm shrouded in secrecy. What could Gabe have seen? he asked himself. The boy never lied. But if there had been someone in the water, whoever it was should have surfaced for air. Puzzled, he wheeled and took several steps, engrossed in contemplation.

"Blade! Look out!" Jenny abruptly shouted.

"Dad!" Gabe screeched.

Blade looked at his loved ones, who had come around the

front of the SEAL, and saw Jenny pointing to the west. He spun, leveling the Commando, hearing the patter of onrushing pads as he rotated.

There were three of them, bounding at the Warrior in a concerted charge, their tails held horizontally. Their coats were a grizzled gray. They stood over three feet high at the shoulder and weighed at least 120 pounds apiece. Flowing over the ground at 30 miles an hour, they growled as they closed on their prey.

Wolves!

A pack of gray wolves!

There was scarcely time for Blade to wonder why the wolves were attacking him. Wolves seldom went after humans unless they were starving or provoked, and the trio bearing down on him appeared to be healthy specimens. But not for long. They were 15 feet away when Blade pressed the trigger and the Commando thundered and recoiled in his arms.

The heavy slugs tore into the pack, perforating each animal repeatedly as the Warrior moved the barrel from right to left. The rounds thudded into the wolves and bowled them over. All three sprawled onto the ground, and only two attempted to scramble to their feet and renew their charge.

Blade wasn't about to let up. He aimed at the pair and fired another burst. One toppled, but the remaining wolf kept coming, and was now less than eight feet from the Warrior's legs.

"Blade!" Jenny screamed.

The Warrior held the Commando steady and kept the trigger depressed, his legs braced, his back to the water. Every shot hit home, smacking into the last wolf's head, dissolving the eyes and the forehead in a geyser of blood and gore.

With a final defiant snarl the wolf fell.

Blade let up on the trigger, his ears ringing from the din of the sustained burst. He edged to the nearest wolf and nudged the body with his left foot, then walked to the other two and checked them for life. All three were dead. Completely mystified by their unexpected attack, he gazed thoughtfully at the last animal. A stillness had descended upon the Northern woods.

Jenny and Gabe ran toward him.

Why? the Warrior asked himself. Why did the wolves try to slay him? If they weren't hungry, what was their motive? Had one of them been shot by a human before and as a consequence they despised all humans? Had they mistaken him for someone else?

A loud splash, accented by the deathly quiet, came from the lake.

Blade turned and beheld a commotion in the water less than ten feet from the shore, as if something large swam near the surface.

"Are you all right?" Jenny asked, hurrying to his side, holding Gabe by the left hand and the Beretta in her right.

"Fine," Blade said.

"Why'd they try to kill you, Dad?" Gabe questioned.

"I wish I knew."

Jenny glanced around nervously. "We should get Gabe back to the cabin. There's no telling what else might be in the trees."

The Warrior nodded. Animals and mutations for miles around must use the lake to quench their thirst, and since most predators were more active at night, he wanted his family safe and sound while the nocturnal beasts were abroad. "To the cabin," he said. "I'll bury these carcasses in the morning."

"Maybe the man in the lake will eat them," Gabe stated.

"Don't start that again," Jenny told him.

Together they returned to the cabin. Blade verified the SEAL was locked, then bolted the cabin door and inspected the metal latch on every window.

"You can leave a window cracked open," Jenny suggested. "We can use fresh air in here to dispel the fish smell."

"Not tonight," Blade replied, slinging the Commando over his left arm as he took a seat on the sofa.

"Why not? Wolves can't open windows."

"Tomorrow night, if we're still here, we'll crack a window.

Tonight I intend to play it safe.''

Jenny's forehead creased. ''Do you know something I don't?''

''No.''

''Did you see something outside?''

''No.''

She pursed her lips, looked at Gabe, and wisely dropped the subject. ''I have a great idea. Why don't we play a game?''

''What kind of game?'' Gabe responded.

''I'll show you in a second,'' Jenny said, and stepped into the bedroom.

''While you're in there, grab another lantern,'' Blade called out.

Gabe came over and sat down alongside his father. ''Are we going to stay here?''

''I don't know yet,'' Blade said.

''What if there are more wolves?''

''Normally wolves leave human beings alone unless they're starving,'' Blade answered, and instantly regretted his lack of tact.

''Were those wolves starving?''

Blade looked at his son and debated whether to lie or tell the truth. Years ago he had resolved never to lie to his children, and he answered accordingly. ''No.''

Gabe considered the information for several seconds. ''Dad, I don't know if I want to stay here very long.''

''We'll see how everyone feels in the morning.''

Jenny ambled from the bedroom, smiling broadly, the picture of cheerfulness. In her left hand was the lantern Blade had requested. She raised her right hand and opened her palm. ''Look at what I found in the top drawer of the dresser! A deck of cards.''

Blade glanced at the cards, then at his wife. Was she really as happy as she appeared, or was she putting on an act for Gabe's benefit?

''We can play cards for a few hours and turn in,'' Jenny proposed. She deposited the lantern on the kitchen counter and faced them. "What will it be? Gin rummy? Hearts? Poop on Your Neighbor?"

Gabe stood, brightening considerably, and grinned. "What's that game we play where we say, 'Go fish'?"

"You want to play that one?"

"Yeah."

Jenny looked at Blade. "Well, Mister Doom-and-Gloom? Are you going to sit there scowling all night, or will you lighten up and join us?"

"Deal me in," the Warrior said, his mouth curling upward. "But give me a minute." He walked to the counter and examined the second lantern, which turned out to be empty, then entered the bedroom to fill the circular tank with kerosene. After lighting the wick he grabbed the handle in his left hand and went out.

Gabe and Jenny were sitting on the floor next to the coffee table. She was shuffling the cards while he watched intently.

"Gabe, isn't there something we must do before we play cards?" Blade asked.

"Like what?" Gabe replied innocently.

"You know what," Blade said.

"What?" Jenny chimed in.

"What do you think?" Blade rejoined.

"I don't—" Jenny started to respond, and her gaze drifted to a point several inches below Blade's belt. "Oh. That's right. Gabe, you haven't gone since we arrived. You must need to go to the bathroom."

"I can wait," Gabe said.

"I can't," Blade stated, "so we might as well go together. Come on. Help me find a suitable tree."

"I don't want to go into the woods," Gabe declared.

"That was a joke."

"Oh."

Blade moved to the door and threw the bolt.

"Why don't you take the flashlight?" Jenny asked.

"I want to conserve the batteries," Blade said. He didn't bother to add that the flashlight was small and the beam of light it projected was thin. The lantern illuminated a greater area, although the illumination didn't extend as far as the flashlight beam, and he preferred to have a wider field of fire if necessary.

Father and son left the cabin and walked to the right, around the southwest corner.

Gabe stared at the inky wall of vegetation to the rear of the cabin and halted. "Let's go right here."

"We shouldn't go this close to the cabin."

"Why not?"

"It's not sanitary," Blade said, and walked to the west, paralleling the towering trees.

Gabe's wide eyes were riveted on the forest. He tried to glue himself to his father's right leg, gripping the fatigue pants with both hands.

"Are you scared?" Blade inquired tenderly, and stopped 30 feet from the log building.

"Nope," Gabe replied quickly, too quickly. He gazed up into the kindly face above him. "That's not true. Yeah, Dad, I'm scared. I'm sorry." His voice wavered as he spoke the last two words.

"What do you have to be sorry about?"

"For being scared. For not being brave like you," Gabe said softly.

"I've been scared plenty of times."

"You have?" Gabe responded in astonishment.

"More times than I care to count."

"But I didn't think you ever got scared. Ringo says his dad is never scared."

"And Ringo is right about his dad. Your Uncle Hickok is one of the few genuinely fearless people I know. Hickok will walk into danger with that devil-may-care grin of his plastered on his ugly puss because he takes everything in stride. Absolutely everything. In fact, I'd go so far as to say that Hickok is probably the bravest Warrior the Family has ever known."

The conversation had temporarily soothed Gabe's qualms.

"Wow!" he exclaimed. "Is Uncle Hickok braver than you are?"

"In one sense, yes."

"I don't understand," Gabe said.

Blade scanned their immediate vicinity, ensuring they were alone. "Let me give you an example. Let's pretend Hickok and I are going to fight a band of raiders."

"How many raiders?" Gabe asked.

"I don't know. The number isn't important."

"Yes, it is," Gabe insisted. "How many?"

"Oh, let's say there are forty raiders."

"Gosh! That's a lot."

"You bet. And it's Hickok and me against all of those raiders. Now let's pretend the raiders have us surrounded and there's nothing we can do but fight. Hickok would tear right into them without a second thought. He wouldn't worry about being shot or stabbed. He wouldn't give any thought to the odds. And it would never occur to him to be afraid. But I'd be different," Blade said, and paused. "I'd be calculating the odds and worrying about being outnumbered and outgunned. I'd be afraid of being injured or killed. Most of all, I'd be afraid that I'd never see your mom and you again. But even though I was afraid, I'd be right by Hickok's side. Despite my fear, I'd do what had to be done. That's the measure of a man's courage, Gabe. When a person admits their fears and confronts their fears head-on, that's true courage."

"Do Geronimo and Rikki and Yama get scared too?"

"Geronimo and Rikki, yes. I don't know about Yama any more. Ever since we came back from the run to Seattle, Yama has been acting like he's invincible."

"Then it's okay for me to be scared?" Gabe asked.

"Yes. Just try not and let your fear get the better of you. Conquer your fears and you conquer yourself."

Gabe nodded knowingly, as if his youthful mind comprehended every word his father uttered. "Can I tinkle now?"

"We'll both tinkle."

They watered the weeds and retraced their steps toward the cabin. Blade saw Jenny watching them through the west window. They were almost to the southwest corner when a tremendous tumult erupted in the lake, a noisy splashing intermixed with a panicked bleating.

"Get inside," Blade ordered, and moved with his son to the doorway where Jenny awaited them. "Stay put," he said, and jogged across the field to the water, the lantern swaying in his left hand and causing the light to dance eerily about him as he ran, the Commando in his right. He discerned the outline of shadowy forms struggling in the lake, perhaps 15 yards from the north shore. The bleating grew weaker and weaker with every passing moment. He tried to identify the source, and the first animals that came to mind were sheep and goats, but he knew the guess was ridiculous because there weren't any sheep or goats within miles of the retreat. The only other likely candidate he could think of was a deer. A very terrified deer.

Blade focused on the thrashing and held the lantern higher, but the radius of the light fell slightly short of the disturbance. He glimpsed a swirling of limbs and heard a final, pathetic bleat, and whatever was creating the commotion sank beneath the surface. He waited, hoping the deer, if such it was, would resurface, hoping to get a clue as to what was going on.

Nothing happened.

"Blade?" Jenny shouted.

The Warrior frowned, gave the lake a last searching glance, and hastened to his loved ones.

"What was it, Dad?" Gabe asked when his father was still 20 feet away.

"I think a deer tried to swim across the lake and didn't make it," Blade said.

"A doe or a buck?" Gabe queried.

"I couldn't really tell," Blade said.

"The poor deer," Jenny commented.

Blade perceived the relief on their features at the mundane explanation. He smiled and motioned at the cabin. "Didn't hear someone say something about a game of cards?"

CHAPTER EIGHT

She moved with an obvious urgency in her stride, her loose-fitting orange dress a distinct contrast to the enveloping night. Her usually calm hazel eyes were troubled and her oval face set in lines of worry. The red hair topping her five-foot frame was stirred by the cool night breeze. She gazed absently at the stars and prayed the man she needed to see would still be up.

There was his cabin!

She stopped for a second, surprised to find him seated in a wooden chair a yard from his cabin door, his head tilted back so he could view the celestial spectacle. "Plato?"

The Family Leader shifted in his chair and looked around. "Who—?"

She advanced and announced herself. "It's me. Hazel. What are you doing out so late?"

Plato stood and regarded her quizzically. "My favorite pastime is to commune with the Spirit at night. I feel closer to our Divine Source when I'm viewing the immensity of creation."

"I understand. I feel the same way."

"And to what do I owe this honor, Hazel?" Plato inquired.

"The chief Family Empath is seldom abroad at this hour."

"I needed to talk to you," Hazel replied, her eyes straying to the cabin. "Is Nadine still up?"

"My charming wife retired a half hour ago. She's keeping the bed warm for me."

"Good. I wouldn't want to disturb her."

"I can get you a chair from inside," Plato offered.

"No. I'm fine."

"Suit yourself," Plato said, and clasped his wiry hands behind his back, waiting for her to broach the subject that had brought her to his doorstep at such an unusual time. They had known one another for five decades, and he realized that whatever prompted the visit must be crucial. As one of the six Family members gifted with psychic abilities, and the most sensitive of the group, Hazel had been of incalculable benefit over the years in periods of crisis.

"Blade and Jenny left on their trip this morning, didn't they?" Hazel questioned.

"Yes," Plato said, concern flaring within him. "Why?"

"Do you know where they went?"

"To a lake about ten miles northeast of the Home, and they don't intend to return for at least two weeks."

Hazel sighed and gestured at the chair. "I could use a seat after all. Do you mind?"

"Help yourself," Plato replied, stepping aside so she could sit down.

"Do you have any way of contacting Blade?" Hazel inquired.

"No."

"He didn't take along a radio?"

"No. He wanted his family to enjoy their trip without any interference. Jenny was looking forward to this vacation and he didn't want anything to spoil it for her."

Hazel stared at the ground.

"Why all these queries involving Blade? Is his family in

any jeopardy?''

"I don't know," Hazel said hesitantly.

"Uncertainty brought you here so late? Explain yourself, Hazel," Plato directed.

She nodded and looked at him. "Yesterday morning, twenty-four hours before Blade departed, Eva came to me and related a disturbing dream she had the night before. The dream baffled her because she dreamt about Blade, which she had never done.

"What was the nature of her dream?"

Hazel coughed lightly and averted her gaze. "Eva said the dream was short but intensely vivid. In it, she saw Blade swimming in a body of water, when suddenly he sank below the surface and kept sinking until he touched bottom. He kept trying to swim back up, but try as he might he couldn't." She paused. "He drowned."

"Why wasn't I informed about this dream?" Plato asked.

"One dream in and of itself is not especially significant. You're undoubtedly well aware of the random nature of most dreams. Quite frequently dreams will be precipitated by the food we ingest before we retire. Or our emotional state will influence the dreams we experience. As a group, we Empaths evaluate dreams in conjunction with other factors to determine the validity of the vision," Hazel related. "Of course, had I known Blade was planning to spend his trip at a lake, I would have attached more importance to Eva's dream."

"Blade wanted the destination kept secret so he could surprise Jenny," Plato mentioned.

"I see," Hazel said.

"The dream alone wouldn't have brought you here," Plato noted. "What else has occurred?"

"Several hours ago I retired. I had spent most of the day assisting the Weavers in making new quilts, and I was very tired. I fell asleep right away, and I experienced a distressing dream."

"Involving Blade?"

"Yes. I saw him driving the SEAL. He came to a clearing and parked, and Jenny, Gabe, and Blade got out to stretch their legs. Jenny strolled near some trees, and when the others had their backs turned, someone or something reached out of the trees and grabbed Jenny, covering her mouth so she couldn't scream. A bit later, while Blade was inspecting the underside of the transport, Gabe was snatched. Blade realized they were missing and went searching for them, and I saw a gun barrel poke out of the underbrush to his rear," Hazel detailed somberly.

"What happened next?" Plato prompted.

"There was a shot and Blade pitched forward, shot through the head. And then I heard a wicked laugh, an evil sort of cackling that became louder and louder until I woke up with a start," Hazel said, and stared at him. "Plato, the dream was exceptionally graphic. I awoke terrified by what I'd seen."

"And you believe Blade and his family are in definite danger?"

"I believe there is a strong possibility, yes. Which is why I came to see you. I haven't been this upset by a dream in years. Taken in conjunction with Eva's vision, there is serious cause for alarm," Hazel stated.

"Damn!" Plato said, venting a rare oath.

"What will you do?"

"My options are limited. Obviously I must send someone after them. But there are no roads into the area where Blade has taken his family. Whoever goes after them will have to travel overland and contend with the wild animals, the mutations, and all the rest."

"Which makes it a job for the Warriors. Send Hickok," Hazel suggested.

"Nathan is in charge of the Warriors in Blade's absence. He must stay here."

"Any of the Warriors would be happy to warn Blade," Hazel said.

"True. But I need someone who can cover the distance between the Home and the lake quickly. Someone who can run for hours without tiring.''

''Yama can,'' Hazel mentioned.

''Yes, Yama is one of the few Warriors whose physique is almost as powerfully developed as Blade's. But Yama has been behaving oddly since that business in Seattle. I'm thinking of someone else, someone as strong as Yama and as dedicated as Hickok.''

Hazel glanced to the south. ''Oh. Him.''

''You don't agree with my choice?''

''On the contrary, if anyone can reach Blade quickly, it would be him.''

''I must speak to him immediately. Do you want me to walk you to your cabin?''

''No, but thanks for the offer,'' Hazel said. ''Before you go I want to apologize. I should have consulted you after Eva's dream instead of waiting this long. I'm sorry.''

''You conducted yourself properly,'' Plato assured her. ''We'll discuss this further tomorrow, if you wish.''

''Fine.''

''Now if you'll excuse me,'' Plato said, and hurried to the south along the row of cabins. Because he had learned to trust Hazel's intuitive premonitions, anxiety seized his mind. He blamed himself for the situation. He was the one who had initially proposed the idea of using the founder's retreat to Blade, so the burden must rest on his shoulders. Any trip beyond the walled security of the Home entailed grave risks, as he well knew. But he'd believed that Blade could handle any problem, any threat. Perhaps he'd been lulled into complacency. Perhaps he'd allowed his confidence in Blade's prowess to subvert his better judgment.

Plato passed Blade's empty cabin and glanced at the darkened windows. If the giant Warrior or his family came to any harm, Plato would never forgive himself. He affectionately thought of Blade as the son he'd never had, and they enjoyed a strong bond of friendship. If Blade died, Plato would be torn to the depths of his soul.

He passed other cabins as he continued southward. The lights were out at Hickok's but on at Geronimo's, and he was tempted to stop and relay the news to Geronimo, but he refrained. Geronimo would undoubtedly want to inform Hickok, and the stubborn gunfighter would probably insist on sending out a rescue team immediately. Plato intended to talk to Hickok in the morning, after a night's rest girded him for the ordeal. Provided he could sleep.

Minutes later he spied his destination, and he paused when he saw the lanterns weren't on. If he knocked now, he might rouse the children. But if he wanted the Warrior to leave at daybreak, then he had to inform the man now. Plato walked to the cabin and rapped lightly on the door. After 30 seconds elapsed and no one answered, he knocked again, louder.

Still no one came.

Plato raised his right hand to knock even harder.

The cabin door abruptly swung inward and the barrel of a Bushmaster Auto Rifle poked out.

"It's only me!" Plato blurted out as the barrel came to within inches of his nose.

"Plato?" a deep voice said, and the Bushmaster lowered.

"Yes. I'm sorry for this intrusion," Plato stated, looking at the Warrior's face, striving to distinguish details in the dark. All he could discern was the Warrior's long, flowing hair and massive wide bulk.

"Is the Home under attack?"

"No, nothing like that," Plato replied. "I need you to go on an urgent mission at first light."

"Where?"

"Blade and Jenny have gone on a trip to a lake ten miles northeast of the Home, and I have reason to believe they may be in danger. You must travel to the lake and ascertain if they are safe."

"I'll be ready to leave at dawn. Has Hickok been informed?"

"No, not yet."

"I can't leave without notifying him."

"I know. I'll meet you at his cabin shortly before first light and clear your departure with him," Plato said.

"Fair enough. You sound very worried about Blade. How serious is it?"

Plato shrugged. "I don't honestly know," he admitted. "The Empaths have given me reason to believe his life and the lives of Jenny and Gabe are imperiled. I just hope you can reach them before it's too late."

CHAPTER NINE

Blade came awake with a start and blinked a few times, clearing his mind of any residual sluggishness, remembering where he was and what had happened. He glanced at the faint sunlight filtering in the windows and shifted in the rocking chair, relieving a cramp in his lower back. Dozing in a chair all night was not his idea of a soothing sleep. He yawned and looked at the Commando in his lap, then at the bedroom door. Last night, before Jenny and Gabe retired, he'd positioned the rocking chair near the kitchen counter. From his vantage point he could see the bed where his wife and son lay sleeping, and he had an unobstructed view of the windows and the entrance. As much as he would have preferred to sleep in the bed, safety was his paramount consideration.

Outside the birds were coming alive and filling the forest with their lively chirping.

The Warrior stood slowly and stretched. He rubbed the prickly growth on his chin as he strolled to the door. He reached for the knob, then caught himself. First things first. Turning to the window on the left, he crouched and peeked

over the sill at the field and the lake. Both presented a picture
of peacefulness. A buck and two does munched on grass in
the field, while a flock of nine ducks swam on the lake.

Blade stood and exited the cabin. He breathed in the cool
morning air and wondered if he had allowed his imagination
to get the better of him the evening before. In the warming
light of a new day the setting seemed utterly harmless. He
checked the SEAL, confirming no one had tampered with the
vehicle during the night. Then he proceeded to the north shore,
cradling the Commando in the crook of his left elbow, and
as he started across the field the three deer took off for the
shelter of the woods, the buck snorting and bounding high and
the does trailing after him.

At the edge of the water Blade halted and watched the ducks
swimming from west to east approximately 50 yards from the
shore. He saw a large fish leap out of the lake, midway
between where he stood and the ducks, and drop into the water
again with a minor splash.

No wonder the Founder had used this spot as a retreat!

Blade was about to head back to the cabin when he
remembered the three gray wolves and turned, expecting to
see the trio of bodies lying where they had fallen.

The wolves were gone.

The Warrior examined the ground carefully. He found
puddles of blood where the three wolves had lain for hours,
but there were no marks to indicate the direction the carcasses
had been dragged. If they *had* been dragged. He made a tight
sweep of the field near the lake, but his hunt for tracks proved
fruitless. The wolves would have been tempting meals for any
hungry animal or mutation, so the absence of the bodies was
not in itself noteworthy. The lack of prints and drag marks,
however, was bizarre. What, he asked himself, could have
lifted the wolves and carted them off? Certainly nothing on
four legs could have performed the feat. Even if a cougar or,
as was extremely unlikely, a bear had lugged the bodies into
the forest, there should have been evidence of some kind.
Neither a cougar nor a bear would be capable of lifting the

body of a full-grown wolf completely off the ground.

Wait a minute.

What was he doing?

Blade chuckled and shook his head, amused at his attempt to construct a menacing scenario out of the simple disappearance of dead wolves. He strolled in the direction of the cabin, admiring the natural splendor of the setting, and gazed to the east at the rising sun. Last night he'd been ready to leave; now he wasn't so sure. He decided to try his hand at fishing and make up his mind about departing after breakfast.

Jenny was waiting for him in the doorway, dressed in a white robe, her hair disheveled. She stifled a yawn as he came around the SEAL and looked at him anxiously. "Anything?"

"Nothing."

"Nothing?" she repeated quizzically.

"The wolves are gone, but anything could have taken them. I'm going to grab a pole and go fishing."

"Is it safe to stay then?"

"For the moment."

Jenny fussed with her hair. "Should we head back to the Home today?"

"I don't know. What do you think?" Blade asked.

"Why don't we stay half the day at least. I mean, except for the wolves and the strange noises we heard, which could have been a deer in the lake, there's no reason to leave. I don't want to cut our vacation short."

"Then we'll stay until noon, possibly longer," Blade said.

"Good. I'll get dressed and wait for you to catch some fish. Don't forget to clean them," Jenny said. She grinned and winked at him, then headed for the bedroom.

Blade slung the Commando over his left shoulder, took one of the fishing rods from the closet in the living room, and returned to the lake. Digging for worms proved to be easy, and during the next 30 minutes he caught five fish. Whistling to himself, he used the end of the fishing line to string the fish and carried them to the cabin.

"Gabe is still asleep," Jenny announced when he walked in the door.

"He was up late last night," Blade remarked.

"Those two hours of cards did the trick. He was laughing and having loads of fun by the time we hit the sack," Jenny said. She stared at the fish and scrunched up her nose. "Why aren't those fish clean?"

"I thought I'd clean them on the kitchen counter," Blade responded.

"You thought wrong. The last sight I want to see in the morning is fish guts."

"I bet Cynthia would clean them," Blade mentioned playfully.

"You're not married to Cynthia," Jenny stated.

"I know. Geronimo has all the luck."

Jenny stuck out her tongue and held up a long, thin knife. "Look at what I found."

"Is that to trim your toenails?"

"No, dummy. You know perfectly well what it's for. Now take those fish out of here."

Blade took the knife, kissed her on the forehead, and went outside, angling to the west. Twenty feet from the cabin he deposited the fish on the grass and knelt. Jenny's quirk about fish had always tickled him. She could skin a deer or pluck a grouse without a problem, but slicing into a fish and removing the stomach and the spine nauseated her. She'd tried on several occasions, and each time with the same results. He remembered a particular instance when she had bisected a trout and peeled the two halves apart, and there was a worm inside the fish, wiggling and squiggling. The shriek she'd voiced had nearly shattered his eardrums.

He laughed at the recollection and went about cleaning the fish, stacking the prepared sections in a pile. As he began inserting the knife into the last fish an ominous event transpired.

The birds in the forest abruptly ceased singing and the insects stopped buzzing.

Blade tensed and glanced at the woods, probing the undergrowth. Every seasoned woodsman knew to beware if the wildlife suddenly fell silent. Usually the silence betokened the presence of a meat-eater.

Even the trees were still, the air momentarily motionless.

Blade released the knife and gripped the strap to the Commando, and as he did the forest again became filled with the sound of the wild creatures. The various birds were especially noisy, singing their welcome to the new day. He waited for another interruption in the rhythm of the woodland, but all appeared well. After a bit he finished the fish and carried them to the cabin. "Here we go," he said when he stepped through the doorway.

"Look who's up," Jenny stated.

Gabe stood by his mother's side near the bedroom door, his eyelids drooping drowsily. "Hi, Dad."

"Hi, sleepyhead," Blade responded, moving to the kitchen and depositing the fish on the counter. "Here you go, honey."

"Thanks. How would you like fried potatoes and toast with your fish?"

"How would you like a nibble on your neck?" Blade answered jokingly.

Gabe glanced at his father. "Why would you want to nibble on Mommy's neck?"

"Now see what you've done," Jenny said.

"Go get dressed," Blade told his son.

"Why would you want to nibble on Mommy's neck?" Gabe repeated.

"That was another joke," Blade explained.

"I don't get it."

"All I meant was that I'm so hungry I could eat Mommy's neck if she doesn't fix breakfast fast," Blade said.

Jenny snorted and went to work on the meal.

"Why would you want to eat Mommy's neck?" Gabe inquired.

"I don't really want to," Blade admitted.

"You're worse than Hickok," Jenny muttered.

Gabe looked from one parent to the other, then shook his head and shuffled to the bedroom. "That was a dumb joke, Dad."

"Do me a favor," Jenny said softly.

"What?" Blade asked.

"When Gabe finally expresses curiosity about the birds and the bees, let me tell him about the facts of life."

"Why you?"

"Because men have a tendency to distort the truth."

"We do not."

"Oh, yeah? Hickok told Ringo that babies are delivered by storks."

"I'm not Hickok," Blade noted.

"No. You'll probably tell Gabe babies are delivered by mastodons."

"Now why would I do something that silly?"

Jenny shrugged as she arranged plates on the counter. "If I knew the answer to what makes men tick, I'd be the wisest woman on the planet. No woman can claim to understand men."

"Why not?"

"Two reasons. One, men and women are two distinct varieties of the same species. From birth and throughout all eternity we're completely different. We can think alike at times, and even appreciate each other on emotional, intellectual, and spiritual levels, but we can't totally comprehend everything because of our separate natures."

Blade waited for her to continue, and spoke up when she didn't. "You said there were two reasons but you only mentioned one. What's the other reason men and women can't fully understand each other?"

Jenny looked at him and smirked. "Men are weird."

"Women," Blade mumbled, and turned, walking idly toward the from door. He was five feet from the entrance when the left-hand window exploded inward, showering shards of glass in all directions, and something thudded into the bookcase. For a second he gaped at the shattered window, astounded, and then his years of training and experience came into play and he pivoted, his ears belatedly registering the crack of the shot, and darted to the kitchen.

Jenny was standing behind the counter, a frying pan in her left hand, her mouth hanging open.

Blade reached the counter and shoved her down. "Get on the floor!" he cried, and out of the corner of his right eye he detected movement. He spun, his heart seeming to pump harder at the sight of Gabe coming from the bedroom, confusion twisting his features, his pants on but his shirt bunched around his neck.

The boy blundered into the line of fire from the left-hand window, not a foot from the bookcase.

"No!" Blade bellowed, and hurled himself at his son, his arms outstretched.

A chip of the remaining glass flew from the window and the second shot boomed outside.

Blade felt a stinging sensation in his right shoulder. His arms looped about Gabe and he pulled his son to the floor, rolling as he hit, taking them to the right. He stopped in the middle of the floor and pressed Gabe flat on his stomach.

"What's going on?" Gabe asked, a tremor in his tone.

"Stay down," Blade instructed him. "Someone is shooting at us."

"Who?" Gabe asked.

"I don't know," Blade said, and glanced at the kitchen counter. "Jenny, are you okay?"

"No."

For a moment Blade thought she'd been hit, and a chill rippled down his spine. "You're not?"

"No, I'm ticked off. I dropped the fish on the floor."

The Warrior didn't know whether to chew her out or laugh, so he compromised and snickered. Then he focused on the left-hand window, wondering if there would be another shot.

"What should we do?" Jenny queried.

"We don't do anything until I assess the situation," Blade replied.

They stayed on the floor for several minutes, but the firing did not resume.

"Don't budge," Blade ordered his son. He crawled to the front door and swung it closed, half expecting the sniper to send a round into the cabin in response, but nothing happened. Using his elbows to pull himself along, he moved to the window and slowly, ever so cautiously rose to his knees.

"Be careful," Jenny advised.

Blade looked over his left shoulder. His wife was lying flat on the floor with her head protruding past the end of the counter. He blew her a kiss, then eased his left eye to the corner of the window. The front of the SEAL, part of the field, and the lake beyond were all visible. He guessed that the sniper was hidden in the tall weeds somewhere between the SEAL and the water. But where? He scrutinized the field.

"Anything?" Jenny whispered.

Blade drew away from the sill and gazed at her, shaking his head.

"Maybe whoever it is has gone," Jenny said without a shred of conviction.

As, if in answer to her speculation, a third sharp report sounded and a bullet punched through the top panel of the door, inches from the roof, sending wood chips flying.

Blade hugged the floor and fumed.

CHAPTER TEN

He covered five miles without incident.

In stature he reached three inches above six feet, but his massive, superbly muscled, broad-shouldered build lent him the illusion of being much taller. His alert brown eyes swept the terrain ahead. He breathed easily, his square jaw set firmly, jogging at a tireless dogtrot. Light brown hair hung to the small of his wide back, braided from the neck down. A camouflage outfit tailored to fit by the Family Weavers covered his solid form. And a pair of Bushmaster Auto Pistols adorned his waist, one in a specially crafted swivel holster on each hip. Slung over his right shoulder was his Bushmaster Auto Rifle.

Five miles or so to go, he told himself.

The day promised to be a hot one, and the warm sunlight combined with his exertion had caked him with sweat. He swiped at beads of perspiration on his brow and skirted a high pine tree.

A startled squirrel scampered out of his path and climbed up the pine, venting its annoyance with a vehement chittering.

He smiled and pressed on, thinking of Naomi, Benjamin,

and Ruth, of their sad expressions when they had seen him
off at the drawbridge. "The Lord will watch over me," he
had assured them, but his words of inspiration had not
alleviated their distress.

Far overhead a hawk circled, seeking prey.

The Warrior came to a hill and headed for the top, his brown
leather boots thumping on the ground. The sound reminded
him of the angry blow Hickok had delivered to the side of
his cabin during the heated argument with Plato. He'd dutifully
stood to one side and listened, knowing it was not his place
to interrupt. Plato had been quite insistent on the need for his
departure, and equally insistent that only one Warrior should
make the journey. Hickok had argued that several Warriors
should go, that there would be safety in numbers. But the
Family Leader had pointed out there was only one other
Warrior who could cover ten miles cross-country at a steady
pace, namely Yama, and Yama was on wall duty. Hickok had
volunteered the services of the hybrid Warriors, the three
mutations. Unfortunately, the hybrids were on a two-day
break, and had ventured to Halma to assist the Clan in
exterminating a wolverine that had raided a few outlying
residences. Plato prevailed, and Hickok reluctantly agreed to
send just one Warrior.

He considered Plato's confidence in his ability a distinct
honor.

A bald clearing crowned the hill, marked by a few small
boulders. A badger squatting below the rim saw him coming
and immediately backed into a nearby burrow, hissing and
squealing.

The Warrior ignored the animal and started to descend the
hill. To take his mind off his family and the mission, he
mentally began to recite his favorite passages from the Bible.
Paslm Eighteen came to mind: "I will love thee, O Lord, my
strength. The Lord is my rock, and my fortress, and my
deliverer; my God, my strength, in whom I will trust; my
buckler, and the horn of my salvation, and my high tower.
I will call upon the Lord, who is worthy to be praised: so shall

I be saved from mine enemies.'' How true, he noted, and then abruptly stopped.

Something had growled.

He lowered his hands to his sides and scanned the brush and trees. A dark four-legged form moved through the undergrowth to his right, a large, bulky thing with a shuffling gait, then disappeared.

Another guttural growl sounded.

The Warrior refused to be delayed. He angled to the left, intending to bypass the creature in the woods. He kept his eyes on the spot where he had seen it last, and consequently he neglected to pay proper attention to the slope he was traversing. His right boot bumped into an object and became entangled. He fell forward, looking down to see the tip of his boot hooked in the supple branches of a knee-high bush, and landed on his hands and knees. His boot was wedged in the bush, but he wrenched his foot free and went to rise.

Just then a terrible roar rent the forest.

He rose, spinning as he straightened, his hands dropping to his Bushmaster Auto Pistols. He'd designed the swivel holsters personally, and the Family Gunsmiths had constructed the pair to fit his requirements. All he had to do was grasp the synthetic pistols' grips and swing the barrels upwards, and both breakaway holsters would part at the seam, allowing him to fire from the hip. He'd practiced and practiced until he could perform the technique swiftly and efficiently, and his practice now served him in good stead.

A raging mutation burst from the undergrowth, a deformed monstrosity of a black bear, its head misshapen, its shoulders forming a hunchbacked peak, its left limbs shorter than its right.

The Warrior stood firm, resolutely facing the charging beast. Both Bushmasters were attached to their swivel holsters by a stud affixed to a slotted metal plate so he could tilt the guns as high as needed. He angled the barrels and squeezed both triggers.

Lumbering and snarling, the bear advanced awkwardly, its

body rising and falling as its uneven limbs made contact with the earth. Because the bear's parents had been affected by the lingering radiation poisoning the ecological chain, the animal had been born with only one eye instead of two. The solitary orb was situated in the center of its forehead, giving the beast a Cyclopean appearance. Its nostrils were half the length they should be and flattened at the end, almost piggish in aspect. Many of its upper teeth were inches too long and jutted over its lower lip, vampirelike. When the first rounds bored into its head and chest, the bear recoiled, roared again, and came on even faster.

He never expected the beast to reach him. There were 30 shots in the magazine of each Bushmaster, and there wasn't an animal living that could absorb 60 rounds and live. Or so he believed.

But the bear, rushing headlong down the slope, took all 60 and never slowed. Crimson-speckled holes dotted its head and torso, yet its spark of vitality was undiminished.

The Warrior realized the bear would get to him when it was only three yards away, and he released the Bushmasters and braced his legs. The mutation slammed into him going at full speed, and the impact lifted him from his feet and sent him tumbling down the hill. He flipped end over end, completely disoriented, until he crashed into the trunk of a tree with a bone-jarring concussion. Dazed, his ribs in agony, he pushed himself to his knees and twisted in time to see the bear still on its feet and coming at him with its jaws wide. He tried to dodge to the right, but the bear plowed into him once more and he was flung back against the tree. This time his head made violent contact and swirling stars engulfed his mind as something heavy pounced on his back.

The Warrior passed out.

CHAPTER ELEVEN

"It's been hours. The sniper must have gone," Jenny commented hopefully.

"Can we try and get in the SEAL now, Dad?" Gabe asked.

Blade glanced at them and pondered their next move. True, six hours had elapsed and it was almost noon. And the last time the sniper had fired had been three hours ago, when Blade had tried to reach the transport. He'd opened the front door and poked his head out, and a bullet had missed him by less than an inch, smacking into the jamb and spewing tiny wood fragments onto his hair. He'd slid back inside and slammed the door shut.

For three hours there had been quiet. Blade had moved Gabe behind the kitchen counter, and his wife and son lay side by side watching him expectantly. "I'll take a look," he told them, and crawled toward the door. His plan to park the SEAL close to the entrance so he could reach the vehicle quickly in an emergency had backfired. Yesterday he had locked the doors to ensure no one could enter the transport during the night, and now those locked doors were thrwarting his efforts to escape. A yard of space separated the SEAL from the cabin. The sniper, after firing those initial rounds, had changed position to cover the front door clearly, shifting somewhere to the east, still hidden in the thick weeds. As Blade had learned when he stuck his head out, the rifleman now commanded a perfect shot at the space between the vehicle and the doorway. In the five seconds Blade would need to step to the SEAL, insert the key, unlock the door, and climb inside, the sniper would be able to squeeze off several shots. Even if Blade tried to sneak out the west window and come around the rear of the SEAL, the sniper would still spot him and cut loose. He was willing to take the risk, but Jenny protested and he'd respected her wishes for the time being.

Blade came to the door and stopped, the Commando in his hands in front of him. Several conclusions were obvious. There was only one sniper. Only one gun had fired each time, with the recognizable blast of a high-powered rifle. Since the person doing the shooting had persisted until midmorning, and was probably still out there, the sniper wasn't about to be discouraged easily. And since the assassin could have waited and picked off one of them when they stepped outside instead of firing randomly through the window, the sniper must be toying with them, playing a bizarre sort of demented game. Cat-and-mouse, and they were the mice.

Blade squatted and clutched the doorknob. If he'd been by himself he would have gone out one of the windows hours ago and tried to circle around and find their assailant, but he knew Jenny and Gabe wanted him to stay. Jenny put on a brave front, but she wasn't accustomed to combat and the strain showed in her eyes and her drawn features. Gabe, surprisingly, had recovered from his first fears and was bearing the strain better than his mother.

He turned the knob, shoved, and flattened.

No shot greeted his action.

Blade raised his head and inched to the doorway. He

extended the Commando barrel out and instantly withdrew it.

Still nothing happened.

Had the sniper tired of the game and departed?

Blade squatted with his back to the right jamb and contemplated. He wondered if the man Gabe had seen at the lake was the same one shooting at them. Perhaps the sniper lived at the cabin and was striving to drive them off. But if that were the case, the man wouldn't prevent them from getting into the SEAL and leaving. Was the rifleman a long raider, a rogue, or simply a solitary psychopath who got his kicks by gunning down others?

"Are you going out?" Jenny inquired. She was kneeling next to the counter, holding the Beretta. Gabe peeked over her left shoulder.

"I may," Blade replied. "Whatever happens, the two of you must stay inside. Agreed?"

"What if you're hurt?" Jenny inquired.

"I'll take care of myself. You two must stay in the cabin, no matter what. I can't cover myself and protect you at the same time."

"We'll stay here," Jenny said.

Blade nodded, bent over, and stepped to the coffee table. He seized one of the legs in his left hand and moved to the south wall, standing between the door and the left-hand window.

"Be careful, Dad," Gabe said.

The Warrior smiled at his family, then whipped his left arm in an arc and spun, flinging the coffee table out the shattered window. As his fingers released the coffee table he darted out the doorway and ducked to the right. Hopefully, the sniper had focused on the table and would need a second to react. Blade raced to the southwest corner and swung around, his back to the west wall.

The sniper hadn't fired!

Blade grinned and sighed in relief. Either he'd taken the

bastard by surprise or the sniper was gone! He headed to the north, pausing to glance in the west window and wave at Jenny and Gabe. Jenny spotted him first, nudged their son, and they both waved and smiled. He ran to the forest and took cover behind a tree.

So far, so good.

If his estimation of the sniper's last position was correct, he should be able to find where the sniper had been concealed in the weeds. With that as his goal, he moved through the woods to the east, staying five yards from the edge of the field. Once past the cabin he could see the section where the rifleman must have been hidden, and he crouched and studied every bush, every clump and patch, for any evidence of the sniper.

Nothing.

Encouraged, Blade crept to the tree nearest the field and hunkered down. A robin winged from a pine tree off to his left toward the lake. He eased onto his elbows and knees and snaked into the field, moving at a turtle's pace, endeavoring to minimize the rustling he caused, pressing on the weeds as lightly as possible.

Somewhere a cricket chirped.

Blade traveled 15 yards, constantly glancing at the cabin, until he reached a point where the space between the SEAL and the front door was visible. He examined the ground minutely, them moved slightly farther east. In two yards he found what he was looking for, an area several yards long and 18 inches wide where the weeds had been flattened by a heavy body lying on them for hours. A flash of reflected sunlight arrested his attention, and he discovered a spent cartridge. He picked up the metallic brass casing and turned it over to check the caliber, which was .30-06. That didn't help him much. There were too many rifles capable of firing .30-06 rounds for him to be able to identify the weapon from the casing. He dropped the cartridge on the ground and swiveled toward the cabin.

What should he do next?

He was tempted to return to his family, pack them in the SEAL, and get out of there. But he had to ensure the sniper was definitely gone before exposing them outside. He elected to conduct a sweep of the field and the lake.

The minutes dragged by as Blade conducted his search, crossing and recrossing the field in a zigzag pattern until he came to the border of the water. He rose to a crouch and surveyed the land rimming the lake. The sniper's disappearance puzzled him. He couldn't bring himself to accept that the sniper had really departed. Since the man had vacated the field, he must be in the forest.

Blade made a beeline for the trees, dashing through the weeds while stooped over at the waist, and he attained the woods without being fired upon. More time passed as he prowled the undergrowth, and after 20 minutes he hiked back to the cabin, finally convinced the phantom rifleman had slipped away. Now he intended to rev up the SEAL and make tracks for the Home. Enough was enough. First Gabe had seen things in the lake, then the wolves had tried to kill him, and now this! Vacations weren't all they were cracked up to be. He might as well be on a run with the Warriors for all the rest he was getting.

The sun had peaked at its zenith an hour ago.

Blade moved along the west wall and rounded the corner. As he walked past the right-hand window he glanced inside and saw Jenny sitting in the rocking chair and Gabe in the straight chair. Both were facing the doorway. Why, when he had specifically instructed them to remain behind the counter, had they disregarded him? He stepped into the cabin and they looked at him in fear, and before he could open his mouth a rifle barrel jammed him roughly in the back of the head.

"Don't move, you big son of a bitch!"

The Warrior tensed at the sound of the familiar voice, the same nasal twang he'd heard the day before at the scavengers' camp.

"Let your submachine gun fall to the floor," the man behind him ordered.

Blade complied, lowering the Carbine slowly.

"Now put your hands on top of your head."

Again, frowning, his eyes on his frightened wife and son, he obeyed.

"You aren't so tough, scumbag," the man said, and came around the Warrior with his rifle leveled.

Blade glared at the weasel, his eyes slits of rage.

"You remember me, don't you? Roy. The guy you beat the crap out of yesterday for no good reason."

The Warrior refused to respond.

"Yeah, you remember me, sucker," Roy declared spitefully. "You thought you were so high and mighty, pounding on me because I looked crosswise at your squeeze. Well, you ain't so high and mighty now, are you, turkey?"

Blade glanced at Jenny and Gabe.

"Sorry, honey," Jenny said. "He caught us off guard."

"You bet your ass I did!" Roy stated, gloating, staring contemptuously at the Warrior. "Do you want to know how I did it?"

"I imagine you'll tell me," Blade responded.

"Damn straight I will," Roy said. He relished having the upper hand and being able to enact his vengeance, and he planned to savor his revenge to the final, sweet drop. "I was hiding in the trees when you went into the field, and while you were out there playing with yourself, I snuck to the west side of this dump. Then when you went into the trees again, I crawled to the front door and pretended I was you." He lowered his voice and spoke in a raspy whisper. "Jenny! It's me! I've been hurt. Help me."

Jenny bowed her head and closed her eyes.

"The bimbo and the kid fell for my trick," Roy said, and cackled. "They ran to the door and I shoved my gun in her belly and told them to listen or else. Pretty clever, huh?"

"It's me you want, not them," Blade mentioned. "Why

don't you let them go?'' He spied Jenny's Beretta and Blackhawk on the sofa.

Roy snorted. ''Do you expect me to let a fox like your woman walk on out of here? You're nuts. I aim to have a lot of fun with her after I'm done with you.''

''You bad man!'' Gabe shouted, tears of frustration welling in his innocent eyes.

''Shut your face, you little snot, or I'll waste you right here and now!'' Roy snapped.

Blade gritted his teeth and measured the distance to the scavenger, gauging whether to make a desperate lunge. The weasel stood six feet away, two far to reach in one bound. If Blade tried, he would be shot. But he couldn't stand by helplessly while his family was abused. ''You followed us all this way?'' he asked, hoping to divert Roy's interest from Gabe.

''Following you was as easy as pie,'' Roy bragged. ''That buggy of yours left a trail even an idiot couldn't lose.''

''Then how did you manage?'' Jenny baited him.

Roy sneered and took a stride toward her. ''Open your mouth again, fuzz, and I'll put a bullet in your hubby. Right in the bellybutton. Do you know what a gut shot does to a man? He'll be in misery for hours, maybe days. He'll beg to be put out of his agony.'' He paused. ''On second thought, smart-mouth me again. I want this prick to suffer before he dies.''

''You realize this is a mistake,'' Blade interjected.

''Yeah. And you made it!'' Roy responded maliciously.

''No, you did. Friends of ours are due to arrive here soon, within the hour. You'll be outnumbered.''

''I don't believe there are any friends coming,'' Roy said. ''You told Jared that you're on a special trip and you don't want anything interfering with it. No, your family is all alone here.''

Blade scowled and absently flexed his arms. The man was a weasel, but a *smart* weasel. Blade couldn't afford to underestimate the scavenger again.

"We have the cabin all to ourselves," Roy noted. "Ain't it cozy?" He laughed wickedly.

"What about an exchange?" Blade asked.

"A what?"

"An exchange. A ransom. You already know the Family has a fully stocked armory. Why don't you trade me for all the weapons you want? They'd fetch a high price on the black market in any town in the Outlands."

Roy's forehead creased as he mulled the proposal.

"Just think. You could be rich. You'd be able to afford all the drink and women you desire. All you have to do is release my wife and son and let them drive to the Home. Someone will be sent with the ransom," Blade said, and looked at Jenny. He intuitively knew what she was thinking. She couldn't drive the SEAL. But the weasel wasn't aware of the fact. And he'd say or do anything to get his wife and son out of the cabin. If he could trick Roy into permitting them to enter the SEAL, they could lock the doors and would be protected by the transport's impregnable body.

"You must *really* think I'm a jerk if you expect me to fall for such a dumbass idea!" Roy declared.

"We'd keep our part of the bargain," Blade stated.

"The hell you would! Your Family would send a bunch of guys to off me. No dice, stupid. We're all staying right here. We'll even spend the night together," Roy said, and chuckled.

Blade envisioned the vile acts Roy had in mind, and his fury mounted. He couldn't tolerate the thought of Roy pawing Jenny. Sooner or later the weasel would get around to tying him up. He had to make his move before then.

"I have to go to the bathroom," Gabe unexpectedly announced.

"Tough, brat. Suffer," Roy responded.

"I'll pee my pants if I don't go," Gabe protested.

"Who the hell cares?"

"You're mean!" Gabe cried, and started to slide off the chair.

"Don't move!" Roy bellowed. He took a step in the boy's direction.

Blade saw his opportunity and leaped, his arms outstretched to swat the rifle aside. As if in slow motion he observed Roy pivot, and he watched the Ruger as the barrel swept up and pointed straight at him. His hands were nowhere near the rifle when the booming retort thundered in his ears and he felt the slug tear into his body.

CHAPTER TWELVE

He came awake slowly, painfully, his head throbbing, his consciousness seemingly floating in a stygian void. The exquisite agony almost overwhelmed him, and he struggled to rouse himself through sheer force of will.

Gradually his memory returned. He recalled the mutation, the monstrous bear. He remembered the fight and emptying both Auto Pistols into the creature. And he recollected colliding with the tree. Twice.

Now he felt the hard ground under his left cheek, and there was a great weight pressing down upon his back. He went to open his eyes, but couldn't.

For a second panic threatened to blossom, but he suppressed the fear and centered his concentration. Why wouldn't his eyes open? he asked himself. It felt like they were glued shut. He tried again, but the best he could do was crack the left eyelid a fraction, just enough to detect a glimmer of sunlight and realize the sun hadn't set. It was still daylight.

The Warrior tried to move his right arm, to wipe at his eyes, but the arm wouldn't budge. The enormous weight on top of

him was pinning both arms. He attempted to slide his body
to the side, but the weight prevented him, pinning him in place.

This wouldn't do.

He took a deep breath and thought, "I am yours, O Lord,
to guide as you will. Grant your mortal son this request. Grant
me the strength of my namesake."

The Warrior pressed both palms on the rough ground and
pushed, his muscles straining. His shoulders and upper arms
quivered. His nostrils flared as he breathed noisily. He
succeeded in raising his head and chest an inch, but the burden
on his back conspired with gravity and his pounding head to
foil his intent. Dizziness washed over him and he sagged, a
small rock gouging into his cheek.

He rested a moment, until the pounding subsided marginally,
and experimented. His effort had not been in vain. Although
his left arm was still pinned, he could move his right, and he
brought his hand to his face and gingerly ran his fingertips
over his features.

His forehead had been split open when his head smashed
into the tree. He could feel the jagged wound, situated in the
middle, running from his hairline almost to his nose, three
inches in length and half an inch wide. The gash must have
bled like a bear—he grinned at the thought—and accounted
for the substance coating his eyelids. Most of the blood had
dried, sticking his eyes shut. Most, but not all. He found a
pool of blood ringing his head, more blood than he would have
thought possible from such a wound, and he surmised the
bear's blood must have seeped down and been added to his
own.

He began peeling the dried blood from his eyelids, a
tormenting process in itself. Every fleck he stripped off made
him wince. His eyelids smarted terribly. In a minute he had
his left eye fully open, and shortly thereafter, after using his
nails to scrape off the blood adhered to his eyelash, he restored
his right eye.

The Warrior took stock.

He was lying within six inches of the tree trunk, his body

aligned due north. The sun was well up in the sky, and he
realized he'd been unconscious for hours. Turning his head
to the left, he saw the front of the bear lying on top of hi
left shoulder. The mutation had fallen across him diagonally
which explained why the greatest weight was on his back and
legs.

No wonder he couldn't rise.

Every second he was delayed increased the danger to Blade
Jenny, and young Gabe. Plato had told him about the Empaths
dreams and stressed the urgency of reaching Blade quickly
Despite the severe wound, no matter how much blood he'e
lost, he had to continue. He had to replenish his deplete
strength and energy.

There was only one way.

He placed his chin on the ground and closed his eyes
allowing himself to relax, and mentally probed deep within h
mind for the spirit spark at the core of his being, the fragmer
of Deity he believed indwelt all men and women. Ever sinc
childhood he'd been profoundly religious. At the Namin
ceremony on his sixteenth birthday, the ceremony institute
by the Founder at which all Family members were encourage
to select their own names from any of the books in the librar
as a means of ensuring they appreciated their historic
antecedents, he'd picked the name of one of the mightie
warriors in the Bible: Samson. Even earlier, at the age o
seven, he'd publicly dedicated himself to the Lord by becomin
a Nazarite.

The order of the voluntary Nazarites extended back int
antiquity. Those who took the Nazarite vow pledged then
selves to live according to the will of the Lord, every minut
of every day. As part of the vow, as a physical symbol of hi
kinship to the Creator, Samson had promised to never perm
a razor or scissors to cut his hair. He'd also taken an oat
never to drink an intoxicating beverage. The original Samsor
Samuel, and John the Baptist were just three of the renowne
Nazarites mentioned in the Bible.

Like his namesake, Samson credited his virile vitality an

steely sinews to the fact he'd never broken his vow. Like the Samson of old, he knew all he had to do was call on the Lord and he would be granted the power to accomplish any task. So he called on the Lord now.

Samson placed both palms on the grass and surged upward, his arms exerting every iota of strength he possessed. His face turned red and his veins bulged. Ever so slowly he managed to rise himself an inch from the ground, then two, and three. Again vertigo engulfed him and he sank down.

He lay there, gathering his energy. If he wasn't weakened by the wound, he would have been able to shrug off the bear effortlessly. But now he had to focus on the indwelling Spirit as never before if he hoped to save his life and convey Plato's warning to Blade.

Samson tried one more time, ignoring the anguish, the torment racking his head, and threw his shoulders and back into the effort. The technique was the same as doing a push-up, he told himself. The only difference being that he was doing the push-up with a full-grown bear on his back.

"Hear my prayer, O Lord. Give me the strength of ten!"

He got his chest six inches off the earth. Every muscle on his body bulged and rippled. The dizzinesss recurred, but he shook his head, clearing his thoughts, striving to be at one with the limitless source of power within him.

"Your will be done, on Earth as it is in Heaven."

Samson grunted, pushing harder, getting his body a foot above the ground, but only from the knees up.

More!

He needed more!

"Hear me, O Lord! Fill me with the might of twenty!"

A current of immense force shot through his torso, recharging his flagging muscles, reviving his resolve. He tilted his head back, his mouth opening in a grimace, and surged upward, the sweat dripping from his brow.

"My cup runneth over!"

For a second his fate hung in the balance. He wobbled, the bear resting on his shoulders and back and threatening to dump him on his face.

Not again!

Samson trembled with the intensity of his monumental exertion. His fingertips were sinking into the dirt, and his knees felt ready to crack. "I am the Lord's!" he cried, and straightened, locking his legs and shoving.

The mutation tumbled to the earth.

The Warrior stood proudly erect, swaying slightly, elated by his victory. Tears of gratitude dampened his eyes, and he gazed at the azure sky, silently expressing his thankfulness. He wanted to spend an hour in proper worship, and he would once the mission was completed.

The mission!

Samson moved down the slope, unsteadily at first, his stride lengthening with every step. The loss of so much blood would slow him down for the next few miles. If another mutation should attack, he might well reach Blade too late, if he wasn't too late already. He estimated he wouldn't reach the lake until after dark.

What was he doing?

How could he be so careless?

He stopped abruptly and replaced the spent magazine in his Auto Pistols with fresh ones from the ammo pouch attached to the rear of his camouflage belt. Then he inspected the Bushmaster Auto Rifle and discovered blood caking one side of the weapon. A proper cleaning was in order, but it would have to wait.

Blade might be in trouble at that very minute.

Samson prayed his friend could hold out until he arrived, and resumed his trek to the northeast.

CHAPTER THIRTEEN

Blade heard the words dimly.

"—least let me bandage him!"

"He doesn't need a bandage, bitch. Just fix my grub before blow the kid's brains all over this cabin."

"My daddy needs a Healer!"

"In a few hours your old man won't need diddly, brat. Now lam up or else!"

Blade breathed shallowly, endeavoring to recall what had happened. Why had he blacked out? Suddenly he remembered; here had been the shot and the shock of being hit, the orturous, searing pain as the bullet ripped through his midriff, ind he had involuntarily doubled over, clutching his abdomen. enny had screamed, and he had looked up to see the stock of the scavanger's rifle sweeping at his head. He'd lost count of how many times Roy struck him. He didn't even recall lumping to the floor.

"Get me a glass of water," Roy directed.

Blade heard dishes rattling and he resisted the urge to open his eyes. He didn't want the bastard to know he was awake yet.

"Quit giving me the evil eye, brat, or I'll tie you up and throw you in the bedroom," Roy snapped. "No. I can't do that. Your mom and me are going to have some fun in there later."

"I hope my dad beats you to a pulp!" Gabe declared.

"Your dad's beating days are over, kid."

"If my daddy dies, the other Warriors will find you. Uncle Hickok will track you down and shoot you full of holes!" Gabe said.

"It's a big world, kid. Your dad's friends won't know where to begin to look."

"Uncle Hickok will never give up!"

"Shut up."

"Uncle Hickok will shoot you in the head!"

Blade heard the sound of movement followed by a sharp slap. He opened his eyes to behold Roy standing over Gabe, who sat on the straight chair with his right hand pressed to his cheek. Pride welled within him at the sight of his son sitting erect, glaring at the scavenger, unafraid.

"Leave him alone!" Jenny yelled, coming around the kitchen counter with a steak knife in her right hand.

Roy pointed the Ruger at her. "Back in the kitchen, whore!"

Blade was lying on his right side, facing the chairs, curled up in a fetal posture. The scavenger's back was to him, and neither Jenny or Gabe knew he had revived. He placed his right hand on the floor and tried to rise. To his surprise he felt little pain. Using both hands he rose to a crouch. He could feel a damp, sticky sensation on his stomach, but he refused to look down until after he accomplished what he had to do.

Jenny had stopped a yard from the counter, her face livid.

"Back in the damn kitchen!" Roy barked.

Blade clenched his fists and slid silently closer to the degenerate. A spasm lanced his abdomen and he gritted his teeth and suppressed an impulse to cry out.

"You know," Roy said as Jenny walked to the counter, "this isn't as much fun as I figured it would be. I thought I'd toy with you turkeys for a day or so. Get my jollies. See the look on your husband's face when I stick it to you. Make all of you *suffer*!'' Roy hissed, and paused. ''But it's not working out the way I planned. The big son of a bitch might never open his eyes. I think I'll snuff the brat right now, then take you into the bedroom for a few hours, bitch.''

''I'd rather die first,'' Jenny said.

''Hey, one way or the other doesn't make any difference to me,'' Roy responded.

''You're sick.''

''Why? Because I take what I want? Because I kill to stay alive? It's dog-eat-dog nowadays, lady. Survival of the fittest.''

''You're disgusting because you enjoy inflicting pain on others. You terrorize and brutalize others to get your kicks. A real man would earn the respect and love of a woman, not take her against her will. But you're not a real man. You're not one of the fittest. You're nothing but a slimy pervert, and one day someone will squash you like the slug you are.''

''What a crock.''

''Mark my words,'' Jenny said solemnly.

''Nobody will ever take me down,'' Roy bragged.

''Wrong,'' stated the low voice behind him.

Roy whirled, bringing the rifle around, shuddering as he perceived the major blunder he'd made.

The Warrior uncoiled from his crouch with the speed of a striking cobra. The knuckles of his right fist caught the scavenger on the chin and propelled Roy into the air. Roy's teeth crunched together and blood spurted from his mouth.

''Blade!'' Jenny shouted.

The Warrior closed in as Roy toppled onto the rug. The scavenger landed on his back and attempted to scramble to his feet. Blade swung his left fist, driving the knuckles into Roy's nose, flattening the nostrils and sending Roy flying into the bookshelves. The rifle sailed to the right.

''Get him!'' Gabe cried.

Roy's elbows were hooked on the third shelf, supporting him, and he uttered a gurgling noise, his head bobbing, and turned.

Blade slammed his right fist into Roy's chest, and everyone in the room heard the loud crack. He followed through with a left. The scavenger buckled and fell to his knees.

"No more!" Roy blubbered. "Please!"

"For Gabe," Blade said, and delivered a right to the scavenger's left temple.

Roy toppled onto his side, the blood pouring over his lower lip, blubbering incoherently. He frantically heaved to his hands and knees.

"For Jenny," Blade stated. His left fist came down on Roy's back with the force of a pile driver.

The weasel was flattened by the blow. He screeched and crawled toward the bedroom. "Don't hurt me!"

Blade sneered and took a long stride, reaching down and locking the fingers of his left hand in Roy's oily hair. His grip slipped once, and then he tightened his hold and hauled the scavenger to a standing position. "This next one is for me."

"No!" Roy whined.

"Yes," Blade said coldly. He drew back his right fist, thinking of the abuse his loved ones had suffered, channeling his rage into the next punch, releasing the full extent of his fury. His fist smashed into the scavenger's mouth at the same instant he released Roy's hair, and the weasel flew backwards and thudded onto his back next to the bedroom doorway, limp and unconscious.

"Yah!" Gabe yelled.

Blade stared at his foe for a moment, then tottered, abruptly feeling weak. He hugged his abdomen and started to bend over.

"Honey!" Jenny exclaimed in alarm and dashed to his side. She looped her arms around his middle and helped ease him to the floor, where he could sit with his back propped against the east wall. "How bad is it?"

"Bad," Blade said.

"Don't move," Jenny instructed him. She ran to the kitchenette and began filling a bowl with water out of a jug they'd brought from the Home.

"Darn. I was hoping to do some calisthenics," Blade quipped feebly.

Gabe scooted to his father and knelt in front of him. "Dad, is there anything I can do?"

"Make sure that scumbag is out for the count," Blade said.

Nodding, Gabe stood and walked toward the scavenger.

"Here we go," Jenny stated, returning with the bowl of water and a clean washrag. "I'll remove your vest." She deposited the bowl and slowly unzipped Blade's black leather vest, frowning when she saw the blood rimming the top of his pants. Gently, exercising the utmost care, she unbuckled his belt and undid the button above the zipper, then eased the zipper down. Blood had soaked the fabric of his pants.

Filled by weariness, Blade leaned his head against the wall. He saw Gabe step behind the counter, then glanced down. "Have you found the entry hole?"

Jenny nodded and licked her lips. She pointed at the finger-sized hole three inches to the left of his navel. "It's stopped bleeding."

"That's good news," Blade said.

"Where's the exit hole?" Jenny asked, reaching gingerly around his back and probing with her fingers.

"I don't think there is one," Blade replied, and grunted.

"The bullet is still inside you?"

"I think so."

Jenny ran her fingers all over his lower back and finally withdrew her hands and placed them on his knees. "You're right. There's no exit hole."

"Damn," Blade said softly.

They both heard a loud, dull dong, as if a fractured bell had been struck with a hammer, and they looked at the scavenger.

Gabe stood over the weasel's head, the largest frying pan he could find in his slim hands. He raised the pan over his head a second time and brought the metal bottom down on the scavenger's forehead with all the strength he could muster.

"That should be enough," Blade said. "He's out for the

count.''

"Maybe he's faking. I should hit him five or six times just to be sure.''

"That's enough,'' Blade reiterated.

Gabe's disappointment showed.

"Tell you what, though,'' Blade added. "Why don't you stand guard over him. If he comes around or moves, let him have it.''

"How many times?''

"Ten or twenty.''

"I hope he moves,'' Gabe said.

Jenny leaned down and inspected her husband's belt, pants, and vest. "The Spirit smiled on you.''

"Oh?''

"The bullet was deflected by your belt buckle into your belt, then passed through the belt and into you. It might not be very deep. If the buckle and the belt hadn't slowed it down, the bullet would have passed clean through and probably shattered your spine.''

"You'll have to dig the slug out.''

Jenny glanced into his eyes. "Me? I'm not a Healer.''

"Gabe certainly can't perform the operation,'' Blade noted.

"But what if I do something wrong? What if I cut a vein or an artery or accidentally hit one of your organs?'' Jenny asked, intimidated by the prospect of doing surgery.

"There's no one else who can do the job,'' Blade stressed. "The Home is too far away for me to risk the ride. Besides, if we wait, infection could set in.''

Jenny swallowed hard. "If I make a mistake I could kill you.''

"You must try, unless you like the idea of being a widow.''

"Don't joke that way. It's not funny.''

"I wasn't joking.''

She stared at the entry hole, nervously rubbing her hands together. "What will I use for instruments?''

"We shouldn't need much. Since I've stopped bleeding and the entry hole isn't very large, we won't worry about stitches.

We'll need something to use as a probe and an instrument to cauterize the wound. Both have to be long and thin.''

''I'll find what we need.''

''The first step is to heat a pot of water to sterilize the instruments.''

Jenny rose without another word and walked to the stove.

Waves of agony rippled over the Warrior and he gasped lightly so as not to cause any anxiety in his wife and son. Had the shot hit an organ? he wondered. If so, he needed to get to the Healers as swiftly as possible. He planned to take off for the Home after Jenny finished tending the wound, and he gazed at the front windows expecting to observe the bright sunlight of early afternoon. Instead there were shadows on the panes. ''What time is it?''

''After six,'' Jenny answered, busy filling the pot.

''In the evening?'' Blade asked in disbelief.

''Yep. You were out about five hours, more or less.''

Five hours! Blade's shoulders slumped dejectedly. He wasn't about to try and drive to the Home in the dark, not in his condition, and Jenny undoubtedly wouldn't finish operating on him until nightfall. He swiveled his head to watch her. ''What happened while I was out?''

''Not much.''

''Did he lay a hand on you?'' Blade queried harshly.

''He pawed me a few times, but he was more interested in gloating and baiting us. He deliberately tried to upset Gabe, to make him cry, but it didn't work,'' Jenny said. ''I'm very proud of our son, and you should be too. He behaved like a man.''

Still standing alertly over the scavenger, Gabe kicked Roy in the head. ''He said bad words to Mom and kept touching her.''

Jenny saw her husband's cheeks flush scarlet and changed the subject. ''I fixed him a meal about half an hour after you were shot, and he was having me prepare another meal shortly before you woke up.''

''He'll never eat again,'' Blade vowed.

"Stop talking and rest," Jenny advised.

Too fatigued to argue, Blade closed his eyes and wished they were all safe and sound back at the Home. With Roy out of commission they'd be safe at the cabin. Relatively safe, anyway. And in his current state nothing less than the walled security of the Home would alleviate his apprehension over not being able to protect Jenny and Gabe.

He glanced at the weasel, thankful the man was an idiot. An efficient adversary would have finished him off, murdered the others, and stolen the SEAL. Fortunately, Roy had been more interested in tormenting them than in attending to business.

"Say! I have an idea!" Gabe declared.

"What is it?" Jenny inquired while searching through a drawer for a suitable makeshift probe.

"I can go for help."

"You wouldn't be able to reach the Home on foot."

"Not to the Home. To those people we met. The nice people who were with the bad man."

"The scavengers?" Jenny said, staring at her son.

"Sure. They're not far. I can find them," Gabe said.

"They're a mile away, which might as well be on the moon for all the good they can do us," Jenny stated.

"I can do it!" Gabe asserted confidently.

"No," Jenny told him.

"But—" Gabe began, bubbling over with enthusiasm.

"No, son," Blade interjected. "It's almost dark, and you wouldn't be able to get to their camp before nightfall. There are more mutations and other predators abroad after the sun sets. You'd never make it."

"I'd try for you, Dad," Gabe said frankly.

The Warrior smiled, his throat constricted by an odd lump, his eyes dampening. "Thanks," he said huskily. "I appreciate the thought. But I want you to stay here with us."

"Okay," Gabe responded reluctantly.

Blade stared at the windows and reflected on his blessings. Despite the inconvenience of holding down two jobs, despite the periodic absences for days and weeks at a stretch, despite the stress his dangerous occupations caused, he had a wife and son who loved him with all their hearts, who would jeopardize their own lives to save his, who valued him more highly than life itself.

What more could any man ask for?

Jenny came over holding two objects in her left hand. "We don't have much of a selection to choose from. I've found forks, spoons, knives, scoops, basting brushes, and a few tools." She unfolded her hand to reveal an eight-inch Phillips screwdriver and a narrow butter knife. "They're both dull."

"They'll have to do," Blade said. "Use the screwdriver as the probe and we'll cauterize with the knife."

"*We'll* cauterize? What's this 'we' stuff? You'll lie there looking handsome and I'll be doing all the work." She wheeled and walked to the stove.

Blade grinned and rested his chin on his chest. His eyelids suddenly seemed to weigh a ton. Strange. He'd been shot several times during the course of his career as a Warrior and never reacted like this. Why did he feel so tired? He thought of the approaching night and wondered if the door had been bolted. When he tried to advise Jenny, however, all he could do was mumble. And seconds later he slumped onto his left side, oblivious to the world.

CHAPTER FOURTEEN

"**W**e need more wood," Jared said.

"Don't we have enough already?" Tammy asked, gazing at the waist-high pile in front of them.

"The wind is picking up, which means our campfire will burn faster. If we run out of wood before dawn, someone will have to collect more. Do you want to walk around in the woods at night?"

"No," Tammy admitted, and faced the others. "You heard the man. We need more wood."

Jared looked at the sun hovering above the western horizon and made his way into the forest to the south, collecting suitble broken limbs as he went along. If only they'd been able to prevail upon Blade to take them to the Home instead of waiting for two weeks! A lot could happen in two weeks. There would undoubtedly be mutations to deal with, and who knew what else. He should have remonstrated with the giant, insisted tht they leave after Harold's burial. Tammy had acquiesced for fear of antagonizing Blade and ruining their golden opportunity to finally locate the famed compound, and he'd gone along with her against his better judgment. Now he regretted his lack of resolve. The prospect of spending another night in the woods was distinctly unappealing.

A five-foot length of branch to his right drew his attention. Jared stepped to the branch and bent down to retrieve it, when out of the corner of his right eye he saw a figure dart from one tree to another less than 30 feet away. He straightened, his pulse quickening, his mouth suddenly dry.

He let the wood he'd gathered clatter to the grass at his feet, and unslung his Marlin. The glimpse had been too fleeting to determine exactly who or what he'd seen, but of one fact he was certain: It wasn't one of his people. He backpedaled, angling in the direction of the camp, the hair at the nape of his neck prickling.

A feminine voice addressed him from the left. "What's this action, lover? We're collecting wood and you're practicing walking backwards?"

Jared glanced around and saw Tammy grinning at him. "We have company," he said.

She dropped her limbs and drew her Charter Arms Bulldog. "Friendly or hostile?"

"I don't know yet."

Tammy joined him and they hurried to the campfire, their eyes on the forest the whole time. Jim and Alice were depositing loads of wood and were about to venture out for more.

"Hold it," Jared said.

Jim took one look at Jared and unslung his Winchester. "What's up?"

"Keep your eyes peeled," Jared directed, and cupped his right hand to his mouth. "Everybody in! Forget the wood! Everybody back to camp!"

They waited expectantly for their companions to appear. Lloyd and his wife Betty emerged from the woods to the north, both carrying branches.

"What's going on?" Lloyd queried.

"Somebody's out there," Jared informed him.

The wood was forgotten as all six clutched their weapons and stared into the trees.

"I don't like standing next to the fire," Jim mentioned. "We make great targets."

"We'll wait for Tom, then take cover," Jared said.

"How many did you see?" Tammy asked him.

"One. Acting like he didn't want me to know he was there. Whoever it is might have been watching us for hours."

"Other scavengers, you think?" Lloyd questioned.

"I doubt it," Jared replied. "This area is too far off the beaten path for most scavengers. Hell, we wouldn't be here if we weren't looking for the Home. If it is scavengers, though, I doubt they'll give us any trouble unless they outnumber us."

"I've heard stories," Betty said. "Tales about hermits and backwoods types who prey on travelers."

"Why do you always look at the bright side?" Lloyd cracked.

"Where's Tom? He should have been back by now," Tammy noted.

"There he is!" Alice exclaimed, nodding to the west.

They saw their friend coming toward them, and they instantly perceived something was wrong. Tom walked in a slow, shuffling gait, his hands at his sides, swaying every few strides. His rifle and revolver were both gone.

"Tom?" Jared said, and took a step toward him.

Their companion came out of the shadows and lurched the final dozen feet. He collapsed onto his knees and arched his back, his mouth forming an O.

"Tom!" Jared reached his friend in two steps and went to loop his left arm about Tom's back, but his hand bumped into an obstruction, an object protruding from between Tom's shoulder blades. "Oh, no!" Jared declared.

Tom pitched onto his face. Everyone saw the slender shaft jutting from his back and the spreading crimson stain on his green shirt.

"An arrow!" Betty stated, aghast.

"And there's more where that came from!" bellowed a deep

voice from the undergrowth to the west. "Drop your guns!"

"Let's get the hell out of here!" Jim said, swinging around to the east.

They all heard the swish and thump, and they all saw the arrow penetrate Jim's forehead and bore out of the rear of his cranium. He stumbled backward for several feet and fell.

"Anyone who tries to run will be shot!" warned the voice.

"Jim!" Alice wailed, recovering from the shock of witnessing her husband's death. "Jim!" She spun to the east and fired two wild shots, working the bolt of her Mossberg rifle furiously.

Again a shaft streaked out of the woods, and again they heard the swishing noise, almost a buzzing, and saw the arrow catch her squarely in the chest, knocking her from her feet. Alice landed on her posterior and gaped at the six inches of shaft sticking from between her breasts. She glanced up at the others, said "Damn!" and died.

"We'll kill you all if we have to!" the voice threatened. "Drop your guns!"

Jared's mind was racing. There were only four of them left now, and there was still no telling how many enemies lurked in the brush. If all four made a break simultaneously, at least two would die. He didn't mind the idea of dying himself, but he couldn't abide the thought of harm coming to Tammy.

The lay of the land wasn't in their favor either. To the south the trees were sparse and the undergrowth thin, affording few hiding places. To the west, north, and east there were more trees, but there were also bowmen, one to the west, another to the east. Escaping to the north was their only option.

"I won't say it again! Drop your guns or die!" the man concealed to the west demanded.

Jared became aware of the others staring at him, awaiting his decision. He looked at Tammy sadly, frowned, and placed his rifle on the ground.

"We should fight!" Lloyd whispered.

"And wind up like Jim and Alice?" Jared responded, and let his revolver fall to the grass.

"You're being smart!" the voice told them. "All of you had better lay your guns down!"

Tammy, Lloyd, and Betty followed Jared's example.

"Now raise your hands over your head!" the man in the woods instructed them.

Jared extended his arms overhead and gazed at the forest, dreading that he'd committed a fatal mistake. He had no guarantee whoever was out there wouldn't slay them on the spot.

Two figures materialized in the brush, approaching warily, converging on the camp from both sides, one from the east, the other from the west. Both held bows. Each had an arrow ready to fly. The man to the west was taller and leaner. They sported scraggly dark hair down to their shoulders, and they wore crude clothing made from animal hides. The tall one had Tom's rifle over his left shoulder and Tom's revolver tucked under his homemade leather belt. A quiver full of arrows hung on the back of each.

"We've got us quite a haul," the tall one said, and laughed wickedly. He halted six feet from the quartet and scrutinized them closely. "Guns *and* women. Not bad."

"Who are you?" Jared asked, then added petulantly, "We aren't doing you any harm."

The tall one snorted. "Do you hear this fool, Silas? He says he wasn't doing us any harm."

Silas stopped eight feet from the campfire and shook his head. "How do some folks manage with such a pitiful shortage of brains, Harvey?"

"Beats me," Harvey replied, smirking at Jared.

"Please! Let us go!" Betty spoke up.

"You must be kidding, lady," Harvey retorted. "The slavers will pay us in gold for the redhead and you."

Jared's mouth curved downward and overwhelming regret flooded his soul. Lloyd had been right. They should never have given in without a fight.

"And all these weapons will keep us in food for months," Silas mentioned.

"Where are you from?" Tammy inquired, intending to distract the pair with conversation, her eyes on the Bulldog lying next to her right foot.

"Here and there," Harvey answered.

"Where are the slavers based?"

"On the moon," Harvey said sarcastically.

"Are there just the two of you?"

"Did you ever hear about what curiosity did to the cat?" Harvey responded.

Tammy realized the pair weren't about to divulge any information, and she thought about how she could grab the Bulldog without receiving an arrow through the chest for her effort. Sooner or later, one of them would lower his bow and reduce the odds against her by half. She knew if she didn't resist now, while she had the chance and her gun was within reach, she might spend the rest of her days in the clutches of a pervert.

"What about us?" Jared asked.

"What about you, asshole?" Harvey replied.

"What do you plan to do with us?"

"Not a thing. There's no market for men. The slavers are only interested in women."

"You're going to kill us!" Lloyd declared.

"Bingo," Harvey said, and released his shaft.

The arrow sped straight into Lloyd's torso, spearing into his heart, spinning him around and dropping him to the ground within a yard of the fire.

"Lloyd!" Betty screamed, and moved to his side. She knelt and placed her hands on his shoulders. "Lloyd!"

Tammy glanced at her Bulldog, girding herself to make the lunge.

"Don't even think it, bitch!" Silas warned, aiming his shaft at her.

Harvey pulled another arrow from his quiver and grinned at Jared. "Guess whose turn is next," he said, and notched the arrow on the bowstring.

Jared saw the tall man draw the string back and snicker.

He heard Betty weeping, and as he riveted his gaze on the razor-tipped hunting shaft he wondered if her plaintive crying would be the last sound he'd ever hear.

CHAPTER FIFTEEN

'**A**re you okay, Mom?''

''I'm tired, Gabe. Very, very tired.''

''Will Daddy live?''

''If the Spirit is willing.''

''When will Dad wake up?''

''I don't know,'' Jenny answered wearily. She walked to
the sofa and sat down, sighing with relief, and stared lovingly
at her husband. Blade was on his back on the floor near the
bookshelves, his midriff tightly bandaged with strips torn from
a clean sheet, covered from his toes to his chin with a brown
blanket. His broad chest rose and fell gently.

Gabe stood next to the rocking chair, watching his father
sleep, obviously worried. ''Should we put him in bed?''

''How? He's too heavy for us to budge. No, he'll stay right
where he is. Besides, we shouldn't wake him, son. He needs
all the rest he can get. Thank the Spirit he passed out earlier
and was unconscious during the operation. I know I would
have caused him a lot of pain if he'd been awake.''

''What should we do about the bad man?'' Gabe inquired,

pointing at the scavenger.

Jenny looked at the battered, blood-caked, unconscious form and pursed her lips. She'd bound him securely, hands and feet, prior to ministering to Blade. Except for an occasional moan, Roy had not displayed any sign of life. Hatred billowed within her, an emotion she rarely experienced, and she wished the man was dead. He'd caused her family so much suffering! She ran her right hand through her hair, recalling the teachings of the Elders that love and compassion were two of the greatest mortal attributes and should be cultivated by all, and she felt a twinge of guilt over her hatred.

"What should we do?" Gabe repeated.

"I'll drag him outside in a minute," Jenny said.

"Will you put him in the SEAL?"

"No. I'll leave him on the ground alongside the transport."

"But what if an animal finds him, a wolf or a mutation?"

"Tough."

Gabe smiled and nodded. "You sound like Dad."

"Thanks for the compliment." Jenny opened her left hand and studied the bullet she'd pried out of her husband, trembling inadvertently as she mentally relived inserting the screwdriver into the entry hole. Five minutes of careful pushing and pressing had failed to locate the slug, so she'd resorted to using her fingers. Blade's skin had been extremely hot to her touch, a symptom of his high fever. She would never forget the soft texture of his flesh as her right index finger slid in and probed about.

"Can I see it?" Gabe asked, moving over and taking a seat on her left.

"Sure," she said, and watched him pick the slug up and examine it. "Thanks for helping me with the operation."

"Any time."

"Never again, as far as I'm concerned," Jenny said. She kissed him on the cheek, marveling at how composed he'd been while observing her pry the bullet out and later, when she'd cauterized the wound. He'd borne the grisly sight stoically and hadn't cried once.

"I think I'll sleep on the floor next to Dad," Gabe remarked.

She was about to tell him he couldn't, but she changed her mind. Since she intended to do the same, how could she justifiably refuse him permission? "We both will."

"When can we leave for the Home?"

Jenny gazed at the windows, noting the descent of twilight. "I don't know, honey. We're stuck here until your father is fit enough to drive. You know I can't."

"You could try," Gabe suggested.

"I've watched your father enough times that I probably could do a fair job, but I'm afraid of crashing us into a tree or a boulder. And what would happen if we were stranded in the middle of nowhere?"

"Aren't we stranded now?"

The question gave Jenny pause. She glanced at Blade, thinking of the consequences if he developed an infection. Gabe's idea tempted her. The Healers would have Blade on his feet in no time. But common sense prevailed. "It's not the same. At least here we can keep him warm and we have plenty of food and water. We're safe in the cabin."

"I'd feel safer in the SEAL."

Jenny stood and crossed to the scavenger, gazing at his crushed nose, split lip, black eyes, and puffy face without a trace of sympathy. She grasped him by the ankles and backed toward the front door.

"Can I help?" Gabe inquired.

"Get the door."

He scooted to the door, turned the knob, and pulled it wide open.

"Thanks," Jenny said. Her shoulders straining, she dragged the scavenger out and aligned him alongside the SEAL, next to the front tire on the driver's side. She stepped inside, bolted the door, and went to Blade to feel his forehead. His temperature seemed stable.

"Are you hungry, Mom?" Gabe queried.

"Are you?"

"Yeah."

"Then I'll rustle us up some food."

Jenny set to work preparing a can of chunky stew for their supper, trying to alleviate her anxiety by keeping busy. She repeatedly glanced at Blade, and memories of their marriage arose unbidden in her mind. She remembered how happy she'd felt when she gave birth to Gabriel, and the joy in Blade's eyes when he held his son in his arms for the very first time. She also thought about the time the Home had been attacked by the vicious Trolls from Fox, Minnesota, and of her capture and subsequent rescue by Blade. He was a devoted father and loyal husband. What woman could ask for more?

Gabe moved the rocking chair close to his dad and sat down, rocking and watching Blade's face. "Mom, can I ask you a question?"

"Certainly."

"Where do we go when we die?"

The unexpected query made her do a double take. She leaned on the counter and regarded Gabe intently. "Why do you ask?"

"I want to know."

Jenny looked at Blade, worried that Gabe might be expecting his father to die. "Well, you've asked a very important question. All down through the ages men and women have wondered about the same thing. There have been a lot of different ideas about where we go after we die, and yet despite the differences they all pretty much agree on one point."

"How do you mean?" Gabe inquired earnestly.

"I'm not an expert, you understand. You should talk to Plato or Joshua. They know more about religion and philosophy than I do. But I do know the Bible teaches that we pass on to Heaven. The Koran says we'll live in Paradise. Most religions agree that we survive this life and ascend to a higher spiritual level."

"What do *you* think?"

"I believe the Elders when they tell us that we'll awaken in the mansion worlds on high. I believe there's a part of us our soul, that becomes one with the Spirit and lives forever."

"Does Daddy believe like you do?"

"More or less, yes."

"So if Daddy dies and goes to the mansions, we'll see him again someday?"

"Yes. When we die, we'll join him on the next level."

"Does everybody who dies go there?"

"The Elders say a person has to have faith to survive."

"What's faith?"

Jenny made a smacking sound with her lips. "You sure ask the tough ones. Faith is belief in the Spirit."

"Do I have faith?"

"You believe in the Spirit, don't you?"

"I think so."

"You've listened to Joshua and the Elders talk about God. Do you believe there is a God?"

"Yep. But I don't know what God is."

"You're still young. Give yourself another fifteen or twenty years. A person can't be expected to wrestle with profound spiritual questions until they're mature enough to understand the answers."

"Huh?"

"You believe there's a supreme Spirit. That's enough for now. You have nothing to worry about because you'll pass on to the next level."

"Good," Gabe said, and gazed at his father. "Dad believes in the Spirit, right?"

"Of course he does."

"And does he believe in the things the Elders say about loving everyone?"

Jenny saw what was coming and smiled. "Yes."

"Then how come he kills bad people?"

"Because they *are* bad people. Your father believes that the spiritual have the right and the duty to protect themselves from those who aren't spiritual, from those who are deliberately evil, from those who enjoy being wicked. That's why the warriors were formed, to protect the Family and the Home from those who would destroy both. Believe it or not, there

are some who want to wipe out our Family. There have always
been those, Gabe, who live a life of spite and hatred, devoted
to destruction,'' Jenny paused. ''Do you understand any of
this?''

''I think so. I hope I can become a Warrior when I'm big
and protect the Home like Daddy does.''

''Maybe you will,'' Jenny responded. She checked the stew
on the stove, pleased with herself for being able to answer
his questions so well. ''The stew is hot. Are you ready to eat?''

''You bet.''

Jenny found two bowls and ladled the piping hot stew into
them. Minutes later she and Gabe were seated on the floor
next to Blade, spooning the broth and vegetables into their
mouths.

''Ummmm. This is tasty,'' Gabe said.

''Thank the folks who made this a hundred years ago.''

Gabe studied the stew for several seconds and his forehead
creased. ''How come canned stuff lasts so long?''

''Some does, some doesn't. We know canned goods are
more likely to be edible if they've been stored in a cool, dry
place. The age doesn't seem to matter, only where the canned
goods are stockpiled.''

They continued eating in silence.

Jenny swallowed the last of her helping and looked at the
front windows. Darkness enshrouded the land, and she could
barely distinguish the huge bulk of the SEAL a yard from the
cabin. ''I'd better light the lanterns,'' she proposed, and
walked to the counter to set down her bowl.

Something thumped against the west wall.

''Did you hear that?'' Gabe asked.

''Probably just the wind,'' Jenny said. She lit the lantern
Blade had placed on the counter first, then the lantern on the
coffee table. As she blew out the match and straightened, the
thump on the west wall was repeated.

''Do you want me to go see what's doing that?'' Gabe asked
hopefully.

''No. We're staying right here.''

"Maybe it's an animal."

"So?"

"I can chase it away."

"It'll go away on its own. We're not going outside unless you have to go to the bathroom."

"Not right now, Mom."

"Then how about a game of cards?" Jenny recommended.

"Sounds great."

Jenny picked up the deck from the coffee table and glanced at her Beretta, which was leaning against the kitchen counter. She doubted the wind accounted for the pounding on the cabin. A curious bear might give a building a few whacks, and curious bears were better left to wander off and amuse themselves elsewhere.

"Did you hear that?" Gabe suddenly asked, standing.

"What?" Jenny replied, cocking her head to listen.

"That," Gabe said.

And she heard it too, a low, pathetic cry from out front, the words barely audible.

"Help me!"

"It's the bad man!" Gabe exclaimed.

"I know," Jenny said, having recognized the voice.

"What do we do?"

"We play cards," Jenny stated, and sat down alongside the coffee table.

Gabe hesitated, his eyes on the left-hand window, waiting to hear the cry once more. But a minute elapsed and nothing happened. "Okay." He took a seat across the table from her. "You deal."

"You trust a cardsharp like me?" Jenny joked.

Gabe chuckled. "You wouldn't cheat."

"Why not?"

"You're my mom."

Jenny laughed and went to cut the deck.

"Help me!"

They both looked at the front door. The plea had been louder and laced with sorrow.

"Shouldn't we help him?" Gabe questioned.

"No. He probably just wants water, and he can die of thirst for all I care," Jenny snapped.

"Help me! Please! Something is out here!"

Jenny twisted, staring out the window behind her. "What did he say?" she asked, although she knew very well what the scavenger had said.

"Something is out there," Gabe said nervously.

"He's lying to make us go out. There's nothing out there," Jenny stated.

"Are you sure?"

"Do you trust that man after what he did to us?"

"No, I guess not."

"Then let's forget about him and play cards," Jenny advised, cutting the deck as loudly as she could.

"Please! There's something out here! It's looking at me!"

"Be quiet!" Jenny shouted angrily. "You're not fooling us! Shut up and leave us alone!"

"Please! I'm not making this up!"

"Quiet!" Jenny yelled.

"Maybe we should take a peak," Gabe suggested.

"No."

"Dad would take a peak."

"Your dad would break his face," Jenny declared. She began dealing the cards out. "Now concentrate on the game and forget about the S.O.B."

"What's an S.O.B.?" Gabe inquired innocently.

Jenny frowned, annoyed at herself, then mustered an easygoing grin. "S.O.B. stands for Selfish Obnoxious Boob."

"Really? I never heard that one before."

"Just don't use it in public."

"Why not?"

"Because some people don't like to be called selfish," Jenny answered. "Now let's play cards."

The scavenger abruptly shrieked in terror. *"Dear God! It's coming toward me! Please get out here! Help! Help!"*

Jenny slammed the cards on the table and stood. The las

cry had bordered on the hysterical. She retrieved her rifle and hastened to the door, loosening the .44 Magnum in its holster.

"Can I come?" Gabe asked, rising.

"Stay here," Jenny said, her hand on the doorknob. She wanted to ignore the man, to believe his cries were a ruse to lure them outside, but the panic in his voice persuaded her he was telling the truth. And no matter how much she despised him, she couldn't sit idly by while an animal ate him alive.

"Be careful," Gabe said.

"I will," she promised, and let go of the knob to throw the bolt. "Lock this behind me."

Gabe watched her step out and close the door quickly. He stared at the windows, hoping to see her appear and wave, indicating that everything was fine, but she didn't. He moved toward the door to obey her instructions, then paused. What if she got into trouble out there? What if she needed to return in a hurry? The smart thing to do was leave the door unlocked.

A muffled exclamation sounded from near the entrance.

"Mom?" Gabe called.

Dark forms swirled past the right-hand window, attended by the noise of a scuffle.

"Mom!" Gabe shouted, dashing to the window and pressing his face to the cool pane. He noticed the looming outline of the SEAL, and could see part of the driver's side thanks to the diffuse lantern light cast through the glass, but the ground near the tire where his mom had put the bad man was plunged in shadows. "Mom?"

His mother did not respond.

"Mom! Where are you?"

Again there was no answer.

Gabe ran to his father and shook Blade's left shoulder. "Dad, wake up. Mom needs us."

The Warrior's eyelids fluttered briefly.

"Dad! Please wake up!" Gabe urged, shaking even harder. A scream pierced the night outside and Gabe stiffened, petrified. His gaze fell on the Commando, propped against the wall near the door, and he dashed to the Carbine and lifted the weapon awkwardly. If his mother was in danger, he would save her! With that thought uppermost in his mind, Gabe flung open the door and dashed into the night.

He took several steps and halted, thinking of his father alone and unconscious in the cabin, and decided to close the door. As he pulled the door shut a second scream sounded from a dozen yards off, in the direction of the lake. "Mom!" he shouted, and ran around the SEAL.

Vague forms were moving toward the water, and there appeared to be a struggle going on.

Gabe noticed that the figure in the middle had light-colored hair. Blonde hair! "Mom! I'm coming!" he yelled, jogging in pursuit, his left leg bumping against the Commando's magazine.

"No!" Jenny cried. "Go back!"

"I'll save you!" Gabe vowed.

"Go back!"

Gabe raced as fast as he could, but the figures outdistanced him. He received the impression the things were carrying his mother. They came to the lake and, without hesitation, plunged in with a loud splash.

"Gabe! Go—!" Jenny yelled, and was abruptly cut off.

"I'm coming!" Gabe responded, already halfway across the field. He saw two dark forms standing at the edge of the water, but his mother had vanished. "Mom!"

One of the things started toward him.

Stunned, Gabe stopped, his eyes widening, watching the vague figure approach. "Who are you?" he blurted. "What have you done with my mom?"

The thing advanced silently.

Gabe raised the Commando barrel and curled his finger around the trigger. "Who are you?" he repeated, striving to note details. But all he could tell was that the thing stood slightly over five feet in height and possessed a slim body. Was it a person, he wondered, or something else?

The thing hissed.

It wasn't a person, Gabe realized, and he braced himself.

"Don't come any closer!" he warned. "Just give my mom back."

Ten yards separated them.

"I'll shoot if you don't stop!" Gabe threatened.

Seven yards.

Gabe gulped and wagged the Carbine. "I'm not kidding. Stop or else!"

The thing ignored him.

"What have you done with my mom?" Gabe demanded angrily. He let the figure get closer, to within five yards, and then tensed his arms and squeezed the trigger. The thundering blast of the submachine gun stung his ears as the Commando sent three rounds into the creature. The recoil drove Gabe backwards and he fell onto his backside, still firing.

The powerful bullets lifted the thing from its feet and hurled the creature to the ground in a heap.

Gabe ceased firing and laughed, astonished at his victory. He scrambled erect and stepped tentatively over to the crumpled form. What in the world was it? More importantly, was it dead? He nudged the body with his right foot, and when the thing didn't move he pivoted and took a step toward the lake.

A cold, clammy hand suddenly seized his left wrist.

Startled, Gabe inadvertently screeched and tried to wrench his arm free, but he couldn't tug loose from the viselike hand. He glimpsed the creature he'd shot rising slowly, and he spun to confront it, holding the Commando by his right hand only. "Let go of me!" he shouted, and fired, able to get off four more rounds before the recoil tore the Commando from his fingers.

The heavy slugs drilled into the creature and slammed it to the earth once again, causing the thing to lose its grip on the boy.

Gabe tottered and stumbled onto his hands and knees. He saw the Carbine clatter to the grass near the creature's legs, and he was about to leap and retrieve the weapon when the thing started to stand.

What *was* it?

He glanced at the lake and spied another creature advancing, and he realized there were too many for him to take on. If he wanted to save his mother, he had to rouse his father at all costs! He straightened and flew toward the cabin, shrieking at the top of his lungs. "Dad! Dad! Help! They've got Mom!"

The cabin seemed so very far away.

Gabe covered five yards and glanced back to see if his pursuers were gaining. His peripheral vision registered something materializing directly in his path, and the next instant he collided with a spongy, yielding body and thin limbs looped about his chest, pinning his arms. He was brusquely lifted from his feet and carted toward the lake.

They had him!

CHAPTER SIXTEEN

"Any last words, jerk?" Harvey asked sarcastically.

Jared extended his arms, palms outward, and took a halting step backward. "Don't!"

"How original," Harvey quipped, and sighted along the arrow.

"No!" Tammy cried.

"What's to stop me?" Harvey cracked.

The answer, spoken in a low tone by the newcomer standing at the edge of the weeds to the south, astounded all of them. "The hand of the Lord."

As one they spun, shocked to behold the massively muscled man in the camouflage clothing who stood there calmly, holding a Bushmaster Auto Pistol in both hands. The firelight illuminated his rugged features and the gash in the center of his forehead. "Drop the bows," he commanded.

"Go to hell!" Harvey snapped.

"You first," the man said, and leveled both Bushmasters and fired.

Harvey and Silas were struck simultaneously. Each was hit

again and again and again, the rounds smacking into their torsos and knocking them backwards. Harvey managed to release his shaft but the arrow went wild. Both men were dead when their bodies thudded onto the ground.

"May the Lord have mercy on their souls," the muscular titan commented.

"Who are you?" Jared blurted.

"My name is Samson. I heard shots and came to investigate."

"You saved our lives," Tammy exclaimed.

Samson scrutinized the bodies littering the clearing, noting the four slain by arrows. "Who are you folks? What are you doing here?"

"I'm Jared, and this is my wife, Tammy," Jared introduced them.

"And this is Betty," Tammy added, nodding at the weeping brunette. "Her husband, Lloyd, was just killed."

"What happened?" Samson inquired.

Jared indicated the two men Samson had shot. "They planned to sell Tammy and Betty to slavers, and they would have succeeded if you hadn't come along."

"You still haven't told me what you're doing here," Samson observed.

"We're waiting for someone," Tammy said.

"A friend," Jared stated. "We can't leave until he returns."

"I'd like to stay and assist you in burying your companions, but I'm in a hurry," Samson mentioned.

"You're leaving already?" Tammy responded. "Why don't you share some food with us?"

Samson walked to the northeast. "I really can't. I'm sorry. Food and rest are out of the question until I've accomplished my mission." He holstered the Auto Pistols.

"Well, we'll be here if you should come by this way again," Jared said. "You're welcome to stop and visit."

"We won't be here if Blade returns first," Tammy mentioned.

Samson stopped in midstride, then turned. "Blade? Do you know Blade?"

"Yes," Jared answered, and as he studied their rescuer, reflecting that the newcomer was almost as big as Blade and equally as deadly, insight dawned. "You're from the Home, aren't you?"

"Yes," Samson confirmed, "and I'm looking for Blade. When did you see him?"

"He came by here yesterday morning. His wife and son were with him. He promised to pick us up on his return trip in two weeks and take us to the Home."

"Why do you want to go to the Home?"

"We hope to be permitted to live there," Jared said.

"So Blade and his family got this far safely," Samson mused aloud. "Thanks for the information." He went to leave.

"Wait!" Jared declared.

"What?" Samson responded.

"I get the impression Blade and his family are in some kind of danger. He helped us out yesterday and kindly offered to take us to the Home. If he's in trouble, we want to help," Jared offered.

"He might be in trouble," Samson acknowledged, "which is why I must reach him as quickly as I can."

"Let us go with you."

"I'll travel faster alone."

"Please," Jared urged. "We don't want to stay here another two weeks. We don't want to stay another day, if we can help it. Five of us have already been killed. Let us come with you and we'll keep up. I promise. And if Blade is in trouble, we can help."

"Please," Tammy implored, clasping her hands together.

Samson hesitated, torn between his duty and his desire to aid the trio. The pleading expressions on Jared and Tammy convinced him of their sincerity, and the sight of the brunette kneeling over her husband's chest and crying pitiably stirred his compassion. He wanted to let them accompany him, but his wound had slowed him down the last few miles and he couldn't afford to dally.

Jared construed the muscleman's silence as a negative response and became angry. "What's with you people from the Home, anyway? We were told all those wonderful tales about how kind and considerate all of you are, but you don't seem to give a damn about anyone else."

"Jared!" Tammy said, trying to cut him off, afraid he would anger Samson.

"I'm letting him have a piece of my mind!" Jared started testily. "We traveled hundreds of miles to live at the Home, and the first two guys we meet from the Family couldn't care less about our welfare. Blade didn't want his precious trip interrupted, and now this clown is going to go off and leave us without a thought to our safety. We're stuck in the middle of the Outlands, for crying out loud! There's just the three of us left. Our dearest friends are all dead. Is it too much to ask to be taken along so we won't wind up like them?"

Tammy averted her gaze.

"No, it's not too much to ask," Samson said.

"What?" Jared responded in surprise.

"You can come with me, but we must leave immediately," Samson stated. "There's no time to bury your dead."

Hearing that statement, Betty looked up, her eyes moist, tears streaking her cheeks. "I'm not leaving until Lloyd is buried."

Jared began retrieving his revolver and rifle. "We've got to go now, Betty."

"I won't leave Lloyd here to be eaten by animals," Betty said angrily.

"And what about the others?" Tammy chimed in. "We owe it to them to bury them properly."

"We don't have the *time,*" Jared insisted.

"Then you go on without me," Betty suggested. "I'll bury my husband and catch up with you."

"You'd never find us in the dark," Tammy said.

Betty shrugged. "If I don't, I don't."

"You wouldn't last ten minutes by yourself," Tammy remarked.

"Without Lloyd, I don't feel much like living anyway," Betty replied softly.

"We can give Lloyd and the others a proper burial tomorrow or the next day," Jared proposed.

"By then the carrior-eaters will have chewed his face down to the bone," Betty said. "I'm not going, and that's final."

"Don't be so stubborn," Jared stated. "Lloyd wouldn't want you to throw your life away needlessly."

Betty folded her arms across her chest and tilted her chin defiantly. "I'm not going."

"Enough!" Samson abruptly commanded and stalked over to them. "This useless arguing is getting us nowhere. I'll compromise this much. Betty, we'll bury your husband right now. But the others will have to wait until after I locate Blade. Is that agreeable with you, Tammy?"

She nodded.

"Okay. Then let's bury Lloyd. With the four of us digging, we can leave in five minutes," Samson said.

Betty, still on her knees, reached out and hugged Samson's legs. "Thank you! Oh, thank you!"

"We'll name our firstborn after you," Jared declared happily, and fell to scooping at the earth with his bare hands.

Samson watched them begin digging, worry gnawing at the back of his mind, hoping he hadn't made a grave error. If the empaths were right, Blade's life was on the line. And the minutes they now wasted in burying the dead man might well turn out to be the very amount of time that would mean the difference between life and death for Blade. If such turned out to be the case, Samson knew he would never forgive himself.

Which would be small consolation for Blade and his family.

CHAPTER SEVENTEEN

Blade came awake with a start and stared at the ceiling, wondering why he was so cold. He remembered passing out, and he looked down at himself, at the blanket covering him, and knit his brow in bewilderment. Who'd put that there? Jenny? His hands were folded on his chest underneath the blanket, and he raised them so he could see his wound. A flicker of surprise affected him when he laid his eyes on his bandaged midriff. Jenny must have operated already, he realized, and glanced to his left.

The living room was empty.

He gazed at the lantern for a minute, watching the orange flame, and wished he was lying next to the fire. A shiver rippled along his body. He placed his right hand on his hot forehead and licked his dry lips. Evidently, he'd developed a doozy of a fever. A glass of water would be nice.

"Jenny?"

Blade waited patiently for her to reply. He assumed his wife and son were in the bedroom, although he wouldn't have expected them to leave him alone.

"Jenny?" he called out.

He wondered about the time and looked out the west window above the sofa, disconcerted to note that it was pitch black outside and therefore must be the middle of the night. Perhaps Jenny and Gabe were asleep. If Gabe had been afraid to sleep alone, Jenny had probably offered to sleep with him, Blade reasoned. And he didn't want to wake them up.

The Warrior placed his hands flat on the rug and slowly pushed himself to a sitting posture, gritting his teeth as pain lanced his abdomen. He inhaled deeply through his nose and pressed his right forearm to his stomach. Gradually the discomfort subsided and he could breathe easily. He knew Jenny would be furious if he set the wound to bleeding, so he stood carefully, inching upward until he attained his full height, allowing the brown blanket to drop at his feet.

A sticky sweat caked his skin and contributed to his chills. He wiped his left hand on his forehead and took a tentative step. Although he felt extremely weak, he could move without provoking too much agony, and he shuffled to the kitchen counter and reached for the water. His gaze strayed to the open bedroom door.

Blade stiffened.

No one was sleeping in the bed!

"Jenny? Gabe?"

The resultant silence filled the Warrior with dread. Where could they be? he asked himself, and hobbled into the bedroom to check it completely. They wouldn't leave the cabin at night. Jenny knew better. He returned to the living room and stood in the middle of the rug, gripping the straight chair for support, scanning the windows and the door, and made two dismaying observations.

The front door wasn't bolted.

And the Commando and the Beretta were gone.

Blade swallowed hard, shaken by the inescapable conclusion his loved ones had ventured outdoors and not returned. Maybe, he rationalized hopefully, Jenny had just taken Gabe outside to go to the bathroom. For a moment he was relieved, until

he realized both lanterns were still in the cabin. Thinking that
she might have taken the flashlight, he stepped to the kitchen
and rifled through the box of supplies he'd brought inside from
the SEAL and deposited on the floor near the cupboard
containing the canned goods. He found the flashlight and
straightened, holding it in his left palm.

There was no way Jenny would have gone out without a
light of some kind.

Unless there'd been an emergency.

Blade slipped the flashlight into his left front pocket and
strode to the front door, forgetting all about his wound in his
anxiety over his family. He saw the Beeman/Krico leaning
on the jamb and grabbed the rifle. The bolt-action rifle wasn't
as lethal as the Commando, but it would suffice. He took hold
of the doorknob and paused as a cold sensation afflicted him,
numbing him momentarily.

The damn chills!

Blade shook his head and opened the door. The cool night
air only compounded his condition, and he shivered violently
as he stepped from the cabin.

Wait a minute.

What was he doing? Trying to get himself killed?

The Warrior went back into the living room and picked up
the lantern off the coffee table. The fever was impairing his
mental clarity. If he didn't get his act together, he'd wind up
in a world of hurt. The lantern held high, he went out, closed
the door, and walked to the front of the SEAL. Not until then
did the fact that someone else was missing occur to him.

Where was the lousy scavenger?

Blade's apprehension mounted. What if Roy had revived and
kidnapped Jenny and Gabe as a means of getting even? After
the beating he'd given the man, Blade would have doubted
the scavenger could kidnap a daisy, let alone his wife and son.
Maybe Roy was a lot tougher than he'd figured. He opened
his mouth to shout Jenny's name, then changed his mind. If
Roy was lurking out there somewhere, he certainly didn't want

to advertise that he was after the bastard.

Which way should he go?

The Warrior walked toward the lake, swinging the lantern from side to side, straining to distinguish details in the gloom. Another thought struck him, and he halted. The lantern would advertise his presence just as much as a shout would. Roy could undoubtedly spy the light from hundreds of yards off. So what difference did it make if he called out? None.

"Jenny? Gabe? Where are you?"

Blade continued to the south. With his attention focused on the lake shore and the treeline, he almost missed the metallic glint in front of his feet. He glanced down and stopped in amazement.

The Commando!

He hastily slung the Beeman over his left shoulder and scooped up his submachine gun. What was it doing lying in the middle of the field? He sniffed the barrel and frowned. The gun had been fired. A quick check of the magazine confirmed that about ten of the 90 rounds were gone.

Someone had put up a hell of a fight.

Blade headed for the lake, the Commando cradled in his right arm.

"Jenny! Gabe!"

Except for the breeze blowing from the northwest, the night seemed preternaturally still.

The Warrior shuddered again, and guessed that his fever must be worsening. His face felt as if it was on fire. But he refused to rest until he found his wife and son. He would scour the area until he located them or dropped in his tracks.

Tracks.

He came to the lake shore and idly looked at the soft soil, not really expecting to find anything important. So the sight of Jenny's Ruger Blackhawk .44 Magnum lying on the ground stunned him. He knelt, set down the lantern, and examined the revolver. The gun was fully loaded, prompting a slew of questions. Had Jenny lost it? If so, why was she out by the lake? If she hadn't lost the weapon, then who had left it lying there? Surely Roy wouldn't have left it behind. But then, the Beeman hadn't been taken. He sighed in frustration and gazed at the ground.

And saw the print.

Blade blinked a few times and leaned down for a closer inspection. Never before had he beheld such a strange track. Imbedded a quarter of an inch in the earth within inches of the water was a four-toed footprint of bizarre dimensions. Eleven inches in length and three inches wide at the heel, the track was unlike any other he'd ever seen, although it vaguely resembled those of a lizard. The heel was short and rounded and the toes were elongated, comprising eight inches of the total length. The middle pair of toes were two inches longer than those on the inner and outer margins of the foot. Because the track was aligned with the toes pointing due south, he knew whatever had made the print had entered the lake.

But what could it have been?

Strains of inexplicable giantism were not uncommon in the postwar wildlife. The Elders speculated that the radiation was responsible, but they didn't know precisely how the growth spurts in various species were produced. Blade had encountered more than his share of oversized creatures during his travels. In Dallas, Texas, he'd even tangled with a nest of giant lizards. So the print in front of him could conceivably belong to a lizard. Except that most lizards he knew of rarely went into deep water.

What else, then?

Blade gazed out over the lake, endeavoring to piece together the puzzling pieces of the mystery. He debated whether to continue the hunt on foot or in the SEAL. In the shape he was in, he couldn't hike very fast and would tire readily. In the transport he'd be able to conserve his energy and cover more terrain, but he wouldn't be able to penetrate the thicker stands of trees. If he—

A crackling noise sounded to his rear, then abruptly ceased

The Warrior rotated, the .44 Magnum in his left hand, the Commando in his right. He searched the field but failed to discern a hint of movement. Was his fever inducing his mind to play tricks on him? He doubted it. There was something hiding in the field, observing him. His instincts told him to be wary, that he wasn't alone.

Blade reached back and tucked the .44 Magnum under his belt at the base of his spine. He lifted the lantern in his left hand and walked slowly in the direction of the cabin, his gray eyes flitting from side to side, scanning the weeds. The lantern illuminated a curious greenish-blue hump approximately 20 feet to the west. The hump glistened in the light, as if wet. He angled toward it.

Suddenly the hump uncoiled and darted into the bushes.

Blade glimpsed a long body, a longer tail, and a flurry of slim limbs, and then the thing was gone, vanished in the night. He started toward the bushes, then paused, leery of being led into an ambush. The contours of the creature were disturbingly familiar, but he couldn't identify the thing from his short sighting.

A loud hissing arose to the east, persisted for five seconds, and ended.

As if in response, more hissing sounded to the west, lasted all of ten seconds, and stopped.

Blade hefted the Commando. There must be more than one of the creatures concealed in the field, and they were communicating with one another. He glanced at the SEAL, then at the lake, and froze.

Something was *rising* out of the water near the shore, standing erect on two legs and stepping onto the land.

Blade placed the lantern at his feet and pressed the Commando to his right shoulder.

Another figure began rising out of the lake, then another, and yet another.

The Warrior rested his finger on the trigger and disregarded the chilly feeling intensifying in his body. At last he knew what

had happened to his wife and son. The creatures had gotten
them. And if Jenny and Gabe had been pulled under the water,
they were udoubtedly dead by now. The notion aroused a
burning rage, and he sneered as he sighted on the foremost
thing and fired a short, controlled burst.

Suddenly creatures popped up all over the field.

Blade saw his initial target topple backwards, and he
swiveled and pointed the barrel at a five-foot-tall form that
had risen in a clump of weeds ten feet to the right. He sent
a half-dozen rounds into the thing's torso and it fell from view.
But there were many more, on all sides, and some hissed as
they converged on him.

What *were* they?

He was about to shoot at a second creature when the one
he'd just fired at reappeared, standing in the same spot as
before. For an instant he believed it was a different creature,
until it doubled over, apparently injured and holding its arms
to its chest, and lumbered straight at him.

The thing had taken direct hits in the chest and survived!

Blade elevated the barrel slightly, going for the head this
time, and let the creature have six more bullets. The impact
flipped the figure into the bushes, and Blade grinned in
triumph. Their heads were their weak spots!

A twig snapped to his rear.

The Warrior whirled, his cockiness replaced by
openmouthed consternation when he saw one of the beings
less than two yards from him. In the second before he squeezed
the trigger, Blade clearly saw its features: a rounded, blunt
head notable for a pair of widely separated, bulbous black eyes
and a slit of a mouth; moist, smooth, greenish-blue skin; a
slender body lacking shoulders and hips; thin limbs, the lower
longer than the upper; four extended digits at the end of its
"arms", five at the end of its "legs"; and a long, flat tail
that helped support the creature as it walked erect. Like the
rest, this one stood about five feet in height.

Blade fired, and he saw the slugs tear into the thing's head and knock it to the ground. He watched it thrash and convulse for a moment, at last confirming what he was up against.

Mutations.

Once, perhaps a century ago, their ancestors had been insignificant salamanders, secretive and nocturnal amphibians equally at home on land or in the water. Once, before the staggering amount of radiation and chemical toxins were unleashed on the environment, the ancestors of these creatures had roamed the woods at night seeking prey. All salamanders were carnivorous.

And there were no exceptions.

There wasn't time for Blade to dwell on the factors contributing to the creation of the giant mutant strain. There wasn't time to reflect upon the irony of humankind's superweapons transforming nature itself into an adversary. There was only time for firing and downing as many as he could.

Blade tried his utmost. He swept the Commando in an arc, blasting four of the salamanders coming at him from the west. Spinning, he sent a hail of lead into three approaching from the east.

Something abruptly grabbed him about the ankles.

Blade looked down and found a salamander on all fours, holding fast to his legs and striving to jerk him off balance. He rammed the barrel into the creature's left eye and fired, the rounds rupturing the orb and the cranium and spraying gore all over his fatigue pants.

The salamander slumped to the earth lifeless.

The Warrior realized they could travel on all fours as well as on two legs, and he stared toward the lake and spied one doing just that, scuttling at him with the speed of a streaking snake. He stitched the thing from head to tail, flipping the creature onto its back.

Many others closed in on him.

Blade downed three more when the inevitable occurred; the Commando went empty.

A salamander charged him, running manlike.

Blade reversed his grip on the submachine gun and swung it as a club, slamming the stock into the salamander's mouth and catapulting it onto the ground. He reached behind his back and drew the .44 Magnum, aimed, and flattened another foe.

Still they came on.

He heard a twig snap and whirled to catch a pair of mutations less than six feet away. Two quick shots killed them both, the .44 Magnum booming.

They surrounded him now.

Blade fired a final time, slaying an onrushing salamander. Two others darted in from different directions, running on all fours, keeping their bodies level with the ground. He attempted to get a bead on one of them, but they moved too rapidly. Only when the pair were almost to him did he perceive that he wasn't their target.

They were after the lantern!

The Warrior tried to lunge and grab the lantern before they could reach it, but the speedier of the duo hit the lantern without breaking stride, using its blunt head to deliver a smashing blow. Tumbling crazily, the lantern went sailing.

The flame went out.

Darkness engulfed Blade. He squinted, endeavoring to locate the salamanders, but he needn't have bothered.

They knew where he was and they came to him.

The mutations hurled themselves at the Warrior, springing at him from every direction at once, seven, eight, ten of them working in concert. More piled on, seeking to overwhelm him by sheer force of numbers.

Blade was driven to his knees by the weight of their bodies. He struck at them, punching with his left hand and clubbing them with the barrel of the Blackhawk, swinging right and left in reckless abandon. They hit him on his head and shoulders and tried to grab his arms. He held his own briefly, until he released the Ruger and tried to draw his right Bowie, leaving his right side exposed.

The hissing salamanders swarmed over the Warrior, burying

him in their moist, writhing flesh. Four of them locked their
limbs on his right arm. Three others succeeded in clamping
their arms around his neck. His legs were yanked out from
under him.

Blade came down hard on his stomach. A pervading
weakness brought on by his exertion, his fever, and his wound
caused him to go briefly limp. Before he could recover, they
seized his arms and legs in unbreakable holds and, en masse,
lifted him into the air.

They had won.

CHAPTER EIGHTEEN

Blade felt them carrying him, felt their cool digits on hi
arms and shoulders and face. He was too disoriented, too tire
and sore, to pay much attention to where they were takin
him. Waves of vertigo tried to swamp him, but he fought then
off, forcing himself to stay awake. His mind seemed sluggisl
For a minute the issue was in doubt, and he came close t
passing out. But just when he thought he would slip int
unconsciousness, the salamanders revived him.

They carried him into the lake.

He heard the splashing as the creatures entered the wate
and the sound sent a current of shock through him. The
planned to drown him, to consume him underwater! Jenny an
Gabe must have suffered the same fate! His fury returned, an
the resultant adrenaline surge restored his full alertness an
imbued him with newfound strength. "No!" he bellowed, ar
attempted to tear his arms and legs from their collective grasj

The salamanders paused to tighten their grips.

Blade bucked and heaved, jerking this way and that, h
muscles bulging, sweat pouring from his skin. He exerted h

...ight to the maximum, ignoring the agony in his abdomen, ...ut there were too many for him.

Moving methodically, the mutations marched into the lake.

The icy water touched Blade's legs first, soaking his pants, ...en drenched his back and began to rise over his chest. He ...ndeavored to slow them down by rocking from side to side, ...ut the creatures were undeterred.

Blade gasped as the frigid water crept higher and higher. ...espair welled within him. If he was going to die, he preferred ... go out fighting, or else expire of old age in his bed with ...is wife at his side. To be helplessly drowned by horrid ...utations seemed an ignoble manner of dying.

The water lapped against his chin.

Blade instinctively held his breath, drawing as much air as ... could into his lungs. The cold water invigorated him and ...ade his skin tingle. His despair gave way to hope. Maybe, ...ce they were underwater, he could break free. The water ...as bound to make him slippery to hold.

Lowering smoothly into the lake, the salamanders ...bmerged completely and swam into deeper water. They ...gled toward the west shore, swimming powerfully, using ...eir hind legs and tails to propel them.

The Warrior struggled for only a few seconds and realized ...eir grip on him was as strong as ever. He conserved his ...ergy, waiting for them to release him and begin their feeding ...nzy, envisioning them attacking him as if they were a school ... firece piranha. Instead, to his growing astonishment, they ...peared to be in a hurry to reach a particular destination, ...t to rip him to shreds.

What were they doing?

His chest started to ache and he wondered how long he could ...ld his breath. Two minutes? Three? Four? He hadn't done ...y swimming on a regular basis in years and was badly out ... practice. Except for an occasional dip in the moat during ...ich he would dive down and touch the bottom, he'd rarely ...d any reason to hold his breath.

...He definitely had a reason now.

Blade peered ahead, trying to spot their destination, but th
murky water restricted his field of vision to within a yard o
his face, and even then he could only perceive dim outlines
The surface of the lake, however, was visible as a lighte
mantle of gray against the backdrop of the night.

The salamanders increased their speed.

Blade grimaced as the gnawing ache in his chest becam
general torment. His fever flared terribly. He perceived a
enormous dark mass materializing in front of them an
deduced they were rapidly nearing the west bank.

Were the mutations intending to climb out of the lake again

The Warrior anticipated them arching upward, but the
swam on a beeline for the bank without slowing or deviatir
their course. His cheeks puffed out and his throat felt as
the pressure threatened to cause him to explode.

A black cavity abruptly loomed in the west bank. Th
salamanders glided into the opening and kicked harder.

Blade had the impression he was rising, and to h
amazement he unexpectedly burst from the water and felt dar
air on his face. He automatically inhaled, his chest expandin;
overcome with relief. The creatures had brought him to the
lair, some sort of underground cavern! He was lifted and pulle
and shoved, then dumped unceremoniously onto soft eart!
The lair was pitch black, but he didn't care.

They'd released him!

And he still lived! Not only that, he still had his Bowie

A smile twisted his features and he rose to his knees. A seri
of splashes arose nearby and he surmised the creatures we
returning to the lake. After a bit the lair became eerily quie
Blade ran his hands through his soaked hair and coughed

"What was that?" a youthful voice asked.

"Quiet," responded a woman who Blade knew better th:
any other on the planet.

The Warrior felt as if a lightning bolt had jolted his bod
He swung in the direction of the voices and experienc
difficulty in finding his own. "Jenny! Gabe!" he finally blurt

out. Their answering cries were literally music to his ears.

"Daddy!"

"Blade?"

"Stay where you are!" Blade told them. He judged his loved ones to be very close, within ten feet of his position, but he didn't want to fumble hastily toward them in the darkness and fall into the water. His left hand closed on his left pocket and found the flashlight still there. "I have a light," he said, and pulled the flashlight from his pocket. Would the thing still work, he fretted, after being submerged? Trembling as much from his excitement as from the chills, he pressed the button.

The thin beam of light played over Jenny and Gabe, who were huddled together eight feet off. Gabe impetuously let go of his mom and scrambled on his hands and knees across the mud floor toward his father. Jenny followed.

Blade took them into his arms and hugged them tight, bowing his head in thankfulness. A constriction in his throat prevented him from speaking until he swallowed and said huskily, "I didn't think I'd ever see either of you again."

Soft sniffles came from Gabe.

Jenny kissed Blade tenderly on the lips.

Although the Warrior wanted to prolong their reunion and embrace them indefinitely, he knew better. Time was precious. The mutations might return at any second. For all he knew, there could be a few lurking nearby. The thought prompted him to move his left hand back and forth and up and down, flicking the flashlight beam around the lair, gauging its dimensions.

The salamander's subterranean abode consisted of an earthen excavation 30 feet wide and slightly under six feet in height. The walls and ceiling were compact dirt, but the floor had been turned to mud by the constant dripping of the creatures. A circular pool of water ten feet in diameter linked the lair to the lake.

Blade spied whitish objects in the far corner and swiveled the flashlight to illuminate them. He almost recoiled when he saw the piles of bones littering the floor. Among the grisly collection were two human skeletons.

"I knew you'd come save us," Gabe commented happily.

"Yeah. What kept you so long?" Jenny quipped, and laid her moist cheek on his.

"You forgot to leave a note telling me you'd gone to visit the neighbors," Blade replied. He kissed her, then released them.

"What do we do now?" Gabe asked.

"We get out of here," Blade said, and patted his right Bowie.

"Take me too," interjected a weak, raspy voice to his rear.

The Warrior swung around and trained the flashlight on the person he discovered lying in the opposite corner from the bones. "Roy!" he blurted out.

"Help me," the scavenger responded. He lay on his back, his wrists and ankles bound, his visage a battered ruin, mud coating his clothing. "Please help me!"

"He wanted me to untie him, but I wouldn't," Jenny said.

"How'd he know you were in here?" Blade asked.

"Those terrible things brought him down first, then me. When they dropped me on the ground I didn't know where I was. I sat in the dark and tried to figure out what to do next. Then they brought Gabe in and I heard him coughing and calling for me. We crawled to each other. That's when the pervert opened his mouth and asked me to untie him," Jenny detailed.

"Please, mister!" Roy begged. "Don't let those things eat me."

"Let them, Dad," Gabe said.

"He deserves whatever happens to him," Jenny concurred.

Blade glanced at them, their features cast in shadows. "I never realized the two of you were so bloodthirsty."

"Do you expect us to show mercy to him after what he did to us?" Jenny countered.

"Yeah. He's scum," Gabe added.

The Warrior sighed and extended the flashlight to Jenny. "Here. Take this."

"What are you planning to do?" she inquired as she took it.

"I'm going to cut him loose," Blade said.

"What?" Jenny queried in disbelief.

"I'm going to cut him loose," Blade reiterated.

"But *why*?"

"Because no matter what he's done—and I'd kill him in a second for the pain he inflicted on us if we weren't in here—he's human."

"So was Jack the Ripper."

Blade rose to a crouch. "Jenny, I can't just leave him there to be eaten by the mutations. I'm a Warrior, not a psychopath. I'll free him and then he's on his own."

"Let me get this straight. You'll cut him loose so the mutants won't eat him, but if you bump into him after we're out of here, you'll kill him?"

"Exactly."

Jenny made a snorting sound and muttered, "Men!"

Blade took a partial step forward, doubled over at the waist, when he heard the water lapping against the edge of the pool and sensed a commotion in the water. "Douse the flashlight!" he directed, and quickly took Jenny and Gabe protectively into his arms.

Blackness enveloped the lair once again.

The Warrior listened to splashing noises, then the muffled tread of something shuffling across the floor. He detected a hint of movement, and conjectured that one of the creatures had returned. His supposition was confirmed moments later when the scavenger uttered a harsh exclamation.

"Get your slimy paws off me!"

Blade could feel the tension in Jenny and Gabe, and he wondered if they could feel his.

"Let go of me!" Roy bellowed.

The Warrior placed his hands on the hilts of his knives.

"Damn you! Let go! What—!" Roy cried, and vented a

strangled, gurgling gasp.

Blade leaned closer to his wife. "When I give you the word, shine the flashlight over there."

"Got it," she said.

A peculiar, squishy, ripping noise arose in the corner, then a spattering noise, as if a liquid substance was spraying over the floor.

Blade realized what had happened and knew he'd waited too long, but he hadn't expected the things to finish Roy off so quickly. He drew the Bowies, whispered, "Now!" and dashed toward the corner as Jenny turned on the flashlight.

The beam revealed a gory tableau. Three mutations were gathered around the scavenger's body. Roy was dead, his head torn from his body, blood spurting from his severed neck. One of the salamanders held Roy's head in its left hand while it gnawed on the jagged stump under Roy's chin. The second creature lapped at the crimson geyser sprinkling the floor, and the third was in the act of stripping off the scavenger's clothes. The sudden illumination made them whirl toward the source. They dropped whatever they were doing and raised their hands to shield their bulging eyes.

Blade plowed into them at an awkward run, his speed impaired by his having to run stooped over. He felt the ceiling scraping his broad shoulders and wished he could straighten to his full stature, but he would have to make do, and make do he did. His left forearm batted the foremost salamander backwards, and the thing tripped over the scavenger's corpse and toppled to the ground. Blade arced the right Bowie out and around, and the keen razor edge slit the second creature's throat from one side to the other. A putrid fluid spurted out. The creature clutched at its neck and sank to its knees. Blade kicked it in the face, and his combat boot sent the thing crashing into the wall.

The third mutation hissed and lunged.

The Warrior met the lunge with both Bowies leveled, impaling the creature in the area of its body where its chest would be if the thing had a chest. He surged his arms upward, cracking the mutation's head on the compact dirt ceiling, then brutally flung the salamander to the right.

Limp as a wet rag, the creature slipped off the Bowies and fell.

Leaving the one Blade had struck with his arm.

The Warrior saw the thing come up and over Roy's body in a savage rush. He tried a new tactic, swinging the Bowies out and in, hacking at the mutation's eyes.

Displaying astounding reflexes, the salamander raised both upper limbs to block the knives. Instead, the Bowies cleaved through both arms. chopping the hands off. The hands plopped into the mud and continued to open and close, even though detached. The creature's lifeblood gushed out the sundered wrists.

Blade sank his left Bowie into the salamander's head between its eyes. He wrenched the knife free and watched the mutation keel over. All three were now on the ground, and only the one with the slit throat still moved, twitching and convulsing, its movements weaker and weaker with each passing second.

"You did it!" Gabe shouted.

"Not so loud," Blade advised. He wiped the Bowies on his pants and returned to his wife and son.

"More of those things may show up at any minute," Jenny noted.

"I know," Blade said, "which is why we're leaving right this instant. Are you both up to another swim?"

Gabe glanced at the pool apprehensively. "I had a hard time holding my breath the first time, Dad."

"Don't worry. We'll swim as fast as we can. And once we're out of the lair and in the lake, we'll swim straight up to the surface. If my calculations are correct, we'll be within yards of the western shore. You won't need to swim as far this time," Blade assured him.

"There are dozens more out there somewhere," Jenny remarked. "Even if we make it out of the lake, what do we do then? Try and take shelter in the cabin? They could break in there easy enough.''

''I doubt they know how to open a door or a window. If they did, they would have broken in on us last night.''

''Or during the day,'' Gabe commented.

''Did you see the way they reacted to the flashlight?'' Blade asked, and went on before his son could answer. ''I suspect they're nocturnal.''

''What's nocturnal?'' Gabe queried.

''They're only abroad at night. Bright sunlight is probably too hard on their sensitive eyes.''

''Oh.''

Jenny gestured at the pool. ''So what do we do once we're out? Hide in the forest until dawn?''

''No. They might be able to track by scent, and we already know their eyesight at night is exceptional. I also don't much like the idea of taking shelter in the cabin. Sooner or later they'll figure out how to get inside.''

''Then what do we do?'' Jenny inquired.

''Our best bet is to reach the SEAL. Once we're inside the transport, we'll be safe. There's no way those things can break into the van.''

''But the field will be swarming with them,'' Jenny noted. ''They'll be all over the area, hunting for food.''

''I know,'' Blade said. ''They must scour the woods in the vicinity of the lake for game during the night, and bring the animals they catch down here to store until they're ready to eat.''

''Maybe those three who killed the bad man had the munchies,'' Gabe mentioned, and laughed.

''Remind me to have a talk with you about your sense of humor, young man, after we return to the Home,'' Jenny stated.

Blade was pleased that they could banter in the midst of such a crisis. The Elder who taught the novice Warriors their trade never tired of stressing the fundamental importance of attitude in a life-threatening situation. Attitude ranked as high as ability and an aptitude for dispensing death. With a positive attitude, a person could face insurmountable odds and triumph or could observe the most sickening violence and retain his or her self-control. Without a positive attitude, the barbarism the Warriors confronted would ravage them emotionally.

"I'm ready when you are, Dad," Gabe declared.

"Okay. I'll hold onto you and your mom will stay by our side," Blade said. He looked at Jenny. "If you want, I'll hold your hand until we're clear of the lair."

"I want."

"Then let's go."

CHAPTER NINETEEN

Samson, Jared, Tammy, and Betty emerged from the forest bordering the southwest curve of the lake and halted.

"What was all that shooting we heard earlier?" Tammy asked.

"I don't know," Samson replied. He didn't bother to add that the gunfire had worried him immensely. He'd engaged in numerous target-practice sessions with Blade at the shooting range in the southeast corner of the Home, and he knew the distinctive, heavy thundering of the Commando Arms Carbine well. The gunfire he'd heard had included bursts from a Commando.

"What's that light?" Jared questioned, staring to the north.

The Warrior pivoted and spied the dim glow at the north end of the lake. According to the information imparted by Plato, the Founder's cabin was located near the north shore. "That's where we're headed," he announced, and moved off.

Jared kept pace on Samson's right while the women trailed behind.

"It seems peaceful here," Betty remarked.

"Appearances can be deceiving," the Warrior said.

"Do you think Blade will be mad that we came along?" Jared inquired.

"No. Why should he?" Samson responded, his attention on the distant light. He held the Bushmaster Auto Rifle in his right hand.

"I don't know. But I got the impression he's not the kind of guy you'd want to tick off."

"He's not," Samson confirmed.

"I also get the impression he's an important person at the Home."

"You certainly get a lot of impressions. Yes, he is."

"In what way?"

"There are eighteen Family members who have been chosen by the Elders to serve as Warriors, as the guardians of the Home. Blade is the head Warrior," Samson elaborated. "The only one who has more authority than Blade is our Leader, and even then only in times of peace. In times of war Blade is in command."

Jared studied the muscular figure next to him. "And you must be one of the Warriors, huh?"

"Yes."

"Do you mind if I ask you something?"

"Heaven forbid."

"What?"

"Never mind. Go ahead. Ask."

Jared cleared his throat. "Are all the men at the Home as big as Blade and you are?"

Samson glanced at his newfound companion, trying to read Jared's expression in the dark. "No."

"Whew! I was beginning to think that all men in the Family are giants and I'd be a midget in comparison."

"No, we're not all giants," Samson said, suppressing an urge to laugh.

"Thank goodness."

"Actually, Blade and I are the runts in the Family."

There was a pregnant pause, and then came Jared's sheepish

response. "You're kidding, right?"

Samson suddenly halted and turned to scan the inky vegetation ten yards to his left. "Listen," he said softly.

Jared cocked his head. "I don't hear anything."

"Neither do I," Samson stated.

"So?"

"So what happened to the insects?"

"The insects?" Jared repeated, and abruptly comprehended. Moments before the forest had been alive with the buzzing and chirping of countless bugs. Now the woods were like a tomb. Even the breeze had abated.

"What does it mean?" Tammy whispered.

"Stay alert," Samson warned, cradling the Bushmaster against his right side.

"You don't have to tell me twice," Tammy said nervously.

The Warrior looked at the brunette. She had spoken only a few times since her husband's burial, and then only when addressed. Her countenance was pale. On several occasions Samson had had to remind her not to fall too far behind the rest as they'd hastened toward the lake. He recognized her symptoms from previous experience. The poor woman suffered from delayed-stress syndrome, as the Elder who'd taught Combat Psychology 101 had described the condition. Anyone who lived through a harrowing ordeal could succumb to a belated reaction when the full shock set in. The trauma of losing Lloyd was almost more than Betty could bear. "How about you? Are you okay?"

"Never felt better," Betty answered caustically.

"I'm serious."

"So am I," she said, and laughed lightly. "Why shouldn't I be okay? Just because I lost the man I loved today? Or because life in this stinking world sucks?" She paused, then launched into a bitter tirade. "I mean, what's the reason we're here? Why are we put on this rotten world to suffer? From the cradle to the grave all we know is pain. Everywhere you turn there's violence and death. If the raiders, the murderers, the robbers, the mutations, the animals, or some disease doesn't get you, it's a miracle. All Lloyd and I wanted out of a life was a peaceful place to raise our children, a place where we wouldn't have to worry about being attacked every time we stepped out the door. A place where men and women treat each other with mutual respect. A place where everyone trusts everyone else.''

"Put your trust in the Lord."

Betty snickered. "Now I *know* you're not serious."

"But I am. Without faith and trust in the Lord, life is a sham.''

"How do you figure?"

Samson gazed at the trees and frowned. "This isn't the proper time or place to discuss this. How about if we continue our conversation later?"

Betty's chin drooped to her chest. "Yeah. Sure. Later," she replied, her words barely audible.

"I'm sorry," Samson told her.

She motioned for him to keep going.

The Warrior regretfully turned his back on her and hiked northward. The silence still shrouded the woods, signifying that someone or something had disrupted the natural rhythm of the wildlife. He wished the Empaths could have been more specific about the nature of the threat to Blade. To be forewarned was to be forearmed, he'd always believed.

A loud splash sounded in the lake.

"Hey, maybe we can have fish for breakfast," Jared commented.

"How can you think about food at a time like this?" Tammy asked.

"It's easy. I didn't have supper."

"No more talking," Samson ordered, staring across the placid water. He wasn't very surprised when one of them ignored him.

"Can I have a drink before we go any farther?" Betty queried.

"It can wait," Samson said.

"Please. I don't feel so good."

The Warrior pursed his lips. If he refused, she might be miffed and would be of even less value in a fight. He pointed at the lake. "Splash some water on your face, but don't drink it."

"Why not?"

"The water might be contaminated."

Betty stepped to the edge of the lake and knelt on her right knee. She extended her right arm and cupped a cool handful, and she was about to raise her arm when a thin form broke the murky surface, hurtling at her with its limbs outstretched, hissing loudly. Her sluggish mind betrayed her. The thing was almost upon her before she could do more than blink. It was that quick.

But not quick enough.

Samson's Auto Rifle chattered when the creature was less than 12 inches from its prey. The rounds smacked into its torso and propelled it backwards into the lake, where the thing promptly sank from view.

"Dear God!" Tammy exclaimed. She moved to Betty's side and assisted the stunned woman in rising.

"What was that?" Jared asked anxiously.

"Your guess is as good as mine," Samson replied, and walked over to the women. "Are you all right, Betty?" he inquired.

She nodded absently. "Yeah. Yeah. Sure."

"We can't stop. We have to reach the light at the end of the lake. Can you keep up with us?"

"Yeah. Yeah."

"I'll take care of her," Tammy offered.

"Be ready for anything," Samson advised them. He hurried in the direction of the cabin, certain their troubles had just begun. The creature in the water had appeared to be manlike, but he'd glimpsed it for only a few seconds. Since no known animal resembled what he'd seen, he concluded the thing must have been a mutation. And where there was one mutant, there invariably were more. Was that the threat? Were there mutants in the lake? "Don't stray near the water," he recommended.

"You don't have to tell me twice," Jared whispered.

The Warrior studied the light ahead, puzzled. There seemed to be a large, squarish object, a boulder perhaps, interposed between the light and the lake. A faint halo outlined a portion of the object.

A twig snapped to his left.

Samson scrutinized the trees, pondering. The insects wouldn't have ceased droning unless there was something in the forest. The things in the lake wouldn't bother the insects at all. Unless, of course, the creatures in the lake were also in the forest. Or, conceivably, there might be two menaces, one in the water, the other skulking in the woods. Which meant walking along the shore qualified as being caught between the proverbial rock and a hard place. But he had no choice. He'd already wasted too much time. It was imperative he find Blade right away.

They proceeded along the western shore until they were 40 yards from the indistinct glow.

"I saw something," Betty unexpectedly declared.

Samson stopped and glanced at her. "Where?"

"In the trees," Betty replied. "I don't know what it was."

Samson wondered if her overwrought nerves explained her sighting. He decided to give her the benefit of the doubt. "If you see anything else, let me know."

"Will do."

The Warrior hiked faster. He wasn't about to dispute her and cause her to regress when she was beginning to snap out of her befuddled state. The incident with the creature must have startled her enough to bring her back to her senses.

In short order they came to a field.

His eyes narrowing in perplexity, Samson studied the odd object now 20 yards distant, bothered by a feeling he should know what it was. And in five strides he did.

It was the SEAL.

How could he have been so stupid? Samson asked himself. He knew Blade had driven to the lake in the transport. Visible above and beyond the vehicle was the Founder's cabin, a sturdy log structure, the front faintly illuminated by a light source inside that streamed through the windows and reflected off the SEAL.

Samson slowed, extra wary now. There was no hint of movement within the cabin. There weren't any shadows playing across the glass panes. And he doubted that Blade's family would have retired so early.

The Nazarite dreaded to open the door. He feared the worst, feared that the delays had prevented him from reaching the scene in time to save his friend. With the Bushmaster Auto Rifle leveled, he approached the cabin, skirting the front end of the SEAL. He tried the transport's door, which turned out to be locked.

"Keep watch," Samson commanded the others.

"You want us to stay out here?" Jared whispered in response.

"Yes."

"I was afraid you'd say that," Jared muttered.

Samson tested the doorknob, and was surprised to discover it unlocked. He twisted the knob and shoved, leaning against the jamb as the door opened. "Blade?" he called. "Jenny? Gabe? Are you here?" When no reply was forthcoming, he glided across the living room to a kitchenette, then gazed into a neat bedroom. The cabin was vacant. He noticed a livingroom window had been completely shattered. He glanced at the flickering lantern, debating his next move.

Jared suddenly cried out frantically. "Samson! Get out here!"

The Warrior grabbed the lantern by the handle and dashed outside to find the three of them standing near the transport's grill and staring into the field. "What is it?" he asked, joining them.

Jared appeared to be almost in shock. He simply nodded. Samson faced the field and felt his skin crawl.

Dozens of greenish-blue horrors with bulbous eyes and long tails were converging on the cabin, advancing slowly, walking erect. Those in the foremost ranks raised their hands over their eyes as the lantern light bathed them.

"What are they?" Tammy asked needlessly of no one in particular, her voice wavering fearfully.

"Mutants," Samson said, scrutinizing the creatures closely. "Amphibians of some sort would be my guess." The things were 15 feet off. He elevated the lantern for a better look.

And a strange thing happened.

The nearest creatures stopped and twisted their heads away from the light, then came on again walking sideways.

"They don't like the light," Samson instantly deduced.

"Let's set the cabin on fire," Jared suggested.

"Be serious," Samson admonished him.

"I was."

"What do you think they want?" Betty asked in a hushed, dazed tone.

"That should be obvious," Tammy said.

"What do we do?" Jared inquired, sounding petrified.

"We call on the Lord for deliverance," Samson stated calmly.

Betty unexpectedly tittered inanely. "While we're at it, why don't we call on the Tooth Fairy? God doesn't care if we live or die. God doesn't care if we suffer."

"You're wrong," Samson said, his eyes on the amphibians.

"Am I? Look at what happened to Lloyd!" Betty snapped, her tone brittle. "Why didn't God save him? Why didn't God spare me the anguish of a life without my husband? I'll tell you why!"

Samson fingered the trigger on his Auto Rifle, trying to concentrate on the tightening ring of mutations. Their appearance had evidently set Betty off again. She needed attention, needed comforting, but he couldn't allow himself to be distracted when they were about to be attacked.

"Better yet, I'll show you!" Betty cried, her voice breaking.

Before Samson or the others could stop her, Betty walked rapidly toward the mutations.

"Betty!" Tammy shouted. "Don't!"

Samson went after her, but he took only a few strides before Betty glanced over her left shoulder, saw him coming, and ran up to the nearest amphibian.

"Betty!" Jared yelled.

The Warrior started to step to the right. He wanted a clear shot at the mutation, which stood within two feet of Betty, its body sideways, staring at her through its spread fingers. "Betty, get back here," he ordered.

"No!" Betty responded. "I'll show you. I'll prove I'm right." She held her rifle level at her waist. Slowly, smiling all the while, she lowered the barrel and extended her right hand to the creature in a friendly gesture. "Hi," she said. "We don't want to harm you."

"Don't!" Tammy exclaimed.

For several breathless seconds nothing happened. The mutations had halted and were watching their fellow, who stood stock still and regarded Betty coldly.

Samson took another cautious stride. Another few inches and he would be able to get off a shot.

Laughing lightly, Betty looked back. "Well, what do you know. I guess I was wrong."

The creature was on her in the twinkling of an eye, its hands clamping on the sides of her head and twisting.

They all heard her spine snap.

"No!" Samson roared, and took three full steps. He squeezed the trigger, gripping the weapon firmly in his right hand to absorb the recoil, and sent six rounds into the lead mutant. The slugs doubled it in half, the impact tearing the thing away from Betty and flinging it to the earth.

Without the amphibian's arms to support her, Betty sank down, her eyes gazing lifelessly at the stars.

Jared and Tammy opened up, their rifles booming.

The Warrior backpedaled, sweeping the Auto Rifle in a half circle, firing a sustained burst. The high-velocity bullets punctured torso after torso, flinging seven of the abominations into the weeds.

Hissing in concert, the rest of the mutations charged. A few dropped to all fours and skittered forward lizard like.

Samson saw an onrushing amphibian, its body held low to the ground, streaking toward him out of the night. He aimed the Bushmaster, leading the creature by a few yards, and fired. The rounds hit the thing in the head and flipped it over.

On all sides the mutations were steadily advancing.

Jared and Tammy expended the ammunition in their rifles and drew their revolvers.

The Warrior came to the front of the SEAL and motioned with the lantern at the cabin. "Inside! Get indoors! We stand a better chance in there!"

They hastily retreated into the cabin and Jared slammed the door shut. "Now what?" he asked. "They have us trapped in here."

"But they can't all get to us at once," Samson said, moving to the counter and depositing the lantern.

"Look!" Tammy cried.

Amphibian faces were peering in at every window, including the open livingroom window, dozens of them, regarding the humans balefully, their mouths thin slits.

"They give me the creeps," Jared muttered. He threw the bolt on the door. "Mutants always do."

"Maybe they won't come in," Tammy said hopefully.

"Reload your rifles," Samson directed them, and stepped to the bedroom doorway. He saw more mutations staring in at the bedroom window.

The cabin was completely surrounded.

"What's that vehicle outside?" Jared asked while feeding cartridges into his Marlin.

"It's called the SEAL. Blade drove it to the lake," Samson

answered.

"Any chance of us getting inside and driving off?"

"No," Samson replied. He began refilling the Auto Rifle's magazine, working swiftly.

"Why not?"

"I don't have the keys," Samson said, his fingers flying.

"Figures," Jared declared. "The way our luck has been running, I'm surprised those things don't try and come in."

A resounding crash came from the bedroom.

Samson whirled, his features hardening at the sight of a mutant using a tree limb to smash the glass out of the bedroom window. He slapped the full magazine into the Bushmaster, took four steps into the room, and let the amphibians framed by the window have it, pouring a withering hail of lead into their bodies.

The creatures jerked and thrashed as they were struck, and four of them dropped on the spot, one sprawling over the windowsill, his arms dangling down.

More crashing arose in the living room, the sound of glass breaking and tinkling to the floor. Then gunshots.

"Samson!" Tammy screamed.

The Warrior darted to the doorway, dreading the worst and confirming his fear.

Amphibians had broken the remaining living room window and were through all the windows attempting to clamber inside, hissing vociferously, as if they were a nest of vipers. Other mutations were battering on the front door.

Jared and Tammy were shooting as fast as they could, but there were too many windows to cover, too many creatures outside pressing to get it, for them to stop them all.

Samson aimed at the west window, at a mutation perched on the sill and about to jump to the floor, and fired from the hip. His rounds slammed into the creature's head and neck and hurtled it into its comrades outside. A thumping noise behind him made the Warrior spin, and there were two amphibians already in the bedroom and springing toward him with their maws wide. He cut loose at almost point-blank range, his slugs nearly tearing them in half.

More were coming in the bedroom window.

A pair of the creatures vaulted through the west window.

And the front door suddenly snapped from its hinges and tilted at a steep angle for a moment before thudding onto the rug, narrowly missing Jared and Tammy.

The amphibians poured into the cabin.

CHAPTER TWENTY

Blade spied the gray expanse of the surface 15 feet above him, arched his back, and kicked his legs furiously, pumping with all his strength. He could feel Gabe's arms around his neck and the tension in his son's body. The fingers of his right hand were interlaced with Jenny's left hand. He flicked his eyes right and left, on the lookout for the salamanders. If the mutations assaulted them now, when they were in the open, underwater, and he had his hands full, their escape would be doomed. They were vulnerable in the water.

A dark form materialized a few feet above him.

Blade stiffened and slowed, prepared to give his own life, if necessary, so his loved ones could flee. But his sacrifice wasn't needed; the form belonged to a large fish. He watched it swim lazily to the east, then resumed his ascent.

Where were the salamanders?

He broke the surface seconds later and gasped, then lifted Gabe out of the water and hauled on Jenny's arm, adding the power in his arm to her momentum so she could reach the surface that much sooner. Her head and shoulders shot out of the lake and she breathed in the cool night air noisily.

Gabe coughed and clung to his father.

"We did it!" Jenny said, elated.

"But we're not out of the woods yet," Blade reminded her. He glanced at the rather steep bank rimming the water at that point, less than ten feet away, and paddled toward land.

Jenny released his hand and swam alongside him. "Are you okay, Gabe?" she asked.

"Yep," the boy replied, then added, "What's all that noise?"

Blade heard the sounds too, the unmistakable blasting of gunfire, an automatic and rifles firing repeatedly. To his amazement, the gunfire seemed to be coming from the direction of the cabin.

"What's going on?" Jenny queried.

"I don't know," Blade told her. He came to the bank and halted, debating whether to try and scale the embankment or to swim to the north where the ground formed the level shoreline he'd fished from. Since he was averse to remaining in the water any longer than was absolutely essential, he opted to climb the bank.

A stout bush, its silhouette an inky outline against the edge of the bank, promised to be the means of their salvation.

Blade estimated the bush to be five feet overhead. He girded his muscles, hunched his shoulders, and surged upward, his right arm fully extended. His fingers hooked onto a branch at the base and held firm. "I'm going to put you down," Blade advised his son, and pulled himself to within a foot of the top. His left arm uncurled and he placed Gabe on the rim. "Don't slip," he said.

"Don't worry. I won't," Gabe replied.

"And now it's your turn," Blade informed Jenny. He locked his right hand on the bush.

"What do you want me to do? I can't reach the top from here," Jenny said, doing the dog paddle.

"Climb up over me," Blade instructed her.

"That bush will never hold my weight."

"We won't know until you try, and we can't stay like this all night," Blade prompted her. "Give it a try."

Jenny snatched at the back of his belt and began to climb, shimmying up him as if he was a sapling.

Blade grunted and clenched his hands tightly. Her knees gouged into his back, then his shoulders, and with a little push of her arms she succeeded in grabbing the edge of the bank. She pulled herself up and rolled onto the grass.

"Made it!"

The Warrior hoisted himself onto the bank and rested for several seconds flat on his stomach, listening to the battle royal transpiring to the north.

Gabe was staring at the cabin. "Golly! Those things are trying to get inside."

Blade rose to his knees, dripping wet and feeling the chills again, and gazed at the eerie scene. He distinguished many amphibian figures moving about the Founder's retreat, their distinctive shapes discernible in the dim light coming through the windows and the door. Now he knew why there hadn't been any in the lake. They were all at the cabin.

But why?

Who was inside?

"You two stay put. I've got to go see what's happening," Blade said.

"You're not leaving us here alone," Jenny responded.

"Yeah," Gabe added.

"I can't agrue. Someone needs my help."

"It could be scavengers," Jenny stated.

"It could be friends," Blade countered.

"Don't leave us, Dad," Gabe requested. "What if there are some of those things out here?"

The Warrior glanced at the cabin, then at the woods. "I have an idea," he said, and took them by the hand. "Come on." He led them to the trees, searching for the one he wanted.

"What are you doing?" Jenny inquired.

"You need to be somewhere safe while I'm gone," Blade responded, and halted at the base of a towering deciduous tree.

A thick limb hung within easy reach. "Here we go."

"Up a tree?" Jenny asked in disbelief.

"I doubt those things are arboreal. Their bodies are probably too slippery for them to be good climbers," Blade replied. He placed his hands under Gabe's arms and swung his son onto the limb. "Hold on tight."

Gabe wrapped his arms and legs around the branch. "I won't fall," he assured them.

"Your turn," Blade said, facing Jenny.

"Promise me you'll be careful."

"Aren't I always?" Blade quipped. He stepped behind her, took hold of her at the waist, and heaved.

She nearly overshot the limb, catching it at the last instant and clinging for dear life. "Were you trying to put me on the moon?"

"The moon isn't out tonight," Blade said, grinning. "Climb as high as you can and don't come down until I return. If a salamander tries to climb up after you, scream your lungs out and kick it in the head if it gets too close."

"Don't take too long," Jenny urged.

"Try not to fall asleep," Blade joked, and raced to the north before he could change his mind. He didn't want to leave them, but he had to see who was in the cabin. As he sprinted, he heard the sound of breaking glass.

The mutations must be knocking out the windows!

He grit his teeth and ran all out, hoping he wouldn't trip in the dark and injure himself. A dull ache throbbed in his abdomen and his forehead seemed to be on fire. Otherwise, he felt fine.

Gunshots thundered in the cabin.

Someone was putting up a hell of a fight. He hoped the mutations wouldn't slay them all before he got there. His trained ear realized the rifles had fallen silent. Only the automatic continued to fire, and moments later it too ceased.

A woman screamed.

Blade reached the field and stopped to get his bearings. Dozens of amphibians were milling about the cabin, and there were undoubtedly more within. He crouched and drew his Bowies, waiting to learn if there was anyone left alive to help.

There was.

The salamanders tramped out of the cabin in groups. The first group carried a struggling woman. The second had a man in their arms, holding him aloft as they rounded the front of the SEAL.

Blade heard a commotion, and then the third group appeared. But they weren't carrying a prisoner. They were swarming around a massive man, a veritable colossus, striving frantically to bring him down, striking and biting in a frenzy. But they might as well have been striking a rock. The man barreled out the door with salamanders hanging from his neck, salamanders hanging from his shoulders, and salamanders clutching at his waist. His malletlike fists pounded right and left, always in motion, knocking the mutations aside as targets presented themselves. The thud-thud-thud of his stony knuckles making contact with amphibian heads resembled the beating of a drum. For every three creatures the man struck, one never rose again. The awesome power in those brawny arms was keeping the salamanders at bay.

Blade's eyes narrowed as the swirling melee came through the door and the man's features were profiled by the light. Astonishment rippled through him on the heels of recognition, and he straightened, gripping the Bowies. The man battling so valiantly was Samson! Blade sprinted toward the cabin. He didn't know how Samson had gotten there, or why, but all such considerations were irrelevant. All that mattered was that a brother Warrior needed his aid. One of *his* Warriors was in trouble, and no force on earth would prevent him from going to Samson's aid.

The first and second groups of amphibians had halted, bearing their prisoners in their arms, and were gazing back at the clash between Samson and their fellows.

Blade realized that Samson was trying to reach the man and woman. He saw Samson and the horde of amphibians come around the front of the SEAL, and affection and pride welled within him. No Warrior had ever acquitted himself more honorably than Samson was doing at that very moment, and Blade intended to ensure that his friend's herculean efforts weren't in vain. He raced past the first two groups, who were so engrossed in the fight that they hadn't seen him coming, and waded into the thick of the conflict.

"Samson!" Blade shouted, and swung the Bowies right and left, slicing into the mutations with a fierce passion, relishing the combat. At last he was able to vent his wrath, and vent it he did, cutting and slashing and stabbing, slitting throats and splitting skulls and severing limbs in a savage exhibition of primal ferocity. The mutants attempting to overwhelm Samson were taken unaware by Blade's onslaught, and over a dozen were dead before the rest awakened to his presence. Some turned on him while the others focused on Samson, and both Warriors were nearly buried under a living wall of amphibian flesh.

Still Blade and Samson fought on, Blade ripping the creatures open with his flashing knives, Samson delivering punch after punch. Convulsing bodies littered the ground.

The group holding Tammy abruptly released her, letting her fall, and entered the fray.

Blade buried his right Bowie in an amphibian's eye, then planted his left in the neck of a creature trying to take a bite out of his leg. He shook a salamander off his shoulders and whirled, the Bowies arcing downward, cleaving the face of a foe to his rear. Always in motion, he pivoted and lanced a hissing monstrosity, then rotated and rent a leaping mutant from its throat to the middle of its chest. Moments later, while evading a lunging salamander, his back bumped into something. Expecting it to be a mutation, he started to turn, and instead found himself back-to-back with Samson, who glanced at him and grinned.

They renewed their struggle; only now they refused to be budged, standing firmly in position, each Warrior dealing with those amphibians that came within his line of vision.

Held in the grip of a dozen salamanders, Jared craned his

neck and gaped at the slaughter. He had never imagined two human beings could be capable of wreaking such carnage. Without warning, the mutations holding him simply let go. He toppled to the ground, landing hard on his right side, and pushed to his knees. The salamanders ignored him. They were piling into the fray.

Undaunted by the increase in the odds against them, Blade and Samson continued to flail away. The head Warrior gutted one of his bestial adversaries, while Samson caved in the skull of another with a blow from his left fist.

A hand touched Jared's right shoulder and he almost shrieked in terror.

"We've got to do something!" Tammy declared, crouching next to him.

"What?" Jared responded, relief flooding through him.

"Something! Anything!"

"All our guns are in the cabin," Jared stated. "Even if we get them, we can't shoot because we might hit the Warriors."

"Then what can we do?"

"Pray they win," Jared replied. And suddenly he thought of something he *could* do. It might not be much, but it was worth a try. "Stay here," he shouted, and ran to the west, bypassing the battle and the SEAL. Amphibian corpses dotted the space between the cabin and the van, and he had to step gingerly over them before reaching the doorway. Heaps of dead lay on the floor. He dodged around and over the mutations, hurrying to the counter. His right hand closed on the handle of the implement that might turn the tide: the lantern.

Jared hastened out, going to the front of the SEAL this time, raising the lantern to illuminate the spectacle.

Blade and Samson were still back-to-back, two pillars of power surrounded by bloodthirsty genetic deviates, slashing and slugging with lethal precision. Dead or dying mutations were everywhere. Fifteen to 20 of the creatures were pressing their attack as vigorously as ever.

Fatigue was beginning to slow Blade's reflexes when the

bright lantern light lit up the immediate vicinity. Several of the amphibians automatically stepped back and covered their eyes, and Blade took advantage of their weakness to strike out with the Bowies and split them open. He saw the remaining creatures start to back away and risked a look at Samson.

Just then the Nazarite broke momentarily free from the encircling deviates and his hands dropped to his Bushmaster Auto Pistols. Denied the opportunity to employ them earlier because of the mutations swarming over him and the press of combat, he now swiveled both barrels and fired, mowing down the creatures in front of him. He spotted Jared near the SEAL and scrupulously avoided shooting in that direction.

The rest of the salamanders bolted.

Samson went after them, shooting on the run, slaying every amphibian he saw.

"Kill them! Kill them!" Tammy yelled.

Blade took a deep breath and observed Samson's pursuit of the creatures. He wanted to join his friend, but his forehead was scorching and his arms and legs felt leaden. A weary sigh issued from his lips and his arms dropped to his sides.

Jared walked up to the giant. "Are you okay?"

"I don't think I need to worry about exercising for a few days," Blade said softly.

"Where's your family?"

"They're safe," Blade said.

"Thank God."

"Yes," Blade said, and glanced at the man. "Thanks for bringing the lantern."

"It was the least I could do."

Blade stared at the lake. Samson had crossed the field, shooting salamander after salamander, and was visible at the edge of the water, firing into the lake. "I intend to come back here soon and make sure all of those things have been wiped out," he mentioned.

"Don't forget to bring Samson along."

"I won't," Blade said, and grinned. "And maybe a couple of the other Warriors. Yama—"

"Yama?" Jared repeated. "Is he as big as you are?"

Blade looked at him. "No."

"Really?" Jared said, sounding delighted at the news.

"Really," Blade confirmed. "Yama is a little smaller than me. He's about the size of Samson."

Jared made a snorting noise. "I knew it," he stated morosely.

"What's wrong?"

"Nothing."

"Are you still looking forward to living at the Home?"

"Yeah," Jared responded, and looked at the stacks of dead covering the ground, then at the Warrior near the lake, and finally at Blade. "But I'm going to feel like such a wimp."

EPILOGUE

'I hear the Healers have given you permission to be up and around.''

En route to his cabin from the armory, Blade turned at the sound of his mentor's kindly voice and smiled. "Hello, Plato."

"I also hear you're leaving tomorrow with Samson, Yama, and Sundance to exterminate any remaining salamanders," Plato said as he came alongside the Warrior.

"Yeah. I'm going to let them do all the hard work."

"I'm truly sorry your vacation turned into a fiasco," Plato stated. "Had I been aware there were mutations inhabiting the lake, I wouldn't have suggested the idea of going there."

"Don't blame yourself. I should have known better. I've seen more of the world than most of the Family," Blade said. "I just wanted to get away from it all. I wanted to make Jenny happy."

"How is she, by the way?"

"Fine. She's decided we'll stay at the Home the next time we want to be alone," Blade replied. "She's learned a valuable lesson the hard way. There's no place like home."

Plato grinned at the bad pun. "And how is Gabe?"

"As rambunctious as ever. The experience has matured him, which is to be expected. I was worried, though, that he'd lose his childhood innocence, his wonder at the world, but he hasn't."

"Children are often more resilient than we give them credit for being," Plato remarked.

"He isn't very fond of salamanders anymore," Blade noted.

They both laughed.

"I've been meaning to ask you a question," Plato mentioned.

"What about?"

"The new couple we admitted to the Family."

"Jared and Tammy? What about them? They're a loving, caring couple, ideal candidates for living here. Samson and I both felt that way or we wouldn't have recommended them," Blade said.

"They're assimilating into the Family quite nicely," Plato agreed.

"What's your question?"

"It concerns Jared. Do you remember the day you arrived back at the Home?"

Blade chuckled. "That was only ten days ago."

"Then you should readily recall Jared's reaction."

"How do you mean?"

"I was near the drawbridge when you returned. I saw all of you climb out of the SEAL while the Family gathered around, and I couldn't help but notice a most peculiar expression on Jared."

Blade placed his right hand over his mouth so Plato couldn't see his grin. He'd talked to Samson about Jared and knew what was coming. "So?"

"So why did he start hugging everyone in sight and keep yelling, 'Midgets! Midgets! Midgets!'?"

DEVIL STRIKE

Dedicated to...
Judy, Joshua, and Shane.
To Sue and Mary and all the fine folks at Golden Gull.
And to Barney, who is warming my lap and purring
even as I type this: Where's a gas mask when I need
one?

PROLOGUE

What were all those vultures doing there?

Horace Greeley applied the brakes and gazed out the windshield, his brown eyes riveted on the dozen or so vultures circling high in the air less than a quarter of a mile away. By his estimation, the vultures were soaring above Jacumba. He thought of the town's population, 63 men, women, and children, and dread seized him.

The presence of vultures could only mean one thing!

Alarmed, Horace floored the accelerator, and the old green jeep jumped forward, its engine coughing. Black puffs of smoke trailed from the tail pipe. He glanced at the loaded Taurus Model 83 on the seat beside him, and wished he had a more powerful handgun than a .38 Special. If worst came to worst, he'd need all the firepower he could muster.

The jeep rounded a curve, and there lay the quaint, tranquil community, sweltering in the intense July heat. Not a soul was in sight.

Horace kept the jeep under ten miles an hour as he approached the outskirts of the town. Even on such a hot day, he reasoned, there should be folks strolling about and kids at play. He wondered if he should make a U-turn and head for help, but decided he needed concrete proof before he could alert the authorities. Vultures were an ominous omen, to be sure, but a slim possibility existed that there might be a perfectly logical explanation for the presence of the carrion-eaters.

Several of the big, ugly birds sank lower and lower and disappeared below the rooftops.

Horace slowed when he came within a hundred yards of the westernmost structures, his anxiety mounting. He might be biting off more than he could chew, he told himself. After all, he made his living as a carpenter, not a policeman or a soldier. He'd served a two-year stint in the Free State of California Army, but his enlistment had occurred 29 years ago, when he was 18.

More of the vultures were sinking to the ground, apparently in the center of Jacumba.

His palms sweating, his mouth dry, Horace stopped 40 yards outside of the town and surveyed the buildings. Most were in need of a paint job. Roofs sagged, windows were missing, and walls were cracked. The dilapidated state of the town typified the conditions found in practically every community located in extreme southern California 106 years after World War Three. Paint, nails, lumber, and especially glass were all hard to come by. The people had to make do as best they could.

A huge white dog, four feet high at the shoulders, materialized between two houses and stared at the jeep.

Horace leaned out the window and waved at the dog. "Hi, there, fella," he called out.

The white dog stood motionless, regarding him coldly.

"Where's your master?" Horace asked.

With a curt bark the dog wheeled and ran off.

"Wait," Horace urged, but the canine ignored him and bounded around the corner of a green house. Horace drove slowly forward, scanning the road and the sidewalks ahead. At the very edge of Jacumba he slammed on the brake pedal.

Son of a bitch!

Sprawled across the sidewalk on the north side of the highway, 30 feet off, partially hidden by a metal trash can on the curb, lay a body, a woman in blue pants and a green blouse.

Horace licked his lips and felt his pulse quicken. Any lingering doubt that a calamity had befallen the town were gone. He could haul butt to the authorities now. He could turn around and retrace his route, head east until he reached Ocotillo, where the Army maintained a garrison. He could, but he didn't.

He wanted to know the answer.

Overcome with curiosity, Horace continued into the town. He stopped alongside the trash can and leaned to the right to stare at the woman. She was prone, her arms outflung, and her forehead rested in a pool of her own blood. Her black hair sagged over her cheeks, screening her features from view. He debated whether to climb out of the jeep and check the corpse, to see if the body was still warm or whether the woman had been dead for hours. Prudence prompted him to stay in the vehicle.

He might be curious, but he wasn't stupid.

Horace squared his shoulders and drove further into Jacumba. He saw more bodies the further he went. Men, women, and even children dotted lawns, driveways, sidewalks, streets, and alleys. Victims were lying in stores and other buildings, visible in the doorways or on the other side of shattered windows. The business establishments had been looted, and discarded merchandise littered the ground.

Raiders maybe?

Whoever had attacked Jacumba had done a swift, thorough job, sweeping through the town before an effective opposition could be mounted. Here and there were indications that a few of the residents had tried to put up a fight. In front of a hardware store near the center of the town a makeshift barricade had been hastily erected, and eight defenders had died on the spot. Further on, a police car had been doused with gasoline and torched, and the smoldering wreck partly blocked the highway on the south side.

Horace skirted the patrol car, staring at the black lettering still readable on the front door on the passenger side. JACUMBA POLICE. SERVICE AND DEDICATION. Near the car, on his back, his arms above his head and handcuffed at the wrists, was a police officer. His legs had been chopped off below the knees, and blood still trickled from the stumps. A red sea enveloped him.

Dear Lord!

Shocked by the atrocity, Horace began to drive past the officer when the impossible occurred.

The policeman's eyes flicked open, he glanced at the jeep,

and his mouth moved soundlessly.

"Damn!" Horace exclaimed, and he halted on the spot. He shifted into park, slid out, and took two strides. His right shoe stepped into the pond of blood and he hesitated, horrified.

"Please," the police officer croaked.

Suppressing his loathing, Horace moved to the officer's side and crouched. "What can I do? I don't know what to do," he blurted out.

"Doesn't matter," responded the policeman, a young man in his twenties with brown eyes and hair. His pale complexion gave him a ghostly aspect.

"I can go for a doctor," Horace offered.

The officer groaned softly. "No time. Nearest doctor is in Mountain Spring. Never make it."

"Oh, God. I wish there was something I could do," Horace said, feeling supremely helpless.

"Can you get word to my parents in L.A.?"

"Anything. Anything at all."

"Merrill and Edith Garforth," the officer said. "Balboa Boulevard. Give them my love."

"I will," Horace pledged, and nodded vigorously. He glanced down at the stumps, at the blood seeping from the severed veins and arteries, and realized with a start that the rest of the man's legs were missing. From the knees to the feet, both were gone.

As if the officer could read Horace's mind, he said, "The dog drug them off."

"The dog?" Horace repeated, stunned.

"The bastard's white dog."

The white dog! A shiver tingled along Horace's spine. "Who did this to you? Who attacked Jacumba?"

A severe coughing fit racked the officer before he could reply. Blood-flecked spittle dribbled from the corners of his mouth. When the fit subsided he closed his eyes and breathed shallowly.

"Garforth?" Horace said, and touched the policeman's right cheek. The man seemed to be on fire. "Damn it all," he muttered, realizing the officer wouldn't last too much longer. Garforth had lost too much blood.

So what should he do?

Horace gazed to the west and spied a large concentration of

bodies at the very heart of Jacumba, evidently where the citizens had made their last stand. As he scrutinized the carnage a peculiar fact became obvious.

All of the vehicles were missing.

He straightened, scanning the street. Why hadn't he noticed it earlier? He'd been through the town on previous occasions, and he knew at least 15 residents had owned either a car or a truck. Except for the squad car they were all gone. Where to? Had the raiders taken the vehicles? He looked at Garforth, mulling what to do.

Something growled.

Horace swiveled to the left, in the direction of the sound, his eyes widening in fear when he saw the white dog less than 20 feet distant, eyeing him balefully, its lips curled up over its glistening fangs. He could see the animal's face clearly, and he shuddered as he perceived the dog's left eye was missing. A discolored, shriveled socket existed in its place, heightening the aura of menace the dog radiated.

The canine growled again.

Stark panic welled up within Horace and he stood frozen in place. He wanted to make a break for the jeep, but he couldn't get his limbs to cooperate with his brain.

The white dog took a stride toward him.

"Run. Don't let the mongrel get you."

Horace glanced at the officer, surprised to find Garforth awake and alert. "I have a gun in my jeep," he said.

"Go for it," the officer stated.

Horace looked at the dog, then at the policeman. "I'll carry you to the jeep."

"Forget me."

"I can't just leave you lying there."

"You don't have any choice," Garforth said weakly. "I'm done for anyway. Save yourself."

"No," Horace responded, amazed at his own obstinacy. He'd served as a clerk in the Army and had never seen a day of combat. The prospect of tangling with the huge dog terrified him.

"Please," Garforth urged, and coughed. "Don't put your life on the line for me. I'll be dead within a half hour."

"I don't—," Horace began. He stiffened when the white dog stalked slowly forward.

"Please," Garforth reiterated. "I failed the people I was sworn to protect. I don't want to have your life on my hands too." He paused. "Please."

For a moment Horace wavered, torn between his fear of the dog and his desire to aid the officer. He knew he wouldn't stand a prayer against the dog without a weapon, but he couldn't bring himself to desert another human being in a time of need. His resolve, however, evaporated the next instant.

The white dog charged.

Pivoting, Horace ran for the jeep, his gaze locked on the onrushing canine. Although the dog had almost 20 feet to cover and Horace only eight, the canine streaked with the speed of an arrow while Horace seemed to be plodding along in slow motion. He expected to feel those viselike jaws clamp on him at any second, and they would have if not for Officer Garforth's bravery.

Rallying all of his rapidly fading strength, Garforth lifted his head and arms and bellowed at the dog, "Try me, you prick! Try me!"

Uttering a feral snarl, the dog swerved, going for the policeman.

Horace reached the jeep and glanced over his right shoulder just as the white dog pounced on the officer. His hand closed on the steering wheel at the same second the dog's sharp teeth closed on Garforth's throat. Mesmerized, Horace saw the officer's flesh rip apart as if the skin was no more than soggy paper.

Garforth voiced a strangled, raspy scream.

The dog snarled.

And Horace clambered into the jeep and slammed the door shut. He simply sat there, quaking, watching the animal vent its primal fury by shaking its head from side to side, ravaging Garforth's neck. The officer's eyes swung toward the jeep, and only then did Horace remember his gun. He grabbed the revolver and pointed the handgun at the dog, reluctant to squeeze the trigger because he might hit the policeman. Instead, he elevated the barrel and fired at a business across the street.

The shot galvanized the canine into action. It whirled and dashed off, making for a nearby alley.

Horace tried to get a bead on the racing beast, but he wasn't a marksman and the dog reached the safety of the alley before he could fire again. Disappointed at his performance, he climbed out and hurried to Garforth.

He needn't have bothered.

The white dog had torn the flesh wide open from the base of the officer's jaw to the bottom of his throat. Jagged strips of flesh rimmed the wound. Garforth's lifeless eyes stared blankly at the heavens.

"Dear God," Horace said softly in dismay. He backed to his jeep, unable to tear his gaze from Garforth. He'd heard stories about the vile atrocities committed by raiders, scavengers, and occasional packs of mutations, but he'd never witnessed the aftermath of a raid firsthand. He knew about the dangers associated with living and traveling along the California-Mexico border, about the riffraff and degenerates who dwelt south of the border and who conducted periodic forays to the north—which was the reason he carried the gun in his jeep. And he'd seen his share of victims, usually lone men or women caught by one of the variety of wild mutants so prevalent since the war, and invariably well after the fact, at their funeral. Never, though, had he beheld a sight as ghastly as the white dog killing Garforth.

The dog!

Horace halted beside the jeep and nervously surveyed the town. If the dog hadn't left, did that mean there could be raiders somewhere in Jacumba? The thought caused him to shiver in terror. He quickly got in and rode westward. Several hundred yards from his position towered a series of poles connected by cables or heavy gauge wires, and it took a few seconds for his dazed mind to recognize the poles and wires as belonging to a telephone system.

World War Three had effectively disrupted all types of mass communications, and virtually destroyed every major public utility in the country. The Free State of California, one of the few states to retain its administrative identity after the war, had restored marginal service to its major urban centers such as Los

Angeles and San Francisco, but the phone lines in rural area were few and far between. Subscribers had to contend with poo service and constant problems. Subscribers also had to b financially well-off, because the cost of phone service was luxury most postwar rural families could not afford.

Horace wondered if the phones in Jacumba still worked, o whether the raiders had cut the lines outside of town to preven the residents from phoning for help. He decided to follow th wires and locate a phone. By staying in the town he riske capture or worse if the raiders were still about, but he coul shave hours off the time a rescue team would take to get ther if a single telephone operated properly. There might be residen who were injured seriously but still alive, and the sooner he got there to assist them, the better. Up ahead vultures flappe skyward.

He came to the very center of Jacumba, where a small tow square and a park, once the gathering place for the peacef inhabitants, had been transformed into a site of unbridle butchery and bloodshed. Bodies were everywhere. Many of th women had been stripped naked and abused. Puddles of bloo shimmered red in the bright sunlight.

Horace stopped, his stomach queasy. He stepped to the aspha and pressed his arms to his abdomen, afraid he would lose h breakfast. He stared at a woman who had been shot in th forehead at point-blank range, and felt bile rise in his mout His gaze shifted to a man whose skull had been split in hal and gagged. Then he looked toward the park and saw the te stakes. His eyes narrowed as he tried to identify the objec impaled on the tops of the stakes. Thirty seconds later he di

And lost it.

CHAPTER ONE

How many would die this time?

The giant clasped his brawny hands behind his back and stared absently at the azure sky, reflecting on the sequence of events resulting in his return to California. Had it only been nine months ago that he'd decided to temporarily disband the Freedom Force? So much had happened in those nine months. He'd fought the Union, the Russians, the Chosen, and others. He'd attempted to come to terms with his dual responsibilities, with being the head of the Freedom Force and the top Warrior. But more important than all the battles and the emotional turmoil were the nine precious months he'd enjoyed with his wife and son. True, the periodic threats had intruded into their lives, had interfered with their happiness. Even with the dangers, he would always cherish the nine previous months as a special interlude during which he'd gotten to spend most of his days and nights with Jenny and Gabe.

He sighed and stretched, his seven-foot-tall frame rippling with raw power, his bulging muscles swelling in prominent relief. A black leather vest covered his broad torso. Green fatigue pants adorned his stout legs. On his feet he wore black combat boots. Strapped to his waist, one riding in a leather sheath on each hip, were two Bowie knifes, the weapons that had become, in a sense, his personal trademark. He brushed at the comma of dark hair hanging above his right eyebrow, his gray eyes focused on the ribbon of road leading to the south end of the Force facility.

The new volunteers were due any minute.

He frowned, thinking of the previous volunteers. The original idea, conceived of by the Freedom Federation leaders, had called for each of the seven factions comprising the Federation to send one volunteer to serve on the Force for a period of one year. In a ten-month span five volunteers had died.

Now they were going to give it another shot.

Worry assailed him, worry about the fate of the new recruits, and he suppressed his anxiety by turning his thoughts to the Freedom Federation. With most of the country, if not the entire world, plunged into barbaric savagery by the war, the Federation stood as humanity's best hope for a future free from tyranny. If humankind was ever to recover from the nuclear holocaust, if the despots, mutants, and assorted raiders were to be overthrown, then the Federation must stand firm in the face of overwhelming odds.

Of all the Federation factions, the Free State of California possessed the greatest military might. The state had sustained only two nuclear strikes during the war. March Air Force Base at San Bernardino and San Diego had both been obliterated. The prevailing winds in the upper atmosphere had blown most of the fallout away from other populated centers, which had allowed the Californians to recover reasonably quickly. After the United States government had collapsed, the leaders of California had reorganized the state into a sovereign entity. The state had seized all U.S. Army, Navy, Marine, and Air Force equipment and material within its borders, and promptly formed the Free State Army. Ever since, California had served as a beacon of progress in a world gone mad.

And California wasn't the only beacon of hope.

The second strongest faction was the Civilized Zone, the official title for the area embracing the former states of Nebraska, Kansas, Wyoming, Colorado, New Mexico, and Oklahoma and the northern half of Texas and part of Arizona. The U.S. government had evacuated hundreds of thousands of citizens into the region during the war. Denver, Colorado, had become the new national capital. But after the government fell part, a dictator had arisen who'd renamed the area the Civilized Zone to distinguish it from the Outlands, the primitive regions where a centralized government didn't exist, where the only law was the survival of the fittest.

The remaining Federation factions were considerably smaller and lacked the mechanized forces possessed by California and the Civilized Zone. In their own right, though, they were formidable adversaries.

In the former state of Montana the Flathead Indians had assumed control. Free, finally, from the yoke of the white man, the Flatheads were living as their ancestors had lived prior to the coming of the first explorers, and they were determined to never be subjugated again.

A tough legion of superb horsemen, the Cavalry, now ruled the Dakota Territory. Their lifestyle resembled that of the frontiersmen of old, and they were as fiercely independent.

In north-central Minnesota, in a subterranean city that had started as an underground fallout shelter and grown over the decades, resided the secretive Moles. Of all the Federation factions, they were the least reliable. The giant suspected that the Moles weren't entirely committed to the Federation. Why else would they have sent such an inept volunteer the last time?

The sixth faction definitely was committed. The Clan lived in the small town of Halma in northwestern Minnesota. Originally refugees from the Twin Cities, they had moved to Halma to be close to the last faction, the one to which the giant belonged.

The Family.

In a 30-acre survivalist compound constructed by a wealthy filmmaker named Kurt Carpenter shortly before World War Three, located on the outskirts of the former Lake Bronson State Park, dwelt the smallest member of the Federation, numerically—but the one with the most influence in Federation councils. The Family, as Carpenter had dubbed his followers, were renowned for their wise leadership and their fearless Warriors, the 18 Family members responsible for the defense of their compound, which was known as the Home. Thanks to the reputation the Warriors had established, the Federation leaders had approached the top Warrior with the offer to head the elite tactical unit they were forming to combat any threats to the Federation's existence.

"And if I'd had any sense," the giant reflected wryly, "I would have told them to take a flying leap off the nearest cliff." Because accepting their offer had turned his life topsy-turvy. Between the two jobs he seldom had time to devote to his wife and son, and the strain on his marriage had drained him emotionally. After losing three Force members within a few days of one another, he'd decided to disband the Freedom Force until after he set his personal life in order, until after he recovered from the ordeal.

Now here he was, about to stick his neck out again.

He must be a glutton for punishment.

The Warrior cocked his head, listening to the distant growl of vehicle engines. Soon, very soon, the jeeps bearing the six volunteers would arrive at the facility built especially for the Force. The governor of California, the man who had initially proposed creating the elite unit, had ordered the headquarters to be constructed north of Los Angeles, near Pyramid Lake. The Force compound encompassed 12 acres. An electrified fence, topped with barbed wire and patrolled by regular California Army troops, enclosed the perimeter. A small runway, a concrete pad 50 yards square which was used by the two VTOLs, occupied the southern sector. Next to the pad stood a hangar. In the middle of the compound were three concrete bunkers aligned in a straight line from east to west. The bunker to the east served as the barracks; the bunker in the center was the command HQ; and the bunker on the west contained supplies. To the north of the bunkers, to be used for training purposes, the land had been preserved in its natural state. A gate situated in the center of the south fence afforded access to the installation.

The noise of the approaching vehicles grew louder.

How many would die this time? the giant asked himself again. He hoped, he prayed, the volunteers would all be competent fighters who would tolerate the discipline he had to impose. The last time around, several of the recruits had given him nothing but trouble.

He thought of his beloved Jenny and young Gabe, and he

anticipated his trip to the Home in two weeks with relish. Gazing to the south, he spotted one of the VTOLs resting on the concrete pad. If not for the two extraordinary aircraft, his monthly visits to the Family would be impossible. Actually, without the VTOLs the Freedom Force itself wouldn't be able to operate. The two jet aircraft were the pride of the California military. Modified so they could carry five passengers and the pilot, and outfitted with extra fuel tanks to extend their range, the jets were used to transport the Force to hot spots. Thanks to their vertical-takeoff-and-landing capability, the VTOLs did not require the lengthy runways utilized by conventional aircraft. The VTOLs could land and take off like helicopters, yet fly with the supersonic speed of a jet.

The giant ended his reflection and placed his hands on his hips. He glanced over his right shoulder at the command bunker, ten feet to his rear, then faced front.

Three jeeps were rapidly approaching.

He remembered the five Force members who had died in the line of duty. Spader, Kraft, Sergeant Havoc, Thunder-Rolling-in-the-Mountain, and Athena Morris had lost their lives so that others might live. Despite the individual shortcomings of a few of them, they had served with distinction when the chips were down.

The three jeeps angled toward the HQ and slowed. A stocky officer seated in the first jeep, in the passenger seat in the front, saw the giant and waved.

The herculean figure nodded in response. General Miles Gallagher didn't qualify as one of his favorite people. A bulldog of a man with brown eyes and crew-cut brown hair, noted for his tenacity and popularity with those under his command, the general had vigorously opposed the formation of the Force. Gallagher had asserted that California could take care of its own problems, that the Force wasn't necessary, but he was too good a soldier to buck his superior, the governor of California, Governor Melnick, who'd appointed the general to be the official liaison with the Force.

Seconds later the three vehicles braked.

General Gallagher hopped out and walked over to the giant, his right hand extended, smiling broadly. "They're all here,

Blade," he said to the Warrior.

"You seem to be in a good mood," Blade noted, shaking the general's hand.

"Why shouldn't I be?"

Blade let go and motioned at the jeeps. "You never were very keen on the Force. I imagine the prospect of reforming the unit has you a bit upset."

"Not in the least," Gallagher replied. "After the Pipeline Strike, as that writer called it, I've come around to the governor's way of thinking."

"You have?" Blade said skeptically.

"There are times when the Force is necessary."

"I must be dreaming. Either that or you had a quart of scotch for lunch."

The general grinned. "I don't drink on duty. You know that."

Blade gazed at the jeeps. "What are they waiting for?"

"I want to introduce them one at a time," Gallagher said, and gestured at the first vehicle. "You didn't make out half bad this time around. And you're in for a couple of surprises."

"Surprises?" Blade repeated.

"You'll see," the general stated enigmatically, and chuckled.

A lean figure emerged from the foremost jeep, a man attired in a black frock coat, black pants, and black boots. In contrast he wore a white shirt. A black, wide-brimmed hat crowned his head. His hair, clipped close to his ears, was brown, his eyes hazel. In height he stood a shade under six feet.

"Blade, I'd like you to meet the volunteer from the Cavalry," General Gallagher said.

The man in black strolled up to the Warrior and offered his hand. "Howdy. The name is Madsen. Don Madsen. Most folks call me Doc."

"Doc," Blade said, measuring the man and liking what he saw: honesty, courage, and self-confidence. But then, the Cavalry was noted for producing self-reliant men and women.

"I've heard a lot about you from Boone," Doc Madsen mentioned, referring to the previous Cavalry volunteer.

"He's a close friend," Blade said. He glanced at Madsen's waist, at a gunbelt riding high on the man's hips. "What are you packing?"

Madsen pulled his coat aside to reveal a pearl-handled, nickle-plated Smith and Wesson Model 586 Distinguished Combat Magnum in a brown leather holster on his right hip.

"Is that the .38 or the .357 Magnum version?"

The Cavalryman smiled. "You know your guns. And this is the .357 Magnum. I like the stopping power."

"You'll have a chance to demonstrate your skill later," Blade told him.

"Why not now?"

"Now?"

Doc pivoted and pointed at a rock lying 40 feet to the east. "See that?" he asked, and drew, his right arm a blur. The Magnum swept up and out and boomed.

Blade saw the rock spin into the air. Madsen's revolver blasted a second time, splitting the rock in half. He looked at the Cavalryman. "Not bad."

"There aren't many better," Doc said. He twirled the Smith and Wesson into its holster. "I've even tied Boone in shooting contests."

"I believe it," Blade said.

A second person climbed from the jeep, an Indian dressed in beaded buckskins. He stared in the direction of the shattered rock, then came forward. Although only five and a half feet tall, he possessed a powerful physique. His wide shoulders and muscular arms hinted at latent strength. Both his shoulder-length hair and his eyes were dark, the hair black, the eyes a deep brown. Dangling from the left side of his leather belt was a large hunting knife in a sheath. In his right hand he carried a spear.

"Hello," the Warrior said, greeting him. "I'm Blade."

"I know," the Indian responded. "My name is Sparrow Hawk."

"Welcome to the Force."

Sparrow Hawk gazed at the bunkers. "I was a friend of Thunder's. His death greatly saddened our tribe. He was highly respected."

"Thunder was my friend too," Blade said sadly. "No one wanted him to live more than I did."

The Flathead regarded the giant for a moment. "I'm honored to be working with you, Warrior." He stepped to the right.

Blade saw someone sliding from the second jeep and he tensed, thinking of Athena Morris and how he had resisted having her on the Force, thinking of how her death had profoundly disturbed him.

A red-headed, green-eyed young woman walked toward him. Clad in plain black pants and a brown shirt, her hair trimmed below her ears, her skin pale from her life underground, she presented the perfect picture of innocence. Five feet eight in height, she walked tentatively toward the giant, gazing up at him in frank astonishment.

"Hello," Blade said.

"Hello, sir," she responded in a soft voice.

"What's your name?"

"Raphaela, sir."

"Call me Blade," the Warrior directed, his brow knitting in bewilderment. "You're from the Moles, I take it?"

Raphaela's mouth slackened. "Yes. How did you know?"

"A lucky guess," Blade said dryly, studying her from head to toe. "How old are you?"

"Twenty-one."

"Did you volunteer for this assignment?"

"Yes, sir."

Blade pursed his lips. "Have you ever killed anyone before, Raphaela?"

She averted her gaze, and her answer was barely audible. "No, I haven't."

"Do you have experience handling weapons?"

"Not much."

"Be specific," Blade instructed her.

"I've used a hatchet to chop wood," Raphaela said sheepishly.

General Gallagher burst into laughter. "A hatchet?" he declared, and laughed even harder.

A crimson tinge crept into Raphaela's cheeks and she clenched her fists at her sides. She looked into Blade's eyes. "I'll pull my weight around here. I promise."

The Warrior folded his arms across his chest. "Why did you volunteer to join the Force?"

"My reason is personal," she responded.

"You do know this is a *combat* unit?"

"Of course," Raphaela stated.

"I take it that you don't have any combat experience," Blade deduced.

"None. But I'm eager to learn."

Blade sighed and gazed at the sky so she wouldn't detect his anger. The Moles had done it again! Specifically, the autocratic leader of the Moles, the vain, temperamental man called Wolfe, had once again failed to send a competent recruit. The first volunteer from the Moles, Spader, a reluctant recruit coerced into joining by Wolfe, had been the first Force member to die.

"Teach me what to do and I'll do it," Raphaela vowed.

"We'll discuss this in my office later," Blade told her.

"I won't go back."

"That decision is up to me."

"I won't," Raphaela insisted.

The Warrior stared at her, surprised at the resolve her countenance conveyed. He read supreme determination in the set of her jaw, in her tight lips, in the flash of defiance in her eyes. "We'll see," he said. "The final decision is mine."

Raphaela frowned and walked to the left.

General Gallagher leaned close to the Warrior and whispered, "Dump her."

Before Blade could comment, a newcomer joined them.

"Whoa, bro! You're the biggest mother I've ever seen!"

Blade glanced at the speaker, a husky black man dressed in a black leather jacket, blue shirt, jeans, and knee-high black boots. Several inches shy of six feet tall, he packed at least 190 pounds onto his athletic form. His features were handsome, his hair styled in an Afro. "Who are you?"

"Leo Wood, at your service," the black said, and extended his right hand. "My friends all call me Lobo."

"Unusual nickname," Blade remarked, shaking.

"I got it back in my gang days in the Twin Cities, before you and those other Warriors bailed our butts out of that stinkin' cesspool," Lobo stated.

"Which gang were you in?"

"The Porns, dude. Who else?"

"As I recall, the Porns were the meanest of the bunch," Blade said.

Lobo shrugged and smirked. "Hell, man. Ain't nobody perfect."

"That's a cop-out."

"Say what?"

"That's an excuse for those who are too lazy to make the effort to improve themselves. We weren't put on this planet to be imperfect, to wallow in our own ignorance," Blade said.

Lobo did a double take, then chuckled. "If you say so, bro. But that mumbo-jumbo is way over my head. All I care about is stayin' alive. Perfect or imperfect don't hardly matter."

"Why do you want to join the Force, Lobo?"

"I'm hopin' to see some action. Livin' in Halma was gettin' downright boring."

The Clansman's words reminded Blade of the previous volunteer from that faction, an immature psychopath who'd delighted in killing, who'd thought only of himself until almost the very end. His mouth curled downward. "Is that the only reason?"

"No. I happen to believe in keepin' the Federation intact. Your Family did a big favor by lendin' us a hand when we were down and out. This is my way of repaying the favor."

Blade's estimation of the Clansman rose several degrees. "Have you had much combat experience?"

"I snuffed a few bozos in the Twin Cities," Lobo stated matter-of-factly. "I'm a whiz with my NATO."

"Your what?"

Lobo reached into the right front pocket of his jacket and withdrew a long, slender black object. "My NATO," he said. "I found this in the ruins of an old knife shop in Minneapolis." He flicked a switch and a gleaming four-inch blade automatically popped out a slot at the top.

"May I?" Blade asked, and held out his left hand.

"Sure, but if you break it I get one of those swords you're packin'," Lobo quipped.

Blade took the knife and examined the craftsmanship. On the black handle, imprinted in white letters, were the words NATO MILITARY. The spring-loaded blade retracted snugly into the slot, where the handle concealed it from view, and flicked out again at a slight press of the switch. "Nice knife."

"Damn straight," Lobo said.

The Warrior gave the automatic back and glanced at the third jeep. A soldier had emerged and was walking forward. Blade's eyes narrowed. The man's features were oddly familiar, and unsettling.

General Gallagher cleared his throat. "Blade, I'd like you to meet the volunteer from the Free State of California."

Recognition struck the giant with the force of a physical blow, and astonishment left him momentarily speechless.

Gallagher nodded at the robust trooper. "His name is Havoc."

CHAPTER TWO

Havoc!

The name brought a flood of memories to Blade, memories of the valiant noncom who had given his own life to save the life of another Force member. Of all the recruits on the first Force, Sergeant Havoc had been the most experienced, a professional soldier whose dedication and discipline were superb. General Gallagher had personally selected him.

And now the general was introducing a man by the same name? A man who bore a remarkable likeness to the original Havoc. A man in a Special Forces uniform with the insignia of a captain on his collar. A man endowed with exceptionally broad shoulders and the build of a classical Greek wrestler. A man with short blond hair and clear blue eyes, who stood two inches over six feet and weighed in the neighborhood of 210 pounds.

"Blade, say hello to Captain Mike Havoc," General Gallagher said. "Sergeant Havoc's older brother."

"I never knew he had an older brother," Blade noted absently, and held out his right hand.

Captain Havoc halted. "Pleased to meet you, sir," he said formally without a hint of emotion on his face. He took the Warrior's hand and squeezed.

Blade shook, feeling Havoc's fingers close on his own, impressed by the officer's strength. The pressure kept building as Havoc squeezed harder and harder, and for a moment Blade wondered if the man was testing him, measuring his might. But the pressure abruptly abated and Havoc released his hand.

"I'm ready for duty, sir," the officer declared, and saluted.

"Welcome aboard," Blade responded, returning the salute.

"I've been eager to meet you," Captain Havoc stated flatly. "I've heard so much about you."

Blade gazed into the officer's eyes. "I'm sorry about your brother. He was a good man."

Havoc grimaced and quickly glanced down at the ground. "Jimmy was the best, sir," he said, his tone laced with anguish.

The Warrior opted to change the subject. "I recall reading in his file that he had several brothers."

"There are two others, sir, both younger. And we have a sister living in Eureka," Captain Havoc said. He recovered his composure and straightened, standing at attention.

"Captain Havoc is ideally suited to be on the Force," General Gallagher interjected. "Like his brother, he's a career military man with an outstanding record. He's a qualified marksman and holds a black belt in karate. As an added bonus, he's been through Officers Training School. Until nine months ago he was Regular Army. He switched over to Special Forces and has been getting high marks from his superiors."

Nine months ago? Blade scrutinized Havoc's visage, strangely bothered by the news. The captain must have switched over to Special Forces shortly after the death of his brother.

"Jimmy was more skilled in hand-to-hand combat than I am," Captain Havoc commented fondly. "He had black belts in karate *and* judo, as well as a brown in aikido. Few men could match him."

"Your family has a strong military tradition, doesn't it?" Blade observed.

"Yes, sir. Our grandfather and father were both career soldiers. We were raised to be patriotic, to be loyal to the Free State of California. We were typical Army brats. Except for our sister, all of us entered the military."

"Well, I'm happy to have you on the team," Blade said.

"You have no idea how much joining the Force means to me," Captain Havoc said. He snapped another salute and moved to the right.

The Warrior glanced at General Gallagher. "You were right about my being surprised."

"The surprises aren't over yet."

"What?"

"I said you're in for a couple of surprises, remember?" Gallagher reminded him, then pointed at the third jeep.

Blade looked, and surprise wasn't adequate enough to describe his reaction. Amazement would barely fit. Total consternation came close. And all he would think of, as the thin form ambled toward him, were two words, repeated over and over: Not again!

Six feet in height, slim as a rail, walking with a graceful, light-footed gait, the last recruit was distinctly different from all the others. He was part feline. The creature that now halted in front of the Warrior and yawned as if bored, the creature attired only in a black loincloth, the creature with a reddish coat of fur all over his body, with a relatively small, oval head and rounded ears, with eerie green eyes distinguished by vertical slits in the center, and with razor-sharp teeth, was a hybrid, a genetically engineered mutation endowed with human and bestial traits in equal measure. "So this is where I'm expected to live for the next year?" the creature said disdainfully, surveying the facility. "Oh, well. I gave my word." He yawned again.

Blade struggled to regain his composure. The last team had included a mutation too, a querulous character by the name of Grizzly who had been a constant source of trouble. Although the Warrior and Grizzly had become fast friends, the aggravation the mutation had caused, stemming in large part from Grizzly's hatred of all humans, had been an unnecessary burden on Blade's shoulders. He hardly wanted to go through all of that again.

"Jaguarundi is the name the damn Doktor gave me," the mutant disclosed, his tone low and raspy. "I prefer to be called Jag."

"Pleased to meet you," Blade said, recalling the infamous geneticist the Family battled years ago.

The Doktor had been perhaps the greatest genetic engineer

of all time. Prior to World War Three, genetic engineering had been the rage of the scientific establishment. Many of the scientists involved had wanted to be the first to develop new species. The government had even granted patents for such creations, and tremendous amounts of money had changed hands. The genetic engineers had been able to tamper with a human embryo, to combine elements in a test tube and produce crossbreeds. By editing the genetic instructions encoded in the chemical structure of molecules of DNA, the Doktor, decades after the war, had bred an assassin corps of animal men and women.

Other mutations stemmed from more conventional sources. The massive amounts of radiation unleashed on the environment scrambled the genetic codes of the wildlife. Animals were born with two heads, or three eyes, or six legs, or any other bizarre combination of warped traits. Equally grotesque were the mutations resulting from the toxic chemicals employed during the war. In particular, the chemical clouds were responsible for transforming ordinary reptiles, amphibians, and mammals into hideous monsters known as mutates. Their bodies covered with pus-filled sores, they stalked the land seeking fresh flesh to consume.

"Are you really?" Jag responded sarcastically, intruding on the Warrior's train of thought. "Pleased to meet me, I mean."

"Why wouldn't I be?" Blade asked.

"Most humans have a difficult time accepting my kind," Jag noted.

"I'll vouch for Blade," General Gallagher said. "He's not prejudiced against mutants."

The cat-man leaned toward the general and smiled, exposing his pointed teeth. "If you don't mind, I like the term hybrid better. Mutant sounds sort of demeaning, don't you think?" he said pleasantly, but there was an edge to his voice.

Gallagher shrugged. "If you want to be called a hybrid, we'll call you a hybrid. It doesn't matter to us."

"It does to me," Jag stated. "Just call me Jag and we'll get along wonderfully."

"Were you one of the—hybrids—who rebelled against the Doktor?" Blade inquired. A number of the Doktor's creations had opposed the madman's oppressive rule, had resisted his domination of every aspect of their lives, and been slain or tossed into prison for asserting their independence.

"Yeah," the cat-man said. "The lunatic locked me in solitary confinement, and I wasn't released until after your Family won the war. I've been living in the Civilized Zone."

"Why'd you decide to enlist in the Force?"

"You had a hybrid on this team before, didn't you?"

"Yes. Grizzly."

"If being on the Force was good enough for Grumpy, then it's good enough for me," Jag said.

"You know Grizzly?"

"We bumped into one another a few times," Jag replied, and gazed intently at the Warrior. "Whatever happened to Grumpy anyway? He never came back to the Civilized Zone after his hitch here was up."

"He went into the Outlands," Blade divulged.

The cat-man blinked a few times. "The Outlands? Why the hell would Grizzly do that? The wackos in the Outlands hate hybrids."

"He told me that he wanted to get away from everything," Blade explained. "He knew how dangerous the Outlands are, but I don't think he cared anymore."

"Why not?"

"Because the woman he loved had died."

Jag appeared startled by the revelation. "Woman? Do you mean Grumpy found a foxy hybrid to take as his mate?"

Blade frowned. "No. Grizzly was in love with a human."

A belly laugh erupted from the mutation. "A human? No way, mister. I knew what he was like. Grumpy hated humans. He thought you were all scum."

"I know," Blade said softly.

The cat-man's expression sobered and he uttered a low hissing noise. "You're really not putting me on?"

Blade shook his head.

"Damn," Jag declared.

Saddened by their conversation, by the discussion of Grizzly and Athena Morris, the Warrior glanced absently to the west, and as he did his eyes happened to alight on General Gallagher.

He saw the most baffling combination of emotions he'd ever seen on the pugnacious officer's face, a curious mixture of apprehension and outright panic. The instant the general realized Blade was looking at him, he forced a smile on his face and stared at the cat-man.

"Mind if I ask you a question?" Gallagher inquired.

"Be my guest," Jag said.

"What kind of mutation are you exactly? I mean, I know the Doktor mixed human and animal embryos together somehow to concoct his pet killers. Grizzly was made by mixing a human embryo with a grizzly bear embryo, or some bullcrap like that," Gallagher said. "Are you part jaguar? I thought jaguars have spots or dots or something. Your coat doesn't have a mark."

Jag took a half-step toward the officer, his arms coming up to his waist, revealing the inch-long tapered fingernails rimming his hands. "I won't tell you this again. *Don't* refer to me as a mutation. I'm a hybrid. Got it? A hybrid."

"Hey, I didn't mean to insult you," General Gallagher retorted defensively.

"No offense taken. *This* time," Jag said, and relaxed his arms. "As far as your question is concerned, I'm part jaguarundi."

"What the hell is that?"

The cat-man's flattened nostrils flared. "Anyone with half a brain knows that jaguarundis are big cats found mainly in South America and Mexico, although their range extends as far north as Texas and Arizona. They're famous for their speed and stealth. And just so you'll know, they don't have a spot on their bodies after they outgrow their kitten stage."

"I just asked."

"And I just answered you," Jag stated, his green eyes narrowing.

Blade took a stride forward, then rotated to face the recruits. "All right. I want you to form a line in front of this bunker."

"In any order, sir?" Captain Havoc queried.

"It doesn't matter," Blade told him. In short order they were arranged as required, with Havoc to the west, then Jaguarundi, Doc Madsen, Lobo, Raphaela, and Sparrow Hawk. They watched Blade expectantly. "I'll make this short and sweet. All of you were probably informed about the Freedom Force. You undoubtedly know that the Force is an elite combat unit designated to respond to any and all threats to the Federation. But you might not have learned that five of the previous Force team perished." He paused. "I don't want to have a repeat of that statistic."

"Who does, dude?" Lobo joked.

Blade stared at the Clansman. "I want to make several aspects of your new life crystal clear. First and foremost, I will not tolerate any breach of discipline. When I give you an order, you will obey it right then and there without griping. When you're in formation, like now, and I'm speaking, you will keep silent unless you request permission to speak."

Lobo swallowed hard.

"Second, this is a military unit. You'll undergo extensive training, and you'll be expected to adhere to certain standards of conduct both on and off duty. If you don't like the idea of regimentation, of taking orders, then the Force isn't for you. You can change your minds now without any hard feelings. No one will think less of you if you don't want to subject yourself to all this."

No one moved or spoke.

"Third, our mission, essentially, is to kill or be killed. We'll frequently be going up against overwhelming odds. If you have any qualms about combat, if you don't think you can kill another human being in the line of duty, then now is the time to head on back to whichever faction you're from and everyone will understand," Blade stated, and looked at Raphaela.

The Molewoman returned his gaze without flinching.

"Does anyone have any questions?" Blade asked them.

"I do," Doc Madsen said. "Do we get to keep our own weapons? I'm partial to my Combat Magnum."

"You'll all be allowed to carry whatever weapons you favor," Blade replied. "You'll also be issued whatever additional arms and gear will be needed on each assignment."

"I've got a question, man," Lobo said.

"What?"

"Where are you hidin' the john? If I don't get to take a lea real soon, I'm gonna piss in my pants.''

Blade sighed and bowed his head. There could be no doubt about it. He *definitely* was a glutton for punishment.

CHAPTER THREE

"**Y**ou're puttin' us on, dude."

"I'm serious, Lobo," Blade responded. He walked to the center of the mats and gazed at the six recruits lined up on the south side. "I did this with the other team too. It's a great way to judge how well you can handle yourselves. So who wants to be first?"

The volunteers exchanged glances. They'd enjoyed a restful night and a hearty breakfast. An hour after their meal the Warrior had instructed the recruits to bring the four gray mats from the supply bunker and arrange them in front of the HQ. Now they looked at one another, each waiting for the other to step forward first. With a notable exception.

Captain Havoc glanced at his teammates, snorted, and strode onto the mats. "Hell, sir, I'll go first."

"Ready when you are," Blade said, and assumed the horse stance.

Havoc adopted the Shumoku-tachi, a T-shaped stance, and brought his arms up, his hands in the Nakayubi-ippon-ken position, clenched into compact fists with the second joint of the middle finger protruding. "No holds barred, sir?"

"No holds barred," Blade confirmed. "The purpose is to simulate an actual combat situation."

"I understand that you fought Jimmy and won," Havoc mentioned.

"We sparred. I came out on top."

"You won't come out on top this time," Captain Havoc declared, and then added, as an afterthought, "sir."

"Begin," Blade ordered, and a second later Captain Havoc flew into him, raining a series of hand and foot blows. Blade retreated several paces, blocking or countering every strike, assessing the officer's ability, and within a minute realized that the captain had been unduly modest. The man might only hold a black belt in karate, whereas his brother, Sergeant Havoc, had attained proficiency in three martial arts systems, but Captain Havoc exhibited a mastery which his sibling would have been hard pressed to match. Blade rated the officer as one of the best he'd ever encountered.

On the sidelines, Raphaela shook her head in disbelief. "They're moving too fast. I can't keep track of their hands and feet."

"I can," Jag said. "They're almost as quick as I am."

"You're rather high on yourself, aren't you?" Doc Madsen asked.

"I have reason to be," Jag stated smugly.

"I wish I did," Lobo said. "If that honky expects me to take him on, he's nuts."

"There is something wrong," Sparrow Hawk commented.

"What?" Doc queried.

"I'm not sure," the Flathead responded. "But the officer is trying too hard."

"Hey, bro, when you're going up against a guy the size of a friggin' tree, you try as hard as you can," Lobo remarked.

"What's happening now?" Raphaela asked.

Captain Havoc had backed the Warrior into the northwest corner and seemed to be on the verge of knocking Blade off the mat. He executed a devastating roundhouse kick, a Migi-nawashi-geri, and had it landed on the Warrior's temple the fight would have been over.

Blade instinctively brought his left forearm up to block the kick, then, before Havoc could pull the leg back, he clamped his left hand on the officer's ankle, using the Eagle Claw technique, and whipped the leg around, using Havoc's own momentum to swing the officer in a semicircle. His hands whipped out and caught Havoc in the back, propelling the captain into the middle of the mats.

Lobo laughed.

The captain stumbled and almost fell. He recovered his balance at the last instant and whirled.

Having taken the measure of his sparring partner, Blade walked toward the officer, about to compliment Havoc for a job well done. Instead Captain Havoc came at him with the fury of an unbridled thunderstorm; every kick cracked like lightning and every hand blow buffeted him as mercilessly as cyclonic winds. Blade resisted the onslaught with considerable effort, bringing all of his might and speed to bear, and as he fought he thought that perhaps, just perhaps, Captain Havoc was being a bit too aggressive. If he didn't know better, he would swear that Havoc's strikes were intended to slay him.

But that couldn't be.

Blade decided to end their contest, and he allowed two blows to land on the left side of his chest and doubled over, in pain but not in *that* much pain, not enough where he couldn't function, not enough to prevent him from suddenly uncoiling when Captain Havoc stepped in to deliver a swordhand chop to the neck. He drove his right hand into Havoc's midriff, a palm-heel thrust into the breadbasket that doubled the officer in half and caused Havoc to sink to his knees.

"Wow!" Raphaela declared.

"You're quite skilled, Captain," Blade stated, catching his breath.

His arms covering his stomach, breathing in great gasps, Havoc looked up and scowled. "Not talented enough, sir."

"You're easily as talented as your brother."

Captain Havoc averted his eyes, took a deep breath, and rose to his feet. He stood at attention, despite the agony lancing his abdomen. "I can understand why you beat Jimmy, sir," he said "I doubt anyone could best you in hand-to-hand combat."

"There are others better than I am," Blade informed him

"That's not possible," Captain Havoc replied.

"It's true," Blade asserted. "There's another Warrior at the Home by the name of Rikki-Tikki-Tavi who has beaten me a sparring a number of times. And I met a Thai once, a particularly vicious genetleman called Kan Tang, who was my equal in every respect. I'm sure I'll meet others from time to time who will be in the same class, and I can't afford to let my expertise go to my head. The day I start to think of myself as the best there is, that's the day someone better will come along and make my wife a widow.''

The officer did a double take. ''You're married?''

Blade nodded. ''And I have a son named Gabe.''

''I didn't expect you to be married,'' Captain Havoc said lamely.

''What difference does it make? Why are you so surprised?'' Blade inquired.

''I'm not. It's just that . . .'' Havoc mumbled, then abruptly regained his composure and bowed to the Warrior as a token of his respect. ''Thanks for the lesson, sir. I learned a lot.''

''We'll do it again soon,'' Blade said. ''I can always use a good sparring partner.''

''I can hardly wait, sir,'' Captain Havoc said. He performed an about-face and walked to the south side of the mats.

''Who's next?'' Blade asked.

''I'll go,'' Doc Madsen stated. He unstrapped his gunbelt and gently laid the holster and Magnum on the edge of the mat.

''I know that many in the Cavalry pride themselves on their boxing ability,'' Blade mentioned. ''Are you a boxer?''

''I'm a fair hand at it,'' Doc acknowledged, coming closer and raising his clenched fists.

''Are you adept at any of the martial arts?''

''I don't go in for any of that fancy dancing,'' Doc replied. He wagged his fists. ''Let's get this over with. And try not to kill me.''

They engaged, exchanging jabs and punches, never really connecting, merely gauging their respective prowess, circling and flicking uppercuts, hooks, and crosses.

On the sidelines, Lobo leaned toward Raphaela and whispered, ''Why don't you go next, foxy?''

''The name is Raphaela to you,'' she responded, ''and you can go next.''

''How about you, Sparrow Hawk? Why don't you go?'' Lobo prompted.

"Please, call me Sparrow," the Flathead said. "And I wouldn't think of depriving you of the honor to be the next one. You must be eager to test your mettle against the famous Warrior."

Lobo studied Sparrow's features for a moment. "Are you jivin' me, dude?"

"What does jivin' mean?"

The Clansman snorted and shook his head in amazement. "Jive means to feed somebody a line."

"A line of what?"

Lobo snickered. "Bro, they sure grow 'em dumb where you come from," he said, then added, "No offense, red man."

"Thank you, my black brother," Sparrow stated solemnly.

"They're done," Raphaela interjected.

Blade and Doc Madsen had finished their sparring and were shaking hands.

"How'd I do?" Doc asked.

"Not bad. I'd say you could hold your own against most opponents," Blade said in praise.

Doc walked over and retrieved his holster. "Will I be learning any of that martial-arts junk while I'm here?"

"When we're not off on a mission there will be daily practice sessions in unarmed combat. Whether you learn anything or not is entirely up to you," Blade said. He smiled at the others. "Okay. Who wants to give it a shot?"

"Sparrow does," Lobo declared, and gave the Flathead a shove, causing Sparrow Hawk to stumble onto the mats.

"I guess you're next," Blade remarked, and grinned.

"Evidently," Sparrow agreed, and glanced back at the Clansman. Lobo seemed to have developed an intense interest in a cloud floating overhead.

"You won't need the spear," Blade mentioned.

Sparrow hefted the finely crafted weapon, consisting of a polished wooden staff six feet in length to which a sharp steel head, triangular in shape, had been affixed. "This belonged to my father, Red Horse. I used it to slay the mutation that killed him."

"My father was also killed by a mutation," Blade divulged somberly.

"How old were you when it happened?"

"Twenty."

"I was only twelve, a boy whose head was filled with childish notions, a boy who didn't realize how hard this life can be," Sparrow said. "I was forced to grow up quickly."

"Do you have any brothers or sisters?"

"Two of each. I'm the oldest."

"What about your mom?"

"She's alive and well and living in Kalispell. Once a month, rain or shine, winter or summer, our family gets together at her house for a feast and fun," Sparrow said, and sighed. "I'll miss those family affairs."

"Your tour of duty is only for a year. You'll be back enjoying their company before you know it."

"Unless I suffer the same fate as Thunder," Sparrow responded. He deposited the spear at the edge of the mat and faced the giant. "Like the Cavalryman, I'm not an expert at unarmed combat. I can wrestle and box a little, but that's about it."

"Then we'll wrestle and box," Blade proposed. "Your objective will be to pin me on the mat. Ready?"

"Why do I suddenly wish I was tangling with a grizzly bear instead of you?" Sparrow joked, and closed in.

Blade grabbed at the Flathead's right wrist, but Sparrow deftly sidestepped and lunged at the Warrior's ankles. Blade felt arms encircle his legs, and he swayed and almost tottered over when Sparrow tried to upend him. He bent down and got his hands on the Flathead's shoulders, and together they tumbled to the mat and wrestled in earnest.

"Go, Sparrow!" Lobo shouted encouragement, then looked at Raphaela. "That midget doesn't stand a chance."

"Sparrow isn't a midget," she replied.

"He's the smallest one here. That makes him the midget of our group," Lobo stated.

"And what are you? Our official mouth?"

Lobo took his eyes from the grappling pair on the mats and faced her. "You're not as wimpy as you pretend to be, lady."

"I've never pretended to be a wimp, Lobo."

"That's how you came across yesterday. But I figure you're

a real sassy momma when the going gets rough.''

"If Blade tries to ship me back to the Moles, he'll find out how sassy I can be," Raphaela vowed.

"Well, since you're such hot stuff, foxy, you can take him on next."

"You go."

"Ladies always go first. Haven't you heard?"

"If you had any manners, you'd be first," Raphaela countered.

Jag unexpectedly hissed lightly. "*I'll* take him on. The two of you can stand here and twiddle your thumbs."

"What's gotten into you?" Lobo asked.

"Nothing a couple of earplugs wouldn't cure," Jag answered.

On the mats, Blade and Sparrow tussled vigorously, rolling over and over, back and forth, each applying hold after hold in vain. The Warrior broke free of every lock, using his superior strength to thwart Sparrow again and again. And although he tried his best, Blade couldn't get a grip on the twisting, wriggling, contorting Flathead. He'd never fought an adversary so slippery, and he was about to call their match a draw when Sparrow tripped over his own feet while scrambling erect. Instantly Blade wrapped his right arm around Sparrow's head, seizing the Flathead in a basic headlock. "Got you!" he said.

"Think so?" Sparrow asked, and wrenched his body in a tight arc at the same second he applied pressure on Blade's arm. Although he couldn't pry the Warrior's arm all the way open, he did succeed in forcing Blade's forearm an inch from his chin. With a backward jerk he popped free and straightened.

"Not bad," Blade said, rising. "You're slipperier than a slug."

"Thanks. I think."

"What are your other strong points?"

"I'm a competent hunter and tracker. And I know herbal medicine, remedies taught to me by the tribal shaman."

"I'm happy to have you with us," Blade said sincerely, then swung to the south. "Next."

Jaguarundi walked onto the mats. "So much for the amateurs. It's time to take on a pro."

"So you're a pro?"

"I'm the best fighter on the team. Go ahead. Test me. Any way you want."

"Fair enough," Blade stated, and waited for Sparrow to reclaim the spear and rejoin the others. "Your objective will be simpler than Sparrow's was."

"Don't go easy on me. You'll regret it," Jag promised.

"Prove you're as good as you say."

"How?"

"Let's pretend I'm an enemy. Your objective is to slash my throat before I lay you out."

The cat-man blinked a few times. "Pick another objective."

"What's wrong?"

"If I get carried away, you're liable to look like shredded venison."

Blade smiled. "You'll never lay a finger on me," he said.

"Pick another objective," Jaguarundi insisted. "You don't stand a chance against my speed."

"Prove it," Blade reiterated, and smirked, deliberately taunting the hybrid.

"Don't say I didn't warn you."

"I won't, *mutant*," Blade stated, emphasizing the last word distastefully, hoping to test the limits of the cat-man's self-control.

Apparently there was none.

Jaguarundi came at the Warrior exhibiting all the primal fury of his namesake, his arms a blur as he tried to rake his fingernails across Blade's neck. A low growl escaped his lips as he fought, growing in volume.

Blade backpedaled a few yards, blocking swing after swing, then stood firm, countering every swipe, focusing exclusively on the hybrid's hands, reacting instinctively. A claw nicked his left wrist and drew a trickle of blood, but he ignored the cut, continuing to block, block, block. His extra foot of height gave him an advantage, compelling Jaguarundi to extend those flashing arms to their limit, making the hybrid work harder. The power in the mutation's limbs astonished him. Though he was seemingly thin and frail, under Jaguarundi's skin flowed sinews of steel. Every blow jarred Blade's arms, and he had no doubt that the hybrid could rip those tapered nails through flesh as easily as one of his Bowies could cleave a wax candle.

As the seconds passed and became a full minute, then two, Jaguarundi became increasingly frustrated by his failure to penetrate the giant's guard. He swung harder, recklessly, his growl a feral vocalization of his simmering rage.

Blade's arms were beginning to tire, his concentration starting to flag. To win, he needed to take the hybrid by surprise, to do something totally unanticipated. Jag undoubtedly expected him to continue standing there, blocking until he was too tired to lift his arms. But what if he did the exact opposite? What if he lowered his guard for just an instant? Would the hybrid be able to check his swing in time?

Perhaps sensing weakness in the Warrior, Jaguarundi pressed his attack with renewed intensity.

And Blade let him. He let Jag swing all out, let those nails come within inches of his face and throat, let the hybrid extend those streaking arms to the limit, and blocked each blow. He blocked a left, an arching right, and another left. Then, as the right lanced toward him, he did the unexpected. He lowered his arms and took a half step backwards, and he saw the stunned expression on Jaguarundi's feline visage as the hybrid's right hand swept downward, missing by half a foot. Before Jag could retract that hand, Blade's hands flicked out and grasped the mutation's wrist. He pivoted, yanking on Jag's arm, throwing his whole body into the motion, sending the hybrid sailing.

Jaguarundi flew to the north edge of the mats and dropped, about to land hard on his back. In midair he executed a graceful flip, his chin tucked into his chest, his arms and legs drawn in tight to his body. When he completed the flip, he uncoiled and alighted on his feet, his arms extended, his green eyes on the giant.

Blade smiled and placed his hands on his hips. "You were a little slow, but I think you'll improve with time."

"And you're all right yourself, for a human," Jag said. A grin creased his thin lips.

"Tell me something, and be honest."

"What?"

"Are you like Grizzly? Are you as prejudiced against humans as he is?"

"Not quite."

"Can you elaborate?"

Jaguarundi walked toward the Warrior. "As I pointed out a while ago, Grumpy believes all humans are scum. I don't go that far. To me, you're all a bunch of meatballs. Crazy, yes. Obnoxious, yes. But I don't hate you."

"That's a relief," Blade said, and chuckled.

Jag halted and regarded the giant in admiration. "You took a chance goading me on. I like a man who's willing to take chances. It means you're not afraid to take life as it comes. I'm looking forward to working with you."

"The same here," Blade acknowledged, and turned to the south again.

"Uh-oh," Lobo muttered.

The Warrior glanced from the Clansman to Raphaela. "Which one of you is next?"

"She is," Lobo declared.

"He is," Raphaela stated.

"Either one of you will do," Blade told them.

"Do I get to use my NATO?" the Clansman inquired hopefully.

"Sure."

"Really?" Lobo replied, beaming happily. He went to reach into the right pocket of his jacket.

"And I'll use my Bowies," Blade added.

Lobo's smile transformed itself into a frown. "No fair, dude. Those knives of yours would hack me to itty-bitty pieces."

"Then why don't we stick to hand-to-hand combat?"

"Why don't you take the chick first?" Lobo suggested.

Blade took two strides toward them, his eyes narrowing. "I don't care which one of you spars with me. But one of you had better step out here now!"

To the surprise of everyone, the Molewoman ventured onto the mats. "I'll go first. If you wait for chicken-heart, we'll be here until nightfall."

Doc Madsen, Sparrow, and Jaguarundi all laughed.

The Warrior scrutinized her from head to toe, then sighed. "Do you know anything about unarmed combat, Raphaela?"

"A little."

"Do you know how to box?"

"No."

"Do you know how to wrestle?"

"Not really."

"Have you ever fired a gun?"

"What's a gun have to do with sparring?" she asked testily.

"Answer the question."

Raphaela winced, as if in physical pain, and sadly shook her head. "But I can learn. I'm a fast learner. I promise."

"I was hoping to get a volunteer with more experience," Blade stated bluntly. "Our training program is thorough, but we can't wait for you to master every aspect before sending you out on missions. And if you make a mistake in the field, it could cost you your life."

"I won't go back to Wolfe!" Raphaela declared angrily. "I deserve to receive the same treatment as the men. Or don't you think women should be in this line of work?"

"Some of my fellow Warriors at the Home are women, women I recommended for the post," Blade disclosed, nipping her argument in the bud.

Raphaela glared up at him. "I demand the right to be tested like everyone else. I want to spar."

"How long do you think you would last against me?" Blade queried softly.

Her eyes roved over his towering physique, over his bulging, contoured muscles, and she frowned. "Not very long."

"Then sparring with me wouldn't be much of a test, would it?"

"I guess not," Raphaela admitted reluctantly, and bowed her head.

"So how about if you spar with Lobo?"

"Say *what*?" the Clansman blurted.

Raphaela looked at the Warrior, incredulity on her countenance. "What?"

"I can use a rest after taking on the other four. How about if you spar with Lobo? Show me what you can do against him and maybe I'll let you stay on the Force for the time being," Blade said. "Is that fair enough?"

She grinned and glanced at the Clansman. "All I have to do is beat him?"

"That's all."

"I'm ready," Raphaela declared eagerly.

"Well, I'm not," Lobo stated, sounding miffed. He joined them on the mats and pointed at her. "This is an insult, dude! Why should I do your dirty work for you? I'm a lean, mean, fightin' machine, and you want me to take on this fluff? Give me a break!"

"Who are you calling fluff?" Raphaela demanded, clenching her fists.

Blade inhaled deeply, suppressing an impulse to laugh, and stared at Lobo. "You don't want to spar with her?"

"No way, man."

"You'd rather spar with me, right?"

There was a slight pause as Lobo struggled to move his lips. "Damn straight I would. A woman ain't no challenge to a guy like me."

"I can imagine how much of a letdown it would be to spar with her," Blade said sympathetically. "And it wouldn't be fair to you. Okay. You've made your point. You can spar with me right now."

Lobo's mouth moved but no words came out.

"It's too bad you feel this way," Blade commented. "You would have done me a favor by sparring with her."

"A favor, huh?"

"Yep."

"If you put it that way, how can I refuse?" Lobo declared. "I'll spar with the bimbo."

"Bimbo!" Raphaela snapped.

"But let me get this straight," Lobo said. "If I spar with her, do I have to spar with you?"

Blade pretended to ponder the question. "No, I guess not. If you spar with her, you won't need to spar with me today."

Lobo looked at her and snickered. "You've got yourself a deal, man. I'll stomp this momma into the ground." So saying, he began shuffling his legs and swinging his arms, moving from side to side, boxing an imaginary foe. "Do you see this, woman?

Do you see these moves? Nobody messes with Leo Wood,''
he bragged, and shuffled some more.

"Is that a fact?'' Raphaela responded.

"You bet,'' Lobo stated, moving faster, boxing rings around
her. "If you know any prayers, now's the time to say 'em.''

Raphaela glanced at the Warrior. "If I beat him, I'm in?''

"That's the deal,'' Blade replied.

"You can forget beatin' me, dingbat,'' Lobo advised her,
weaving and punching, gliding and sliding, a shuffling fiend
if ever there was one. "You're history, bitch.''

And he was still shuffling away when Raphaela planted the
instep of her right shoe between his legs.

CHAPTER FOUR

Blade sat in a gray metal folding chair behind his desk in the HQ bunker, going over the forms he had to fill out on each recruit. He lifted his head when the sound of a vehicle braking to a stop outside reached his ears. The outer door creaked open, then slammed shut, and footsteps thumped on the stairway leading down to his office. "Come on in, General," he called out.

The office door opened and there stood General Gallagher, a black briefcase in his left hand, a mystified expression on his face. "How did you know it was me?"

"You always slam doors. It must stem from your childhood."

"My childhood?"

"Yeah. You were probably assaulted by a doorknob when you were an infant."

Gallagher entered the office, his forehead furrowed. "Not that I recall," he said seriously, then broke into a grin. "How's it going, Blade? It's been a week already."

"It seems like a month."

The general took a seat in one of the two chairs in front of the desk and placed the briefcase on the other chair. "How are the new people doing?"

"Okay," Blade replied.

"Just okay?"

"Each of them has strengths, areas of expertise, they can

contribute to the team. They're eager to learn, and they're not as temperamental as the first group.''

"Break them down for me," General Gallagher said.

The Warrior leaned back and locked his hands behind his head. "If you want. I'd say that Captain Havoc is the best all-around recruit, which is understandable considering his prior experience. He's just as lethal as his brother was, and he's bigger and stronger. He also has the added plus of being an officer, of having command seasoning. But . . ." He hesitated.

"But what?"

"There's something about him that bothers me," Blade divulged.

"What?" Gallagher asked, leaning forward.

"I can't put my finger on it."

"Is he being insubordinate?"

"No."

"Creating problems with the others?"

"No. They tend to look up to him because of his military background and they respect his judgment," Blade said.

"Then I don't see what the problem is," General Gallagher said, puzzled.

"Anyway, I'm thinking of making Havoc my second-in-command. I didn't appoint one on the last team and I should have."

"Mike will be honored, I'm sure."

"Then there's Jaguarundi. Thank the Spirit he's not like Grizzly! He gets along well with the others, although he does think he's better than everyone else. He has sensational speed, his vision is twice as good as ours, as is his hearing, and he can track by scent. He'll be invaluable," Blade said.

"What about the Cavalryman, Madsen?"

"Doc is steady and reliable. He's fast on the draw and he's an accurate shot with a handgun or a rifle."

"What did he do before he volunteered to join the Force?" Gallagher queried. "Was he a rancher like Boone?"

"He was a gambler."

"A what?"

"Doc gambled for a living. The VTOL brought a one-page letter from Kilrane, the leader of the Cavalry, on the last shuttle flight. He provided a few details about Doc's past. It seems that

Madsen has a reputation as a gunfighter.''

"I don't know if I like the idea of having a gunfighter on the Force,'' General Gallagher remarked.

"We're in the business of killing, General. A gunfighter fits right in.''

"But gamblers are shiftless sorts. Why would a man like him want to enlist?''

"Maybe he's tired of being shiftless,'' Blade speculated. "I don't know. But I'm not about to object to having him. I believe he'll do fine.''

"And the Indian?''

"Sparrow is an exceptional tracker and hunter, and next to Jaguarundi he's the best at living off the land. He's honest and dependable, a lot like his predecessor,'' Blade said.

"What about Leo Wood?'' Gallagher asked.

Blade grinned and shook his head. "Lobo is the wild card. He's erratic. He never seems to know when to keep his mouth shut. And if I don't know better, I'd swear the man is a coward.''

"You don't think he is?''

"No. For several reasons. The Clan wouldn't send someone who was unreliable. I know their leader, Zahner, well, and I had a long talk with him after the first recruit they sent, Kraft, turned out to be an immature psychopath. Zahner promised me he wouldn't repeat the mistake,'' Blade said. "Lobo has potential. We've sparred a couple of times now, and he's a natural-born fighter. His reflexes and timing are exceptional, and he's good with that knife of his.''

"Then what's his problem?''

"The man will always take the path of least resistance. He goes out of his way to avoid doing work, to avoid expending effort of any kind. And where there's an element of danger, he'd rather flee than fight.''

"And you want him on the Force?'' Gallagher questioned skeptically.

The Warrior smiled. "Yeah. I do. He'll be my balancing factor.''

"You're what?''

"The voice of caution.''

"Hmmmph," General Gallagher muttered, evidently unconvinced. "It's your show. Do what you want." He paused. "How do they rate on the firing range?"

"Havoc, Doc, and Sparrow are the best shots. Jag has never used a weapon in his life, but he's learning fast. Lobo couldn't hit the broadside of a barn with a bazooka. Raphaela is fair. She's been practicing every chance she gets."

"What about her? Do you intend to keep her on the Force?"

"Yes."

"Even though she's the worst of the lot?"

"Yes. Initially, I was all set to give her the boot. But the more I've observed her, the more I believe she can do the job. The lady has spunk, General. True grit, as a buddy of mine named Hickok would say. She'll stay," Blade stated.

"I hope you don't live to regret your decision," Gallagher said.

"Time will tell. Speaking of which, it's nice to have the time to train them properly, to hone their skills. If you remember, the first team had to go out on a mission on short notice and we lost one man," Blade said.

General Gallagher cleared his throat and gazed at the ceiling.

"I couldn't believe it when you walked in here last time and told me I had two weeks to prepare the unit," Blade went on. "At least I'll have all the time I need to train this team, right?"

The general didn't answer.

"Right?" Blade repeated, his hands lowering to the desk.

"Well . . ." Gallagher said.

"Don't say a word!" Blade declared, and held up his right hand. "I don't want to hear it."

"Look, we both know the best training is actual experience in the field," Gallagher said.

"I don't want to hear it," Blade reiterated.

"I have this terrific idea."

"Go tell it to a great white shark."

"At least listen to what I have to say," Gallagher urged.

"I'd rather not."

General Gallagher sighed and gestured with both arms. "Look, I'm not about to suggest that you take the Force into a combat situation."

"You're not?" Blade said suspiciously.

"No. What good would it do? You have the final authority on whether the Force accepts an assignment. The only reason I was able to persuade you to send out the first Force prematurely was because of the urgency of the mission. This new idea isn't urgent in any respect."

"It's not?"

"No. So will you hear me out?"

The Warrior scowled and rested his chin in his hands. "I know better, but go ahead."

"Thanks," Gallagher said. "What I have in mind is more of a scouting and tracking assignment. Before I can explain, I have to provide some background."

"Be my guest," Blade stated halfheartedly.

"For decades, ever since the war almost, California has had problems with raiders along its southern border. There are checkpoints on all the roads and highways, and fence has been strung along certain sections. But it's impossible and impractical to fence in the entire border."

"I can imagine," Blade remarked listlessly.

"Raiders are constantly coming up from Mexico and attacking our communities and towns," General Gallagher disclosed. "Our Army patrols and border guards can't be everywhere at once. No matter how hard we try—and we try, believe me— bands are always slipping across the border, conducting raids, and returning before we can apprehend them."

"Why doesn't the government of Mexico do something?"

"Because there isn't a centralized government in Mexico anymore. According to the records, the Mexican government fell to pieces about a year after World War Three broke out. There were massive riots in Mexico City when the food shortages drove the populace over the edge. And there were insurrectionists stirring everyone up, Communists and other jerks. The government couldn't handle the mobs, especially after widespread panic set in. For all we know, Mexico isn't even called Mexico now. We just call it that out of habit," Gallagher elaborated.

"How does all of this tie in with your mission for the Force?" Blade inquired.

"About two weeks ago a bandit gang, the worst of the lot, came across the border and attacked a small town called Jacumba. A California resident named Horace Greeley, who was on his way from Brawley to visit a friend living west of Jacumba, drove into the town shortly after the raiders left. He found a police officer barely alive and saw the white dog—"

"The white dog?" Blade said, interrupting.

"I'll get to the dog in a bit," Gallagher said. "Greeley found all the residents dead, butchered. Most of the women had been raped. Even the kids were killed."

The Warrior's features clouded.

"In the center of Jacumba, in a small park, Greeley found the evidence we needed to identify the leader of the band," Gallagher related.

"What evidence?"

"Ten stakes with female breasts impaled on them."

Blade straightened, his hands slowly lowering to the desktop. "What kind of sicko could conceive of such a thing?"

"The bastard responsible for the raid on Jacumba is a Mexican bandit called El Diablo. The Devil. His followers are known as the Devils of Baja. El Diablo has been conducting raids for the better part of twenty years, and he always leaves his calling card at the scene after killing everyone and looting to his heart's content."

"The breasts of women impaled on stakes?"

General Gallagher nodded.

"What else do you know about him?"

"Informants have told us there are upwards of ninety men and women in his band. His real name, by the way, is Celestino Naranjo. What he did before he took to murdering innocent people is anyone's guess. He's reportedly in his late forties. And for the past eight or nine years he's been traveling with a white dog, a huge beast that's missing its left eye."

"Why haven't you sent in a team of Rangers or Special Forces commandos to take care of him?" Blade asked.

"Don't think we haven't tried. Twice we sent special units across the border on his trail. They never came back."

"Then you certainly don't want the Force to tangle with the Devil. We're not ready yet."

"No. But I'm hoping you'll agree to try and find where El Diablo has his headquarters," General Gallagher said.

"You're kidding."

"Hear me out," Gallagher said quickly. "This wouldn't be a combat mission. All you would have to do is track El Diablo into Baja California, locate his base of operations, and report back to me. Once I know where the son of a bitch holes up, I'll convince Governor Melnick to send in an air strike."

Blade shook his head. "Too risky. The new recruits haven't been together long enough to mesh as a unit, and they'd need to be in top form to take on the Devil."

"But that's my whole point. I'm not asking you to take him on. I don't want the Force to engage the Devils. All you have to do is track El Diablo to his lair. How hard can that be? After all, you have a mutation and an Indian on your team. And Captain Havoc is no slouch in the tracking department either."

"I don't know," Blade said uncertainly. "What if something goes wrong?"

"You'll take a radio along. At the first sign of trouble, send out a message. I'll have the VTOLs waiting near the border to fly in and retrieve you. What more could you want?"

The Warrior leaned back and pursed his lips.

"This could be an ideal training exercise for your new people," General Gallagher stated. "You'll be in the field, where you can put the volunteers through their paces, without any danger. Or virtually none."

"I like the idea of a field exercise," Blade admitted, "but this still sounds too hazardous."

"Think it over. Take a few days to decide."

Blade tapped his left hand on the desk. "Didn't you say the raid on Jacumba took place two weeks ago?"

"Yes."

"There you have it. We'd never be able to follow a two-week-old trail. We'll have to pass on the mission," Blade said.

"The trail would be impossible to follow if the Devils traveled on foot, but they don't. El Diablo's band uses souped-up, stripped-down, converted cars and trucks. He takes every vehicle he can lay his grimy hands on and has them converted into makeshift dune buggies," Gallagher detailed.

"Into what?"

"Dune buggies. They're real popular at the beach, and they work like a charm on desert terrain. They're rugged and as lightweight as possible, and they're outfitted with oversized tires. Dune buggies can go practically anywhere," Gallagher said. "Even though the trail is two weeks old, there are bound to be enough tracks for Sparrow and Jaguarundi to track."

"Why don't you send in another Ranger or Special Forces team?"

"They're good, but there are very few Indians in either and no mutations whatsoever. The Force has an edge in that respect."

Blade frowned, striving to formulate another valid objection. "When would you want us to depart?"

"Whenever you felt you were ready. I wouldn't take longer than a week to decide, though. I doubt even Sparrow and Jag could follow a trail over three weeks old."

"I just don't know."

Sensing he had won, General Gallagher gazed at the floor and grinned. When he looked up, he displayed a straight face. "I've brought maps of the area in the briefcase and the intelligence file on El Diablo and the Devils. Read it. Study the maps. Whatever you decide will be fine by me." He rose and clinched his argument with the appeal he had saved for last. "I hope you'll agree. Just think of all the lives, all the innocent men, women, and children we could save if we can eliminate El Diablo. He killed twenty-six kids in Jacumba alone."

Blade thought of Jenny and Gabe and wished he'd stayed at the Home.

CHAPTER FIVE

"**W**here the hell are we, dude?"

"In Baja California."

"I know that," Lobo stated stiffly.

"Then why'd you ask?" Captain Havoc responded.

"What are you giving me a hard time for? All I want to know is where exactly we're at?" Lobo said, stepping over a large rock in his path. He gazed at the camouflage backpack riding between the officer's broad shoulders and waited for an answer.

"We're approximately ten miles south of the border," Havoc told him.

"Is that all? I feel as if I've been hikin' for days," Lobo groused.

Havoc consulted the watch on his left wrist. "We've been hiking for three hours and ten minutes. At a snail's pace, I might add."

"Who asked you?"

Captain Havoc glanced over his left shoulder. "Do you ever wake up in a good mood?"

Lobo hefted the M-16 he carried and eyed the officer resentfully. "What's that crack supposed to mean?"

"All you ever do is complain."

"I do not," Lobo declared. "And you shouldn't be bad-mouthing me, sucker. I'm not the kind of guy you want to mess with, not if you want to stay healthy."

"What will you do? Pay Raphaela to beat me up?" Havoc said, and laughed.

"The only reason the bitch won is because she cheated," Lobo declared angrily.

"She sure nailed you good."

"Don't remind me."

A soft chuckle came from behind the Clansman. "You may never be able to have kids, pardner."

Lobo looked back at Doc Madsen, who followed five feet to his rear. "My balls are made of iron, man. That sneak kick of hers hardly fazed me."

"Then why were you on your knees on the mat, holding yourself and begging her to spare you?" Doc responded.

"It was all an act. I didn't want her to get me riled. I was afraid I'd lose my temper and stomp her butt," Lobo said.

"You're amazing," Doc stated.

"You bet your ass I am."

"Yep," Doc stated, and nodded. "You're truly amazing. I've never met anyone like you. How do you sling so much bull and keep such a straight face at the same time?"

Captain Havoc snickered.

"What is this? Pick-on-Lobo day or something?" the Clansman snapped. "Why is everyone always on my case?"

"Because you ask for it," Havoc said.

"You're nuts," Lobo replied. He wiped his left hand across his perspiring brow and squinted skyward at the blistering sun. "Damn, it's hot. I've never been anywhere as hot as this."

"It's called a desert," Captain Havoc quipped.

"And what are those mountains over there?" Lobo inquired, pointing to the east at the barren foothills and arid peaks beyond, not more than a mile distant.

"That range is known as the Sierra San Pedro Martir," Havoc answered.

"They seem to be gettin' closer," Lobo observed.

"Boy, you don't miss a thing, do you?" Havoc cracked. "Yeah, the mountains are getting closer because we've been angling to the southwest for the past two hours."

"Do you think this El Diablo has his base in those

mountains?'' Lobo asked.

"It wouldn't surprise me," Havoc said. "This section of the Baja is sparsely populated. Except for a few scattered villages, there are thousands of square miles in which a smart bandit could hide his headquarters."

"What if we bump into him?" Lobo queried nervously.

"Our mission is to track him to his lair, remember?" Havoc reminded the Clansman. "We're not supposed to engage the Devil."

"But something could go wrong. His band might spot us," Lobo said. "What then?"

Doc Madsen snickered. "You wouldn't have anything to worry about, Lobo."

"Why not?"

"I reckon Raphaela would protect you."

The Cavalryman and the officer laughed uproariously. Both were looking at the Clansman, and failed to notice the giant blocking their path until Havoc sensed his presence and abruptly halted.

"Fill me in on the joke," Blade stated, his hands on his hips, an M60E3 general-purpose machine gun hanging by a heavy leather strap under his right arm. A pair of ammo belts crisscrossed his massive chest. Under his left arm, in a shoulder holster, rested a Colt Stainless Steel Officers Model 45. Secured to his back was a camouflage backpack identical to Havoc's. Attached to his belt at the small of his back was a full canteen. The Bowies, as ever, were on either hip. Crammed in both front pockets were grenades.

"We were just havin' a little fun," Lobo said.

"Advertise our location, why don't you?" Blade declared, his tone laced with sarcasm.

"You didn't tell us not to talk," Lobo defended them.

"We're in enemy territory, hunting for a guy who takes pleasure in mutilating others, who has been responsible for the deaths of hundreds. Should I have to tell you to keep the noise down? I mistakenly assumed you were smart enough to figure that out for yourselves," Blade said, and glanced at Captain Havoc. "You should all know better."

The officer bit his lower lip, his features hardening, and gazed down at the ground. "I'm sorry, sir. I assure you it won't happen again."

"The same here," Doc Madsen said. He reached up and pulled his hat lower over his eyes. "I guess the heat is making us a bit careless." His fingers tugged on the strap to the M-16 suspended over his left shoulder. Like the others, he wore a backpack, only his was twice as long and half again as wide.

"Do you want someone to spell you with the radio?" Blade asked.

"Nope. I'm doing fine," Doc said, "although I wish I'd taken your advice and worn a pair of those Army boots instead of my own. Mine were made more for riding than walking."

"Live and learn," Blade remarked. Consistent with his long-standing policy of permitting the Force members to wear their own clothing unless the circumstances dictated otherwise, he'd not made an issue of their attire. He'd required each one to bring an M-16, and they all had Colt pistols except Madsen and Jag. Blade's clothing consisted of his vest and pants. Lobo had his leather, and Doc his own clothes. Captain Havoc, naturally enough, had opted to wear fatigues, as had Raphaela, who now stood at the rear of the line, her face caked with perspiration, an M-16 held loosely in her right hand, her weariness transparent. "How are you holding up?" Blade asked, looking straight at her.

"I won't have to worry about losing those five pounds I wanted to lose," Raphaela replied, and grinned. "I feel like I'm being roasted alive. How do animals live in this heat? And how can those two wear coats?" She nodded at Madsen and Lobo.

"It's easy," Doc informed her. "My frock coat and Lobo's leather jacket help to keep us cool."

"Cool? You guys must be sweating like pigs."

"Yeah. But the sweat evaporates, and the evaporation cools our bodies," Doc said.

"I guess I should have brought a coat," Raphaela cracked. "Silly me."

"We'll take a break as soon as Jag and Sparrow return,"

Blade let them know.

"Hallelujah, bro," Lobo declared, and gazed past the Warrior. "Here they come now."

Blade turned and spied the hybrid and the Flathead emerging from a ravine 500 yards to the southwest. They were running side by side, conversing as they ran. Both wore backpacks and had M-16's slung over their arms. Sparrow also carried his prized spear.

"Maybe they found the Devil's hideout," Lobo commented hopefully.

The Warrior watched the pair approach, silently sharing the Clansman's expectation. The mission had progressed satisfactorily so far—so far—but he felt uneasy, a feeling he attributed to his apprehension over taking the new Force into the field with just two weeks' worth of training under their belts.

The seven days since General Gallagher first proposed the assignment had passed quickly, perhaps too quickly. There had been drills and training exercises every day from dawn until dusk. Marksmanship, hand-to-hand combat, military strategy, calisthenics, weapons-familiarity classes, and other activities were crammed into the schedule. Every day at four in the afternoon the team studied survival techniques. The basics of military discipline were instilled in them.

They'd learned well, Blade had to admit. Captain Havoc, of course, had breezed through the classes. Doc Madsen and Sparrow had applied themselves industriously. Jaguarundi, although he viewed some of the exercises as a patent waste of his time, had cooperated without argument. Raphaela had worked the hardest at mastering the techniques and learning the lessons. Predictably, Lobo had adopted a disinterested attitude and expended only enough energy to get each job done.

And then, only last night, the two VTOLs had flown the Force to a point at the border southwest of Jacumba where General Gallagher waited with a convoy of soldiers. A temporary base camp, consisting of four dozen tents, had been set up to serve as Gallagher's command post. After a briefing and a night of fitful sleep, the Force had assembled before dawn. As the first rays of light etched the eastern horizon, they'd departed on the trail of El Diablo.

Now here they were, deep into the domain of the bandits, sweltering in the Baja desert, hot but alive. Blade held the M60 at his left side and waited for his point men. He stared at the large tire impressions imbedded in the earth to his left, recalling the information Gallagher had imparted about dune buggies. The vehicles were supposedly lightweight, but whatever made those prints had been gigantic.

What could it have been?

Sparrow Hawk and Jaguarundi drew closer, and finally halted in front of the giant. Sparrow's buckskins were coated with dust. A layer of sweat coated Jag's fur.

"Did you find the Devil's stronghold?" Blade inquired immediately.

"No," Sparrow replied.

"The trail leads up into the mountains," Jag said. "We followed the tracks for four miles and found a water hole where they made camp. They continued to the east."

"There's a water hole four miles from here?" Blade said, and scratched his chin. "We'll make camp there too. What have you learned about their forces?"

"There are fifteen vehicles. Eleven are the size of an average car and they leave light prints. Four vehicles are huge and heavy. They leave the biggest tire tracks I've ever seen," Jag stated, "and that includes the tracks made by the convoy trucks back at our base camp. The vehicles responsible must weigh tons and be enormous. I can't imagine what they could be."

"I've noticed the same tracks," Blade remarked. "They're quite puzzling." He paused. "Did you see anyone? Any raiders?"

"We saw no one," Sparrow responded. He gazed out over the flat expanse of desert, then at the mountains to the east. Both were bisected by periodic gullies and ravines. The vegetation consisted of scrub brush and stunted trees. Boulders dotted the landscape. "All we encountered were a few birds, snakes and lizards."

"Do we get that break you promised?" Lobo interjected.

"I've changed my mind," Blade said.

"Figures," the Clansman mumbled.

"Since the water hole is only four miles off, we'll keep going until we reach it."

"Any chance of you carrying me piggyback?" Lobo asked.

Blade ignored him and glanced at Captain Havoc. "Contact General Gallagher and inform him of our plans."

"Yes, sir," the officer said, and walked over to Doc Madsen. "Let me have the radio."

The Cavalryman slipped the oversized backpack from his shoulders and gently eased it to the ground. "There you go."

In less than a minute Havoc had the radio out and was adjusting several dials. He flicked a silver toggle switch and raised the square microphone to his lips. "Bravo-Echo. This is Lima-Oscar-Victor-Echo."

Static crackled from a small speaker on the right side of the housing.

"Bravo-Echo. This is Lima-Oscar-Victor-Echo," Havoc repeated, and scanned the dials, insuring the settings were correct.

"Maybe they're not listening," Lobo said.

"Our frequency is being monitored constantly," Blade told him. "General Gallagher is ready to send in the VTOLs at a word from us."

Lobo made a snorting sound. "All he has to do is *hear* the word."

"May I make a suggestion, sir?" Captain Havoc queried.

"Go ahead."

"We shouldn't be standing out in the open like sitting ducks. Why don't you head on out and I'll catch up as soon as I raise the general?"

"I don't want to leave you alone."

Havoc smiled. "I can take care of myself, sir. It shouldn't take more than a few minutes."

The Warrior cradled the M60 and surveyed their barren surroundings. "All right. But you have five mintues and no longer. We'll go slowly." He paused. "Give your backpack to Doc."

Havoc complied, then squatted next to the radio. "See you in a bit."

Blade motioned with his right arm and the Force hiked to the southwest.

"Be careful," Raphaela warned the officer as she passed him.

"Always," Captain Havoc replied. He fiddled with the dials while surreptitiously watching his teammates leave. When they were 30 yards away and well out of hearing range, he spoke into the microphone again. "Hotel-Alfa-Victor-Oscar-Charlie here."

"Report, Captain," barked the stern voice of General Gallagher through the speaker.

"We're heading for the water hole, sir," Havoc informed his superior.

"Any sign of the Boob Boy yet?"

"Negative, sir."

"What about the Goons?"

"Negative again, sir."

"Damn."

The speaker crackled for several seconds.

"Has the Jolly Mean Giant displayed any suspicions?" Gallagher asked.

"No, sir. He doesn't suspect a thing."

"Don't be too sure, Captain. Never underestimate him. His mind is the equal of his muscles."

"If you say so, sir," Captain Havoc said crisply.

"I mean it, Captain. I'll hold you accountable if he discovers the real reason for this mission."

"He won't, sir," Havoc stated. "And if you don't mind my saying, sir, you give him too much credit."

"How so, Captain?"

"If he's so damn great, how come he let my brother die?"

A sigh came from the speaker. "I know how close Jimmy and you were, Mike. But don't allow your feelings to interfere with your better judgment."

"You know me better than that, sir."

"If I didn't have complete confidence in you, I wouldn't have selected you for this job," General Gallagher said.

"I know, sir. You have my gratitude. I want revenge so bad I can taste it."

"Control yourself, Captain. We'll do this my way or not at all."

"Yes, sir."

"If my plan succeeds, you'll avenge your brother and I'll finally be rid of the Force for good."

Captain Havoc grinned. "I can hardly wait, sir."

CHAPTER SIX

Blade didn't like the location of the water hole.

Situated in the mountains on the south side of a spacious clearing, at the base of a sheer 200-foot cliff, the oval depression in which spring water had collected was 15 feet across and appeared to be eight feet deep. The north side of the clearing bordered a steep incline composed of loose rock, too steep to be easily scaled. Only from the east and the west could the water hole be approached. To the west, the route the Force had followed, a wide gully meandered from the base of the foothills to the clearing. To the east the gully continued up a slight grade. Four hundred feet from the water hole was a low crest obscuring whatever lay on the far side.

The Warrior glanced at the cliff, then the steep incline, bothered by the feeling of being hemmed in. If the Force should be attacked now, their mobility would be severely impaired. He squinted up at the top of the cliff, wondering if there were enemy eyes up above spying on them.

"Is everything okay?" Raphaela asked.

Blade looked to his right, where she stood with her canteen in her hands, and nodded. "Relatively speaking, yes."

"I get the impression you're worried."

"This whole mission worries me," Blade said, and gazed at the other Force members. Doc, Lobo, and Sparrow were lounging next to the water. Jaguarundi stood a few yards to the east, scrutinizing the terrain. Captain Havoc was standing a few feet to the Warrior's left, listening intently.

"Why, sir?" the officer inquired.

"Because I still have doubts about our readiness for an assignment of this nature. Most of you are quite capable in your own right, but we haven't learned how to mesh as a team yet. Until we can, every time we venture into the field we take our lives in our hands. In our line of work inexperience and a lack of coordination can be fatal, and I don't want to lose any of you," Blade stated.

"Is that a fact?" Captain Havoc responded, his face impassive.

"It's nice to know you care about us," Raphaela said to Blade.

"In the final analysis I'm responsible for your lives," Blade said. "My decisions can determine whether you live or die. I lost five members of the first Force, and I don't intend to repeat that tragedy."

"How did the others die?" Raphaela questioned.

"They all gave their lives in the line of duty. Most died in combat. One, Athena Morris, a highly respected journalist who wrote reports on our missions for the newspapers, died accidentally when she fell out of a hospital window."

Raphaela's forehead creased. "She fell out a window?"

Blade nodded. "She was under sedation at the time. Athena had been injured during our assignment in Alaska, and the doctor gave her strong medication. Apparently she opened her window to get fresh air and slipped." He frowned. "She was on the seventh floor."

"And she wasn't pushed?" Raphaela asked.

"No," Blade replied.

"They're certain of that?"

"Yes." Blade stared at her. "Why?"

"Oh, I don't know," Raphaela said, and shrugged. "It just seems strange that she would simply fall out a window. She was a regular member of the Force, right?"

"Yeah."

"Then she went through training, didn't she?"

Blade nodded. "She even trained with the Rangers before joining the Force so she would qualify."

"Then she must have been in top condition. Even though she was drugged, I can't see her falling out a window."

The Warrior sighed. "I had a hard time believing it too. But General Gallagher assured us they had conducted a thorough investigation and there was no hint of foul play."

"General Gallagher wouldn't lie. She must have fallen then," Raphaela conceded.

Blade stared at the sky, recalling the funeral, the sight of Athena's coffin being lowered in her grave. Unfortunately, due to the damage done to her head and torso, the coffin had been sealed at the viewing prior to the burial. He remembered the tormented expression on Grizzly, the hybrid who had loved her. Now poor Grizzly was somewhere in the Outlands, an outcast in a savage land, filled with remorse and anger. Someday soon, Blade decided, he would hunt Grizzly down.

"How long will we stay here, sir?" Captain Havoc inquired.

"It's about noon now. We'll rest for an hour," Blade replied. He walked to the east, heading for the crest. "I'll be right back."

"Mind if I join you?" Jaguarundi asked, coming alongside the giant.

"Be my guest," Blade said. He studied the ground underfoot as they ascended the rise, noting the overlapping tire tracks. "El Diablo uses this gully on a regular basis."

"That'd be my guess," Jag concurred. "The walls conceal his vehicles. He can travel all the way to the desert without exposing his band."

"And by using the gully he makes aerial observation extremely difficult," Blade noted.

"He's one devious son of a bitch."

Blade twisted and gazed at the rim of the cliff, disturbed by the sensation of being watched. "This setup stinks."

Jag glanced at the Warrior. "You too, huh?"

"Yep."

They covered a hundred feet in silence.

"You know," Jag commented, "I don't much like having to wear a backpack and tote an M-16. I'm best at infighting, where I can employ my nails."

"Your nails wouldn't do you much good against a machine gun," Blade said.

"True, not unless I could get close," Jag said. "How did Grizzly take to using a weapon and wearing a backpack?"

"He liked to rely on his strength and claws and he hated wearing anything."

Jag chuckled. "That sounds like Grizzly." He licked his dry lips. "Gallagher told me there are hybrids living at the place you come from, the Home."

"Gremlin, Ferret, and Lynx. They've been at the Home for nearly six years."

"What do they do there?"

"They were selected to be Warriors," Blade divulged. "Do you know them?"

"Not personally. I heard about Lynx, about the time he tried to assassinate the Doktor. He was famous. But there were fifteen hundred hybrids in the madman's Genetic Research Division, and I didn't know them all."

"You should visit the Home some day. I'm sure Lynx, Ferret, and Gremlin would like to meet you."

"Maybe I will," Jaguarundi said. "What's it like there anyway? I've heard stories about your Home being a Utopia."

"Utopia? Sir Thomas More would probably disagree. The Family does live according to certain spiritual ideals, and the Home is the ideal environment in which to live, but we have a long way to go before we attain perfection," Blade stated. "We are trying to live harmoniously, though, which is more than can be said about ninety-nine percent of the world."

"Are you religious?"

"Yes."

"Really?"

"Why do you sound so surprised? Are you an atheist like Grizzly?"

"I'm surprised because I never expected a guy with your reputation to believe in any of that metaphysical stuff. As for me, I don't know what I believe. Most of the hybrids in the Genetic Research Division didn't believe in any spiritual jazz. Why should they? All of them were created in a test tube," Jag said. "When a person discovers they were whipped together in a little glass vial, it distorts their outlook on life in general.''

"Are you speaking from your personal experience?"

"Yeah. It blew my mind when I was told the Doktor created me. I felt artificial, alien, as if I didn't belong on the planet. I wanted to crawl under a rock somewhere. And my attitude wasn't helped much by the fact that most humans looked down their noses at us. Some of the hybrids became intensely bitter.''

"Like Grizzly."

"Like Grizzly," Jag agreed. "I couldn't quite bring myself to hate humans because I saw that many of you were in the same boat we were, living miserable lives, drifting from day to day, under the thumb of the dictator, Samuel the Second. Of course, that was before your Family and your allies defeated Sammy and the Doktor.''

"So now you view us as a bunch of meatballs," Blade said.

"Most humans are."

They neared the crest.

Jag grinned. "But I'll make an exception in your case. You're all right for a human.''

"Gee. Thanks," Blade said, and slowed as the rim became visible. The ground curved downward from the crest rather abruptly. A patch of green became visible on the far side, then grew larger until a sea of green foliage came into view. He stepped to the top and gazed in fascination at a lush, verdant valley, an oasis of life ringed by high, dry peaks.

"Wow," Jag commented.

Blade estimated the valley to be 20 miles from west to east and half that distance from north to south. His vantage point afforded him a bird's-eye view. In the middle of the valley, beckoning like a shimmering blue beacon, was a sizeable lake. Less than a mile from the crest, wafting heavenward on the breeze, were a half-dozen thin gray ribbons. A dirt road started at the base of the grade, swung slightly to the south, then bore due east.

"Do you want me to investigate that smoke?" Jag asked. "It might be El Diablo's campfires.''

The Warrior pondered for a moment. Scouting the valley made sense. He didn't want the Force to blunder onto the enemy stronghold. And none of the others, including Sparrow, were as stealthy as the hybrid. "Find out where the smoke comes from," he directed, "but stay alert. It goes without saying that the Devils are dangerous."

"If I find them, I'll bring back one of their heads as a souvenir," Jag boasted.

"Just get back in one piece. We'll wait at the water hole for you."

"On my way," Jag said, and jogged toward the trees. "I should return within an hour."

"Don't rush. And don't get caught."

"Never happen."

Blade watched the hybrid until Jag was lost from sight in the trees. Then he turned and walked toward the water hole. The others were talking and, from the harried look on Lobo's face, poking fun at the Clansman. A smile creased Blade's mouth and he nodded in satisfaction. This new team was a distinct improvement over the old unit in terms of their getting along together. The first Force volunteers had been prone to constant bickering and petty squabbles. These people were relating marvelously, and he hoped nothing would transpire to disrupt their accord.

What was that?

A flicker of movement drew Blade's attention to the north, to the incline covered with loose rock. He spied something perched on top, something huge and reptilian, and it took a second for his stunned mind to belatedly register the magnitude of the creature.

Dear Spirit!

A hideous lizard of gargantuan proportions squatted on four short, thick limbs, its baleful eyes fixed on the unsuspecting Force members by the pool. A blunt, black head, sinister in aspect, reared above a stocky body. The tail, tapered and clublike, twitched from side to side. Both the body and the tail were yellow with irregular black bands and were covered with prominent scales. From the tip of its nose to the end of its tail the lizard measured ten feet in length. Its head was poised six feet above the ground. A long red tongue darted from its mouth and retracted.

In a flash of insight Blade recognized the creature. He'd seen photographs of such lizards in books in the Family library when he was younger, and he'd always been intrigued by the species. Not many lizards were venomous carnivores. And only one kind was known as Gila monsters.

An ordinary Gila monster reached two, maybe three feet in length. The enormous specimen staring hungrily at the Force was a byproduct of World War Three, a consequence of having the biological chain tainted by gene-warping radiation and chemical-warfare toxins. Cases of giantism had become quite common. Everything from cockroaches to alligators now came in a jumbo size.

Blade pivoted and went to yell a warning to his teammates, but even as he did the Gila monster launched its bulky body from the top and hurtled down the incline. "Look out!" Blade bellowed, and gestured at the monstrosity.

The five at the water hole glanced up at the Warrior, then swiveled to the north. Lobo and Raphaela gaped in astonishment. Doc and Sparrow started to unsling their M-16s. Only Captain Havoc reacted instantly by raising his M-16 to his right shoulder and dashing toward the incline.

Blade raced to intercept the mutation. He saw the Gila monster gain momentum as it slid down the slope, its heavy body stirring a swirling cloud of dust into the air.

Captain Havoc fired on the run, making a beeline for the beast, the backpack containing the radio bouncing on his shoulders.

Still too far off to shoot effectively, Blade covered the grade in prodigious leaps. The dust cloud enveloping the Gila monster shrouded all of the lizard except for its head, but the thing was clearly picking up speed as it slid lower and lower.

Havoc reached the base of the incline and sighted on the monster's head.

"Get out of the way!" Blade shouted, realizing the Gila monster wouldn't be able to be stopped in time.

Heedless of his safety, Havoc stood firm and squeezed off a burst. The lizard was a mere 15 feet from him when he threw his body to the right, away from its path. But the next second the mutation changed direction, slanting toward the officer, and before Havoc could fire again the creature pounced.

CHAPTER SEVEN

He loved the forest.

Jaguarundi followed a narrow game trail in the direction of the spires of smoke. His keen ears noted the chirping of birds and the buzzing of nearby insects. To his nostrils came dank, earthy scents and animal odors: rabbit, squirrel, coatimondi, deer, and others. If the odors, sounds, and the tracks on the trail were any indication, the valley was a wildlife paradise. He skirted a tree, saw a straight stretch ahead, and ran full out, not fatigued in the least by the trek across the desert. He reveled in being able to exercise, to use his muscles, and in the incredible speed he could attain.

The Doktor had once arranged a contest to determine which of his many hybrids was the fastest. He'd gathered all of those endowed with exceptional fleetness of foot and raced them around a regulation track, running them six at a time and clocking their speed. After four hours, after the slowest were eliminated, the Doktor had lined up the six best and fired his signal gun.

Jag relived that race as he sprinted through the woods. He'd tried so hard to win, to achieve special recognition, to prove to himself that he was the best hybrid in at least one category. And he'd almost succeeded. The puma-man had given him trouble early on, had stayed with him for a third of the race, and then, as with wild cougars, the puma-man had folded, unable to maintain his top pace for the long haul. Cougars could outrun deer, but only for short distances. So Jag had blown him away and left him far behind. By all rights Jag should have won.

Should have.

But didn't.

After he had passed all the others, after he had outlasted the puma hybrid, when he was halfway around the course and no one was ahead of him, seemingly out of nowhere streaked the one mutation even he couldn't beat, the one capable of running at a top speed of 70 miles an hour, the one who would be honored as the fastest hybrid alive: the cheetah-man.

Jag recalled his intense disappointment at coming in second. Oh, the Doktor had praised him in front of the assembled Genetic Research Division and told everyone that he had been clocked at 52 miles an hour. Fifty-two. Eighteen less than the cheetah hybrid. But being second had upset him, deprived him of any sense of accomplishment. To his way of thinking, those who succeeded in life were the swiftest and strongest. Life went to the sure and the quick. Those who came in second were left with table scraps.

One small consolation, a source of much pleasure, was the fact he could run faster, jump farther, leap higher, and track better than any human alive. He might not be the best, the strongest, the swiftest hybrid alive, but he could run rings around every human in more ways than one. And since humans generally distrusted or despised genetically engineered mutations, he felt considerable satisfaction at knowing he excelled them physically. Only once in his entire life had a human bested him.

Blade.

The enigmatic giant.

The Warrior who, incredibly, did not appear to be prejudiced against hybrids. One of the few humans Jag had met who could look him in the eyes without betraying a trace of uneasiness or bias. One of the . . .

The chattering of automatic rifle fire erupted to his rear.

Jag began to slow and looked over his right shoulder, alarmed, realizing his teammates must be under attack. He took three more strides and started to rotate, to hasten to their aid.

Something grabbed him.

A constricting loop tightened about his left ankle, throwing him off balance, and although he attempted to right himself and jerk his ankle free, although his reflexes were outstanding, he couldn't prevent whatever held him from hauling him from the ground and whipping him 20 feet into the air. The M-16 slipped from his shoulder and fell into the brush. Upended, he swayed back and forth.

A trap!

He'd been caught by a damn animal trap!

Jag craned his neck to see a rope around his ankle. Someone had placed a snare along the game trail, probably a hunter hoping to bag a deer. The rope dug into his fur and skin, causing him minor discomfort. From his ankle the rope rose nine feet to a stout limb overhead, over which it looped and then slanted down to the top of a bent sapling, where it had been securely tied, ten yards to the north.

A lousy snare!

How stupid could he have been!

Jag relaxed, hanging limp, trying to control and reduce the swaying. He gazed at the trail below, listening to the continued gunfire from the vicinity of the water hole. Terrific! His companions were fighting for their lives and he was stuck in a snare. Frustrated, he waited for the swinging to subside. How quickly he could escape depended on the toughness of the rope. His fingernails were quite sharp, but he would need precious time to saw through the strands. Perhaps he could snap the rope. The drop to the ground didn't bother him. A fall of 20 feet was child's play.

A twig snapped to the east.

Jaguarundi twisted and searched for the reason. He didn't have to search very hard.

Eighteen feet off stood a boy of 12 or 13 dressed in a white shirt, white pants, and sandals, armed with a machete in his right hand. His dark eyes gawked upward. "*El tigre!*" he exclaimed, and began to back away.

"Cut me loose, kid," Jag snapped.

The boy's mouth opened wide enough to swallow an apple whole and his eyes tried to bulge out of their sockets. He switched the machete to his left hand and quickly crossed himself. "*Madre de Dios!*" he cried, and burst into a string of words in Spanish.

"Look, kid, do you speak English?" Jag asked, keeping his voice calm and friendly.

The boy only stared.

"Do you speak English?" Jag repeated.

"*Si, señor,*" the boy said softly. "A little."

"Good. Do you hear those gunshots? My pals need me. Cut me down."

"What *are* you?" the boy asked in awe.

"Never mind that," Jag said impatiently. "Just cut me down so I can go to my buddies."

"No, *señor.*"

"What?"

"I can't cut you down. I must tell *mi padre.*"

"Don't tell anyone," Jag stated. He smiled and motioned for the boy to come closer. "Look, kid. I won't hurt you. Cut me down and I'll be on my way."

"No, *señor,*" the boy responded, and unexpectedly spun on his heels and raced to the east.

"Come back here!" Jag shouted. "Don't leave me like this!"

But the boy didn't even look back. In moments he was out of sight.

"Damn it," Jag muttered. He didn't know how long it would take the kid to tell his father, but others were bound to show up soon. He had to escape from the snare and fast. Slowly, tensing his abdominal muscles, he bent in half at the waist and raised his arms, reaching for the rope. Endowed with a slim, supple form and capable of contorting his body in a manner that dazzled most humans, he easily flattened his chest against his legs, lunged, and grabbed his left ankle. An inspection of the rope confirmed that it would be extremely difficult to cut with his nails. Since there wasn't any time to lose, he took hold of the rope and pulled himself upward, climbing higher until he was vertical again. And still he climbed, all the way to the overhead limb, where he paused.

Now how should he go about this?

Jag wrapped his left arm around the limb, then his right, and gracefully swung his legs up. He reclined on top of the limb and listened for more shots, but the guns had fallen quiet. Concerned, he eased his left leg up and his left hand lower until he could loosen the rope and slide his ankle free.

All right!

Elated, he stared at the grass and weeds far below and debated whether to simply jump or use the rope to slide down. Since time was critical he decided to jump and rolled from the limb. The vegetation blurred as he plummeted, and he landed on his feet with his thigh muscles absorbing most of the impact. He straightened and took two strides.

"Stop!"

The barked command brought Jaguarundi up short and he turned, amazed to discover the boy had already returned. The youth wasn't alone. Three men stood 30 feet away, and all three had rifles trained on him. Like the boy, the men were dressed in plain white cotton shirts and trousers. All three wore wide-brimmed straw hats. The tallest of the trio also wore a red poncho.

"If you move we will shoot!" the tall one warned.

Jag hesitated, and glanced at the trees and brush to his left and right. He could probably duck into cover before they could fire. Probably. But there were three guns, and if just one of the Mexicans made a lucky shot it would be all over. He frowned and elevated his arms to demonstrate his peaceful intentions. "I don't mean you any harm."

"It's true!" the man in the red poncho exclaimed. "What Miguel told us is true. *El tigre* speaks English!"

The shortest of the three men spoke at length in Spanish and gestured at Jag several times.

"Look, I don't have time for this," Jag declared. "I must go to my friends."

"You are not going anywhere," stated the man in the poncho. He walked forward, the others flanking him, regarding their prisoner intently. "What are you? You look like a cat but you talk like a man."

"I'm a hybrid."

"A what?"

"Do you know anything about genetic engineering?" Jag asked.

The tall man shook his head, his gaze roving over Jag's features in astonishment.

"No, you wouldn't know much about science, would you?" Jag muttered, and sighed in frustration. "I'm part man, part jaguarundi."

"You are a demon," the man declared.

"Be serious, mister. What's your name anyway?" Jag inquired hoping familiarity would breed friendliness.

"I'm Emiliano, Miguel's father."

"My name is Jag."

The Mexicans halted 15 feet from him, their rifles still leveled.

"You have a name?" Emiliano responded in surprise.

"Why wouldn't I? I'm a person, not an animal."

"We don't know *what* you are," Emiliano said.

"I'd like to go now."

Emiliano shook his head. "That is not possible. We must take you to our village."

A scowl twisted Jag's mouth. He wanted to dart into the forest, but those three unwavering rifle barrels deterred him. There hadn't been any more gunfire to the west, which was good, but the rest of the Force could well be dead for all he knew.

"You will come with us, *señor*," Emiliano said. "We don't want to shoot you, but we will if we must."

"How far is your village?" Jag asked.

"Not far," Emiliano replied, and jerked his head to the east. "We were out setting traps for game." He glanced at the dangling rope. "We set that one fifteen minutes ago, and were working on another one a little ways up the trail when my son ran to us and told us about the talking cat-man." He shook his head in wonder. "I would never have believed it, but Miguel is a decent boy. He always tells the truth."

The little snot! Jag thought, but he wisely kept his opinion to himself.

Emiliano wagged his rifle, a Winchester Model 70. "Now you will walk in front of us to our village. If you try any tricks we'll shoot."

"How about if we compromise?"

"*Señor?*"

"There are companions of mine at a water hole to the west. They might be in trouble and I'd like to go see. Take me to them and I promise no harm will come to you," Jag proposed.

Emiliano turned to the other two and apparently began translating the request.

Jag watched expectantly, anxious to return to Blade. If the peasants refused to take him to the water hole, he was determined to make a break—rifles or no rifles.

The shortest Mexican started shouting at Emiliano while the third one shook his head.

"I'm sorry, *señor*," Emiliano said, facing Jaguarundi. "Were it up to me, I might be tempted to trust you. But my compadres are not so inclined. They say we should take you to our village and show you to the *patrón* when he returns."

"The who?"

"Our master, *señor*. The one who rules our village. Some of his men are there now," Emiliano said, his tone oddly strained, as if talking about his master upset him.

"I can't go with you," Jag said.

"We will kill you if you don't," Emiliano warned.

"You'll try," Jaguarundi corrected him, and then Jag made his move, hoping the Mexicans wouldn't be as quick on the trigger as professional soldiers would be, hoping also that the conversation had lulled the trio into a state of complacency, that their trigger fingers were relaxed instead of tense and ready to squeeze. He plunged into the undergrowth on the south side of the game trail, and the vegetation closed about him as the three rifles cracked. Bullets ripped through the foliage, but none struck him. Instantly he poured on the speed, dodging trees and dense thickets, vaulting over logs, small boulders, and other obstructions. He planned to travel due south for several dozen yards, then cut to the west. He doubted the peasants were competent enough to track him, but they knew he wanted to head west and might try to intercept him. By swinging to the south and looping westward, he could easily elude them.

Another shot sounded to his rear.

Jag grinned. It was probably the short one venting his spleen and wasting a round. He went around a tree and up a low knoll. At the top he paused to glance back. As he'd anticipated, there wasn't any sign of pursuit. The trio and the boy must be on their way to the village to relate their harrowing encounter with the fierce El Tigre! He snickered and continued his circuitous route to the water hole, thinking of the term Emiliano had used to describe him.

Demon.

Funny, wasn't it, how humans were so quick to condemn anyone different from them? How the mere sight of a hybrid could drive an ordinary human into a raging fury or terrify the human witless? At the very least, most humans reacted with fear and suspicion to all hybrids, which to Jag's mind was highly ironic when he considered that human scientists were responsible for the creation of the genetically engineered creatures the humans feared. But then, human logic always had eluded him.

There seemed to be a clearing up ahead.

Jag checked to the north once again, but the three Mexicans still hadn't materialized. He wondered what would have happened if he'd allowed Emiliano and company to take him to the village? Would he have been stoned as a vile abomination? Set ablaze and consigned to some human hell?

The trees abruptly thinned.

Jaguarundi slowed, realizing he'd been mistaken. There wasn't a clearing; it was the dirt road. He weaved past a huge boulder and a tree and ran to the middle of the road. Now he would be able to make good time.

"What the hell are you?"

The harsh words brought Jag around, his features creasing in consternation when he discovered an armored vehicle, a camouflage-painted dune buggy, parked alongside the trees on the north side of the road approximately 30 feet to the east. Four burly men in camouflage fatigues, each armed with a machine gun, were standing in front of the dune buggy.

One of the quartet, a man sporting a full brown beard, swung his machine gun to cover Jaguarundi and sneered. "Twitch and you're history, you son of a bitch!"

CHAPTER EIGHT

Captain Havoc saw the Gila monster spring at him, saw the lizard's mouth swing wide, and knew in the next second that he would feel the beast's iron jaws clamp into his body. And they would have too, if not for the loose rock underfoot, because on his next step, as he frantically threw himself farther to the right, he slipped and fell, sprawling onto his stomach, his arms outflung. Something heavy brushed against his backpack, and dirt and dust whirled all around him, obscuring the ground.

A dull thud came from behind him.

The thing had missed! Havoc exulted, and he began to push to his feet. He got to his hands and knees, and then what felt like a battering ram smashed into his left side, lifted him from the ground, and sent him sailing through the air to crash onto a jagged boulder.

Excruciating agony lanced Havoc's chest and his right arm became momentarily limp, forcing him to release his M-16. He doubled over, clutching his side, in torment, dreading that his ribs might be busted. He gasped and struggled to compartmentalize the pain, to do as the martial arts instructor at the Special Forces Academy had taught him.

Other M-16's were firing now, punctuating the dust with muzzle flashes and lead, and somewhere in the cloud the Gila monster hissed and snapped.

Havoc managed to get to his knees. He heard Lobo shout

excitedly.

"Watch out for its tail! Watch out for its tail!"

A gun boomed, not the metallic burp of an M-16 but the deeper blast of a large-caliber revolver. Doc Madsen's Magnum.

Gritting his teeth, Havoc heaved to his feet and glanced around for his M-16. But all he could see was the swirling dust, dust that now caught in his throat and nostrils and made him cough and gag. He shuffled forward, feeling the pain begin to subside. Maybe his ribs weren't broken after all.

A huge form loomed in front of him and a guttural growl rent the air.

The Gila monster!

Havoc backed away from the mutation and drew the Colt Model 45 on his right hip. He steadied his arm, took a bead on where he imagined the beast's head should be, and fired three times.

An enraged bellow greeted the shots, and suddenly the Gila monster materialized less than eight feet from him, its head perforated with bullet holes and oozing streaks of strangely dark blood.

Havoc bumped into a boulder, the same one he had landed on, and halted. The mutation took a lumbering step toward him. He emptied the clip into the creature, going for the eyes, thinking he might be able to kill the monstrosity if he could plant a slug in its brain.

But the lizard came on. Slowly. Inexorably. Its gaze was riveted on the officer.

Havoc braced for the final attack. He had a 15-inch survival knife tucked inside his right combat boot, and although the knife would hardly dent the mutation's scales, he resolved to fight until his last breath, and crouched so he could draw the weapon from its sheath.

A towering figure suddenly ran between the officer and the lizard and cut loose with the M60 clasped in his steely hands.

"Blade!" Havoc blurted out.

The Warrior didn't bother to acknowledge the greeting. He fired into the Gila monster's blunt head, round after round after round, and the mutation recoiled and hissed, its tongue protruding from between its bony lips. More rounds ripped into the sensitive tongue and drove the brute over the edge. Hissing horribly, it thrust itself at the Warrior but was met by a wall of lead. Blade kept the trigger depressed, stitching the creature's forehead, noting that its movements were becoming sluggish and uncoordinated. Just when he thought the ammo belt would go dry, the Gila monster wheezed and collapsed two yards from his combat boots.

Blade ceased firing.

For all of five seconds there was silence.

"Blade? Havoc? Sparrow? Where is everybody?" Raphaela called out from close at hand.

"Havoc and I are here," Blade responded, lowering the smoking barrel. The dust started to clear and he could see her approaching. But where were the others? If the Gila monster hadn't chomped on them, a stray bullet might have caused a casualty.

"Here I am," Doc Madsen said, moving toward the Warrior.

Captain Havoc stood and walked to the Warrior's right side. "Thanks. You saved my life."

"You'd do the same for me," Blade replied.

Havoc pursed his lips and stared at the dead creature. If not for the damn mutation, the Warrior wouldn't have saved him. Thanks to the Gila monster, he was now in debt to Blade, and the last thing in the world he wanted to be was in debt to the man responsible for the death of his younger brother. He would have to put his scheme for revenge on hold. His sense of justice demanded that he repay the obligation to the Warrior before he repaid Blade for Jimmy's life.

"That is the *ugliest* sucker I've ever seen," Lobo declared, joining them. "It reminds me of a date I had once with Big Butt Biddel. The woman could break rocks just by lookin' at 'em."

"Such a feat isn't possible," Sparrow chimed in, coming around the rear of the lizard.

"Why do you take everything so literal?" Lobo asked.

"Why, Lobo, I didn't know you knew the meaning of the word," Doc joked. "Do you mean to tell us you've been hiding some brains between those ears of yours?"

Raphaela, Havoc, and Sparrow laughed lightly, dispelling the tension from their harrowing experience.

Lobo chose to ignore them and glanced at Blade. "Hey, dude, where's the kitty-cat?"

"I wouldn't call Jag that to his face, if I were you," the Warrior advised. "I sent him to scout the valley over the rise. We spotted smoke."

"El Diablo, you think?" Doc asked.

"We won't know until Jag returns," Blade said, and scanned them. "Is anyone hurt? Anyone nicked?"

"I'm fine," Raphaela said, and the rest nodded.

Except for Lobo.

The Clansman looked down at his pants and did a double take. "Well, I'll be damned."

"What?" Blade inquired.

"I thought for sure the sucker ripped my pants when it tried to gobble me down," Lobo stated, and kicked the carcass. "There I was, rushin' to help Havoc, when the thing came at me, hissin' and roarin' and shootin' fire from its mouth—"

"Did he say roaring?" Doc asked, interrupting.

"Did he say fire came from its mouth?" Raphaela chimed in.

"I believe Lobo must have mistaken the Gila monster for a dragon," Sparrow said. "This area is famous for its dragons."

Lobo stared at each of them in turn. He shook his head and tilted his nose in the air. "Fine, turkeys! Just be this way! If you don't want to hear how I barely came out of the fight alive, I won't tell you."

"We don't want to hear," Doc said.

"Ingrates," Lobo snapped, and headed for the water hole.

"Get set to move out in one minute," Blade instructed them. He saw an M-16 lying on the ground to his left and retrieved the weapon. "Who does this belong to?"

"That's mine, sir," Havoc said, taking the assault rifle.

"Why are we leaving when Jag hasn't come back yet?" Raphaela asked.

"Because someone in the valley might have heard all the gunfire. If so, they'll send a party to investigate. We don't want to be here when they come, so we'll take cover in the forest on the other side of the rise and wait there for Jag."

"But how will he find us?"

"We'll stay at the edge of the trees where we can keep our

eyes on the crest. He has to come that way to reach the water hole. We'll spot him, don't worry.''

''Good. I wouldn't want to lose him. He's been nice to me and I like him,'' Raphaela said.

Blade glanced at her, her words bringing to mind the romance that had blossomed between Athena Morris and Grizzly and the tragic conclusion of their relationship. He speculated on whether a similar situation was developing between Raphaela and Jaguarundi, and decided he was making a mountain out of the proverbial molehill. Just because Raphaela liked the hybrid as a friend didn't necessarily indicate she was falling in love with him.

He hoped.

''Was the radio damaged, Captain?'' Doc inquired.

''I don't know. I'll check,'' Havoc responded. He knelt and unslung the backpack. A hasty inspection verified the radio to be intact and functional. ''It's okay,'' he announced.

''We wouldn't want to lose our link with the outside world,'' Blade commented, then looked at Sparrow. ''Let's head out. You take the point.''

''On my way,'' the Flathead said, and jogged toward the top of the grade.

Blade turned his attention to the officer. ''Trade backpacks with Doc again. He'll carry the radio for a while.''

''I can manage, sir,'' Havoc said.

''The Force isn't a debating team,'' Blade stated, and grinned. ''That Gila monster roughed you up a bit. Doc will take the radio and give you a breather.''

Captain Havoc started to protest, but changed his mind. The Warrior only had his best interest at heart. Which stunk. Because Havoc was trying as hard as he could to despise the man, and Blade kept doing things that caused him to admire the Warrior more and more.

''You can bring up the rear,'' Blade said.

''Glad to, sir,'' Havoc dutifully replied. He took Doc's backpack, gave the Cavalryman the radio, and waited while the others headed for the crest. After a last scrutiny of the Gila monster he started up the grade, his eyes on the Warrior's muscular back, mulling his dilemma. What was he going to do?

He'd been on an assignment in northern California, involved in operations against a wicked drug lord—futile operations at that—when he'd learned about the death of his brother. Because of the remote location and the clandestine nature of his activities, the word didn't reach him until four days after Jimmy had been buried. He'd requested an emergency leave and rushed to Los Angeles, to the Force Facility, where his brother, the woman journalist, and the Indian had been buried. Except for the perimeter guards, no one else was there. The grave site, on top of a low hill in the northern sector of the facility, had seemed so desolate and inappropriate as the resting place for a man once so full of life and vitality.

General Gallagher had arrived while he was at the site, and from the general Havoc had learned that, due to a flat tire on a stretch of secondary road between L.A. and the Force compound, Havoc's mother and two other brothers hadn't arrived in time for the burial. The thought of Jimmy being lowered into eternity without a single family member on hand to mourn his passing was profoundly disturbing.

But not nearly as disturbing as the additional information Gallagher had imparted.

Havoc had been stunned to learn his brother had died on an unauthorized mission in Canada, of all places. According to General Gallagher, the Force had been en route from Alaska to California when the pilot of their VTOL intercepted a distress signal and pinpointed the approximate location. And although Canada was not a Freedom Federation member, although the team had fought long and hard in Alaska and needed a rest, Blade had ordered the pilot to land so they could aid whoever was in distress.

How unprofessional.

Captain Havoc frowned, remembering the details of his brother's death. Jimmy had given his life to save the life of another member of the Force, the former volunteer from the Cavalry, a man named Boone. Such a sacrifice would have been typical of his brother, a supreme example of Jimmy's dedication, a fitting end for a man who devoted his life to safeguarding others.

Except that if Blade had adhered to procedure, if the Warrior hadn't needlessly endangered the lives of the unit by violating proper military protocol, if the Force had returned to California on schedule instead of becoming involved in a battle with pirates, Sergeant James Havoc would still be alive. As the head of the Freedom Force, Blade bore the responsibility for the life of every man and woman on the team, and the Warrior had made a serious mistake in judgment by deciding to land in Canada, a mistake that had cost Jimmy his life.

Mike Havoc gazed absently at the ground.

General Gallagher, on that chilly day nine months ago, had stressed the injustice of Jimmy's death. The general had also emphasized how he felt the Force was a waste of manpower and resources, how California had managed quite well for a century without the need of a tactical strike team. Gallagher had sympathized with Havoc, and had even gone so far as to imply Blade was directly to blame for the loss of five members of the unit, not just Jimmy. But even though Gallagher wanted to close the Force down, he couldn't do so unless he could gather proof of the Warrior's incompetence to present to the Federation leaders.

Havoc remembered saying, "I'll get the proof you need, General."

"How?" Gallagher had asked.

"By joining the Force when it regroups. I'll volunteer to be California's representative on the team, and I'll watch over Blade like a hawk. As soon as I catch him in a slipup, as soon as I can gather concrete evidence, we'll kill two birds with one stone. You can persuade the Federation leaders to disband the Force, and I'll avenge Jimmy's death in a small way by forcing Blade to step down in disgrace."

General Gallagher had beamed triumphantly.

The plan had seemed so simple, so perfect.

But now Blade had saved Havoc's life and displayed concern for the Force team. The man obviously, genuinely cared about his people.

No wonder I feel guilty! Havoc told himself. He had to suppress the feeling and concentrate on exposing the Warrior as too inept to handle leading the Force. After all the trouble General Gallagher had gone to in prevailing upon Blade to take the team into the field prematurely, thereby increasing the likelihood of a disaster that would demonstrate conclusively that the Force wasn't needed, Havoc couldn't let the general and himself down.

Yes, sir.

One way or the other, he would have his revenge on Blade.

One way or the other, the Freedom Force was finished.

CHAPTER NINE

Talk about going from the frying pan into the fire.

Jaguarundi froze and watched the quartet walk toward him. He'd been able to evade several peasants armed with rifles, but he knew he'd be no match for four experienced bandits carrying machine guns. They'd nail him before he could cover ten yards.

"Can you talk?" demanded the guy with the brown beard.

"Just because someone is covered with hair doesn't mean they're a Neanderthal," Jag quipped.

The quartet stopped and regarded the cat-man in amazement.

"It's one of them muties," declared the man on the left.

"I didn't know mutants can speak like us normal folks," observed the lean one on the right.

"I've heard about some that can," said brown beard. "They're bred in little glass bottles."

"You're puttin' us on," stated the man on the left.

"El Diablo told me about them," brown beard said.

"Where'd he hear about 'em?" inquired the lean one.

"A deserter from the Civilized Zone Army joined us for a while about ten years ago, I think he was the one who told El Diablo."

"And this is one of those critters, Mercer?"

"Yep," Mercer replied, and wagged his machine gun at the mutation. "Am I right?"

"I never dispute a man who has a gun pointed at me," Jag said.

Mercer's eyes narrowed. "Am I right, sucker?"

"You're right," Jag answered.

"Why is that thing wearin' a backpack?" asked the lean one. "Is it animal or human?"

Mercer advanced and jabbed the barrel of his weapon into the cat-man's abdomen. "Do you have a name, gruesome?"

"Gruesome? I happen to think I'm rather adorable."

Anger contorted Mercer's features, and he raised his Heckler and Koch MP-5 and took a bead on the mutant's nose. "Don't play games with me, asshole. The next time you mouth off, you're dead. If you think I'm kidding, just try me."

Jag said nothing.

"Now what the hell is your name?"

"Jag."

"What's in the backpack?"

"Rations. Plastic explosives. A first-aid kit. Spare ammo."

"Ammo for what?"

"My M-16."

Mercer stared at the creature quizzically. "I don't see an M-16. What'd you do, lose it?" he cracked.

"Yeah."

The lean one took a step closer. "What kind of rations do you have?"

"Cans of disgusting crud known as K rations. Personally, I'd rather eat hog swill."

"Take off the backpack," Mercer ordered, "but do it real slow or you'll have to round up a new nose."

The three others snickered.

Jag slowly removed his backpack and held it out.

"Give me that," the lean one snapped, and grabbed the backpack. He knelt, opened the flap, and rummaged inside. "It's just like the critter said." He withdrew a can of K rations. "Let's have us some food."

"You know better, Wells," Mercer said, stepping away from the captive and lowering his MP-5. "We turn all of that stuff over to El Diablo."

"He won't miss a few lousy cans of food," Wells remarked.

"You know the rules," Mercer stated.

Wells looked at the pair behind him. "What about you two? What do you say?"

One with a balding pate nodded at Mercer. "He's right, Wells. We turn the backpack and its contents over to El Diablo. He'll distribute the goodies among the Devils. You know the way it works."

Wells jiggled the backpack. "But there's not that much in here. We might not even get a share. Let's take some now."

"No," Mercer said.

"What a bunch of chickens," Wells groused, and dropped the can into the backpack.

"I'd rather be a live chicken than a dead jackass," Mercer declared. "You haven't been a Devil very long, Wells. You're not as committed as the rest of us."

"Committed? I won't kiss El Diablo's shoes, if that's what you mean," Wells responded.

"El Diablo takes care of his people," Mercer commented. "Each of us gets an equal share of the proceeds from the raids. None of us ever goes hungry. We have clean clothes on our backs and a roof over our heads. Any woman we want is ours for the taking. And all we have to do is waste a few turkeys every so often. Do you realize how good we have it?"

"I thought I did when I joined six months ago, but after the raid on Jacumba I'm not so sure."

"Why not?"

"Did you see what he did to those women?" Wells asked, and grimaced at the memory.

"El Diablo has his reasons," Mercer said.

"I'd like to hear them," Wells stated.

"Whatever you do, don't ask him about it," Mercer advised. "Not unless you're tired of living."

"Speaking of asking questions," Jag interjected, "do you mind if I ask a few?"

"Yeah. Keep your mouth shut," Mercer replied.

"What harm can there be in a few questions?" Jag persisted brazenly, striving to concoct a ruse he could use to trick them into lowering their vigilance enough for him to attempt an escape. "Besides, I heard you mention El Diablo."

"So what?" Mercer queried.

"He's the reason I'm here."

"What?"

"I came to this valley to see El Diablo," Jag said, and smiled to assure them of his sincerity. "I've heard a lot about him and I'd like to join his band."

"*You* want to join the Devils!" Wells blurted out.

"Why not? They let you in, didn't they?" Jag retorted with just the right dash of sarcasm.

Wells glared, then took a step toward the hybrid. "Why, you rotten freak! I'm going to pound you to a pulp."

Mercer moved between them. "Cool it, Wells!" he directed. "You're not laying a hand on this mutant. We'll hold him until El Diablo gets here, and he'll decide what we're going to do with him. Hell, El Diablo might even let the freak join."

"El Diablo is on his way here?" Jag inquired, thinking of the atrocities perpetrated in Jacumba and endeavoring to keep his voice calm at the prospect of meeting the man referred to by the residents of southern California as the Butcher of the Baja.

"Yep," Mercer said, and jerked his left thumb in the direction of the armored dune buggy. "We were on our way to our post at the water hole near the entrance to the valley. You must've passed it on your way in."

Jag nodded.

"Well, our engine crapped out on us. I think the carb is on the blink. It's been giving us a hard time for a couple of weeks," Mercer related. "We radioed in for instructions and were told to sit tight until the mechanics got here. Next thing you know, we hear all this shooting to the west and the north." He paused. "You wouldn't happen to know anything about that, would you?"

"No," Jag fibbed.

Mercer shrugged. "El Diablo will get the truth out of you. We called in about the shooting and he's on his way with reinforcements. They should be here any minute."

As if in confirmation of the man's statement, Jaguarundi's keen ears detected the distant growl of vehicle motors approaching from the east. Frustration welled within him. If he didn't escape before El Diablo arrived, he might *never* see his companions again. But there was nothing he could do as long as the quartet had him covered. He frowned and glanced to the north, thinking that he'd be better off being the prisoner of the peasants.

Thirty seconds elapsed before Wells cocked his head and said, "Listen. I hear them coming."

"I hope it doesn't take the mechanics very long to fix our wheels," Mercer mentioned.

"What happens if El Diablo asks about Higbie and his crew?" asked the balding one.

"We tell him the truth," Mercer responded. "I like Higbie, but I'm not putting my butt in the slinger for him."

"El Diablo will have a fit," Wells predicted.

"Excuse me," Jag interjected.

"What is it?" Mercer asked.

"Do you ever call El Diablo by his real name? Somebody told me it's Celestino Naranjo."

Mercer's forehead creased. "Where'd you hear that? Not many people know his real name."

"I heard it from an old man in Mexicali," Jag lied, referring to a town on the border, thankful that Blade had required each Force member to study a map of the region before they departed their facility.

"Yeah, I guess some of the old-timers would know about it," Mercer said. "But whatever you do, don't use his name around him or you'll be sorry you did."

"Why?"

"The last jerk who accidentally used his name was skinned alive and staked out for the ants."

"But why?"

"I can't say. Just take my word for it."

Jag digested this new information, listening with growing anxiety to the vehicles drawing ever nearer.

Wells motioned at the mutation and laughed. "If El Diablo skins this bastard, I'm going to ask for the pelt and give it to Rosita."

"You've been spending a lot of time with that whore," Mercer commented.

"She's special," Wells said.

"Bullshit. She's a lousy *puta*."

"I'm warning you. Don't insult her."

"How can you insult a whore?" Mercer responded.

Wells reddened and his lips compressed. For a moment he seemed to be on the verge of springing at Mercer, but the timely arrival of six dune buggies compelled him to check his anger.

Jaguarundi stared at the vehicles as they came around a curve to the east driving in single file. All six were roofless and outfitted with makeshift armor plating, and each one had been painted in a brownish camouflage pattern. Dust, sand, and mud coated them. Four men rode in each vehicle.

The lead dune buggy braked within ten feet of the quartet. Out vaulted an imposing figure of a man dressed all in black. He straightened to his full height of six and a half feet and rested his immense hands on the pair of stainless-steel revolvers strapped around his thick waist. A wild mane and bushy beard of black hair framed a craggy face bronzed brown by constant exposure to the sun. Clear blue eyes scrutinized the four men, then shifted to the hybrid without betraying a hint of surprise.

With a tremendous mental effort, Jag willed himself to stay composed, to return the man's penetrating gaze without evincing any nervousness, acutely conscious of the power and authority the man radiated.

"What have we here?" demanded the newcomer in a deep, booming voice.

A large white dog, perhaps the biggest dog Jag had ever laid eyes on, jumped from the dune buggy and moved to the left side of the man in black. The dog's left eye was gone.

"We caught him, sir," Mercer explained. "He's one of those mutants."

"What was your first clue?" El Diablo responded, and walked right up to the cat-man. "*Habla español*?"

"He speaks English, boss," Mercer said.

"Does he indeed?" El Diablo stated.

"Fluently," Jag boldly declared. "On occasion I also meow." To his relief, and to the apparent astonishment of the four Devils, El Diablo threw back his black mane and laughed uproariously.

"*El gato* has a sense of humor!" the man in black stated. "I like that." His features abruptly hardened. "What are you doing in *my* valley, cat-man?"

"He said he wants to join the Devils," Mercer said.

El Diablo frowned and stared at the underling until Mercer shifted uncomfortably. "Did I ask *you*, Tim?"

"No, sir."

"Then keep your mouth shut. You'll have a chance to speak in a minute."

"Yes, sir."

Jaguarundi scanned the faces of the quartet, and in every one he saw the unmistakable trace of suppressed fear.

"You want to join the Devils?" El Diablo asked suspiciously, his cold blue orbs boring into the hybrid.

"If you'll have me," Jag answered.

"Where are you from, cat-man?"

"The Civilized Zone. I was created by a genetic engineer called the Doktor twenty-one years ago."

El Diablo nodded. "I know about the Doktor. I know he made a lot of mutations for his Genetic Research Division."

Jaguarundi blinked a few times. El Diablo was remarkably well informed, more so than Jag would have considered possible given the man's life as a border bandit in a remote region of northern Mexico. He had to be careful what he said. "Then you probably know the G.R.D. disbanded after the Doktor died. I've spent the past six years drifting across the Southwest. I heard about you and decided you might be a man after my own heart."

"Is that right?"

"You're a man who isn't afraid to take whatever he wants. You've established a reputation as a smart leader, someone worth working for, a guy who knows his business. You've been raiding California for something like two decades and haven't been caught yet."

"And I never will be caught," El Diablo asserted. He reached down and patted the white dog on the head. "What do you think, Pancho."

The dog growled, its baleful right eye fixed on the hybrid.

"Pancho doesn't trust you, cat-man."

"He doesn't know me," Jag responded, attempting to project a casual tone.

El Diablo grinned. "True enough. But I don't trust you either, *amigo*. What's your name?"

"Jaguarundi."

"Well, cat-man, you amuse me. I will allow you to live a while longer until I decide whether you are telling me the truth. For now you will keep quiet and do exactly as you're told."

"Yes, sir," Jag said.

"To business," El Diablo stated, and turned to Mercer. "I'm most puzzled, Tim. Perhaps you can enlighten me."

"Boss?"

"You called in to say you were having engine trouble, correct?" El Diablo said in a condescending manner.

"Yes, sir. It's the damned carburetor," Mercer said, and pointed at the parked dune buggy. "We got that far."

El Diablo scratched his chin, then nodded. "I can see how far you got. What puzzles me is how you can be here when Higbie is back at the cavern."

"Sir?"

"Higbie and his crew were on watch at the water hole and you were supposed to relieve them," El Diablo said. "Your dune buggy broke down, so by all rights Higbie should still be at the water hole instead of at the base." He paused, his voice lowering ominously. "Do you follow me so far?"

"Yes, sir," Mercer replied promptly.

"Did you tell Higbie to leave his post without waiting for his relief?"

"No, boss, I didn't."

"How fortunate for you. So he took it on himself. Did you speak to him when he drove by on his way to the cavern?"

"I told him the mechanics would be here to fix our buggy in fifteen minutes," Mercer divulged.

"But Higbie didn't turn around and go back to the water hole, did he?"

Mercer looked at the ground. "No, sir."

El Diablo placed his left hand on Mercer's shoulder. "I appreciate your honesty. Higbie was the one who didn't follow procedure, so Higbie is the one who will pay the price."

Perplexed, Jag listened attentively. He gathered that another dune buggy crew had been posted at the water hole, but they'd left before being properly relieved by Mercer and company. He couldn't comprehend why El Diablo was making such a big deal out of the shift relief and ignoring the report of gunfire.

The black-haired leader glanced at the second vehicle and waved his left arm. Two men in gray coveralls, each carrying a metal toolbox, climbed out and hurried to the disabled dune buggy. "I'll have another squad take your place at the water hole," El Diablo told Mercer. "And I hope you won't ever make the same mistake Higbie has made. You know how I feel about those who fail to adhere to regulations."

"I know. Believe me. But what about those shots we heard?"

"What about them?"

"Don't you intend to investigate, boss?"

"Why should I when I'll receive an accurate report from the Cocopas?" El Diablo rejoined. He looked at Jaguarundi. "Were you involved in the shooting?"

Jag hesitated. If he lied to El Diablo and the man found out, he'd be terminated. But if he could continue to string the butcher along, could continue to buy time, the odds of getting away with his life rose dramatically. "I don't know anything about the gunfire to the west, but several peasants tried to kill me north of here."

Mercer scowled. "You told me that you didn't know a thing. You lied to me, you son of a bitch."

Jaguarundi shrugged. "Sorry, but I didn't want a trigger-happy flunky to blow me away before I had a chance to talk to El Diablo. And I'm not about to lie to him."

"How nice," El Diablo said dryly. "Should I be flattered?" He snickered and patted his dog. "I think he's lying, Pancho. How about you?"

Again the white dog growled.

"Let's find out," El Diablo stated, and gazed past the prisoner.

Jag turned, stunned to discover two men standing ten feet to his rear at the edge of the forest on the south side of the road. Both were Indians, but they were as different from Sparrow Hawk as night from day. Instead of buckskins they wore simple tan loincloths. Each had a hunting knife on his right hip, and each was armed with a bow and a quiver full of arrows on his back. Their black hair hung to their shoulders. They stood about five feet in height and were stocky in build. He studied them, annoyed that they had managed to get so close without his hypersenses detecting them.

El Diablo walked over to the Indians and conversed with them in a guttural, melodic tongue. The Indians spoke impassively, their arms at their sides.

Jaguarundi wanted to run for the trees. His intuition blared a warning in his mind, and he felt an overwhelming foreboding of impending peril.

A minute later El Diablo returned, smiling, relaxed, his eyes twinkling. "Do you know who they are?" he asked Jag.

"No. How could I?"

"They're Cocopah Indians. Their tribe has lived in this territory for hundreds and hundreds of years, and they'll probably still be here long after we're gone. I have a treaty with them. For a few weapons, utensils, and food each month, they've agreed to post guards to keep an eye on the western approach to my valley," El Diablo related. He turned and pointed at the 200-foot-high cliff located to the south of where the water hole lay. "Do you see the escarpment there?"

"How could I miss it?"

"Believe it or not, there's a narrow path to the top. Only the Cocopas know how to climb up there, and they keep two men watching the gully at all times. If anyone approaches the valley, they signal. It's impossible for any enemy to take me by surprise," El Diablo said, and paused. "Not that enemies haven't tried. Twice soldiers from California came for me, and each time I gave the gringos a taste of their own medicine."

Jag's mouth suddenly felt very dry.

"We have a system set up. They use hand mirrors to signal my crew at the water hole or me. Just a while ago, for instance, they signaled that an armed party was coming up the gully. Just now they told me that this party wasted a mutation, a Gila monster. Then the six members of the party went into the woods."

Relief soothed Jaguarundi's nerves. At least the other Force members were still alive.

"Do you know what else they told me?" El Diablo inquired.

"I have no idea."

"Guess."

Jag looked at the bandit leader, wondering if he was joking. A fake grin curled the man's thick lips.

"Come on. *Por favor.* Guess."

Acting on the spur of the moment, refusing to be intimidated and angered by the mocking visage in front of him, Jag smirked. "They told you that I'm one of the party they saw."

"Right the first time," El Diablo stated gruffly, and struck.

Jaguarundi never saw the blow. He felt excruciating agony in his stomach and doubled over, gasping for air. A brittle laugh fell on his ears, and then his left temple exploded in a combination of pinwheeling lights and exquisite torment. He sank to his knees, only dimly conscious.

"Sweet dreams, *bastardo*!" El Diablo said.

He never felt the third blow.

CHAPTER TEN

"**I** think I saw two men," Sparrow Hawk whispered.

"You *think*?" Blade responded, glancing to his left at the Flathead.

"They moved like shadows," Sparrow explained. "They were there one instant, gone the next."

"Where?" the Warrior asked.

Sparrow motioned with his spear to the south. "Near the dirt road. They were traveling eastward."

"To the east?" Blade repeated, perplexed. If two men had been sent to investigate the shooting, they should be heading to the west, to the water hole, not in the opposite direction.

"Hey, dude," Lobo said from his position six feet to the right of the giant. "How long are we waitin' here?"

"Until Jaguarundi returns," Blade replied.

"What if he doesn't?"

"Then someone six months from now will find our moldy bones right at this spot," Blade quipped.

"You're warped, man. Totally warped."

"Coming from you, that's a compliment," Blade said.

"Huh?"

"Never mind. And keep your mouth shut until further notice," Blade instructed the Clansman. He looked past Lobo at Raphaela and Captain Havoc, who were strung out in a line to the north, then gazed to the south beyond Sparrow at Doc

Madsen. He'd arranged them in a skirmish line, certain the occupants of the valley would dispatch someone to check on the gunfire. But minutes had elapsed and no one had appeared.

Very strange.

Blade leaned his back against a tree and pondered his strategy. By all rights, if El Diablo used the valley as a base of operations, the Force should have encountered guards and patrols. He was particularly surprised there hadn't been a single guard at the water hole, the logical spot to post one. Either El Diablo was incredibly lax in his security precautions, which seemed highly unlikely since the raider had operated successfully for decades, or the security setup must be ingeniously elaborate. He gazed at the rise to the west, thinking of the water hole on the other side, and wondered if he had missed something.

"Blade!" Sparrow stated in a hushed voice.

The Warrior swung around.

"Someone is coming," Sparrow declared, and nodded to the east.

Blade listened and heard the hurried footsteps of several people approaching rapidly. He extended his left arm, palm down, and wagged his hand toward the ground. Immediately the team dropped flat and he followed suit.

None too soon.

Four people dressed in white came running along a game trail. Three were adult males, the fourth a young boy. The three men wore white sombreros and one had on a red poncho. All the men carried rifles, the boy a machete.

Blade saw them run between Sparrow and himself to the edge of the forest, less than ten feet away. There they stopped and stared at the grade leading to the crest, evidently mystified to judge from the expressions on their faces as they surveyed the trees and the grade. They began talking in Spanish.

Could *these* be the guards?

Blade crawled toward them, creeping with all the stealth of a crafty, hungry fox after succulent game, adapting his body to the flow of the terrain and screening his passage with the intervening vegetation. He drew within two yards and rose slowly to a squat, then clutched the M60 and straightened. "Don't move!"

The four Mexicans spun, shocked by the ghostly advent of the giant, and two of them pointed their rifles in his direction. But they promptly lowered their weapons when five other figures stepped forward armed with assault rifles.

"Don't kill us!" cried the man in the red poncho, who took a protective stride in front of the boy. "We won't shoot!"

"Drop your guns," Blade commanded.

The man in the poncho snapped directions to his compadres, and all three let their rifles fall to the grass.

"I take it you speak English?" Blade said to the apparent leader.

"*Si, señor*. I do. My name is Emiliano."

"Where are you from?"

"Our village is about a mile east of here, *señor*."

"What are you doing here?"

"We were chasing *el tigre*. A cat-man."

Blade recalled the rifle shots his team had heard earlier, while crossing the crest, and he tensed. "Did you shoot at the cat-man?"

"Yes, *señor*," Emiliano answered honestly, and suddenly wished he hadn't when an angry black man stalked toward him and aimed an M-16 at his head.

"This sucker shot Jag?" Lobo declared. "I say we waste the bum."

"*I'm* in charge," Blade reminded him stiffly, "and I'll decide our course of action. So clam up."

Lobo stopped and glared at the peasants.

"Do you know *el tigre*?" Emiliano asked timidly.

"He's our friend," Blade divulged.

"I don't think we hit him, *señor*. We're simple farmers, not *solados*. We hunt and trap game to put food on the table for our families, but only because our *patrón* takes most of the grain and vegetables for his men. We are not very good shots."

"Where did you see the cat-man last?" Blade probed.

"He ran to the south. But we knew he wanted to go to the water hole, so we came this way to try and catch him."

"Why would simple farmers take it upon themselves to capture a hybrid?" Blade questioned, and stepped closer.

"To please our *patrón*. He might pay us for such a creature or let us keep more of the food we grow for our families,'' Emiliano said.

"Who is this *patrón* of yours?"

"El Diablo, *señor*."

"El Diablo takes your harvest for his men?" Blade asked, elated at the discovery. If the village turned out to be the bandit's base, once Jag returned the Force could make tracks for California with the mission successfully accomplished.

"Yes, he does," Emiliano replied. "El Diablo barely leaves enough for the people of my village to live on. And as his band grows, he takes more and more each year."

"You don't sound too happy about it."

"Would you be, *señor*?"

"No," Blade acknowledged. "I guess I wouldn't. Why haven't your people revolted?"

Emiliano spoke in Spanish to the other two men and all three laughed lustily.

"Did I say something funny?" Blade queried.

"Forgive us, *señor*. My people have wanted to rebel for many years. But Celestino is too strong now. We would be wiped out."

"Do you know how El Diablo got his start?"

"Yes, *señor*. Celestino was born in our village."

"And the village is his base of operations?" Blade inquired hopefully.

"No. His base is a vast *caverna*. I can show you where it is located."

The Warrior sighed and gazed to the east. So much for concluding the assignment anytime soon. Finding the exact site of the bandit's headquarters was essential to the projected air strike. His only recourse lay in having Emiliano guide him there. He stared at the peasant and saw the boy peeking at him from behind Emiliano's legs. "Your son?"

"Yes, *señor*. His name is Miguel."

"I have a son about half his age."

"Where are you from, *señor*, if I may ask?"

"You may not," Blade replied, "but I will tell you this. We're not your enemies. We won't harm you or anyone in your village. All we're interested in is El Diablo and the location of his base.

If you cooperate with us, we'll let you go.''

Emiliano studied the Warrior for several seconds, assessing the giant's character. ''I believe we can trust you, *señor*. We will do as you say.''

''Fine,'' Blade said, and glanced at Lobo. ''Collect their rifles and bring the guns along.''

''Me? Why do I have to lug them around?''

''Because I told you to do it. You can carry them in your arms or crammed up your nose. Take your pick.''

''I'll carry them,'' Lobo said sullenly.

''Sparrow, take the point. Havoc, you're rear guard. Get cracking, people,'' Blade ordered, and waited for the Flathead to advance ten yards along the game trail before he gestured for the peasants to proceed.

Emiliano took Miguel's hand and they led off, followed by their two friends.

The Warrior fell in alongside Emiliano. ''I have some questions to ask you.''

''To be expected, *señor*.''

Blade watched Doc, Raphaela, and Lobo form a single file behind the Mexicans, then focused his attention on the trail ahead. ''Do you know El Diablo well?''

''Very well. We grew up together in Jalapa, our village. Celestino and I played and laughed and enjoyed many good times in our childhood. Back then our village was peaceful, a great place to raise a family. Most of the men farmed or tended goats and sheep and cattle. This valley is very fertile, just right for growing crops. We don't get much rain each year, but the water hole, the lake in the middle of the valley, and our springs are all fed by an underground source,'' Emiliano detailed, and smiled. ''Before Celestino turned bad, this was heaven.''

''Heaven?'' Blade repeated, recalling his discussion with Jaguarundi about Utopia, and grinned. Why was everyone always looking for a heaven on earth when the true source of happiness sprang from within them?

''That is the right word, isn't it, *señor*?'' Emiliano queried. ''It has been years since I talked much in English.''

''Where did you learn to speak the language?''

''From our priest, Father DeCamillo. He was a very kind,

wise man.''

"Was?''

"Si. Celestino killed him.''

"Why?''

"Because the priest spoke out against him. Father DeCamillo publicly branded Celestino as evil and tried to stir the people up against him, so Celestino made an example of the priest. The Devils dragged the father into our town plaza, lashed him to a post, and whipped his flesh down to the bone. They left him there to die a slow death.''

"And no one tried to help the priest?''

"What could we do, *señor*? This took place almost twenty years ago. Celestino had fifteen or twenty men in his band then, and there were only forty or so people in the whole village. Half were women and children. Of course the men of my village wanted to help Father DeCamillo, but Celestino's men had machine guns and we had a few lousy rifles. We would have thrown our lives away,'' Emiliano said sadly. "Now there are seventy-two in our village. We have grown stronger, but so has Celestino. He has eighty-seven Devils at his command, and they have enough guns and explosives for an army.''

"I'm surprised El Diablo hasn't driven your people from the valley,'' Blade commented.

"Celestino wouldn't do that, *señor*. He has a soft spot in his heart for the village where he was born. His men are forbidden to kill any of us. He needs us, needs the food we grow to feed his band. And too, he needs houses for his *putas*.''

"His what?''

"His whores. He has brought in dozens of women from Mexicali, Tijuana, and elsewhere to service his band. He doesn't permit the *putas* to live at the *caverna*, although many of them spend the night there when the Devils want them.''

"How far is the base from your village?''

"That depends on whether you take the road or take the path through the forest. You see, *señor*, there is a lake eight miles to the east of our village. Five miles north of the lake, in the cliffs overlooking the valley, is the *caverna*. The road goes from our village to the lake, then to the *caverna*. That's thirteen miles. But if you cut through the forest it is much shorter,'' Emiliano said.

"Will you show me the path?" Blade requested.

"*Si, señor*. But you would be wise not to take it."

"Why?"

"The path is—how do you say it?—booby-trapped with mines and guns and such."

They hiked in silence for a minute. Blade felt happy at finally knowing the exact location of El Diablo's headquarters. Now all he had to do was verify what Emiliano had told him. The peasant seemed to be reliable, but he'd learned from experience not to be too trusting, especially when the lives of the Force members were at stake. "What turned Celestino Naranjo bad?"

Emiliano sighed. "There is a sad story. He was nineteen or twenty at the time, and he'd been married only a few months to a lovely woman from our village, Maria. Celestino had always wanted to live in California, and he took Maria and packed all of his belongings in a cart pulled by two burros and headed north."

"I don't understand," Blade interrupted. "Why did he want to live in California?"

"Because of all the stories he had heard from his grandfather about how *magnificio* California was. His grandfather, *señor*, was a gringo like yourself but with red hair."

"A Californian?"

"*Si*. He got into some trouble with the law and fled south, and by luck he happened on our valley. We knew nothing of his past and let him live in our village, and he turned out to be a good man. He married one of our women and had several children, and they grew up to be decent folks, hard workers. The eldest son and his wife gave birth to Celestino. All during his younger years, Celestino was urged by his grandfather to go live in California, the land of promise, where very few people are truly poor and a man can get rich if he works hard. So Celestino took his new bride to the land he had dreamed about for so many years."

"And what happened?"

"A tragedy, *señor*. Maria was killed by some gringos. Celestino came back a changed man, filled with hatred for California and Californians. Shortly after that he started his band. He went to the border towns and recruited the roughest men and a few women to be his *soldados*. He formed his own little army, and ever since he had been raiding across the border, killing Californians.''

So now Blade had a motive for El Diablo's actions. In a way he felt sorry for the man.

''Twice before, soldiers from California came to destroy Celestino, and each time they were caught and executed in a horrible manner. If he catches you, *señor*, I would advise you to tell him you are from somewhere other than California. You might live longer.''

''Thanks for the tip,'' Blade said. He looked ahead and saw that Sparrow had halted and was gazing at something above the trail: a rope, one end of which had been draped over a tree limb and the other end tied to a sapling. ''What's that?''

Emiliano coughed lightly. ''A snare we set this morning. The cat-man was caught in it, but he escaped.''

''Are there other snares along this trail?''

''We were setting up a second one when Miguel told us about the creature we had caught.''

''So we don't have to worry about stepping in an animal trap?''

''No, *señor*. There are no more traps on this trail.''

Blade took several strides. Suddenly he perceived movement in the vegetation on both sides, and the next instant armed figures attired in camouflage fatigues burst from cover and trained their weapons on the Force.

CHAPTER ELEVEN

Exquisite pain caused him to groan.

Only then did Jag realize consciousness was returning slowly. His temples throbbed. A dull ache in the pit of his stomach reminded him of the sucker punch delivered by the cruel prick with the black mane, and his eyelids fluttered as he struggled to rouse himself.

"Hey, this turkey is comin' around," declared a low voice to his right.

"Should we let the boss know?" asked a second person, a woman.

"He doesn't want to be disturbed."

The woman snickered. "Can't say as I blame him."

As Jag's feline eyes snapped open, he became aware that his arms were tied above his head and that his body was sagging against a hard surface. He blinked in the bright sunlight, taking stock. The Devils had lashed him to a wooden post imbedded in the ground in the middle of what appeared to be a village square. All around him were single- and two-story buildings made of adobe. Small balconies on the upper stories fronted the square. On a few of the balconies and staring out many of the windows were men, women, and children who regarded him with intense interest.

"Welcome back to the land of the living, freak," said the man on his right.

Jaguarundi twisted his head and found a beefy man in camouflage fatigues standing a yard off. He glanced to his left to find
a raven-tressed woman similarly attired. Both held machine
guns.

"You've been in dreamland, ugly," the woman commented.

Jag licked his lips. "I'd say this is more like a nightmare."

"Would you like anything?" inquired the man.

"Water would be nice."

The Devil looked up at the sun, then wiped his left hand across
his sweating forehead. "Wouldn't it, though?" he responded.

Both guards laughed.

Jag straightened and stretched his leg muscles, his lips a thin
line, and gazed overhead. Strips of leather had been used to
bind him to a metal ring secured near the top of the post.

"Don't go gettin' any ideas," the beefy man admonished.
"We were ordered to blow you away if you try to bust loose."

"And we'll do it too," the woman added.

"Where am I?" Jag asked, and surreptitiously set to work
flexing his fingers and insuring full circulation was restored to
his arms.

"In Jalapa," the woman said, and ran her right hand through
her black hair.

"Where?"

"A village."

"In the valley?"

"Yeah."

The man chuckled and leaned toward Jag. "And don't think
we'll let you grow lonely either. Your buddies will be here
before too long. Of course, they might not be in one piece."

Jag stiffened. "What do you mean?"

"After El Diablo flattened you, he sent ten Devils into the
forest after your friends. He gave them instructions to bring
your buddies back alive, if possible, for questioning," the guard
disclosed. "But he told Mercer and the boys not to sweat it if
they have to blow your pals away."

Apprehension seized Jaguarundi for all of ten seconds, until
he thought of Blade's unparalleled prowess at dispensing death
and the fact the others weren't exactly pushovers either, with
the possible exception of Lobo. He grinned.

"You think it's funny?" the guard asked in surprise. "The Devils are as mean as they come, jerkface. The ten El Diablo sent in will make mincemeat of your friends."

"Care to make a bet?"

"You ain't got nothin' to bet, stupid."

"He's playing with our minds," the woman interjected. "He knows his buddies are as good as dead."

A commotion broke out on the east side of the square. Jag turned his body and saw El Diablo emerging from a building, laughing and swaggering. In each arm he had a pretty woman. Trailing behind him came eight Devils. The group ambled toward the post, chatting amiably. Jag glanced to the north and spotted the six dune buggies parked along a side street.

"So *el gato* is awake?" El Diablo stated boisterously, and shoved the woman aside. "Has he given you any trouble?"

"None at all, boss," the beefy guard responded, and nickered. "He thinks his buddies are going to waste the squad you sent after them."

"He does, does he?" El Diablo said contemptuously. He halted ten feet from the post and sneered. "In addition to being a liar, you're a braggart and a fool."

"Takes one to know one," Jag said, for lack of a better retort.

The mirth displayed by the group promptly evaporated and the two guards edged away from the post.

El Diablo took two strides forward. "Yes. You definitely have a big mouth and an attitude problem. I think it's time that someone taught you a lesson, mutant."

"Hybrid."

"Huh?"

"I prefer to be called a hybrid."

The white dog appeared, weaving through the Devils to stand at the bandit leader's side.

"Who cares what you want, mutant? I sure as hell don't," El Diablo said. Then he rested his hands on his big revolvers. "Do you know what a bullwhip is, *amigo*?"

A knot formed in Jag's gut and he clenched his hands.

"I didn't hear you?" El Diablo remarked mockingly.

"Yeah," Jag answered.

"You do? Good." El Diablo held out his right arm and

snapped his fingers. A tall Devil stepped over and placed a coiled bullwhip into his grasp. He beamed and allowed the whip to unwind slowly onto the ground. "Can you guess what comes next?"

"Touch me and you're dead."

El Diablo laughed. "What?"

Jag stared directly into the butcher's eyes and spoke in a raspy growl. "If you use that whip on me, I'll kill you. Somehow, some way, I'll get you."

"Tough talk, cat-man, for someone who is tied to a whipping post."

"Mark my words," Jag stated harshly. "No one lays a hand on me and lives."

"Now you have me trembling in my boots," El Diablo said and the Devils cackled. His countenance sobered, became a grim mask. "I need answers, *amigo*, and you're going to provide them."

Jag deliberately turned his back to the raider and waited, endeavoring to calm his jangled nerves, to keep his body relaxed.

"Who sent you?" El Diablo asked. He waited several seconds for a reply, then snapped impatiently, "Where are you from?"

Jag kept silent, scarcely breathing, the hairs on his back tingling.

"Who sent you?" El Diablo repeated.

"Your mother," Jag responded, and then inadvertently cried out and arched his spine as the most intense anguish conceivable flooded his brain with tidal waves of torment. He dimly heard the crack of the bullwhip.

The assembled Devils sniggered.

"You were sent to kill me, weren't you?" El Diablo queried.

Jag gulped and braced his body, or thought he did, but there was no defense against the burning lash slicing deep into his left shoulder blade. He automatically pressed into the post, and his sensitive nostrils registered the stale scent of dried blood.

"Look, *amigo*, I can go on like this all day," El Diablo stated. "Why not make your life easier and tell me everything I need to know?"

"Get screwed!" Jag hissed.

"I just did," El Diablo said, and guffawed.

"Give it to the bastard, boss," the beefy Devil urged.

"I intend to, Garvey," El Diablo replied, and lit into the mutation with a vengeance, his steely right arm wielding the bullwhip effortlessly. Again and again and again he struck, until he lost count of the number of times. The crack-crack-crack of the lash attained a regular cadence.

His teeth gnashed together, his body quivering and trembling in unadulterated agony, Jaguarundi fought with every iota of his willpower to prevent crying out. Each stroke of the whip, each time the lash cut into his flesh, seared him to his core. He gripped the metal ring and held on fast, his legs threatening to buckle. A moist sensation, undoubtedly his blood seeping from his wounds, crept down his back. He closed his eyes and breathed in great ragged gasps, hoping the torture would end soon.

But it didn't.

El Diablo flicked the whip over and over, observing with glee the spreading red stain matting the mutation's fur.

Jag's legs were becoming weaker and weaker and his back seemed to be on fire. Until that very moment he'd never known the true depths of suffering. Slowly, despite his efforts, his body began to slip downward.

Some of the Devils were making coarse jokes and laughing.

Please let it stop! Jag mentally shrieked. He knew El Diablo must be deriving pleasure from the whipping, and the insight gave him an idea. Would the butcher exert himself on an unconscious victim? He went completely limp, dangling from the ring, shamming unconsciousness. The lash bit into him once more, then again. He resigned himself to a third stroke.

It never landed.

"The tough guy passed out!" Garvey declared, and cackled.

"Strange," El Diablo commented. "I didn't take him for a weakling."

Jag heard footsteps approach.

"These mutations must not be as formidable as I was led to believe," El Diablo stated. "The wild ones have more *cojones*."

"What should we do with him, boss?" Garvey inquired. "Want us to waste the son of a bitch?"

"No. He hasn't answered my questions yet. Untie him and we'll take him with us."

"Yes, sir."

Jaguarundi felt hands slip under his arms from behind, and became aware of someone else working on the leather straps.

"Be careful," said the man to his rear. "I don't want to get blood all over my uniform."

"What's the big deal over a little blood?" Garvey responded. "You can always have a *puta* wash your uniform."

"I don't want the freak's blood to touch my skin. Who knows what it'll do? It might give me a rash or make hair grow all over my body."

"On you it would be an improvement, Carlos."

"Up yours, *amigo*."

Jaguarundi could feel the leather straps loosening, and he let his arms drop, his mind racing. The objective of the mission was to locate El Diablo's base of operations so the California Air Force could conduct an air strike and wipe the scum out, and apparently El Diablo intended to take him to the base. Provided he lived long enough, he could always try to escape later and find Blade. But what if—and the thought brought on an adrenaline rush—what if he took care of Celestino Naranjo right then and there? Would the Devils disband if their leader died? He had no way of telling, and he really didn't care very much if they disbanded or not. All he wanted was to sink his nails into El Diablo, to repay the bandit chief for the indignity of the whipping. All he desired was sweet, sweet revenge, and he might never have a better opportunity.

"Should we dump this wimp in your buggy, boss?" Garvey asked.

El Diablo nodded. "Place him in the back seat."

"Yes, sir."

Jaguarundi cracked his eyelids as the man supporting him started to turn. He saw Garvey in front of him. Off to the right, conversing with several Devils, stood El Diablo, the bullwhip coiled in his right hand. Off to the left was the female Devil.

"Give me a hand, Garvey," Carlos said. "This freak is heavier than he looks, *compadre*."

"You're gettin' soft in your young age," Garvey responded.

"You're a fine one to talk," Carlos quipped.

Jag inhaled, filling his lungs, and when the beefy guard went to reach for him, when none of the Devils were paying attention, he straightened and swung his right arm, his fingers hooked into rigid claws, and slashed his fingernails across Garvey's neck, splitting the man's beefy neck from one side to the other. He glimpsed Garvey's shocked visage and a geyser of blood spraying from the severed throat, but there wasn't time to witness more because he was already tearing himself loose from the other Devil, Carlos, and spinning, his left hand coming up and around. His nails raked Carlos's face, gouging both brown eyes and ripping through the nostrils, and the Devil screamed and frantically stumbled backwards.

"Look out!" someone shouted.

Jag pivoted toward El Diablo, gratified to see the hint of incipient terror in the man's eyes, and he took a bounding stride, intending to reach Naranjo before any of the Devils could intervene.

But intervention came from another source.

A hurtling white form, snarling savagely, flashed out of nowhere and smashed into Jag's chest, bowling him over. Glistening teeth fastened on his right forearm. He rolled to the right, his own growls mingling with Pancho's, and buried his left hand in the white dog's throat. Battling furiously, they continued to roll back and forth, the dog striving to tear Jag's forearm apart while Jag endeavored to shove the canine from him to give himself room to maneuver.

"Shoot the freak!" a man yelled.

"No!" El Diablo bellowed. "You'll hit Pancho."

Jag winced, racked with pain, the dog's jaws grinding his flesh to the bone. He realized he wouldn't be able to dislodge the animal and instantly opted for another tactic. If he couldn't separate them, he'd close in. He leaned forward and sank his tapered teeth into Pancho's neck, tasting the hair and the salty skin and tangy blood. His jaws clamped shut and he wrenched his head backwards, tearing a three-inch gash in the canine's throat.

Undeterred but enraged, Pancho released the hybrid's forearm and snapped at his face.

Jag jerked to the right, barely evading the crimson-caked mouth. He swiped at the dog's good eye, but missed. Pancho scrambled erect and Jag did likewise, his concentration totally focused on his feral opponent.

Which was a mistake.

Arms looped around Jag's own as someone tried to pin them. He twirled, throwing his adversary off balance, and the female Devil sprawled to the ground at his feet, on her hands and knees. Jag pounced, his left hand grasping her chin, his right behind her head. He viciously yanked and twisted and heard her neck pop. Before he could straighten, Pancho was on him again, leaping in from the left and barreling him from his feet. He managed to get his hands on the dog's blood-soaked neck, and then he came down hard on his back and shoulders with Pancho's bestial features inches from his nose. Fetid breath assailed him as he heaved, sending the canine flying. Instantly he leaped erect, or tried to, and a thin, cord-like object wrapped itself around the base of his throat.

The bullwhip!

Jag took hold of the whip and tugged, but already he was being pulled to his knees. He grimaced and attempted to unwrap the lash from his neck, sensing he was too late, knowing he'd blown his chance, that the delays had been too costly. A boot thudded into the small of his neck, causing him to arch his back, and he saw something, a machine gun stock maybe, sweeping at his head. The blow staggered him and he reeled crazily.

Not again!

Another machine gun stock came down on him with all the force of a ten-ton meteorite and the lights went out.

CHAPTER TWELVE

Blade reacted instantaneously. He leveled the M60 and fired from the hip at three figures on the right side of the game trail, catching the trio before they could squeeze off a shot, the rounds perforating their chests and flinging them into the undergrowth. He dived for the ground and barked, "Take cover!"

Bedlam ensued. The Force members and the seven remaining foes in fatigues cut loose at one another while the four peasants tried to find shelter from the flying lead.

Blade saw Sparrow Hawk dart behind a tree, then glanced over his left shoulder in time to see the two Mexican men get hit. So did Lobo, who dropped the three rifles and clutched at his chest while falling and screaming at the top of his lungs. Raphaela and Captain Havoc dove into bushes.

Leaving Doc Madsen still on the trail. An enemy had popped out less than two yards from the Cavalryman and trained a machine gun on him. Doc instinctively raised his arms, his M-16 in his left hand, and cast the weapon away. In that millisecond, as the machine gunner's eyes were watching the M-16 fall into the weeds, Doc's right hand dropped to his Smith and Wesson in a blur of motion. The machine gunner perceived the danger and his finger began to apply pressure on the trigger, but in the fraction of time it took for his brain to send the mental signal to his hand and his finger to start to squeeze, Doc's Magnum came up and out and boomed.

The machine gunner took the slug squarely in the forehead and catapulted rearward.

Doc spun and dashed toward a nearby thicket, but he was still three yards off when a machine gun chattered and a half-dozen rounds smacked into his backpack and flung him to the earth.

Damn!

Blade rolled into high grass and scanned the surrounding woods. Everyone had gone to cover. If his count was correct, there should be six adversaries left. Logic told him they must be Devils. He crawled stealthily to the east, searching for targets.

A desperate, gurgling shriek wafted from up ahead, from near the tree Sparrow had ducked behind. The shriek ended abruptly.

Blade's eyes narrowed as he studied the wall of vegetation. Had that been Sparrow or one of the Devils? He spotted a bush moving on the opposite side of the trail and tensed.

A woman in fatigues appeared, crouched over, holding an assault rifle, an AK-47.

The Warrior angled the M60 at her, but someone beat him to the punch. An M-16 chattered and the woman flung her arms out and fell. He looked back and realized the shots came from where Raphaela had disappeared. The lady certainly pulled her weight, as she'd promised.

An eerie hush descended on the forest. Even the birds and the insects were silent.

Blade moved to a towering tree and eased his body up, pressing his left side against the trunk. There were four Devils remaining, and he wondered, hopefully, if they would withdraw now that they were outnumbered. He peeked out.

No such luck.

A tall Devil materialized 20 feet to the north, a Colt AR-15 pressed to his shoulder, and fired three times.

The Warrior ducked back and heard the bullets thud into the trunk. He eased to the edge of the tree, intending to return fire, but the sight he beheld rendered retaliation unnecessary.

Captain Havoc stood behind the tall Devil, his left arm wrapped tightly around the man's throat, his right burying a survival knife in the Devil's chest. Once. Twice. And twice more. The Devil collapsed, spurting blood, and Captain Havoc lowered him to the ground. The officer looked at Blade, grinned, and vanished into the forest.

Three to go.

Blade crouched, and sidled away from the game trail into a patch of shoulder high growth. He spotted a shadowy form creeping among a stand of saplings 20 feet from his position, and froze.

The Devil hadn't seen him!

The Warrior flattened, never losing track of the man in the stand. He let go of the M60 and inched his right hand to the corresponding Bowie on his hip. The knife slid clear easily, and he held the hilt firmly and waited.

Casting anxious glances in all directions, the Devil walked from the saplings, cautiously nearing the hidden giant.

Blade held his breath and stayed motionless. He spied someone moving a few yards to the Devil's rear, and Sparrow came into view holding the spear in his right hand.

As if sensing the Flathead's presence, the Devil pivoted.

Sparrow let fly with the heavy lance, his powerful body unwinding in a supple, practiced motion. The spear sped true, its steel point penetrating the Devil's chest on the right side, and completely transfixed the bandit's torso. The man grunted, released his machine gun, and clutched futilely at the lance. His legs buckled and he sank to his knees, blood pouring from both corners of his mouth.

Blade rose slowly, smiling in appreciation of Sparrow's skill.

The Flathead saw the Warrior and nodded. His eyes strayed past Blade and suddenly widened in alarm.

Knowing that one of the Devils must be behind him, Blade threw himself to the right, twisting as he did, sliding the Bowie into its sheath as he elevated the M60 with his left hand. Ten yards to the west, grinning confidently in anticipation of mowing him down, were two Devils, one sporting a full black beard, the other on the lean side, both with their weapons leveled and ready to fire. Blade braced for the impact of their bullets.

Which never came.

From behind *them* an M-16 discharged a short burst and the

tops of their craniums erupted skyward, spraying flesh, hair, and brains over the vegetation. In unison the men toppled, landing side by side on their stomachs.

Blade gazed at the brush to their rear, expecting to see Captain Havoc or Raphaela. Instead, to his amazement, he discovered Lobo kneeling beside a bush. "You!"

"Me, dude," the Clansman said, rising with a smirk on his face. "Those two were the last of the bunch, right?"

The Warrior nodded absently. "Aren't you hurt? I saw you go down."

Lobo strolled forward, beaming slyly. "I faked it."

"You pretended to be shot?" Blade asked in disbelief.

"Sure. I figured those creeps weren't about to waste any more ammo or pay much attention to somebody they thought they'd wasted."

"Quick thinking," Blade complimented him.

"Of course," Lobo said. "Like I keep tellin' everybody, I'm a lean, mean fightin' machine."

"You're not all that lean, partner," interjected a newcomer, as Doc Madsen came through the brush. Tucked under his left arm was the large backpack containing the radio.

Blade walked over to the Cavalryman. "Are you all right?"

"I was nicked in the side," Doc said, and lowered the backpack to the ground. "One of them had me dead to rights, but he shot at me from an angle and the radio took most of the rounds. It's ruined."

"Now we can't call for help," Lobo declared.

Blade frowned, then looked up from the punctured backpack. "Where are the others?"

"Right here, sir," Captain Havoc stated. He emerged from the woods to the north with Raphaela a few feet to his left.

"Are you both okay?"

"We're fine," Raphaela answered, studying the Warrior's features. "How'd we do?"

"You did outstanding," Blade replied.

She smiled and hefted her M-16. "That wasn't so hard. Bring on El Diablo."

Blade glanced at the officer. "I want every Devil checked."

"Right away," Havoc replied, wheeling. "Give me a hand,

Raphaela,'' he said, and they moved together.

"Without the radio we might as well head home," Lobo remarked. "If you ask my opinion."

"I didn't," Blade stated. He looked over his right shoulder and observed Sparrow Hawk drawing the blood-soaked spear from the hapless bandit. The loss of the radio irritated him immensely. Now they couldn't rely on the VTOLs to bail them out if they got into serious trouble. They also couldn't radio in the location of El Diablo's base. If they found the head-quarters, they would have to trek all the way to the border to relay the news.

He sighed.

For a mission that wasn't supposed to involve combat, they were seeing a lot of fighting. If he hoped to avoid further conflict, his best bet was to head for California right away. But they couldn't leave without Jaguarundi. Besides, the ten Devils had been waiting for the Force, an ambush undoubtedly devised by El Diablo himself. After all the gunfire at the water hole, the bandit leader, and everyone else in the valley for that matter, must know the Force was in the vicinity. So running away wouldn't do any good. El Diablo might send his dune buggies after them and run them down in the open desert.

What a mess.

Blade scratched an itch next to his right ear and mulled his options. Since heading for California was out of the question, and since they were stranded in enemy territory anyway, he decided the wisest course of action entailed striking directly at the raider chief. The survival of the Force depended on eliminating El Diablo and decimating the Devils. He looked around. "Has anyone seen Emiliano and his son?"

"We are here, *señor*," the farmer announced, approaching from the south with Miguel. "We ran as fast as our legs would carry us." He scowled. "My *compadres* did not run fast enough."

"I know," Blade said.

"I am so sick of El Diablo and his *asesinos*."

"How would you like to see them driven out of your valley permanently?"

"That would be a dream come true for all of my people,"

Emiliano replied. "But who is to do it? You? I admire your bravery, *señor*, but you do not have enough *soldados*. Celestino still has seventy-seven Devils. You are greatly outnumbered."

"We don't have any choice. Either we attack him, or we wait for the Devils to hunt us down. Personally, I'd rather take the fight to El Diablo," Blade stated.

"I'm with you, Blade," Doc declared.

"Count me in," Sparrow added.

Lobo gazed from one to the other. "Let's not do anything hasty, dude. Can't we talk about this?"

"No," Blade said, and faced Emiliano. "What about you? Will you help us? Feel free to say no. You have a family, and they might suffer if we don't succeed."

Emiliano placed his right hand on Miguel's shoulder. "I am tired of all the killing. I am tired of never having enough to fill our bellies while Celestino takes most of our crops. He was my friend once, but no more. I will do whatever you want."

"Thank you," Blade said sincerely. As a husband and a father himself, he could readily appreciate the supreme risk Emiliano was taking. He glanced at Lobo. "I want you to collect all the weapons from the dead Devils and pile them right here."

"All by myself? Can't Chicken Hawk lend me a hand?"

"Get cracking," Blade ordered, and motioned with his right arm.

Grumbling under his breath, Lobo walked off.

"Do you have a plan?" Doc inquired.

"We'll take this a step at a time," Blade answered. He stared at Emiliano. "Does El Diablo keep Devils posted in Jalapa?"

"There are Devils there all the time, but I don't know if they are posted, as you say. They mainly come to the village on their days off to spend time with the *putas*. Sometimes the *putas* go to their base."

"How many Devils are at the village at any one time?"

Emiliano shrugged. "It varies, *señor*. Sometimes only a few. Sometimes a dozen or more. And there are days when almost all the Devils flock into Jalapa for special celebrations."

"Have you ever been to their headquarters?"

"No. Celestino does not allow any of the villagers except the whores into the *caverna*. The base is well guarded all day and all night."

Blade pondered the information. "Okay. The first step will be for you to lead us to your village."

"Gladly, *señor*."

The Warrior spotted Captain Havoc and Raphaela walking toward him. "Are all of the Devils dead?"

"As doornails, sir," Havoc replied.

"Help Lobo collect all their weapons," Blade directed them, and turned to Emiliano. "Will your people join us in our fight against El Diablo?"

The farmer stared at the bandits Lobo had slain. "I honestly can't say, *señor*."

"Aren't they as tired of El Diablo as you are?"

"*Si*, most are. But as I told you before, we are not skilled at killing. Celestino knows we do not pose a threat to him, which is why he lets some of us keep our rifles for hunting and protection from the monsters."

"How many rifles are there in Jalapa?" Blade inquired.

"Fifteen or so, I think."

"That's more than enough. Follow me on this. I have six competent fighters with me. If we distribute the weapons we're confiscating from the ten Devils to villagers who don't own a gun, then add in fifteen riflemen, we'll have thirty-two people. El Diablo only has seventy-seven left. We could finish him once and for all."

"Perhaps. But seventy-seven is still more than thirty-two. The people in my village will not like the odds."

"The odds may never be better," Blade told him. "You've been waiting for almost two decades for a chance to destroy the Devils, but they keep growing stronger and stronger. El Diablo is too powerful for your people to topple by themselves. Now you have us to aid you. With our assistance, under our guidance, we can defeat him."

Emiliano scrutinized the giant's rugged, honest features. "I believe you, *señor*, but I can not predict how my people will decide."

"Lead us to your village. Call a meeting and present the issue to them. Put it to a vote. I hope your people will join us, but if they don't we'll do the job ourselves. It's El Diablo or us," Blade said, and paused. "To the death."

CHAPTER THIRTEEN

He became aware of the loud metallic growl of an engine and felt a swaying motion, then realized his wrists and ankles were bound securely. Pain dominated his being: pain in his head, pain in his right forearm, and pain all up and down his back. He opened his eyes to find himself in the back seat of a modified dune buggy.

"You're a tough bastard. I didn't think you'd revive so soon."

Jaguarundi glared at the smirking countenance of El Diablo, who sat in the front passenger seat a mere foot away. "You should have killed me when you had the chance."

"You'll die soon enough, cat-man," the bandit chief stated confidently.

Jag glanced at the driver, then at the Devil seated on his left with an M-16 pointed at his side. "Where are you taking me?"

"To my headquarters," El Diablo replied.

Jag twisted and stared at the dust swirling into the air from the vacant dirt road to their rear. "Where are the rest of the Devils you had with you?"

El Diablo grinned. "I left them in the village as a reception committee for your friends, just in case they get past Mercer and his squad."

"They'll get past Mercer."

"Don't underestimate my Devils, *amigo*. They caught you, didn't they?"

"Only because I was careless, because I wasn't watching where I was going," Jag said, and gazed at the stretch of road ahead. The blue lake he had seen from the western crest lay a quarter of a mile off. "Where is your headquarters?"

"You'll find out soon enough," El Diablo said. He reached out and patted the dash. "What do you think of my dune buggies?"

"The bigger the boy, the bigger the toys," Jag quipped.

"My dune buggies are not toys, mutant. I got the idea when I visited California. My mechanics have built my fleet of buggies almost from scratch, modeling them after the kind I saw on the beach. I used the same general design, but I have a back seat installed in each vehicle and lightweight armor plating fitted to the doors and hood. They're fast and they get great gas mileage."

"Where do you obtain the motors, tires, and all the other parts you need?"

"From the vehicles I steal in California."

Jag looked at the driver, his brow knitting. "But how do you bring your stolen vehicles to his valley? An ordinary car or truck wouldn't make it across the desert, and you certainly don't have time to strip the vehicles at the border."

"True," El Diablo said. "You'll understand once we reach my headquarters."

"With all the raiding and killing you do, I'm surprised you found time to visit the beach," Jag mentioned sarcastically.

El Diablo's features clouded. "I went to the beach with my wife on my first trip to California."

"You're married?" Jag asked in surprise.

"I was," El Diablo said sadly. "But I made the mistake of taking my beautiful wife, Maria, to California. My grandfather had always told me that California was the land of opportunity." He snorted derisively. "And fool that I was, I believed him. Maria and I were in Los Angeles two days—two lousy, stinking days—when we took a picnic lunch to the beach."

"What happened?" Jag prompted.

El Diablo stared at the floor and frowned. "A group of young gringos in dune buggies drove up to the spot we had picked. There was no one else around. They taunted us, these gringos did, both the men and the women. They insulted us, called us spics and greasers. One of them, a woman, called Maria a whore.'' His voice lowered. ''Maria tried to keep me calm, but I lost my temper and hit the woman. All of them attacked me and I was knocked out. When I came to, I found Maria nearby. She had been raped. Each of the men had taken a turn with her.'' He stopped and took a deep breath. ''They'd beaten her as well.''

''Did she die?'' Jag asked softly.

''*Si*. She was damaged inside. I sat by her side in the hospital for a day and a half, holding her hand and watching her fade.''

''Did the police catch the ones responsible?''

''Are you kidding?'' El Diablo snapped, his head coming up. ''Do you really think the *policía* cared about the death of a Mexican woman? Do you think they gave a damn what happened to a greaser?''

Jag said nothing.

''Needless to say, I did not remain in California, the land of opportunity,'' El Diablo said contemptuously. ''I came back to my village filled with hatred for all Californians.''

''And you've been venting your hatred ever since.''

El Diablo glanced at the hybrid. ''Do you blame me?''

''No,'' Jag said, thinking of the prejudice and bigotry he had encountered. He'd lost count of the number of humans he'd met who hated him simply because he was different, who'd detested him because he was a mutation. If he had a gold coin for every time a human referred to him as a freak or with some other equally unflattering term, or for every time a human gave him that certain glance hinting at concealed revulsion or dislike, he'd be able to open his own bank. He'd learned to accept the fact that humans were a naturally intolerant species, although he'd never fully appreciated that their intolerance extended to one another. The irony made him want to laugh. Humans were equal-opportunity haters. They even despised each other.

As if El Diablo could read the hybrid's mind, he leaned toward his prisoner and said, ''You should be able to understand the way I feel, *amigo*. You're a mutant. I bet you've had to put up with bigots all of your life. Am I right?''

Jaguarundi nodded.

"You may not believe this, *amigo*, but I admire you. You and I have a lot in common. More than you can know. And when I saw you come at me back in the plaza, I knew you were also brave. I respect bravery, in a friend or in a foe."

"And you kill them anyway."

"A man does what he has to do. But I'll tell you what. From here on out, even though I'll kill you in the end. I will not insult you by calling you names. How is that?"

"Damned decent of you. I'm all choked up."

El Diablo glanced at the driver and sighed. "Do you see, Stimson? You try to be nice to some people, or whatever he is, and all they do is hand you sarcasm."

"I see, boss," Stimson responded.

"Why don't you stop?" Jag asked.

"What?"

"Why don't you stop conducting your raids? You've avenged Maria many times over. What can you hope to prove by continuing to butcher innocent men, women, and kids? Agree to disband the Devils and give up raiding border towns, and the authorities in California will stop sending teams down here to eliminate you," Jag said.

A crafty grin creased the bandit chief's lips. "So you admit you are from California!"

"I haven't admitted a thing."

El Diablo chuckled. "But you have, *amigo*. I now know that your friends and you were sent by the rotten gringos in California to kill me. As I suspected." He laughed and slapped the top of his seat.

"We weren't sent to kill you."

"You protest too much, cat-man," El Diablo said, his eyes twinkling in delight. "I knew my little sob story would draw the truth out of you."

Jag's eyes narrowed. "You made up the whole story?"

El Diablo shook his head. "Every word I spoke was true. And yes, I have been avenging Maria ever since. I will continue as long as there is breath in my body. For nearly twenty years I have killed gringos because they are a blight on the earth. Gringos are worse than a plague of locusts. It was gringos who violated my wonderful Maria, who treated her as if she were filth. Gringos took the love of my life away from me, and for such an atrocity I will make them pay until my dying day.''

"But the ones you're killing aren't the ones who assaulted Maria and you."

"What do I care? Gringos are gringos. I hate them all."

"Which makes you no better than the scum who raped Maria," Jag commented.

El Diablo's right hand flashed out and smacked the hybrid across the mouth. "How dare you!" he roared, his face livid. "How dare you compare me to those murdering swine!"

Jag tasted his blood in his mouth and licked his sore lips. "The truth hurts, huh?"

"I thought you understood me. I was wrong," El Diablo said. "Your impudence will cost you, *amigo.*"

"One of us will have to pay a price," Jag stated. He gazed at the landscape on his side of the dune buggy, the wind whipping his fur. If his hands and feet weren't tied, he would have vaulted from the vehicle and risked being shot before he could hide. He wondered how Blade and the others were faring, and he hoped they wouldn't try anything foolish—such as trying to rescue him. He'd gotten himself into the fix he was in, and he'd get himself out.

He hoped.

The dune buggy drew close to the lake, then followed the curving road to the north. The woodland had thinned out as they neared the lake, and now the countryside consisted of scattered stands of trees amidst rolling fields of lush green grasses and wildflowers. Herds of long-horned cattle grazed at random. The idyllic, pristine setting belied the evil breeding in the valley.

The road straightened, and the driver pressed on the accelerator. Larger clouds of dust spewed from the oversized tires, leaving a billowing wake to mark their passage.

Jaguarundi sat quietly, savoring the opportunity to replenish his energy and recover slightly from his wounds. He speculated on the possible fate El Diablo had in store for him, positive the bandit leader would devise a gory end. He longed for the chance to use his nails on the son of a bitch. If the Devils slipped up just once, if they untied him and he was anywhere close to El Diablo, he resolved to terminate the bandit no matter what the cost.

After several miles the grasses were supplanted by forest again. Magnificent peaks formed an irregular wall on the northern horizon.

Jag stared at the mountains, deducing their destination must be in the range ahead. His hunch was verified minutes later when a fortified compound appeared.

"Home, sweet home," El Diablo announced.

The dirt road led to a massive iron gate situated in the center of a 12-foot-high chain-link fence. Two guards stood in front of the gate, machine guns slung over their shoulders. Beyond the fence, perhaps 50 yards distant, reared a cliff the equal of the one situated near the water hole. But with a major difference. The lower third of the cliff, eons ago, had been washed out by the erosive flow of a river long since dry or torn out by a geologic upheaval of cataclysmic proportions, leaving an enormous cavern. The opening alone rose 100 feet and was 70 feet wide. Inside the cavern, visible through the fence, were dune buggies, wooden buildings, and dozens of Devils engaged in various tasks. All the ground past the fence had been paved.

El Diablo looked at his prisoner. "Surprised?"

"Impressed. No one could spot your headquarters from the air unless they knew exactly where it was," Jag replied.

"Even then it would be hard to find," El Diablo said. "And a plane or helicopter couldn't fly too close to those peaks up there anyway, because of the wind and updrafts."

"Very shrewd."

"Thank you, *amigo*. My grandfather told me all about aircraft, and I learned my lessons well, no?"

"Yes."

The driver braked as they drew closer to the gate.

Jag watched the two guards hurrying to throw the iron barrier wide, and a question occurred to him. "Where did you find the camouflage fatigues the Devils all wear?"

"We took them from an armory in California, near El Centro. To me, California is one big store. I take whatever I when need it. Clothes, fuel, weapons, you name it."

The gate swung out and the driver drove into the compound. Astonishment rippled through Jag when he spied the three tremendous vehicles parked just inside the cavern, in the shadows on the right-hand side. They were gargantuan in size, enormous double-decker trailers attached to truck cabs so immense that each one of them could fill a small house. The cabs and the trailers were supported by tires larger than a dune buggy. All three cabs had been painted brown. The trailers were a dull gray.

"What are *those*?" Jag asked.

El Diablo chuckled. "You wanted to know how I bring the vehicles I steal in California to my base? Now you know. Those are my transports. I load the cars and trucks onto the trailers and transport them here. They're not as fast as the dune buggies, but they can negotiate any terrain. They are *magnificio*, don't you think?"

"I've never seen anything like them," Jag admitted. He saw two tanker trucks parked on the other side of the three transports. "Is there fuel in those tankers?"

"Of course."

Occupying the middle of the cavern were the green buildings. Two long, low barracks were situated toward the opening. Behind them was a two-story structure. Along the left wall were 14 dune buggies.

"The *caverna* extends back into the mountain for two hundred yards," El Diablo said. "At the rear is a spring that supplies our drinking water. My Devils have all the comforts of home in the barracks. And we have enough weapons and explosives stored in the tall building to repel the California Army if necessary." He smiled and nodded in self-satisfaction. "I picked the perfect base."

"So it would seem," Jag said, and happened to glance off to the right at the fence. Forty feet from the gate, at the base of the fence, hidden in a bowl-shaped hole scooped out of the earth, was a 50-caliber-machine-gun emplacement. He shifted and gazed to the left. A second machine-gun emplacement, located the same distance from the gate, insured that anyone attacking the compound would be caught in a withering cross fire.

El Diablo noticed the direction of Jaguarundi's gaze and grinned. "Even if your friends manage to get this far, none of them will ever see California again."

CHAPTER FOURTEEN

Not so much as a fly stirred in Jalapa.

Blade crouched in the shelter of a tree, the M60 in his hands and ready for action, and scrutinized the small town. There should be people abroad, but there weren't any. There should be children playing in the streets and dogs yipping, but there wasn't a child or dog in sight. Jalapa resembled a ghost town.

There could only be one explanation.

It was a trap.

The Devils were waiting for the Force, Blade deduced. He looked to the right at Captain Havoc, Lobo, and Raphaela, who were all behind trees of their own, then to the left at Sparrow Hawk and Doc Madsen. They were watching him, waiting for the command to move in. He hesitated, apprehensive over the likely outcome if he was overestimating the team's ability. They'd survived one ambush, but the remaining Devils weren't about to roll over without a fight. The battle was just beginning.

He stared at the flat roofs of red tile, his mind on Emiliano and Miguel. They were waiting in a clearing 50 yards to the west and guarding the weapons confiscated from the ten Devils. Emiliano had wanted to come along, to take part in the fight, but Blade had put his foot down and flatly refused to bring the farmer. He regarded Emiliano as too valuable a contact to gamble losing the man.

The warm afternoon sun on his face brought the Warrior out

of his reflection.

Girding himself, Blade motioned with his right arm, and took off across the narrow field separating the forest from the village, a 40-foot-wide strip of grass and shrubs. He zigzagged, darting from shrub to shrub, his eyes scanning the buildings for any hint of movement.

No Devils appeared.

No gunshots sounded.

Puzzled, he came to a dirt street and dashed across it to the front of a house, flattening against the wall next to the closed door. A window, lacking a glass pane, was to his right. He saw the others reach the cover of adjacent homes, then ducked down and peered in the window. Simple furnishings adorned an empty room. He was surprised to discover the floor consisted of hard-packed dirt.

Where were the inhabitants?

Blade straightened and glanced to the south, wondering if the Devils had evacuated the villagers. Hundreds of yards away, bordering Jalapa's southern boundary, were tilled fields ranging for as far as the eye could see, fields in which corn, wheat, beans, sundry vegetables, and other crops were growing.

The Warrior moved around the northwest corner of the home and proceeded into the village, hunched over, his eyes constantly probing for enemies. He passed empty building after empty building.

"Where is everyone?" Raphaela whispered from right behind him.

"Your guess is as good as mine," Blade replied.

"The Devils are expecting us, aren't they?"

"Either that or the villagers took the day off to go skinny-dipping in the lake," Blade said, and abruptly halted as the noise of a vehicle engine arose to the east. He listened for several seconds as the noise gradually receded, indicating the vehicle must be departing Jalapa on the road Emiliano had mentioned.

"What's that?" Raphaela asked.

"Beats me," Blade said, and looked back to check that everyone was still with him.

Raphaela smiled up at him, then suddenly tensed and threw herself at his chest, knocking him aside as she raised her M-16 and trained the barrel on the upper window of a building on the left side of the street, not more than 25 feet off. She squeezed off a burst.

A strangled screech came from the window, and a moment later a man dressed in camouflage fatigues toppled out, his arms outflung, his face peppered with red dots, his machine gun falling from limp fingers. He fell to the street with a pronounced thud.

Blade glanced at the dead Devil, then at Raphaela. "Thanks. You saved my life."

She smiled sheepishly. "I saw the sun gleam off his barrel."

The others converged on them, each one alert for another sniper.

"Damn! That was close!" Lobo commented.

"It's a good thing you didn't send her back to the Moles," Doc remarked with a grin.

Blade nodded. Raphaela was turning out to be a major asset to the team. Which proved that the old clichés were invariably correct. What was that one again? Oh, yeah. Never judge a book by its cover. He gazed at them and wagged the M60. "Remember your training. Don't bunch up. Spread out. Give yourselves room to maneuver. Don't make it easy for the opposition to bag us."

They promptly obeyed, fanning out.

The Warrior advanced farther into the village. There were bound to be more Devils lying in ambush, and he strained his senses to detect them before they sprang their trap. He came abreast of a squat house and looked inside through the open door. A pot and a thin, flat, circular piece of dough were lying on the floor near the doorway. The occupants, evidently, had departed in haste.

Another motor roared to life to the east, only this one was much closer.

Blade halted and surveyed the street ahead. At the end there appeared to be a public square of some sort. Even as he looked, a dune buggy swung into the street from the square and raced toward the Force.

"Look out!" Raphaela shouted.

Two grinning Devils were in the dune buggy. The guy on

the passenger side leaned out with an AK-47 clutched in his hands. He smirked and leveled the weapon.

"Take cover!" Blade bellowed, and dove into the house on his right. He heard the machine gun open up as he came down on his elbows and knees, heard rounds smacking into the walls, and he scrambled erect and faced the doorway.

The dune buggy was just speeding past.

Blade stepped to the door and sent a dozen rounds after the vehicle, gratified to see the shots rip into its rear end. The thundering engine reverberated in the confined space between the buildings. Combined with the blasting of the M60, the din was enough to drown out every other sound.

Which almost cost the Warrior his life.

With his attention on the dune buggy racing to the west, Blade didn't realize there was imminent danger from another source until he glimpsed Sparrow Hawk framed in a window across the street. The Flathead was gesturing frantically with his right hand, *pointing to the east.* Blade spun, and he barely registered the sight of a second dune buggy hurtling toward them when the Devil on the passenger side cut loose with an assault rifle.

Damn!

Bullets plowed into the outer wall on the right side of the doorway. Instead of retreating into the shadows, Blade automatically did the unexpected; he stepped into the center of the street, trained the M60 on the dune buggy, and let them have it. The big machine gun bucked in his arms as he poured a veritable hailstorm of lead into the grill, hood, and driver. A short swing to the left stitched the pattern of slugs into the other Devil, and the man screamed as his chest was transformed into a series of miniature crimson geysers.

The driver slumped over the steering wheel and the dune buggy veered into a house on the right, smashing through the wall and coming to an abrupt rest as a portion of the roof collapsed upon it.

Blade whirled and saw the first dune buggy returning for another run. He planted his feet firmly and fired.

Three blocks off, the driver gunned the engine and came at the giant head on, undaunted by the rounds puncturing the front of his vehicle.

Captain Havoc suddenly materialized in a second-floor window a few dozen feet in front of the buggy. He looked down, smiled, and pulled an object from his right front pocket.

Blade knew what was coming. He saw Havoc pull the pin, and he pivoted and dashed to the doorway, his eyes on the hand grenade the officer tossed directly onto the onrushing vehicle. His head and shoulders were just clearing the jamb when the grenade went off. The explosion rocked every building on the street, rattling cabinets and causing dishes to crash to the floor. Blade sprawled onto his stomach and rolled, seeing flaming fragments sail past the doorway. He surged to his knees and peeked out.

The concussion had flipped the dune buggy—what remained of it—onto its back. Fire engulfed the twisted wreckage. Bits of the two Devils were scattered about. A severed arm lay a few yards to the east. Near the corner of a house a smoldering leg leaned against the wall, propped upright, as if waiting for the owner to reclaim it.

Blade surveyed the street. Satisfied the Devils were momentarily holding back, he moved into the street.

The other Force members joined him, each one tense, each one primed for combat. They kept at least a yard between them.

"I guess we taught those wimps," Lobo commented when they were all assembled.

"Yeah. *We* did," Havoc said, and chuckled.

"Move out," Blade instructed them. "And stay frosty."

"You don't have to tell me twice, dude," Lobo responded.

They headed for the center of Jalapa, warily checking every house they passed. An unnatural silence hung over the village. Behind them the burning dune buggy crackled and hissed as the flames consumed the vehicle.

Blade stopped a few yards shy of the town square and scrutinized the layout. In the center stood a wooden post. Adobe structures ringed the plaza. There wasn't a living soul in sight.

"I don't like it," Doc Madsen said. "We're being watched. I just know it."

The Warrior nodded. He felt the same way. But if he wanted to lure the Devils out into the open, if he wanted to wipe out every last bandit in the village, he had to take calculated gambles. Such as boldly striding into the square. The short hairs at the nape of his neck tingled as he walked toward the post. His unit followed. All except one.

"This definitely sucks," Lobo mentioned softly. "After all we've been through, I'd better get a month off when we get back to L.A."

"Dream on," Raphaela said.

Blade glanced over his left shoulder, noting their positions. Lobo and Raphaela were right behind him, then Havoc and Sparrow. Surprisingly, Doc Madsen had hung back and was standing near the corner of the last building, scanning the roofs. Why?

The Warrior received his answer seconds later when the Devils set the next phase of their trap into motion. Four bandits, each on a different roof, one to the east, south, west, and north, popped up and opened fired on the exposed Force members at the same instant that two dune buggies sped out of a street at the northeast corner of the plaza.

"Scatter!" Blade barked, and swung to the northeast, focusing on the dune buggies and hoping the others could take care of the Devils on the roofs.

He needn't have worried.

Out of the corner of his left eye Blade saw Doc Madsen spring out of the side street. The Cavalryman's M-16 was slung over his left shoulder, and as he came into the open he drew his Smith and Wesson Distinguished Combat Magnum.

The other Force members were returning fire while running a serpentine course for cover.

On the roofs, the four Devils were concentrating on the racing figures near the middle of the square. Not until it was too late did they awaken to the fact that another man had entered the fray.

Doc held the Magnum low, next to his waist, and as he ran clear of the buildings to the west he twisted and fired without consciously aiming. The Devil on a roof three doors up threw his hands to his head and fell from view. Doc spun, beginning a complete revolution, and as he faced north he fired again, the shot unerringly accurate, catching the Devil to the north in the throat, and still Doc spun, now facing to the east and snapping off his third round, and he continued his turn, coming around to the south, the Magnum booming once more. The Devil to the east and the one to the south dropped simultaneously.

Leaving the dune buggies.

Blade tracked them with the M60 and was about to squeeze the trigger when they parted, the first bearing to the right, the second to the left. The Devils began firing, foolishly sweeping their weapons back and forth, spraying lead wildly instead of trying to nail a specific target. He bent in half and dashed to the wooden post. It wasn't much cover, but it would have to do. He leaned against it, scarcely noticing the fresh blood stains on the wood, and watched the dune buggy on the right as the vehicle swept around the square. He waited, hearing total bedlam rock the west side of the plaza as his teammates poured their concentrated fire into the second vehicle.

The Devil in the front passenger seat of the first dune buggy got off a few hasty rounds, trying to hit the giant next to the post.

Blade ducked as the shots hit the post, chipping off slivers, and dove straight out, flattening on the ground and firing as he landed. Both the driver and the other Devil thrashed and jerked when their bodies were punctured again and again. The driver released the wheel and the dune buggy slanted to the right, ramming into a two-story structure and grinding to a halt with its engine running.

What about the other one?

Blade rolled onto his back and leaped to his feet.

The two Devils in the second dune buggy resembled sieves. Scores of holes dotted their heads, necks, and torsos, oozing blood. Both of them were sitting with their heads tilted back and their mouths hanging open. The vehicle had coasted to a stop mere inches from a wall.

Blade surveyed the plaza. Havoc and Raphaela were to his right, rising from the ground. Doc Madsen was reloading his Magnum. Lobo and Sparrow were off to the left, slowly approaching. "Anyone hit?" he called out.

"Me," Havoc responded. He walked over, his left arm pressed to his side, a spreading red stain on his left shoulder.

"How bad is it?" Blade asked.

"It stings like hell," Havoc said, and grunted.

"Let me help you," Raphaela offered, slinging her M-16 over her right arm. "I'll bandage the wound."

"That's not necessary. I can manage," Havoc responded.

"Let her help," Blade directed, then glanced at Doc Madsen. "Take Lobo and Sparrow with you. Check the whole village. Make sure there aren't any more Devils lurking around."

"I doubt it man," Lobo spoke up. "We whipped their butts but good."

"Go anyway," Blade said flatly.

"You've got it," Doc said, and led the other two to the north.

Captain Havoc had dropped to his right knee and was allowing Raphaela to assist him in removing his backpack and fatigue shirt. "Looks like this isn't my day," he commented.

"You're still alive," Blade reminded him. He stepped closer to inspect the bullet hole. A round had penetrated the fleshy part of the officer's shoulder, just above the collar bone, and gone completely through. Muscles and sinew had been torn, and the hole was bleeding moderately, but the wound wasn't life-threatening.

Raphaela removed her backpack and rummaged inside for her first-aid kit. "I'm pretty good at patching people up. I have four younger brothers and three younger sisters, and I've had to tend them more times than I care to remember."

"That's quite a family," Havoc remarked.

Blade scanned the buildings ringing the plaza. "Bandage him quickly, Raphaela. The Devils could return any minute."

"Yes, sir."

"I tend to agree with Lobo, sir," Captain Havoc said. "Call my feeling gut instinct, but I don't think they'll try and take us out for a while."

"You hope."

"There's something I don't quite understand," Raphaela mentioned as she laid the first aid kit on the ground and opened it.

"What's that?" Blade asked.

"Now bear in mind I don't know a lot about guns and bullets and whatnot," Raphaela stated, removing a bottle of antiseptic and a box of bandages, "but I distinctly recall you telling us that those dune buggies have armor plating on them.''

"True," Blade said.

"Then how come your shots bored right through that armor as if it was paper?''

"Two reasons," Blade replied, pleased by her inquisitive mind, by the interest she displayed in her new line of work. "First, the armor plating on the dune buggies isn't the same type you'd find on, say, a tank. It's not as thick, not as heavy. The Devils put lightweight armor plating on their vehicles so the dune buggies wouldn't lose any speed or maneuverability. You've got to remember that El Diablo is a quick-strike artist. He likes to sweep into a town, kill everybody in sight and grab whatever he needs, then pull out before the Army arrives. Speed is essential to his operation.''

"What's the second reason?" Raphaela asked, using a wad of gauze to dab at the blood on Havoc's shoulder.

"The armor plating on the dune buggies is mainly intended to stop rifle and small-arms fire, not heavy machine guns. My M60, for instance, uses a variety of ammo. It takes ball, tracer, armor-piercing, and even blank ammunition if I want. I can mix and match as I desire. And since I knew El Diablo relied on modified dune buggies, every third round in my ammo belts is armor-piercing.''

"Thanks for explaining. I think I understand now."

Blade heard footsteps to the north, and swiveled to find Lobo running toward them. "What's up? More Devils?"

"Nope," the Clansman responded, slowing as he neared them. "Doc sent me back to tell you what he found.''

"Which was?''

"A dune buggy parked on a side street.''

"Does it run?''

Lobo glanced at Raphaela and Havoc. "It's in one piece. There's no key, but that won't stop me. I can hot-wire the sucker, if you want.''

"I want. Drive it back here.''

"Okay, dude." Lobo wheeled and jogged off.

Captain Havoc stared at the Warrior. "What do you have in mind, sir?"

"We need transportation.''

"Are you thinking what I think you're thinking?"

Blade looked at the officer and nodded. "We're going to attack El Diablo's base."

"What?" Raphaela exclaimed, pausing in her ministrations. "Just the six of us?"

"I hope the villagers will help us, but one way or the other we're eliminating that butcher and his band."

"But the odds," Raphaela said. "Wouldn't it be smarter for us to head for California and get reinforcements?"

"No. I doubt El Diablo will allow us to leave this valley alive, and even if we did escape he'd undoubtedly send his dune buggies to catch us on the open desert, where we wouldn't stand a chance. So we take the fight to him now, when he'd least expect us to go after him."

"You *hope* he's not expecting us," Captain Havoc noted. "If he is, he'll prepare quite a reception."

"That's a risk we'll have to take," Blade said.

"What about Jag? Shouldn't we wait for him to return?" Raphaela asked.

"I am thinking about Jag. We should have met up with him by now. He was supposed to check on the source of the smoke we saw, which was this village. The people were fixing their midday meal."

"Maybe Jag is hiding in the forest," Raphaela guessed.

Blade shook his head. "He's not the hiding type. After he got away from Emiliano, he would have circled back to us. He would have had no trouble picking up our trail and overtaking us."

"What do you think has happened to him?"

"I suspect the Devils have him," Blade stated, and turned to the north once again when he spied Doc and Sparrow approaching on the double. "What is it? Where's Lobo?"

"He's working on the dune buggy," Doc answered. "We found something we figured you should know about."

"Tell me."

The pair stopped.

Doc pointed to the north. "There are two bodies in a building about a block from the plaza. One is a woman, the other a guy. They're both Devils."

"How did they die?"

"The woman had her neck broken," Doc answered.

"And the man?"

Sparrow responded this time. "His throat was slashed. The incision, though, is too ragged to have been made by a knife. I've seen such cuts before on deer slain by a mountain lion."

"Jag," Blade said.

Sparrow nodded. "I believe so."

"Then the Devils do have him," Blade declared harshly, and gazed to the west. "This settles it. As soon as Lobo gets the dune buggy running, we're going after El Diablo."

"Jag could already be dead," Raphaela said.

"Maybe. Maybe El Diablo will toy with him for a while," Blade said. "In any event, we're not leaving a single Devil alive."

Doc nodded. "I wouldn't have it any other way."

The Warrior ran his right hand through his hair and sighed. "Our orders were to track El Diablo to his lair and avoid engaging the enemy. Well, due to circumstances beyond our control we don't have any choice. And since we don't, since we're dealing with scum who have slaughtered hundreds of innocent people over the years, since those scum have captured and probably killed a teammate, the standing order of the day will be short and simple." He looked at each of them. "No mercy whatsoever. Is that understood?"

Everyone nodded.

Blade noticed Captain Havoc staring at him with a strange expression. "Is anything wrong?"

"No," the officer said. "I was just thinking that you're a man after my own heart."

"You sound surprised."

Captain Havoc nodded. "I am."

CHAPTER FIFTEEN

"**W**hat do you think of my little army, eh?" El Diablo asked proudly.

"Offhand, I'd say they suck," Jaguarundi responded defiantly, then smiled sweetly at the four Devils who stood to his right with their weapons trained on his torso. "Present company included, of course."

"You shouldn't push me, cat-man," El Diablo said. "Your end will come that much sooner."

"Maybe I can't stand the suspense," Jag quipped. He gazed at the four rows of Devils standing at attention in front of the barracks, their backs to the cavern, then to his left at the bandit leader. "What's with the formation? Are you planning to give them a pep talk?"

El Diablo had planted himself a few feet from the middle of the first row, facing the Devils, his hands clasped behind his back. He glanced at the hybrid. "Have your fun while you can. In a little while you won't feel like laughing."

"Promises, promises," Jag said, and for the umpteenth time surreptitiously tried to snap the rope binding his wrists. But the rope held fast. At least his legs had been untied, so his scheme to eliminate El Diablo before the Devils finished him off had a slim hope of succeeding.

"Do you want us to shut this creep up?" one of the guards asked.

"Let him prattle," El Diablo replied, and turned to the assembled Devils. "Higbie, front and center."

A weasely man with oily dark hair stepped from the second row and came around to stand in front of El Diablo. Over his left shoulder hung an M-16. "Yes, boss?" he asked nervously.

"Did you pull a shift at the water hole today?"

Higbie licked his lips and mustered a feeble smile. "Yeah, boss. You know I did. I was in charge of the morning shift."

"Did you wait to be properly relieved?"

Jag almost laughed when he saw the color drain from Higbie's face. He observed that every Devil was watching the proceedings intently.

"Sort of," Higbie answered.

El Diablo glowered. "What the hell does 'sort of' mean?"

"I waited ten minutes past the time I should have been relieved, then I went to find out why my relief hadn't shown up," Higbie responded.

"And what did you find?"

"Mercer's dune buggy had broken down. He told me the mechanics would be there to fix it in fifteen minutes."

El Diablo lowered his hands to his sides. "And what did you do then?"

Higbie swallowed hard. "I figured we'd come on back. Mercer wasn't that far from the water hole, and I assumed he'd be at his post in thirty minutes at the most."

"You *figured*? You *assumed*?"

"I didn't think a few minutes could make that much of a difference."

"You didn't?" El Diablo said sternly. "Then allow me to explain the consequences of your negligence." He twisted and pointed off to the west, at the escarpment visible above the trees. "Why do you think I went to so much trouble to seek out the Cocopas and arrange for them to post men on top of that cliff? For my health?"

"No."

"Could it be because the only approach to the valley is from the west? Could it be because anyone who is after us has to pass by the water hole and that cliff?"

Higbie shifted nervously. "Yeah."

"And why do you think I keep a crew posted at the water hole twenty-four hours a day?" El Diablo questioned.

"So the Cocopas can signal them and the crew can intercept anyone who tries to enter the valley."

"Brilliant!" El Diablo said. "Now follow me on this next part. Intruders came to our valley today. The Cocopas saw them coming. But the Indians couldn't signal the crew at the water hole because *it wasn't there*." He paused. "You'd already left. You'd already deserted your post."

Higbie said nothing.

"Fortunately, they could still signal *me*. I'm lucky it isn't cloudy today. I'm also lucky Mercer heard all that gunfire and radioed in."

"Everything turned out for the best," Higbie ventured.

"Did it?" El Diablo responded skeptically. "Then why are the intruders still loose in my valley? Why haven't I heard from Mercer or the squad I left in Jalapa?"

"I don't know."

"You don't know," El Diablo repeated mincingly.

"I'm sorry, boss. I really am," Higbie said.

"Being sorry doesn't cut it," El Diablo declared. "You deserted your post, pure and simple. I can't blame the three men who were there with you because you were in charge. The fault is yours."

Higbie started to speak, but he seemed to experience considerable difficulty in mouthing his words. "What are you going to do?"

"What do you think?" El Diablo replied, and placed his hands on his revolvers.

Jag saw Higbie flinch and take a step backwards. Suddenly El Diablo drew those stainless-steel revolvers, and they had to be two of the biggest revolvers Jag had ever laid eyes on. The barrels alone were 12 inches in length, tilted upwards at Higbie's head. Both guns thundered, the twin blasts deafening, sounding for all the world like the roar from a cannon. The bullets bored into Higbie's forehead and burst out the top of his cranium, spraying his hair and brains on the Devils in the foremost row. Higbie stiffened, his mouth moving wordlessly, and pitched onto his face.

None of the other Devils moved.

Jag watched blood and brains seep from the gaping cavity in Higbie's head.

"I won't tolerate fools," El Diablo stated. He swung toward Jag and extended his arms. "What do you think of my handguns?"

"They'd come in real handy if you ever tackle a dinosaur."

El Diablo grinned and hefted the revolvers. "I took these from a rich *bastardo* in California. Have you ever heard of the .454 Casull?"

"No," Jag admitted.

"They were manufactured before the war, *amigo*. The Californian told me these are the world's most powerful handguns," El Diablo boasted.

"Higbie would probably agree."

The bandit leader laughed and slid the revolvers into their holsters. "Now to our next piece of business," he said. "The contest."

"Contest?" Jag didn't like the sound of that.

"Yes," El Diablo responded, then turned as a brown-haired man wearing glasses and a white smock hurried toward him, skirting the Devils on the left. "Yes, Doctor?"

"Carlos will live. I can repair his nose, but his eyes are another matter," the physician said in a deep voice.

"Screw Carlos. What about Pancho?"

"Your dog will be fine. I've stitched the wound in his neck. In a month Pancho will be as good as new."

"Excellent!" El Diablo stated happily, and glanced at the mutation. "Where are my manners? Doctor Vankellen, I'd like you to meet the son of a bitch who tore up Pancho and Jarrod. This deviate is Jaguarundi."

"A genetically altered monstrosity," Doctor Vankellen said. "I've always believed his kind are an abomination and should be exterminated."

"My sentiments exactly," El Diablo agreed, and chuckled. "Leave the extermination to me and go tend to Pancho."

"Do you want me to keep him sedated? He's coming around."

"No sedation, Doctor. I'll need Pancho in a while. I intend

to give him the chance to get even with the freak.''

"As you wish," Doctor Vankellen said, and departed.

El Diablo glanced at Jag. "I found the good doctor in a bar in Mexicali, stone drunk. He'd just had his medical license taken away for a few minor infractions and leaped at the chance to become wealthy working for me."

"You're a regular humanitarian."

"Why are you so bitter, *amigo*? You're not dead yet."

"But I'm sure you'll remedy that soon," Jag remarked.

"As soon as Pancho revives," El Diablo said. "Poor Pancho. You hurt him, hurt him bad. He was lucky you didn't tear open an artery or a vein."

"How'd the mutt get here? He didn't ride with us."

"No, I sent Pancho and Carlos on ahead with my best driver as soon as you were knocked out. I was worried Pancho might die."

"But you weren't worried about Carlos?"

El Diablo shrugged. "Why should I be? He's one of my men. He knows the risks."

Jaguarundi scrutinized the Devils for several seconds. "You know, I just noticed that two-thirds of your Devils are from north of the border. Why?"

"It amuses me to use gringos to destroy gringos."

"And they don't care that you hate gringos?"

El Diablo nodded at the Devils. "Those who join me are in it for the gold and silver they receive, for their share of the loot, or just because they like to kill and rape. They couldn't care less about my personal feelings as long as I treat them fairly. Besides, my Devils are not the social cream of the crop. Any one of them would shoot their own mother if the price was right."

"So they're all as warped as you are."

"They all know that if a person wants something out of this life, the only way to get it is to take it."

Jaguarundi scanned the four rows of hardened faces and scowled. "Yeah. Birds of a feather flock together. Isn't that the saying? You all deserve to die together."

"And who's going to kill us, cat-man? You?"

"The ones who will come after me."

"Do you really believe your friends will survive the ambush I set for them in the village?" El Diablo asked.

"Yep."

"Such confidence is touching. You must know them very well."

"No," Jag said. "But I think I know the man who is leading them, and if I'm right he won't rest until you're six feet under. He's not the kind to leave a job half finished."

"Who is this formidable hombre?"

"Wouldn't you like to know?" Jag retorted.

The bandit chief made a few smacking sounds with his tongue. "Such nastiness is uncalled for. I can see that you are eager to begin the contest. What a pity. Just when we were having such a marvelous *conversación*. Oh, well."

"I'm not in much of a mood for a contest right now," Jag said. "Maybe tomorrow we can play a game of chess."

"I'm partial to Russian roulette myself. And the contest I have in mind is one a creature such as you will find more interesting then a dull game of chess."

"What kind of contest is it?"

El Diablo grinned and gazed at the Devils. "*Machetazo*, front and center! Pronto!" he bellowed.

Jag saw a tall figure move from the fourth row of Devils and move briskly forward. The man who stepped into view stood well over six feet in height and was endowed with a barrel of a chest and thick arms. His hair and mustache were black, his eyes an icy green. Several scars marked his cheeks and chin. Oddly, the man wore a machete on each hip. He halted and saluted.

"*Si*, El Diablo?"

The bandit chief gestured at the hybrid. "How would you like to demonstrate to the cat-man why we call you Machetazo?"

"It would be my pleasure," the man said, and sneered at Jaguarundi.

"Do you need time to prepare?" El Diablo asked.

"A few minutes to apply the oil."

"Then go. But hurry back."

Machetazo did an about-face and headed for the nearest barracks.

"What was that business about oil?" Jag inquired.

"You will see, *amigo*," El Diablo said, and laughed. He abruptly barked a series of orders in Spanish.

Jag watched the four rows perform a drill they must have practiced many times. In precise military fashion, the first row marched to the left while the second tramped to the right. The two rows went a few dozen yards in a straight line, then executed a right-angle turn so that both columns were marching to the south. Twelve yards farther away both turned again, toward one another, and in no time at all the two rows met and halted. The third row then followed the first, and the last row took off on the heels of the second. When their maneuvers were completed the Devils had formed into a large square with Jag, El Diablo, and the four guards in the middle. The Devils all faced inward and stood at attention.

"I've trained them well, no?" the bandit leader commented.

"They can march without tripping over their own feet. Big deal," Jag cracked.

"Why do you persist in mocking me?"

"I'd rather tear your throat out, but at the moment I'm rather . . . tied up," Jag said.

"You must have a death wish, *amigo*."

"I wish you'd untie my hands."

"They will be untied as soon as Machetazo returns. But you would be well advised to restrain yourself. Should you try to attack me, those four men will slay you instantly. You had better concentrate on the contest."

Jag stared at the four Devils, at their weapons. "I guess you have the upper hand, for now."

"For now and forever," El Diablo said. "I did not become the most feared and respected *bandido* in the Baja by being careless."

"Respected? Don't make me laugh. I doubt your own mother respects you."

El Diablo's lips compressed and he took a stride toward the mutation. "You dare! Don't ever mention my mother again."

The enraged intensity of the raider's reaction surprised Jaguarundi. After the beating and the whipping, after the treatment he'd received from El Diablo and the Devils, Jag took particular delight in baiting them. He longed to pay them back for the pain he'd suffered. At that moment he recalled the advice Mercer had given him concerning El Diablo's real name, and he decided to provoke the bandit chief even more. "Why not, Celestino? Is your mother sorry she raised a dirtbag like you?"

Bright scarlet flushed El Diablo's features. He sputtered and seemed about to go berserk. Instead, he brutally lashed out with the back of his right hand.

Jag felt the blow land on his mouth, snapping his head around. He stepped backwards and shook his head, clearing his thoughts. "Is that the best you can do?" he asked scornfully.

"No one speaks that name in my presence!" El Diablo declared. "Celestino Naranjo no longer exists. He died the day Maria Santiago died."

"I wonder how Maria would feel if she could see you now," Jag commented.

"*Silencio!*"

"What are you going to do if I don't shut up? Kill me?" Jag asked, and laughed.

El Diablo's hands swooped to his revolvers and he started to draw. The barrels were almost out of the holsters when he froze, his eyes gleaming fanatically. "No. This would be too easy. I want you to die a slow, lingering death." He gazed past the hybrid, then smiled. "And here is just the man to do the job."

Jaguarundi pivoted.

Striding toward them was the man called Machetazo. He had removed his fatigue shirt, revealing an awesome physique rippling with layers of well-developed muscles. His chest and arms glistened; they were covered with oil. In each hand he held a gleaming machete.

El Diablo chortled. "Now the contest can begin!"

CHAPTER SIXTEEN

"**H**ow far do we have to go?" Doc Madsen asked.

"It's five miles from the lake to the base," Blade answered, his eyes on the dirt road ahead as he steered the dune buggy into a curve to the north.

Doc looked at the tranquil lake and spotted ducks swimming near the western shore. The scene reminded him of the beautiful rolling hills in the Dakota Territory and the many hours he'd spent hunting and fishing. Next to gambling and dallying with the ladies, he especially liked to spend hours in the woods or on a pond or lake after game. "Will we get some time off when this is all over?"

Blade glanced at the Cavalryman, who sat on his right, and nodded. "Most likely. Why?"

"I've been on the Force less than a month and already I need a vacation," Doc quipped. "I'd like to get some fishing in."

"I'll gladly go with you," Sparrow offered. He sat on the Cavalryman's right, his right hand on the roll bar, the spear clasped between his legs. "I enjoy fishing."

"You've got a deal, partner."

"What about you three in the back?" Blade interjected. He twisted and stared at Havoc, Raphaela, and Lobo, who sat from right to left across the rear seat.

"I've never been fishing. I wouldn't know what to do," Raphaela said.

"That wasn't what I meant," Blade said. "How are you holding up?"

"It's cramped as hell back here," Lobo groused. "I can barely move. I feel like one of those little smelly fish I saw in a tin can once."

"We'll be there soon," Blade said.

"Not soon enough," Lobo responded.

Blade swerved the dune buggy to avoid a pothole. He straightened the steering wheel and gazed at a mountain range in the distance. How could he have allowed General Gallagher to talk him into accepting such a dangerous assignment? he asked himself. After what happened to the first Force, he should have known better. If Jaguarundi died, and odds were that the hybrid had already been slain, then he had to accept the responsibility. The full responsibility. He possessed the authority to turn down any mission Gallagher proposed, and he should have learned his lesson from his experiences with the first team. Never—never, never, never—take a unit into the field until after the unit has been thoroughly trained and functioned flawlessly together.

"I have a question, sir," Captain Havoc announced.

"Ask it."

"You gave us several reasons for taking the fight to El Diablo. Which one, to you, is the most important? Is it because the Devils *might* have Jag as their prisoner? Is it because you know we can't get back to the border without the dune buggies catching us? Or is it because you simply want to put an end to the butcher once and for all?"

"Which reason is the most important?"

"Yes, sir. To you personally," Havoc stressed.

"Strange question."

"I'd just like to know. If you don't object to answering, sir," Havoc said.

"I have no objections," Blade stated, and glanced quickly at each of them before returning his attention to the road. "All of the factors you mentioned are important considerations. But by far *the* most important reason is that the Devils may have caught Jag." He paused. "Whether he's alive or dead is, in a way, irrelevant."

"You don't care if the kitty is alive or wasted?" Lobo asked.

"Of course I do. I want to find Jag alive. I never want to lose another Force member again. If he's still in one piece, we'll rescue him. If the Devils have killed him, then we'll make sure they pay for the deed," Blade said.

"You bet we will," Doc vowed.

"The point I'm trying to make is this," Blade continued. "You're all part of a team now. I know that most of you have never worked as part of a unit. This is a whole new experience for you. But I expect each and every one of you to adhere to a basic directive where the Force is concerned."

"Which is?" Captain Havoc inquired.

"The Force comes first," Blade replied. "The welfare of your teammates must be the single most important issue to you, what matters the most at any given time. Whether we're on duty or off, whether we're on a mission or at the Force facility, you must put loyalty to the other Force members above all else."

"What about my mom, dude?" Lobo quipped. "I'd say she comes in first."

"This isn't a joking matter," Blade admonished. "I'll use an illustration. As all of you know, I'm from a survivalist compound in northern Minnesota known as the Home. Eighteen of us have been selected as Warriors, and it's our responsibility to protect the Home at all costs. The Warriors are a very tight-knit group. We're always ready to back each other up, to lend a hand when needed, to go the extra mile. Any one of us would gladly walk on burning coals to save the life of another Warrior."

"You want us to walk on coals?" Lobo asked.

"Not literally, but the same principle applies," Blade said. "We must stand by each other through thick and thin. We must never abandon a fellow Force member, never leave them in the lurch, never desert a teammate or leave them behind. A mission isn't over until all of us have been accounted for. And this is the main reason we're going to hit El Diablo's base. We're not leaving this valley until we find Jaguarundi. We've only known him a short while, but Jag is part of the Force. No matter what it takes, we're going to locate him."

A silence greeted his comments.

Blade waited for them to respond. Their next statements would prove crucial in determining their inherent fitness for the Force. An elite tactical unit had no place for overly individualistic, egocentric members.

"Sounds fair to me," Doc Madsen spoke up. "I hitched aboard this outfit for the duration, and I want all of us to last the whole year."

"I would not think of deserting my companions, my brothers and sister in combat," Sparrow Hawk said solemnly.

"Count me in, man," Lobo chimed in. "I know I wouldn't want any of you turkeys to leave me behind somewhere."

"I'll never run out on any of you," Raphaela promised.

Blade looked back at the officer. "And you?"

Havoc averted his gaze and coughed. "I feel the same way you do, sir."

"I trust I've answered your question satisfactorily," Blade remarked.

"Better than I would have hoped, sir."

The Warrior started to speak, then changed his mind. An element about Havoc's attitude bothered him, but he couldn't isolate the cause. His intuition told him the officer was testing him in some manner. But how? And why? Did Havoc doubt his competence to lead the Force? If so, for what reason? If Havoc didn't believe him to be an able leader, then why had the officer volunteered for the Force? Captain Mike Havoc possessed an impeccable military record and, on paper at least, rated as the best of the new recruits. But Blade felt compelled to view the officer as one big question mark.

"So what's your plan, dude?" Lobo queried. "Are we gonna drive up to their base and ask for El Diablo?"

"We'll play it by ear," Blade said.

"Excuse me for bringin' this up, but aren't you supposed to be the genius at strategy?" Lobo asked. "All you can say is that we'll play it by ear?"

"Since I don't know the layout of the base, I can't plan an attack, now can I?"

"Well, if you want to quibble, I guess not," Lobo conceded.

"What about the villagers? Do you figure they'll throw in with us?" Doc Madsen wondered.

"The villagers have been under El Diablo's heel for decades. Rebelling against him will be difficult for them to do," Blade said. "I don't know if Emiliano will be able to convince them to join our cause."

Lobo snickered. "Convince them? First the turkey has to find them! Those jokers probably headed for the hills when all the shootin' started."

"You can't blame them for wanting to stay out of the line of fire," Blade observed. "They're farmers, not fighters."

"Ain't that the truth."

"Why must you be so critical all the time?" Raphaela asked the Clansman.

"Who's critical, lady? I'm being realistic, is all," Lobo told her.

Blade stared at the mountains ahead, searching for any sign of the bandit headquarters. Emiliano had instructed him to be on the lookout for a cavern situated at the base of a cliff. A thought occurred to him and he tensed. Would El Diablo post guards on the cliff? Or would the raider be too complacent after so many years without any trouble except for the two teams sent in by California? In any event, the dust from the dune buggy could probably be seen for quite some distance.

The Warrior slammed on the brakes.

"What's wrong?" Doc inquired.

"Why are we stoppin'?" Lobo wanted to know. "We're not there already, are we?"

"No," Blade said. "Everybody out. We're going the rest of the way on foot."

"Say *what*?"

"You heard me. Everyone out of the dune buggy," Blade stated. He lifted the M60 from the floor beside his seat. "We have a few miles to cover on the double."

"Do you mean we have to *run*?" Lobo asked.

"You can crawl if you want," Blade said. "Just so you keep up with the rest of us." He shifted into park and uncrossed the loose wires dangling under the steering column. The engine promptly sputtered and died. "You did a great job of hot-wiring this buggy, Lobo."

"Why'd I go to all the trouble if we have to run halfway there?"

"The exercise will do you good," Blade stated. He climbed from the vehicle and stretched.

The others followed suit, the Clansman grumbling under his breath.

Doc Madsen gazed at the peaks rimming the valley to the north. "We shouldn't have more than a mile or two to go. We'll be there in no time."

"Just a mile or two, huh? I'll hardly work up a sweat," Lobo cracked.

Captain Havoc chuckled. "If you expend half as much energy moving your legs as you do flapping your gums, you'll be the first one to the base."

The Warrior motioned with his right arm. "Let's head on out. Stay alert. And remember the order of the day. No mercy." He turned and led off.

Lobo waited until the rest were already jogging northward before he reluctantly trailed after them. He stared at the mountains and rolled his eyes. "Just my dumb luck! I get hooked up with a fitness freak."

CHAPTER SEVENTEEN

"**T**he rules are simple," El Diablo said, and laughed. "There are no rules, cat-man. Either you kill Machetazo or he kills you. You fight until you drop. And if you're thinking that you'll try to escape once we untie your hands, think again. The Devils will mow you down if you try. *Comprende, amigo*?"

"Yeah," Jag responded sullenly.

The bandit chief turned to his assassin and intentionally spoke in English so the hybrid would understand. "I don't want him finished right away, Machetazo. Toy with him a while. Cut him a hundred times. Make the freak suffer before he dies."

"As you wish," Machetazo said.

El Diablo looked at one of the four guards standing near Jag. "Garcia, take these three and drive into Jalapa. The men I left there should have radioed in by now. See what happened."

Garcia, a lean man sporting a short, neatly clipped mustache, saluted. "We will report back promptly."

The quartet departed.

"And now to the fun and games," El Diablo stated eagerly. "Whenever you are ready to begin, Machetazo, do so."

"What about my wrists?" Jag asked, extending his bound arms. "This won't be much of a contest if my wrists are tied."

"They won't be," El Diablo assured him. He grinned and walked over to the row of Devils forming the eastern side of the square.

The assassin looked at Jaguarundi. "Would you care to make your peace with your Maker?"

"The Doktor is dead."

"What?"

"Never mind," Jag said.

Machetazo shrugged and held out his right machete. "Align the rope under the blade."

Jaguarundi complied, noting the keen edge on the weapon. Each machete measured two feet in length, not including the black handle. The Devil handled them with supreme ease. "What's with the oil you smeared all over yourself?"

"In case you get close."

Before Jag could elicit more information, Machetazo rested the machete on the loops of rope binding his wrists and sliced back and forth gently, once in, and out.

The ropes parted and fell to the asphalt.

"Damn!" Jag exclaimed. "That thing is sharp."

"There are none sharper," Machetazo bragged, and lowered the machete to his side.

"I suppose you've hacked quite a few to death with those overgrown butter knives?"

"Your insults will not work."

"I don't know what you're talking about," Jag said innocently.

"You hope to anger me with insults," Machetazo said. "You hope I will lose control and become careless." He grinned. "I *never* lose control."

Jag shrugged. "You can't blame a guy for trying."

"And to answer your question, I have disposed of twenty-nine foes with my machetes. You will be number thirty."

Jag rubbed his wrists to restore the circulation and backed way several paces, giving himself room to maneuver. He heard dune buggy kick over, and a moment later Garcia and company were bypassing the assembled Devils en route to the front gate. He idly watched the guards throw the gate wide, then frowned as the dune buggy roared toward the lake. There went four more blade would have to contend with.

A glimmer of light came at him from the right.

Jag threw himself backwards, realizing his momentary preoccupation had given his adversary an opening. A stinging sensation lanced his right shoulder, and then he was in the clear, blood pouring from a nasty slash, his fingers hooked into claws and ready to strike.

Machetazo had made no effort to press his advantage. He smiled and raised his left machete, staring at the dripping blood. "You should never take your eyes off your enemy," he admonished.

"You caught me with my guard down. Try me now," Jag hissed.

"I will," Machetazo said, and flew into the hybrid with the speed of a whirlwind. His arms flashed and whipped the machetes in a dizzying pattern of shimmering silver as he advanced slowly, step after measured step, never overreaching himself, as methodical as a machine.

Backpedaling hastily, Jag evaded the swinging blades conscious of El Diablo and the Devils watching from the sidelines. They were waiting for him to slip up, for the assassin to deliver another cutting stroke. Because Machetazo was under orders to prolong the contest, the fight might go on indefinitely increasing their pleasure.

True to his boast, Machetazo exhibited superb self-control He swung the machetes too fast for the eye to follow, always maintaining a distance of four feet between the hybrid and himself, close enough so he could connect if the hybrid slipped yet not so close that the mutant could slip under one of his swing and pounce. Slowly, inexorably, he drove his opponent toward the southeast corner of the square.

Jag evaded swipe after swipe, ducking and dodging and twisting and spinning. Once a blade brushed his left ear. Twice he was nicked on the arms. His enhanced reflexes enabled him to avoid a crippling thrust. He racked his brain for a ploy to gain the upper hand.

Something.

Anything.

But as long as he fought on the defensive, as long as Machetazo had the initiative, as long as he conducted the fight according to *their* rules, he couldn't expect to come out on top

To win, he had to capitalize on *his* strengths, to compel the assassin to fight on *his* terms.

How?

The answer was so obvious, he grinned.

Surprised, Machetazo abruptly stopped swinging and halted. "You are amused?"

"Yeah," Jag replied. "You're a funny guy, Seymour."

"My name isn't Seymour."

"Sure it is. Seymour Stupid. I'll call you S.S. for short."

"In a few minutes you won't have a mouth to use to call anyone names," Machetazo declared arrogantly.

"I'm just getting warmed up, yo-yo," Jag said, and did the unexpected. He whirled and raced directly at the line of Devils, many of whom started to unlimber their weapons, mistakenly thinking they were being charged, but at the last possible second Jag spun again, reversing direction to dash at the startled assassin.

Machetazo raised his right machete, intending to split the hybrid in half.

But Jaguarundi had other ideas. Six feet from the assassin he vaulted into the air, his steely sinews propelling him in a high arc, his momentum carrying him clear over Machetazo.

The assassin swung but missed by a foot and a half.

Jag saw the glistening machete sweep underneath him. He held his arms out from his sides and performed an acrobatic flip, his supple body uncoiling gracefully, and landed lightly two yards from his foe. He wheeled and smirked. "How was that, Seymour?"

"I have never seen the like, freak."

"And you never will again."

"Why is that?"

"Because I'm tired of letting you second-rate psychos walk all over me. It's payback time," Jag stated.

"We shall see, *bastardo*," Machetazo said, and rushed the hybrid.

Jag retreated, covering the ground twice as swiftly as the killer, and when he was almost to the line of Devils he halted and repeated the same tactic: running toward Machetazo and sailing up and over as if endowed with the power of flight. He alighted and turned, amused at the budding frustration on the assassin's face. "What's the matter? Do you prefer your victims weak and helpless?"

Machetazo glared. "No one makes a fool out of me."

"Why should anyone else bother when you do such a great job all by yourself?"

The Devil hissed and sprang forward, both machetes upraised, going for a double slice.

Which was the careless mistake Jag had waited for, the blunder that would cost Machetazo the battle. With a rapid bound Jag ran at the assassin and held his arms out, as if about to execute another spectacular flip, only this time he didn't flip, this time he simply pretended to leap skyward but instead angled his legs down and in, his knees locked and his feet stiff, and struck his brawny foe in the chest, bowling Machetazo over.

Curses erupted from the surrounding Devils.

The blow brought the assassin down hard on the asphalt, on his back, jarred to the bone, and he immediately started to rise again, placing his clenched hands on the ground to shove upward, and in so doing left himself wide open.

Jaguarundi landed to the assassin's left. The instant his feet touched the asphalt he closed in, sinking the sturdy nails on his right hand into Machetazo's neck, tearing through flesh and blood vessels effortlessly, then wrenching his hand out.

Blood, skin, and gore spattered the ground as Machetazo bellowed in fury and surged erect, swinging his left machete wildly.

Jag retreated out of the range of the machete and smiled. "Slowing down in your old age, huh?"

"My neck!" Machetazo snapped, pressing his left forearm against his wound in a futile attempt to staunch the flow of blood. He uttered a string of obscenities in Spanish.

"Ready for round three?" Jag asked.

A familiar voice suddenly intruded from the direction of the row of Devils to the east. "Enough!"

Machetazo pivoted. "No, *patrón*! He is mine!"

El Diablo came toward them, his hands on the world's mos

powerful handguns, scowling. "The contest is over, Machetazo."

"No! *Por favor, patrón*! I have a little scratch, that's all."

"You are bleeding to death, *estúpido*."

"Please!" Machetazo begged. "Don't shame me in front of all the Devils."

El Diablo halted and gazed at his band. He pondered for several seconds, then sighed. "All right, my friend. You have served me well for many years. I grant your request. But don't humiliate me by losing or you will wish you had never been born."

"Thank you, *patrón*. I will honor you with my victory," Machetazo declared.

The bandit leader returned to the line of Devils.

"And now, mutant, we will end this farce," Machetazo vowed.

"You've got that right," Jag responded. "You're boring me to tears." So saying, he raced toward the north side of the square, moving at his maximum speed, his body almost a blur. The Devils standing in the north row stood firm, expecting him to repeat his earlier strategem of turning and attacking Machetazo. Only this time he didn't. This time Jag had another idea in mind. This time he intended to lose himself in the vast cavern until he could devise a means of escaping.

The Devils in the northern row awoke to the ploy too late to stop him.

Jag grinned and winked and launched his lithe body aloft, flying over their heads and coming down before even one of the Devils had so much as turned. He took off, racing toward the parked dune buggies, hoping the Devils would be reluctant to fire for fear of damaging their vehicles.

"After the son of a bitch!" El Diablo thundered. "I'll have your hides if the cat-man gets away!"

Jag weaved from side to side just in case, and the precaution saved his life. One of the Devils squeezed off a short burst, the bullets thwacking into the asphalt within inches of his legs.

El Diablo came to his rescue. "Don't fire, you idiots! You'll hit our buggies. Surround him. He can't go anywhere. The fool is trapped in here.''

Hoping the bandit chief was mistaken, Jag bounded ever nearer to the row of vehicles. He glanced back. The Devils were pounding in pursuit, but they were 30 feet away.

"Faster! Faster!" El Diablo commanded.

Jag gritted his teeth and channeled all of his energy into rivaling the wind with his seemingly winged feet, flying over the ground as if he was a literal embodiment of greased lightning. He came to the dune buggies and darted past the first three, then ducked between the next pair and hunched down, pausing for a second to look at the oncoming Devils, wondering how he could possibly evade so many. True, the cavern was enormous, but there were dozens of bandits and they probably knew every nook and cranny.

"Get him!" El Diablo urged on the Devils.

Jag growled and resolved to resist with his dying breath, if necessary. His fiercely independent nature wouldn't let him submit without a fight. His pursuers were now 20 feet off, shouting and yelling as they bore down on the buggies. He started to turn, about to run deeper into the cavern, when the first explosion rocked the base.

CHAPTER EIGHTEEN

"That's Jag!" Raphaela whispered in alarm.

"No foolin'," Lobo responded. "I thought it was an alley cat."

"Quiet," Blade ordered, his eyes on the clash between Jaguarundi and a Devil armed with two machetes. He counted the four rows of bandits enclosing the combatants and discovered there were 53. Which meant, according to his calculations, that most of the Devils were at the base. Perfect. He didn't want a large body of reinforcements to arrive after the battle was joined.

"Blade," Sparrow said softly.

The Warrior glanced to his right. The Flathead, Doc, and Havoc were crouched in the nearby undergrowth. To his left were Lobo and Raphaela. They were 20 yards from a chain-link fence and about the same distance to the west of an iron gate. A pair of Devils stood outside the gate, their attention on the fight. "What?" he responded.

"Look real closely at the bottom of that fence, about forty feet from the gate on both sides," Sparrow said.

Blade did as the Flathead suggested, and for several seconds he saw nothing unusual. Then he detected movement on the east side, a head moving from right to left for a few feet. The head faced inward. Whoever it was, the man must be watching the match between Jag and the muscular Devil.

"Trenches, you think?" Doc speculated.

Frowning, Blade looked at the same point on the western section of fence and spied two heads, both turned toward the fight.

"My guess would be machine-gun emplacements," Captain Havoc commented. "From where they're situated, they have a perfect field of fire."

Blade nodded slowly. "We'll have to take them out first."

"What about the dune buggy that passed us a ways back?" Doc inquired. "Do you think it will come back?"

"With the way our luck has been runnin', it'll come back with a zillion more Devils," Lobo whispered. "We were just lucky we saw the sucker comin' and hid in the woods."

"They'll find the dune buggy we abandoned," Raphaela mentioned. "What if they radio in to the base?"

"We don't have much time," Havoc said.

"I know," Blade agreed, aware that every one of them was regarding him intently, waiting for him to decide on a plan of attack. He motioned for them to converge in a huddle. They obeyed quickly and quietly. "All right," he began. "We have to hit them fast and hit them hard. Havoc, take Doc and Sparrow with you. Use grenades and take out the machine-gun emplacement on the east side of the fence. I'll take care of the other one. When it goes, you do yours."

"What about those two guards at the gate?" Captain Havoc asked.

"I'm getting to that. Sparrow will dispose of them at the same time we hit the machine guns. Once those emplacements are out of commission, we go through the gate. Kill as many Devils as you can. Do as much damage as possible. Above all, remember that we don't leave without Jag."

Lobo looked toward the compound. "We'd best boogie. The dude with the carving knives is givin' Jag a hard time."

Blade looked at each of them. "Okay. Let's do it."

Captain Havoc, Doc Madsen, and Sparrow headed to the east, crawling on their elbows and knees, skirting the bushes and trees in their path.

"I would have liked to have gone with Havoc," Raphaela remarked wistfully.

"He doesn't need you to hold his hand," Lobo said.

Blade gazed at the fence. The gate guards and the machine gunners were still preoccupied with the duel. He saw Jag vault clear over the Devil swinging the machetes and marveled at the hybrid's prowess. If only Jag could keep the fight going for a few more minutes! "Follow me," he directed, and slid forward under cover toward the west gun emplacement.

A black-tailed jackrabbit darted from a patch of weeds ten feet to the left and leaped off to the northwest, the brush crackling and rustling with its passage.

The Warrior glanced at the guards and the machine gunners, but not one of them appeared to have heard. He relaxed slightly and advanced to within 15 yards of the western emplacement, then halted. Havoc and the others would require at least two minutes to get into position, maybe longer considering they had to cross the dirt road to enter the forest on the east side. His gaze shifted to the match.

Jag and the Devil were conversing. Suddenly the hybrid raced at his foe and performed another graceful high jump, sailing up and over the Devil.

Blade grinned. The jackrabbit he'd seen could take jumping lessons from Jaguarundi. He slid his left hand down and reached into his pocket for a grenade. The metal felt cool on his palm.

There was a flurry of activity in the compound. Jag delivered a flying kick to the Devil, knocking the man down, then sank his nails in the man's neck.

The Warrior held the hand grenade in front of his face and stared at the circular finger hole at the end of the metal pin. He deposited the M60 flat on the ground and transferred the pineapple to his right hand.

All set.

A lot of angry shouting came from the other side of the chain-link fence.

Blade gazed at the Devils. A man dressed all in black, wearing a revolver on each hip, exchanged words with the machete-user. Could the guy in black be El Diablo? All of the other bandits wore camouflage fatigues, and it made sense that the leader might wear distinctive apparel.

Jag unexpectedly dashed to the north.

What was he doing now?

The Warrior tensed when he intuitively perceived that the hybrid wasn't going to stop, and he almost laughed aloud when Jag flew over the row of Devils and headed for the dune buggies. He rose to his knees, hefting the grenade, and watched the Devils give chase. No one, absolutely no one, was paying the slightest attention to the area outside the fence. He couldn't have asked for a better opportunity.

Now!

Blade pulled the pin, then swept his arm in an overhand arc, flinging the hand grenade outward and upward. The sun glinted off its metallic surface as the grenade sailed over the chain-link fence and descended into the machine-gun emplacement.

Someone vented a gruff oath.

The Warrior flattened and placed his arms protectively over his head, and the next second the grenade detonated with a thunderous whomp, showering dirt and machine-gun parts and body fragments in all directions. Instantly Blade pushed erect, the M60 leveled, and sprinted toward the iron gate. He saw Sparrow Hawk pop up within a dozen feet of the guards and blast both into eternity with his M-16.

A second explosion tore apart the machine-gun emplacement to the east.

"Party time, dude!" Lobo yelled excitedly.

The idiot! Blade thought, and then there was no time for thinking because he came to the gate, stepped over the pair of perforated guards, and grabbed the bar securing the barrier. He wrenched the bar aside, hurled the gate open, and stood framed in the entrance.

Almost in unison, the Devils in pursuit of Jaguarundi had stopped and whirled at the sound of the detonations. They gaped at the smoke and dust-shrouded fence in consternation, belatedly comprehending that their base was being attacked.

El Diablo's bawling voice spurred the bandits to action. "To the fence, you assholes! The Californians are here! Move!"

Blade advanced several strides into the compound. Lobo, Raphaela, and Sparrow came in behind him and fanned out to the left. Moments later Havoc and Doc entered and moved to the right. "Find cover," Blade instructed them. "I'll draw their fire."

The Devils regained their composure and surged in the direction of the iron gate.

With a lopsided grin creasing his lips, Blade walked toward them through the swirling dust, his finger caressing the trigger, eager to cut loose. And cut loose he did when he spotted the foremost Devils jogging straight at him. The machine gun boomed and bucked, and he let his massive arms absorb the recoil as he whipped the barrel from right to left. Screams of despair and agony arose from the bandits as the heavy slugs tore through their heads, torsos, and limbs.

Eight, nine, ten dropped with the initial burst.

And still the Devils charged, their confidence stemming from their superior numbers. They fired as they ran, concentrating on the giant figure near the gate.

Blade flinched when a searing pain lanced his right shoulder. He grit his teeth and ignored the torment, continuing to sweep the M60 from side to side, mowing more foes down.

Captain Havoc suddenly materialized on the right, his right hand hurling a grenade into the midst of the Devils.

A flash of brilliant red and orange attended the concussion that ripped asunder five of the onrushing bandits. An acrid aroma filled the air. Most of the remaining Devils scattered, seeking shelter. A few knelt and fired from where they were.

Another grenade went off. Screeching Devils were sent flying. A severed arm flopped to the asphalt, the fingers reflexively fluttering.

Blade hunched over and angled to the right, firing from the hip, felling another Devil. He saw several gray canisters tumble end over end out of the dust and land on the ground near the spot where he had been standing, and he dove and came down prone, his chin tucked to his chest, his left arm over his face, expecting multiple deafening blasts. Instead, he heard a loud hissing sound and looked at the canisters.

Smoke bombs!

Some of the Devils has tossed smoke bombs!

A curtain of enshrouding smoke spewed from each of the three canisters and spread out rapidly, blanketing the immediate vicinity. Other smoke bombs descended out of the murky cloud on all sides.

Blade's brow knit in perplexity. What were the Devils trying to accomplish? Gunfire crackled all around him, indicating the bandits were still resisting mightily. By throwing up a screen of smoke, the Devils only made it harder on themselves to spot the Force members. The Force would also have a hard time of it, but the smoke would work to their advantage because they were outnumbered.

So using the smoke was stupid.

Unless . . .

Unless someone planned to use the smoke screen to effect an escape.

But who?

El Diablo?

The Warrior rose and ran into the smoke, swinging the M60 back and forth. A pair of Devils, both women, appeared directly ahead and he squeezed the trigger. The rounds bored into their midriffs and hurled them to the ground, the one on the right convulsing violently. Blade paused to get his bearings, worried about the possibility of a stray bullet accidentally striking one of his own unit. Maybe there was a method to the Devils' blunder after all. If the Force couldn't—

A heavy body rammed into Blade from the rear, slamming into the small of his back and driving him forward onto his knees. He twisted, striving to bring the M60 to bear, but a pair of husky hands gripped the barrel and yanked the machine gun free before he could tighten his hold. He shoved to his feet and spun.

A couple of yards away stood the Devil Jaguarundi had fought, a man endowed with a tremendous build. Blood trickled from a ragged wound in his neck. His green eyes seemed to mock the Warrior, and his hands hung next to his machete handles.

Blade went to draw the Officers Model 45 in his shoulder holster, then hesitated when the Devil made no hostile moves.

The Devil grinned and gestured at the Warrior's waist, at the Bowies. "Man to man, eh, *hombre*? Just you and Machetazo."

The Devil was offering him a fair fight! For a second Blade wavered, tempted to take the man up on his offer but keenly aware that his companions might need his assistance, might be in dire need of the firepower he could supply with the M60, and in that second of indecision he gave the Devil the opening to close in.

Machetazo's right machete streaked out of its sheath and whisked at the Warrior, only instead of going for a death stroke, the Devil aimed his blow at the giant's right hand, forcing the Warrior to lower the hand or lose it at the wrist.

Blade backpedaled and drew the Bowies as Machetazo quickly slid the left machete free and took the offensive. Blade countered a flurry of savage swipes, the Bowies and the machetes clanging when they connected. He blocked a side slash from the left, then parried an overhand thrust at his head. The Devil displayed a masterly skill, almost the equal of the Family's renowned martial artist and self-professed "perfected swordsmaster," Rikki-Tikki-Tavi.

Almost, but not quite.

The Bowies and machetes connected with increasing frequency as the tempo of the combat increased. The steel weapons clashed and pealed without breaking or chipping in testimony to the superb craftsmanship exhibited in their construction.

The greater lengths of the machetes compelled Blade to slowly retreat while seeking a means of dispatching his advesary. But every swing of his was checked, every intricate pattern designed to penetrate the Devil's guard thwarted.

Machetazo suddenly pressed his onslaught with renewed vigor.

Blade took a stride backwards, foiling a double underhand thrust at his abdomen, deflecting the machetes outward and for a heartbeat leaving his opponent's stomach unprotected. He stepped swiftly in between the Devil's arms, drove his arms down and in, and buried his Bowies to the hilts in Machetazo's stomach.

For several seconds the tableau froze, suspended in time, the two of them silhouetted against a backdrop of billowing smoke.

Blade felt the Devil sag as crimson spittle flecked Machetazo's mouth. He pulled the Bowies out and moved away, watching blood and abdominal fluids seep from the knife holes.

Incredibly, Machetazo grinned and shook his head. "You are quite good, *hombre*," he said weakly, and tottered to the right. His legs gave out, bringing him to his knees, and he released the machetes. "Finish me. *Por favor.*"

His features hardening, Blade wiped the Bowies on his pants, replaced them in their scabbards, and scanned the asphalt for the M60. The smoke limited his visual field to two and a half yards at best, and he had to take several paces to the right before he found the machine gun, which he promptly scooped up.

Machetazo gasped and swayed. "Hurry. Please."

Blade walked over to the bandit, stuck the barrel of the M60 in the Devil's left ear, and fired.

CHAPTER NINETEEN

Jag wanted to shout for joy when he saw the charging Devils halt and whirl. The two explosions along the fence had drawn the attention of the bandits away from him. He edged to the front of the closest dune buggie, exhilarated by his deliverance. All he had to do was circle around the Devils and rejoin his teammates, and with that goal in mind he padded into the open, heading for the buildings in the center of the cavern. He hoped none of the bandits would notice him. A glance at the iron gate showed him the Force members were entering the base. More explosions occurred.

He felt like cheering.

Instead he ran to the corner of the second barracks and ducked from sight, then turned and peered out. The Force and the Devils were firing furiously, creating a strident din. The noise rendered his usually acute ears ineffective in detecting soft sounds.

Such as the patter of canine feet on asphalt.

Jag heard the throaty growl and tried to rotate, but the white dog sprang from behind him and fastened its razor teeth on his right shoulder, tearing the fur and the skin and hauling Jag onto the ground.

Pancho snarled and leaped clear.

Jag rolled to the right, endeavoring to put space between the mongrel and himself. He managed to get to his knees, and the white dog came straight at his chest and tried to bite his face off. Jag threw his arms up and caught hold of the dog's neck, preventing those slavering jaws from ripping into him.

Frustrated, Pancho went beserk, thrashing and kicking and snapping in a frenzy.

With the dog's fetid breath assailing his nostrils, Jag felt his own rage mounting. He lanced his nails under the folds of Pancho's fleshy neck and squeezed. If he could only sink his teeth in as well! But Pancho fought with a desperation born of animal cunning. The dog had been hurt once before and wasn't about to repeat the mistake by giving Jag a shot at its neck. He lunged to the left, carrying the entire canine to the asphalt, and tried to slide his body on top of Pancho's.

The white dog writhed from under the hybrid's legs and strained to stand, its sole good eye balefully fixed on its enemy.

Its sole good eye?

And suddenly Jag knew how he could win, at least how he *might* win if his left hand was quicker than Pancho's jaws, and he abruptly let go of the dog's neck and speared his hand at the dog's good eye.

Pancho yelped when the sharp tips of the hybrid's nails punctured the remaining eyeball.

Jag heaved, flinging the canine to the asphalt, and jumped erect, prepared to meet another rush. But the white dog was lying down, blood pouring from the ravaged eye, and frantically wiping at the useless orb. Jag moved closer, intending to put the dog out of its misery.

"You rotten son of a bitch!"

The exclamation caused Jag to spin to the south, knowing who he would see.

El Diablo, standing eight feet away and holding both revolvers. Three Devils flanked him. Beyond them, blossoming and swelling rapidly, billowed a cloaking veil of smoke. Gunshots cracked within the hazy shroud.

"At least I'll have the satisfaction of killing you before I leave, freak," the bandit chief snapped.

"You're leaving?" Jag responded in surprise. "The great El Diablo is tucking his tail between his legs and running?"

"Those who fight and run away live to fight another day."

Jag tensed his legs, calculating the odds of reaching the raider before he fired. "I never would have expected this," he said, stalling, buying precious seconds in which to formulate a plan. "You're a murdering, psychopathic pig, but I never took you for a coward."

El Diablo chuckled. "Thank you for the compliment. As I have told you several times, I am not a man who takes unnecessary risks. I did not think your compadres would get this far, but now that they have I must proceed accordingly. I expect they have powerful explosives with them, and if just one eludes my Devils this cavern will be blown sky high. So a few of my followers and I will drive away before the end comes, then wait down the road to ambush your friends if and when they leave."

"You don't seem to have a lot of confidence in your Devils when the chips are down. I thought you said they were good."

"They are, within their limitations. But my loyal followers are *bandidos*, low-life gangsters and criminals of every kind I took out of the gutter and gave a chance to become rich. I've trained them well. Unfortunately, they're not invincible," El Diablo said, and smiled. "So where would you like to be shot? In the head, which would be the quickest way to die? Or should I shoot you in the belly and make you suffer?"

"Why don't you holster those guns and take me on hand-to-hand?" Jag proposed.

"You must be kidding. My fists against your nails? What chance would I have?"

Jag smirked and took a step forward. "None."

El Diablo cocked the Casulls. "I have never wanted to kill anyone as much as I do you."

Jag braced for the shots. He saw four Devils racing toward the bandit leader.

"El Diablo!"

"What is it?" the raider replied, turning his head to look over his right shoulder.

"We have used the last of the smoke canisters," the foremost Devil said. "Anything else, *patrón*?"

"Find the gringos and kill them."

"*Sí, patrón.*"

The quartet wheeled and sprinted toward the smoke.

"And now for the grand finale, eh?" El Diablo stated scornfully, and took a bead on the hybrid's chest.

A fleeting millisecond of dread seized Jaguarundi, a dread he instantaneously suppressed, his mind racing lightning fast as he stared down those twin barrels. He realized he couldn't get to El Diablo before the bastard squeezed the triggers, but he might be able to avoid being killed if he could hurl himself to the right just as Naranjo fired.

"Adios, freak," El Diablo said, and grinned.

Jag girded himself, his eyes riveted to the bandit chief's trigger fingers, waiting for the first hint of movement. But the fingers didn't begin to apply pressure, and he wondered what El Diablo was waiting for, whether thè raider was toying with him. The reason for the momentary reprieve became clear the next second when the white dog walked unsteadily past him and halted, whining pitiably, its right eye a grisly pool of blood.

El Diablo paused, his eyes narrowing, and the Casull barrels dipped a few inches. "Pancho?"

Pancho swung toward the sound of his master and whimpered.

"Pancho!" El Diablo cried. He took a stride toward his dog.

Jag stared in fascination at the genuine concern etched on Naranjo's features. He curled his fingers and prepared to leap, to take advantage of the distraction, when an M-16 chattered from somewhere to his rear and to the left.

The rounds thudded into El Diablo and the three Devils, the impact causing all four to stumble backwards and collapse, their chests dotted with crimson splotches.

Jag blinked a few times in disbelief, then pivoted.

"Are you all right?" Captain Havoc asked, running up, his M-16 held loosely in his right hand.

"Fine," Jag blurted. "Where did you come from?"

"I just set charges on two tanker trucks along the east wall. We have three minutes to locate the others and get the hell out of here before this place goes up," Havoc disclosed.

They started to head for the smoke cloud, but a strained, harsh command brought them up short.

"Don't move!"

El Diablo was on his knees, the revolvers trained on Jag, red rivulets trickling from the five bullet holes high on his chest

"I'll still take you with me, eh?" he said, and fired.

Jaguarundi had already galvanized into action, diving to the right, only not swiftly enough to beat the Casulls. An invisible hand hammered into his left thigh as exquisite pain speared through his body, and he found himself hurtling rearward to sprawl onto the asphalt on his right side. He'd been shot! Stunned, he twisted, anticipating that El Diablo would finish the job.

Captain Havoc never gave the bandit the chance. He took two strides, dropped the M-16, and launched himself into a forward roll, his wide shoulders and backpack serving as the fulcrum on which his body flipped. With impeccable execution he arched his legs down and in, his right combat boot slamming into El Diablo's face and knocking the man to the ground, dazed. Havoc completed the roll and came up on his knees next to his foe.

El Diablo, on his back with his legs bent under him, struggled to rise.

Havoc's right arm shot out in an open palm thrust. The base of his palm caught his foe on the chin and slammed El Diablo's head to the asphalt, bending the bandit's neck, exposing the throat. Havoc swept his right hand to his combat boot and drew his survival knife, then reversed direction and lanced the tip of the serrated blade into El Diablo's neck just below the lower jaw, burying the knife all the way.

Celestino Naranjo gurgled and gazed, wide-eyed, at the cavern roof. A gusher of blood spurted from his mouth and his body quivered. He tried to lift his head but couldn't. "Maria!" he cried, and died.

Captain Havoc reclaimed his M-16 and moved to the hybrid's side. "Can you walk?"

"I don't know," Jag admitted, looking down at the wound. Only one of the shots had hit him, the bullet boring into the rounded curve of his left hip and bursting out the other side. The pain assaulted his senses.

"I'll help you," Havoc offered. He slipped his left arm under his companion's right armpit and hauled Jag to his feet. "We've got to haul butt."

"I wish you wouldn't use that word."

The officer laughed, then shifted to the south at the sound

of drumming footsteps.

Sparrow Hawk, Raphaela, and Lobo were hastening toward them.

"What's wrong with Jag?" Raphaela shouted.

"He took a hit," Havoc responded.

"Is it serious?" Sparrow asked.

"He'll want to go to the bathroom standing up for a while."

Jag glanced at the cloud of smoke, startled to perceive that the firing had ceased. "Did you bag all of the Devils?"

"A lot of 'em," Lobo answered. "The Devils are a bunch of wimps. They're not even in our class."

"Tell that to *them*," Jag said urgently, and nodded at the cloud.

Nine Devils were emerging from the grayish-white blanket, and at the sight of the Force members they voiced a hearty yell and charged.

Captain Havoc glanced to the right and the left. The dune buggies and the barracks were too far off. They would have to make their stand in the open. "Get down!" he yelled, and pulled Jag to the asphalt as the others flattened.

A lanky figure attired in a black wide-brimmed hat and frock coat came out of the smoke to the east of the Devils. Apparently the M-16 in his left hand had gone empty. His right hand snaked to the Smith and Wesson Model 586 Distinguished Combat Magnum on his hip, and the blur of his arm was punctuated by three swift retorts. At each shot a Devil fell.

The six bandits still on their feet spun and rushed the Cavalryman, squeezing off rounds as they did, but they only managed to fire a few before yet another figure appeared.

A strapping giant materialized alongside the gunman, and in his hands he held one of the most reliable machine guns ever manufactured. The M60 blasted, spitting flame and lead, a rain of death that burned dozens of holes through the outgunned Devils. They danced and jerked and screamed, geysers of gore spraying from their torsos, and perished en masse. When all six were lying still on the ground the giant finally let up.

"Damn! That dude is awesome," Lobo commented in the silence that ensued.

Havoc glanced at his watch and stiffened. "Everyone out o

the cavern! We have a minute and a half!'' He lifted Jag and together they hastened toward the iron gate. The smoke was beginning to dissipate and a vague outline of the chain-link fence was visible on the southern perimeter.

''A minute and a half until what?'' Lobo inquired as he rose.

''Until the plastic explosives on the tanker trucks go off,'' Havoc informed him.

''Say what?'' Lobo blurted out, and raced for the entrance. Blade and Doc Madsen jogged to meet their associates.

''What happened to Jag?'' the Warrior asked.

''Save it,'' Havoc said. ''We've got to get out of here.''

''You've set charges?'' Blade asked, noticing the officer's urgent attitude.

Havoc nodded. ''A minute and twenty seconds until detonation.''

''Then let's get in gear,'' Blade said. He allowed the M60 to dangle by its leather strap from his right shoulder, stepped in close, and took the hybrid from the officer, hoisting Jag into his huge arms before a protest could be lodged.

''What the hell do you think you're doing?'' Jag exclaimed indignantly.

''What does it look like I'm doing?'' Blade retorted. He sped to the south.

''I can manage, thank you,'' Jag asserted.

''Maybe you can, maybe you can't. We don't have time to find out.''

''This ain't fair,'' Lobo complained, keeping pace on the giant's right.

''What isn't?'' Blade responded. He glanced around to insure all of them were hard on his heels.

''You wouldn't carry me piggyback, but you'll carry him.''

''You weigh more.''

''Are you callin' me fat?''

''No.''

''Good.''

''Just chunky.''

They poured on the speed, racing through the diminishing acrid blanket, bypassing dozens of corpses in their path.

Jag looked back only once. He saw the white dog standing

next to his slain master, licking El Diablo's face, and he felt a twinge of regret that he hadn't finished the dog off.

"Devils!" Lobo shouted.

Jag swung forward and spied nine or ten Devils fleeing down the dirt road. Either they had witnessed El Diablo's death, or had overheard Havoc's comments about the explosives, or were simply preserving their own lives. In any event, he was glad to see them go. Oddly, for the first time in many years, he didn't feel in the mood for more killing.

The Force reached the open gate and hastened away from the sprawling compound.

Captain Havoc began a countdown. "Seven-six-five-four-three-hit the dirt!-one!"

Each one of them was diving for the ground when the initial blasts transpired, the detonation of the tanker trucks. A fireball of enormous porportions engulfed the transport trucks and the buildings, and seconds later the explosives and weapons arsenal stored in the two-story structure went off with an earth-jarring blast. The fireball grew, expanding outward, and a hurricane-force wind toppled the iron gate and the chain-link fence. More explosions followed, lesser blasts, adding to the smoke and fumes and heat. The roof of the cavern cracked, then split wide and crashed down on the legacy left by a man whose consuming hatred had finally consumed him.

At that moment, as the cavern rumbled and thundered and crumpled, one of the Force members had an observation to make on the entire affair.

"Far out, dudes! I guess we taught those turkeys."

EPILOGUE

"**H**ow are you feeling?" Blade asked.

Jaguarundi looked up from the nature magazine he had been reading and smiled. "I can't wait to get out of the sack."

"The doctor says you're to stay in that bed for another two weeks."

"Cut me some slack. I need to get up and move around."

"You do, and you'll open the wound," Blade said, and halted next to the bunk, one of three aligned along the north wall of the Force barracks. "If you get out, I'll strap you back in."

Jag sighed and placed his left hand behind his head. "Of all the places to be shot. I'll never hear the end of it."

"Has Lobo been getting on your case?"

"The man has a pitiful sense of humor. The thing is, he really believes he's brilliant."

Blade grinned. "Lobo does add a little spice to the new unit."

"Where are the others anyway?"

"Havoc is giving them karate lessons. When I left them, he had just kicked Lobo for a loop."

"Damn. And I'm stuck in bed."

"Has General Gallagher been in to see you yet?" Blade inquired.

"Yeah. Once. He offered his sympathy, but I got the impression he wasn't very sincere."

"The general has been behaving strangely ever since we

returned," Blade said. "So has Havoc, come to think of it. He's moodier than his brother."

"Life's too short to spend it being moody," Jag stated.

"Can I quote you?" Blade quipped.

"I mean it. My personal philosophy is to make the most of every minute, to enjoy life to the fullest, to take what comes and make the best of it," Jag declared. "You can't sweat the small stuff."

Blade nodded and beamed. "You must be right. I heard Lobo say the same thing just the other day."

"Thanks heaps."